"Sophia," he said, taking her hand and holding it between both of his. "It's a beautiful name. I enjoy the sound of it."

~~~⌒◯◯⌒~~~

"I enjoy the sound of it, too, James—when *you* say it." Her voice simmered with beguiling allure. "I would like it even more if you said it again."

All at once he felt as if he were falling from a very high place. Apprehensions pierced through him, for none of this was going as he had planned. *"Sophia."*

He gazed down at her hand and turned it over. With his finger he drew a little circle in her palm. He felt her body shudder, and her stimulation shivered through him as well.

He hungered for more. So much so, it ached. It was damned inconvenient. This was a business arrangement. She knew it. He knew it. He should not forget that.

Yet his attraction to her was mounting at a shockingly brisk pace . . .

Other **AVON ROMANCES**

Coming Soon

And Don't Miss These
ROMANTIC TREASURES
from Avon Books

JULIANNE MacLEAN

TO MARRY THE DUKE

AVON BOOKS

An Imprint of HarperCollins*Publishers*

This is a work of fiction. Names, characters, places, and incidents are products of the author's imagination or are used fictitiously and are not to be construed as real. Any resemblance to actual events, locales, organizations, or persons, living or dead, is entirely coincidental.

AVON BOOKS
An Imprint of HarperCollins*Publishers*
10 East 53rd Street
New York, New York 10022-5299

Copyright © 2003 by Julianne MacLean
ISBN: 0-06-052704-8
www.avonromance.com

First Avon Books paperback printing: June 2003

Avon Trademark Reg. U.S. Pat. Off. and in Other Countries, Marca Registrada, Hecho en U.S.A.
HarperCollins® is a registered trademark of HarperCollins Publishers Inc.

Printed in the U.S.A.

10 9 8 7 6 5 4 3 2

*As always,
this one is for you, Stephen,
for being my hero every day.
And special thanks to
my fabulous new editor, Kelly Harms,
my gorgeous agent, Paige Wheeler,
and my dear cousin, Michelle,
whose friendship I could not do without.*

Chapter 1

The London Season, 1881

With a sigh of resignation, Sophia Wilson realized she had unwittingly hurled herself not only across an ocean to London, but from a sizzling-hot frying pan into a fierce and fiery blaze. She was about to enter the Marriage Mart.

She moved with her mother into the crowded London drawing room, elegantly adorned with silk tapestries and bouquets of roses tied with ribbons, and a host of other useless knickknacks skillfully arranged to make perfect idleness the only option. Squeezing her fan tightly in her gloved fist, she prepared herself— after a month of intense English etiquette training—for the introduction to the earl and countess of something-or-other, then dutifully smiled her best smile.

"That wasn't so terrible, was it?" her mother whispered afterward, assessing the room as she spoke.

Sophia could almost hear her mother's thoughts aloud as she formulated the evening's strategy: *An earl here . . . a marquess there . . .*

The weight of Sophia's responsibility hung over her then, like an iron chandelier dangling from a single screw, ready to drop at any moment. She was an American heiress, and she was here in London to ensure her family's acceptance into high society back home and ultimately change their lives forever. She was here to marry an English lord.

At least, that was what she had promised her mother when escape had become her only hope. For Sophia had turned down four proposals in the past year—very good ones, in her mother's frequently professed opinion—and her mother had begun to bang her head against the wall. The last gentleman had been a Peabody, and good gracious, a Wilson marrying a Peabody would have been a *coup* like no other. It would have secured an invitation to the Patriarch's Balls. Mrs. Astor—*the* Mrs. Astor—might even have paid the bourgeois Wilsons a call. The high-society matriarch would have hated it, of course.

All this marital desperation because Sophia's family was one of many *new* families to try to break into the impenetrable old New York society. *Arrivistes,* they were called. The *nouveaux riches.* They knew what they were, and they all wanted in.

Sophia gazed despondently at the hordes of strangers in the room, listened distractedly to the cool, reserved English laughter, if one could call it laughter. Her sisters certainly wouldn't.

She sighed, reminding herself how important it was to find a man she could love before the end of the Season. She had made a deal with her mother so the poor woman wouldn't make herself ill again. The only way her mother would let Sophia off the hook regarding the Peabody proposal—without having an "episode" and calling the doctor again—was with the promise of a bigger fish. Since bigger fish were found exclusively in London—bigger fish with titles, no less—here they were.

Sophia only hoped she could find a romantic fish, a handsome fish, a fish who would love her for herself, not her money.

"Allow me to present my daughter, Miss Sophia Wilson," her mother said as she introduced her to a group of ladies, each with daughters of their own by their sides.

For a moment, the Englishwomen were silent as they took in her appearance—her Worth gown, her emerald-cut diamond pendant, her diamond-cluster drop earrings. None of the English girls wore such extravagant jewels, and they gazed at her with envious looks on their faces. Sophia felt suddenly like a fish herself—very much out of her familiar waters.

"You're from America?" one of the women said at last, flicking open her fan and fluttering it in front of her face, waiting somewhat impatiently for Sophia's reply.

"Yes, from New York. We're guests of the Countess of Lansdowne."

The countess, as it happened, was also American, and in New York, she was known as one of the very best "social godmothers." She had married the Earl of Lansdowne three years previous and had somehow managed to fit into London society as if she had been born and raised here. The Wilsons had known Florence in New York before she had married the earl. Florence, too, had been on the outside looking in, had received the cold shoulder one too many times, and now took great pleasure in thumbing her nose back at those same high-nosed Knickerbockers. She secured her revenge by assisting the so-called *upstarts,* like Sophia and her mother, up the long and often slippery social ladder, and sending the families home to New York with impressive English titles in their bursting beaded reticules.

"Yes, we're familiar with the countess," the taciturn Englishwoman replied, exchanging a knowing nod with her companions.

No more was said, and Sophia did her best to smile, the evening suddenly stretching before her like a long, monotonous road with carriages halted and lined up for miles.

At that moment, a hush fell over the room, followed by a few scattered whispers: *It's the duke . . . Is it the duke? . . . My word, it is the duke.* All heads turned toward the door.

The majordomo's deep, booming voice announced, "His Grace, the Duke of Wentworth."

As Sophia waited for the duke's entrance, her American opinions about equality bucked in her head. *Duke or ditch digger, he's still just a man.*

She rose up on her toes to see over people's heads and get a peek at the highest-ranking peer in the room, but leaned back when one of the young English girls in her group whispered in her ear: "Avoid him if you can, unless you want to marry into a nightmare."

Sophia faced the girl, who paled and took a step back, discouraging any further conversation.

Shaken by the girl's comment and more than a little curious about it, Sophia turned her attention back to the door. Women were curtsying. Through the crowd, she could see skirts billowing onto the floor. Finally, someone stepped aside, and Sophia found herself gazing across the room at a most impressive and magnificent man.

Dressed in a black suit with tails, white shirt, and white waistcoat, he prowled into the room like a hungry panther, nodding politely but impassively at all those who were curtsying and bowing in his path.

While Sophia gazed at his strong, arresting face—all smooth planes and sharp angles—her heart began to flutter in her breast. It was as if she were looking at a great work of art, feeling robbed of breath by an inconceivable thing of beauty. It seemed impossible that anyone could have created such a face; and yet, someone had. A woman. A mother, who had years ago given birth to divine perfection.

She continued to watch him, taking in everything about him—his self-assured bearing, his calm, aloof presence.

His hair was midnight black, thick and wavy and spilling freely onto his broad shoulders. Long and disordered, it was distinctly unfashionable. Scandalous almost. Sophia raised a delicate eyebrow. No one in New York would ever be seen in public in such a feral-looking state, she thought, but this man was a duke, and he could no doubt do as he pleased. No one would dare contradict him or cut him.

That's what made London different from New York, she supposed. One could be eccentric if one was blue-blooded, and nothing could take away from one's social standing.

The crowd was silent—in awe it seemed—as the imposing man made his initial sweep about the room. Then the assembly resumed its quiet conversational hum.

Sophia, however, was not yet ready to take her eyes off the tall, compelling man. She couldn't get over the way he moved, with such smooth confidence and grace. Catlike.

His green eyes were catlike, too, she noted. Clever and discerning. Cynical and dangerous. Sophia shivered with a confusing mixture of excitement and fear. Instinct told her she would not wish to cross him.

As he moved with a fair-haired gentleman to the other side of the room, Sophia turned to the young woman beside her. "What did you mean," she whispered to her, "about the nightmare?"

The woman gazed over her shoulder to glance at the duke. "I shouldn't have said anything. It's merely drawing room gossip."

"Were you teasing me?"

The woman's breast rose and fell with apparent frustration over the fact that Sophia would not relinquish her inquiry. "No, I was warning you." She leaned in and whispered, "Some call him the Dangerous Duke. They say he has a black heart."

"Who says?"

The woman's brow furrowed with deeper frustration. "Everyone. They say his family is cursed. A cruel lot, all of them. Just look at him. Wouldn't you agree?"

Sophia turned to gaze in his direction again. She watched his eyes. He slowly blinked, gazing with disdain at everyone who passed in front of him. "I wouldn't know."

Yet her instincts warned her that he was indeed a dangerous man. There was no light in his eyes, only darkness and what looked like a deeply buried, simmering contempt for the world.

She did not wish to meet him, she quickly decided.

Judging by the height of her curiosity and her fascination with him—more importantly, the way her insides were presently fluttering with foolish, juvenile butterflies—it would be a mistake. She wasn't certain she would be strong enough to keep those butterflies from gaining control over her intellect, and she needed to choose a man with her head, not her passions, for she had always believed that passions could not be trusted.

She gazed back at him again and watched him bow elegantly at a lady as she passed by, then felt her skin prickle.

Yes, he would undoubtedly be very dangerous to Sophia.

Regaining her composure, intent to return to the conversation at hand, Sophia glanced uneasily down at her mother.

Heavens. She, too, was staring over someone's shoulder at the duke.

A surge of dread pushed through Sophia.

Her mother was salivating.

James Nicholas Langdon, the ninth Duke of Wentworth, Marquess of Rosslyn, Earl of Wimborne, Viscount Stafford, stepped out from behind a potted tree-fern and gazed intently across the crowded drawing room. Lady Seamore's ivory plumed fan clacked open to obscure his view, and with some irritation, he tilted his head to the side to see around her.

For something had caught his eye.

"Who is that woman?" he asked the Earl of Whitby, who stood behind him, absentmindedly twirling an emerald ring around on his finger.

"She's the American," Whitby replied. "The one they call 'the Jewel of New York,' with the dowry big enough to support Buckingham Palace. Or so I'm told."

James stared at those engaging, blue eyes, the full impertinent mouth. "*She's* the heiress?"

"You sound surprised. I told you she was beautiful. Didn't you believe me?"

Without replying to the remark, James watched the golden-haired beauty glide across the room toward Lord Bradley, their host. Introductions were made, and the American woman's eyes flashed as she smiled. She wore a silver-and-chestnut silk brocade gown that caught the light, and pearls at her neck, with an obscenely large diamond pendant that dangled in the cleft of her engaging bosom.

He let out a jaded sigh. "Another American, here for the peer-hunting season. How many is that, now? Three, four so far? What are they doing—writing home to all their friends on the frontier? Telling them to please come quickly, there are titles to be had for those who can pay?"

Whitby moved to stand beside him. "You know as well as I do that Bertie enjoys a novelty, especially one with wit and beauty, and what the Prince wants, the Prince gets."

"And the Set is only too happy to oblige him."

At that moment the heiress laughed, revealing perfect, straight white teeth.

Whitby raised his chin at her. "She and her mother are residing with the Countess of Lansdowne for the Season."

"The Countess of Lansdowne, of all people," James replied dryly. "Another American huntress—one who has already bagged her title. She'll coach the new recruit, I suppose." James knew the countess all too well, and subtlety was not her strong suit.

James and Whitby walked together across the room. James wasn't even sure why he had decided to come here tonight. He despised the London Marriage Mart, for he was not seeking a wife, nor did he wish to seek one. He loathed being pursued by the avaricious mothers of single daughters, who would marry their babies off to a reputed monster just for the pleasure of knowing their own blood would run in the veins of a future duke.

Yet this evening, something had lured him out into society. . . .

James paused beside the marble mantel, draped with a gold-fringed valance and topped with a vase full of carefully arranged white feathers. He couldn't help looking at the American again, all flash and glitter.

"You've met her?" he said.

Whitby watched her as well. "Yes, at an assembly three nights ago."

"And what about the Prince?"

"He met her last week at the Wilkshire Ball. He danced with her twice—in a row I might add—and from what I hear, her silver salver has been overflowing with ivory cards ever since."

James leaned an elbow upon the mantel and watched her converse easily with their host.

"You're not declaring an interest, are you?" Whitby asked, sounding surprised.

"Of course not. I rarely declare anything."

But perhaps tonight, he thought, there was some element of *interest* shifting around inside his head. Shaking things up. She certainly was exceptional to look at.

He let his gaze wander leisurely down the length of her gown, over the soft curves of her body. Such slender arms she had, beneath those long, tight white gloves.

His experienced eyes roamed over her graceful hand—holding on to a champagne glass, sipping from it all too rarely—along to her dainty elbow, then up to her smooth, opulent shoulders and across her enticing collarbone. Her full breasts were tightly constrained by the close-fitting evening gown, and he imagined what they would look like, free from the constraint and falling out into his waiting, hot-blooded hands.

"Is your mother still nipping at your heels about taking a wife?" Whitby asked, interrupting his private observations.

James brought his mind back around. "Daily. Though I doubt I'll have to answer questions about any Americans. Mother enjoys running the house too much. She's hoping for some little insignificant chit— British, of course—who won't complain or attract any attention, one who'll be content to stay in the shadows."

James nodded amiably at Lady Seamore as she passed by on her way into the gallery, where a recently acquired Rembrandt was on display. It was widely known in the best houses of London that the painting had come from the Marquess of Stokes—who had been forced to sell off a cartload of art to keep his estate from falling into disrepair. (And it was indulgently whispered in drawing rooms everywhere that his wife had not spoken a single word to him since.)

"An American, especially one as flashy as her," James added, trying not to think any more of the Marquess of Stokes and his money problems, for it hit too close to home, "would be Mother's worst nightmare. My worst nightmare, too, I suppose. If I ever decided to marry, I would choose a woman who would fade into the wallpaper and let me forget that I'd *been* married."

A group of gentlemen in the far corner laughed at some private joke, then the room fell to a conversational murmur again.

"You're the only peer I know who says '*if* I was ever to marry,'" Whitby commented. "You are such a rebel, Wentworth. You always were."

"I'm not a rebel. I just don't have it in me to be anyone's doting husband. I want to put it off as long as possible, or perhaps even avoid it altogether."

"Oh, how hard could it be? You live in a house big enough that you'd never have to see her, except when you wish it."

James scoffed at the simplicity of Whitby's opinions. "Women are a little more complicated than that, my friend. Most don't like to be ignored, especially if, God forbid, they fancy themselves in love with you."

Whitby nodded at a gentleman as he passed, then leaned in closer to James. "A wife can be a business matter, if you handle it right."

"Perhaps. But I am fortunate enough to have a younger brother to fall back on if I wish it, as far as an heir is concerned. Martin will definitely marry. He's not like me or Father. He's softhearted and he enjoys falling in love."

For somehow, Martin had escaped what James had inherited—the passionate nature that had dragged his ancestors into a dark, inhuman hell on earth. James couldn't help hoping that his younger brother's calmer nature would put an end to the cycle of violence. At times, James felt as if he was merely holding down the fort, so to speak, managing the dukedom until Martin was old enough and wise enough to understand that he was the family's greatest hope—the most promising link in the hereditary chain.

Whitby conceded, and James knew he had distracted the man from asking any more intrusive questions.

The heiress turned to glance his way then, and he found himself locked in a titillating moment of acknowledgment.

They gazed at one another. God, her eyes were enormous. Feeling his brow furrow with bewildered awe, James noted the paradox of her full, dewy lips. They were sweetly innocent, yet at the same time brimming with bewitching, irresistible sexuality. He found himself imagining all kinds of things he would like to do in the dark with those appealing, wet lips.

A base, masculine instinct to take the steps necessary to indulge himself with her shook him from the inside out and unnerved him exceedingly. He had not felt a pull quite like it in years. Since he was a defiant adolescent, to be exact. These days, he never played games with young, marriageable women. He kept his affairs discreet and respectable—limiting himself solely to lovers who were already married.

After a time, the heiress nodded cordially toward him. He inclined his head in return, then she calmly returned to her conversation with Lord Bradley.

That was it.

She touched her host's forearm, reacting to something he had said. Lord Bradley glanced down, quite evidently shocked at her informality. He recovered fast, however, with an ardent blush and a new sparkle in his eye that made him look ten years younger.

James felt the corner of his mouth turn up slightly.

Indeed. He couldn't remember the last time a woman had stirred the long-buried embers of his susceptibilities.

For a fleeting, reckless moment, he ignored his principled inner voice—the voice that told him to look away—and thought he might like to meet her after all. To be properly introduced that is, and see where a casual acquaintance might lead. He had been complaining of boredom lately.

But was it really boredom? he wondered with some uneasiness. He wasn't altogether certain. He'd become so adept at strangling his desires that he couldn't really remember what they felt like anymore.

Better that than the alternative, he thought, further reminding himself that he was still the son of a hot-tempered beast and the grandson of a paranoid killer, and to unleash his passions—passions of any kind—would be perilous.

With that, he quickly crushed the impulse to meet the heiress and prudently joined a group of gentlemen in the gallery discussing politics.

Mrs. Beatrice Wilson watched helplessly from across the crowded drawing room as the handsome Duke of Wentworth walked out. She glanced up at her daughter, Sophia, conversing attentively with an aging marchioness, blissfully unaware of anything going on around her. In particular the departure of the most prestigious and difficult catch in all of London. Hadn't Sophia noticed that he was leaving the room?

When the marchioness excused herself, Beatrice led Sophia to a quiet corner. "Darling, let us go and find the countess. You *must* be presented to the duke. What's the matter? Why are you looking at me like that?"

Sophia pressed a hand to her forehead. "Mother, I'm afraid I don't feel very well."

"You don't *feel* very well? But the Duke of Wentworth is here, and from what I've heard, he rarely attends drawing rooms. We cannot let this opportunity pass us by."

It had been a long year of struggles for Beatrice Wilson, who was growing tired and weary of the exertion. Sophia, in her innocence, did not understand the importance of her marriage—how crucial it was that she marry *well*. She did not know that romance and passion would not last through the years. She still believed that she should marry for love and love alone, and that nothing else mattered.

Beatrice loved her daughters too much to let them make poor choices and have to live unhappily with those choices. Beatrice wanted security for her girls, safety, and she knew how easily money could come and go, and how easy it was to be cast out of good society when the money *went*.

British titles, however—there was something that would last. Here in the aristocracy, all a woman had to do was birth her babies, and her child's social position would be guaranteed.

"Are you ill?" Beatrice asked, touching her daughter's forehead.

"I might be. I don't think tonight is a good night to meet the duke. Can't we go home?"

There it was again—that immovable resistance. Sophia had always been strong-willed.

There was, however, something else tonight—something different in Sophia's disposition. Beatrice wished she could put her finger on it. "Didn't you like the look of the duke? I thought he was very handsome."

Her daughter considered the question. "To be honest, Mother, I didn't. He is not the sort I'm looking for."

"How can you make that judgment without even speaking to him? It will not do any harm to be introduced. Then you can decide whether or not you like him."

"I don't want to be introduced."

"Sophia, you must give the man a chance. You cannot afford to be so picky. The Season will not last forever, and your father has invested a great deal to—"

"Mother, you promised you would let me make my own choice."

Beatrice's heart squeezed painfully at the reminder. Yes, she had promised.

Feeling drained and in no mood for a battle, Beatrice cupped her daughter's chin. If she wasn't feeling well, she wasn't feeling well. What could be done? "Let's get our cloaks then."

She walked out with her daughter, wondering if she should have stood her ground and insisted upon an introduction to the duke. Once again, she felt the uncomfortable weight of her shortcomings. Her husband had always said that she was too easy on her daughters, that she spoiled them. But how could she help it, when she loved them so very much?

The next morning, James went thoughtfully to his own study to read the *Morning Post* and deal with correspondence. As he settled into his chair and leaned back, his gaze fell upon the oak-paneled wall, and for some reason he thought of the American heiress.

He wondered what she would accomplish while she was here—what chubby little impoverished lord she and her mother would snare. They certainly wouldn't have any problem charming the ones they wanted. Lately, the American girls were putting the average country squire's daughter to shame. The Americans, after all, were off traveling the world, learning science and art and languages from the best tutors money could buy and seeing for themselves the beauty of the Tempietto or the Sistine Chapel, while the English girls were being educated by a governess or two in a drafty, second-floor schoolroom in the rural English outback.

James was suddenly angry at himself. He was probably one of many gentlemen sitting in his study this morning, staring at the wall and thinking of *her* . . .

No more.

Efficiently, he dealt with the first letter on top of the huge pile, then reached for the next. It was from one of Martin's instructors at Eton—the headmaster in fact.

James read the note. Martin was in trouble again. He'd been caught with a bottle of rum and a laundry maid in his room. The headmaster intended to suspend Martin, and wished for instructions as to where the boy should be sent.

No, not Martin.

Tipping his head back in the chair, James contemplated how to handle this. Martin had always been the quiet, well-behaved child. What was this about?

Perhaps it was simply the natural recklessness of youth. "Boys will be boys," some said.

James, who had always kept his distance from his family and had no intentions of altering that habit, knew he was not the person to provide guidance to Martin. James had been the victim of harsh discipline all his young life, and he would not put himself on the other side of that fence. Nor did he know of any other alternative methods, for he knew only the example set by his father.

After some considerartion, he decided to send Martin to their aunt Caroline in Exeter—his mother's sister—who would be better equipped to deal with this kind of thing. James penned the necessary letters, then firmly swept that problem from his mind and reached for the paper folded on his desk, still warm from the butler's iron.

He had just glanced at the front page when a footman knocked and entered, carrying the gold-trimmed salver. He held the small tray out to James. "This just arrived for you, Your Grace."

James took the letter and recognized the handwriting. It was from his agent, Mr. Wells. The footman departed and James broke the seal.

My Lord Duke,

I regret to inform you that there has been some damage to the roof over the state room. A few days ago, it sprung a leak, causing some unsightly stains in the carpet and furniture. The carpenter I sent for was a rather portly man, and the roof collapsed quite violently under his weight. We now know that the roof was thoroughly rotted, which leads me to wonder how the rest of it will fare over the coming winter.

As you are aware of the state of the finances, I will refrain from repeating the gravity of the situation. I am only hoping you will make a decision regarding the sale of the French tapestries in the west wing, as well as the works of art we discussed in the gallery.

James closed his eyes and pinched the bridge of his nose to fight the tension throbbing in his head. He wondered why all these problems were accruing now, like some kind of test.

He squeezed his left hand, making a fist to ease the pain of a childhood injury that still ached after more than twenty years. He stared intently at his palm, then turned his hand over, remembering the impossible weight of the trunk lid, then—like he always did—he pushed those memories away.

Should he sell the French tapestries? he wondered. They would probably bring in enough to cover the roof repairs.

His mother would not weather the gossip well, though.

Even if James did sell them, however, what after that? The lake needed to be dredged, and his mother's and Lily's pin money had been cut back to almost nothing. On top of that, they were slipping into debt more and more each year. Expenses were rising, revenues were falling. Land just didn't bring the kind of profits it used to, thanks to the worst agricultural depression of the century.

He'd already raised the rents. He would not do it again.

James took a deep breath and let his thoughts return to the American heiress. He remembered the ostentatious diamond that hung between her delectable breasts. That diamond alone would clear up last year's entire deficit.

He stared unseeing at the lace-covered window beside his desk and thought about what Whitby had said about taking a wife—that it could be a matter of business if one handled it right.

Wouldn't it make sense, then, to marry a woman who was as determined as he was to marry for something other than love? A title for instance?

Lord, it was the one thing he'd always despised—that hungry look from women who wanted him because he was a duke.

That's what his mother had wanted when she'd married his father. She'd been blinded by the pomp and ceremony that followed him everywhere, and look where it had taken her. To hell and back.

He leaned forward in his chair. Most likely, the vivacious American heiress was nothing like his mother. He suspected the girl could take care of herself. She had a certain independent quality about her.

Would that be a good thing or a bad thing in a marriage? he wondered. He'd always wished his mother had been stronger against his father. . . .

Perhaps he could go to the Weldon House ball this evening after all. The American was sure to be there. Not that he'd made any firm decisions of course, or because he was fancying her. He was not so easily swept away, nor did he ever plan to be. He would never allow it. He'd spent his entire life training himself to avoid passion and the loss of one's senses that accompanied it. He was as fixed and unyielding as a rock.

So what was there to worry about? He wasn't capable of any kind of true, deep love for a woman. Not with his upbringing.

He decided then that his attendance at the ball would be a reconnaissance mission. A matter of business, for the fact remained that he had to save the estate and the dukedom from financial ruin, for if he didn't, not even Martin would be able to solve the family's deeper, more ancient problems.

Perhaps if James could fix what was wrong in the short term, the next generation might provide the heir to end the madness. Maybe a loveless marriage to a wealthy, socially ambitous heiress would be a means of treading water. If James didn't lose his head, like his father and his other ancestors had, he would be doing a great service to his family. Something that could turn out to be the saving grace they all so desperately needed.

It was decided then. He would see her again and close his eyes to her beauty and charm. What she looked like or how she behaved would not be part of his criteria. For the good of all—the heiress included—his motives would remain mercenary.

Chapter 2

Sophia's stomach flip-flopped with nervous anticipation as the carriage approached the grand, gothic Weldon House. All the windows of the stone mansion were lit up in the night, and gentlemen with top hats and ladies on their arms strolled up the long red carpet that led to the front door.

Across from Sophia in the dimly lit carriage sat her mother, wearing yet another brand-new Worth gown of pink satin and gold lace, and Florence Kent, Countess of Lansdowne—who wore a deep blue silk gown trimmed in *galon d'argent* and glass pearls, adorned with a striking embroidered sunburst on the skirt.

"Now remember," Florence said as she pulled on her gloves, "the Marquess of Blackburn will be here, as well as the Earl of Whitby and the Earl of Manderlin— all unattached and looking. They are your first priority this evening, Sophia. There's also a baron ... from

Norfolk. I can never remember his name. "

Sophia's mother interrupted. "What about the duke? Will he be here?"

Florence gave Beatrice a surprised look. "He rarely comes to balls. And I wouldn't set your sights that high. I'm beginning to think he's made of stone. No one has been able to move him. Oh, look, it's our turn."

Relieved that the countess had dismissed the duke as a potential groom, Sophia remembered what the English girl had said about him: *Avoid him unless you want to marry into a nightmare. They say his family is cursed.*

Cursed in what way? she wondered.

The coach pulled up in front of the house, and the door swung open. A liveried footman assisted the ladies down onto the walk, and together, they made their way up the long red carpet, crowned overhead by a striped awning, to the front door.

They had to pause there in the doorway behind another couple, while they waited to move into the hall and greet their hosts. The lady in front of them turned her head and smiled, then faced forward again, leaning into her escort to whisper, "It's the American."

Sophia felt a sudden rush of anxiety, as if she was flailing in dangerously deep waters. For a fleeting moment, she wanted to turn around and run back to the coach and tell the driver to take her home. Not just to Florence's house, but to America. To her sisters. To the easy way they were with each other, and the way they laughed and giggled and humored their mother. What were the girls doing now? Were they sleeping in their beds? Or were they awake and telling tales in front of the parlor fireplace?

The line finally moved and Sophia greeted the hosts

on the curved marble staircase, then made her way up
to the withdrawing room to remove her cloak and tidy
her gown and hair.

Her mother tugged on her arm, and Sophia—so
much taller than her little mother—leaned down.

"Remember, if you discover the duke has come, tell
me immediately. I will spare nothing to have you presented to him and to get you a dance with him. Just one
dance. You owe me that much, Sophia."

Sophia swallowed hard, trying to control her displeasure at the thought of her mother sparing "nothing."

"Mother, if you could just leave it to me and stay out
of it and let things happen naturally—"

"Stay out of it?" her mother whispered. "How can I
stay out of it when I am your mother, and I want the
very best for you? I know you want the fairy tale,
Sophia, but sometimes fairy tales in real life . . ."

She stopped at that, and Sophia was glad, for the
thought of her mother trying to "hook" that devilish
duke tonight made her want to sink through the cracks
in the floor and not come out until morning.

She decided then that she would not allow herself to
be "presented" to him like a raspberry custard on a
platter, there for him to sniff and taste, to see if he liked
her flavor. Tonight, *she* would be in control, and if she
decided she wanted to meet the duke, she would meet
him when she was good and ready—with her head
steady on her shoulders and her feet planted firmly on
the ground.

As was becoming of a duke, James arrived at the
dance late and strolled into the ballroom with his dancing gloves on. His cool gaze swept the room, which

sparkled with massive brass chandeliers hanging low, and the glitter of gold lace on richly colored gowns. The floor was polished smooth and shiny like a reflecting pool, and couples were swirling around the room, turning and dipping to the magnificent flow of a Strauss waltz.

James felt the gazes follow him as he meandered through the crowd, past eager-looking young ladies with dance cards and short pencils dangling from their wrists, their fans swaying languidly in front of their flushed faces. Whitby spotted him from across the room and, with a flourish, raised his champagne glass in salute. Within moments, the earl was making his way past leafy palms and ferns, around the perimeter of the room.

"You came after all," he said, arriving at James's side. "This is a change for you, out two nights in a row. Reminds me of the old days."

Whitby and James went back many years, their friendship beginning at Eton and peaking when they were both expelled for building a giant slingshot that sent a stone smashing through the headmaster's office window.

James thought back to those days. He'd had a lot of anger in him then, and so had Whitby. That's what had brought them together, he supposed.

"You came to see her again," the earl said.

"Who?"

"The American, of course." At least Whitby had the presence of mind to lower his voice.

"She's making the rounds again tonight, is she?" James replied in a disinterested tone, wondering if he should request a spot on her card.

"Naturally." Whitby raised his glass toward the

dance floor. "Over there. In burgundy. Dancing with that baron from Norfolk . . . oh, what's his name? I can never remember it."

The man's name was Lord Hatfield, but James kept silent, for his attention was totally and completely fixed on the vision coming toward him, swirling and spinning, smiling and glistening.

She drew closer, then he heard the *swish* of her silk gown, smelled her perfume, and just as she twirled in front of him, their eyes met. There was that look again—that haughty, indifferent little smirk.

By God, she was a magnificent creature.

Then he considered making a wife out of her. She would certainly *not* fade into any wallpaper he'd ever seen, and judging by the way his body was reacting to her now—buzzing to life like a brand-new, flickering electric lamp—he knew any hope that this could be a business matter was thoroughly ridiculous.

Bloody hell, he was not interested in any kind of marriage that stirred passions, regardless of its profitability. In fact, he'd always been wholly determined to avoid anything like that at all costs. Surely there were other ways to manage his finances.

"Lucky baron," Whitby remarked, after she'd gone by.

"Why don't you dance with her then? Or have you already?"

"Not yet. Soon, though. I took the last spot on her card."

So her card was full. There would be no dancing with the heiress tonight. *Probably for the best,* James thought. If he knew what was good for him, he would dance with a few wallflowers, then take his leave.

The waltz ended and he and Whitby wandered

around the room, stopping to chat with the Wileys and the Carswells and the Nortons. They reached the far corner and took champagne glasses from a passing footman.

At that moment, they each noticed the heiress turn from her conversation with Lord Bradley and take a direct path toward them. Her mother came hurrying along behind her.

"Good heavens, is she coming over here?" Whitby said with some alarm.

It was a well-known fact that a lady never dashed at a gentleman in a ballroom; she waited quietly for him to speak to her.

Americans, James said to himself, with an amused shake of his head.

Whitby straightened visibly as she approached.

"Good evening, Lord Whitby," she said. Her voice was deep and sultry, like velvet. Just as James had imagined it would be. "It's lovely to see you again."

The orchestra started up again, with a minuet.

Whitby smiled, and James could sense his friend's strong interest in the woman before them. Her mother came up late behind her, looking flustered.

"Wentworth," Whitby said, "may I present to you Miss Sophia Wilson and Mrs. Beatrice Wilson, of America. His Grace, the Duke of Wentworth."

Miss Wilson offered her gloved hand.

Did she know that she was breaking another rule? That unmarried ladies do not offer their hands to dukes—and especially not in ballrooms?

"Your Grace, I am honored." She did not curtsy.

James held her hand briefly. He knew a mistake like that could pulverize a young woman's social prospects in an instant.

Did she even care?

Probably not, for she must know that it was that very quality among her fellow countrywomen here in London—those who made the most of their "uniqueness" by breaking all the rules—that amused the Prince of Wales and had turned these beautiful American heiresses into such curiosities. "The honor is all mine, Miss Wilson."

He kissed her hand.

"I believe I saw you at the Bradley assembly last evening," she said.

James made a slight bow. "Indeed, I was there for a short time. You left early, however."

"I'm flattered that you gave my presence a second thought."

She was certainly bold, James thought, and right in front of her mother. He glanced down at the small woman with the enormous jewels around her neck, her eyes round and questioning, as if she were struggling to follow what was going on. James wondered what to make of her.

"Are you enjoying your visit to London, Mrs. Wilson?" he asked the woman.

"Yes, Your Grace. Thank you," she replied, seeming flattered that he had asked. Her voice had a sharp, thorny quality to it.

The young heiress wore a pleasant expression as she gazed down at her mother. Then, with disinterest, she turned her attention back to James, and he guessed that this was all for her mother's benefit, to satisfy the woman's desire to present her daughter to a duke.

"And where is your home, Your Grace?" she asked. "What part of the country?"

"Yorkshire," he told her.

"I've heard it's lovely in the north."

He made no further comment, and there was an awkward, uncomfortable silence.

"Do you have siblings there?" she asked.

"I do."

"Brothers or sisters?"

"Both."

"How nice. Are you very close to them? Do they travel to London with you when you come?"

Whitby cleared his throat as if to say something, and James somehow knew his friend was going to correct the heiress on her behavior, for she had made another mistake.

James suspected it was just as unimportant to her as the last one.

"Miss Wilson," Whitby said quietly, "perhaps someone should inform you that such personal questions may be acceptable in your home country, but here in England, they are considered rudely intrusive. I only mention it now as a friend, to save you some embarrassment. Has no one told you that?"

He said it kindly, as gently as possible, but still, the mother appeared quite horrified at the situation. Her daughter, however, revealed nothing of the sort.

"Yes, I have been told." She snapped open her fan and flapped it leisurely in front of her face. "But I thank you all the same."

Whitby made a slight bow as if to say "you're welcome," and all James could do was try not to laugh out loud and say "Bravo!" to the girl. Perhaps Whitby was right. Perhaps James was more of a rebel than he thought, for why else would he be so impressed by such a display. She had smirked at the English social code and didn't seem to give a damn. That's why Bertie was so taken with her—because of her daring nonconformity. It kept him entertained. It was a good thing, too, for if not for the Prince's enthusiastic endorsement, she would be finished.

James gazed down at the frazzled mother, who had gone pale and seemed to think all was lost. He simply had to ease the poor woman's mind.

"I was disappointed to hear that your dance card is full," he said to Miss Wilson. "Perhaps next time I will arrive in time to—"

A look of panic flew across her mother's face. "Oh! No, Your Grace! Her card is not full! I've kept one dance open. The last one."

Somehow he was not surprised. James smiled. "Then would you be so kind as to allow me to fill it?"

"Oh, yes! Yes!" The mother grabbed clumsily for the card at her daughter's wrist, tugged it downward and quickly penciled in his name.

The small woman's cheeks flushed with what he could only describe as a mixture of triumph and ravenous hunger. There it was again. Nothing new, though English mothers of marriageable daughters usually did a better job at hiding it than this one.

Miss Wilson smiled politely. "I'll look forward to it, Your Grace."

He settled his gaze on her. *No, you won't.*

Just then, a gentleman appeared out of nowhere, took her hand, and led her to the center of the floor. James watched her intently as she began a *Quadrille*.

Mrs. Wilson excused herself and ventured off toward a group of ladies, and James was left standing with Whitby, who immediately chided himself.

"What was I thinking? Correcting her like that?"

James laughed. "She certainly took it well."

"Ah, but I wouldn't be surprised if she decided to cross me off her card tonight. Damn my idiocy. I was hoping to make a good impression. But really, I wouldn't doubt that she caused a few horrified swoonings just now, refusing to curtsy to you. Unless she wants to be cast out of London altogether, she really should be familiar with our manners and customs."

"I do believe she is, Whitby. She just does what she likes." Before James walked away, he patted the earl on the arm, and added quietly, "Good luck with that one. You'll need it."

He decided at that moment, to give up the idea of any kind of match with her—dowry or no dowry—for somehow, she had managed, in that brief, casual encounter, to again stir what had for years been consciously and contentedly still.

Near the end of the night, James found his mother standing by the door where there was a breeze, fanning herself and looking displeased.

"I saw you talking to the American," she said right off.

"Lord Whitby made the introduction."

"Hardly. I saw her march right up to you, bold as brass." She glanced in the other direction. "Those Americans are always introducing *themselves*."

Hands clasped behind his back, James stood in a relaxed position beside his mother. Neither of them said anything for a time. They simply watched the dancing.

"Lord Weatherbee's daughter is out, you know," his mother said. "Have you spoken to her this evening? She's a charming little thing. Shame about Lady Weatherbee. Passed away last year."

The Dowager Duchess knew she should never push young girls in James's face. She knew how much he loathed it, and that to do so did more harm than good. She was trying to be subtle now, but he knew what she was doing. He did not reply.

"Look, there's Lily," the duchess said. "Dancing with that baron. Unfortunate, isn't it, how short he is?"

James smiled at his sister as she went by, dressed in a cream gown trimmed in gold. She looked like she was enjoying herself.

A few minutes later, the final dance of the evening began. He'd been waiting for it—rather impatiently, he had to admit.

He let his gaze calmly sweep the room and spotted the heiress at the precise instant she spotted him. He smiled and inclined his head, she smiled in return, and he took a step to go to her. Just then, his mother—whom he had completely forgotten just now—took hold of his sleeve.

"You're not going to dance with her, are you?" she asked, the lines on her hard face deepening with concern.

James retrieved his arm from the duchess's grasp. "You forget yourself, Mother."

She released him and took a step back, her face pale with pent-up frustration at not being able to stop him.

Her displeasure had no effect on James, however, for since he had become a man, they both knew she could not control him. Beatings in the schoolroom were no longer possible, and God knew, he felt no obligation to please or appease her. No desire to make her happy or proud.

James let the altercation roll swiftly and smoothly off his back, then straightened his tie and started off across the room toward the heiress.

Chapter 3

After giving Miss Wilson a moment to lift her train, James closed his gloved hand around hers and stepped into the "Blue Danube" with confidence and grace. He did enjoy dancing, and he was pleasantly surprised at the ease with which the heiress followed his lead. On her feet she was as weightless as a cloud floating upon a strong summer breeze. She smelled like flowers; he wasn't sure what kind, only that they reminded him of spring when he was a boy—of the rare afternoons he was permitted to go off on his own, over the green grass and heath and bracken, down to the pleasingly calm, secluded lake.

He hadn't thought of such things in a long time.

They danced the first few moments without speaking or making eye contact. He began to wonder what kind of life she led. What sort of house she lived in, what kind of education she'd had. She had asked him if he had siblings. He wondered the same of her now. If

33

so, how many? Did she have sisters or brothers? Was she the oldest? Did they look alike? Where did she get her confidence and her beauty? She certainly didn't get her height from her mother. Perhaps her father was a tall man.

"You dance very well," he said at last, when she finally looked him in the eye.

"Only because you are a strong lead, Your Grace. It's easy to follow you." She said nothing more, and he found it strange that she was not talking. He'd seen her converse with every other partner this evening. She had always been talking and smiling and laughing.

"Why won't you look at me?" he asked, eager to dispense with the gentlemanly courtesies—for he was hardly a gentleman at heart—and get straight to the point.

Her astonished gaze darted up at him. "Most of the other ladies aren't looking at their partners."

"But you've been looking at your partners all evening. Why not me? Do you dislike me? If so, I should at least like to know the reason—even if it is completely warranted." He spun her around to avoid bumping into another couple.

"I don't dislike you. I barely know you. You simply strike me as a man who doesn't enjoy light conversation. Beautiful turn, Your Grace."

"Why would you think such a thing? Do you believe yourself clever enough to judge a man by taking one look at him?"

"You're very direct, aren't you?"

"Why bother with niceties when plain speaking is so much more efficient."

She gave him a brief glance that told him he had surprised and challenged her, then she took a moment to consider his question. "Well, Your Grace, since we are being forthright, I will acquaint you with the fact that I have heard the London gossip—that you are called the Dangerous Duke—and I therefore feel compelled to exercise some caution with you. On the other hand, I do possess a mind of my own, and I have always been reluctant to believe every piece of idle chatter that lands before me. I wanted to decide for myself what kind of man you were, so I watched you this evening. I ascertained that you haven't smiled once all night, except at that lovely dark-haired woman a few minutes ago—the one in the cream-and-gold dress. You don't seem to enjoy socializing, and from what I understand, you rarely come to balls and assemblies. From that, I gather you don't have much to talk about, or much interest in what others have to say."

Good God, what an answer.

But there was more.

"And as far as being clever enough to judge a man by taking one look at him," she said, "let it be known, Your Grace, that I took more than one look at you. Both tonight and last night."

More than one look. Was she flirting, or just trying to support her superbly categorical rebuttal? Probably the latter, he thought, remembering all that she had said. Still, there was a fine line between candor and seduction, once the barriers of polite behavior were breached.

James pulled her a little closer. "All gossip about me aside, haven't you ever heard the old adage that still waters run deep?"

She considered that. She seemed to always think before she spoke. "And do you believe you are like those deep, still waters, Your Grace? Hidden and unexplored?" She narrowed her eyes playfully. "Or perhaps dark and abyssmal?"

They whirled past a statue of Cupid spouting water into a little pool. James couldn't help smiling. He wanted to laugh! No woman had ever entertained him quite like this. "That depends. Which do you prefer?"

For a long moment she was silent, then she laughed. An infectious, bright, American laugh. He'd managed that, at least. He spun her around again, and she followed him flawlessly.

Sophia, trying to catch her breath, gazed up at the handsome man leading her around the floor. She felt like she was flying. Her heart rate was accelerating, and she wasn't sure if it was the exercise—dancing and swirling around the room at such stupendous speed— or the preposterous subject matter of a conversation like this, with a man she knew had been labeled "dangerous" by good society.

He spun her around at the edge of the dance floor, then moved toward the center.

Sophia became all too aware of how large and strong and magnificently male he was. His shoulders were broad beneath her tiny gloved hand; he even smelled virile—musky and clean. And what skill on the dance floor! This was by far the best dance of the night.

The duke smiled down at her. Something enticingly wicked flashed in his eyes. It excited Sophia and planted in her an exotic desire to flirt and act recklessly. Maybe this was why they called him dangerous. He had the power to deliver irreversible ruin to someone like her.

"Ah," he said, "I can see a light in your eyes. You are reconsidering your first impression of me, and you are beginning to find me moderately charming."

Sophia could not stop herself from smiling. "Only moderately, Your Grace, but no more than that."

She felt his hand move a mere inch up her back, and wished her brain would behave. There was no need even to notice where his hand was from one second to the next. Or how it made her skin erupt in tingling gooseflesh.

"Well, that is a start, at least." He twirled her around again.

Sophia tried to change the subject, for she was beginning to feel dizzy, and not from the dancing. "As I said before, I heard you don't often come to balls. I hadn't expected to see you tonight." *Nor had I wanted to, for I was afraid of exactly this.*

He grinned. "What was it you said to me earlier this evening? Oh yes: 'I'm flattered you'd given my presence a second thought.'"

Sophia sighed. "You're a very unique man, Your Grace."

James pulled her a little closer—as close as the rules of polite behavior allowed. He was pushing the limits, though, and it sent a hot spark through her veins. She had never felt anything like it. It was all-encompassing. Thrillingly naughty.

He gently squeezed her gloved hand in his. Lord, his hands were so big. Warm, even through the gloves. She had never imagined that dancing with a man could be so impossibly knockdown, electrifying to her senses.

"Unique am I? You're too kind. What flattery."

She gave him another smile.

The waltz was coming to an end, and disappointment muddled James's thoughts. He found himself quite unable to accept that this would be the last time he would talk with Miss Wilson, and surprised that he even cared. He hadn't expected to enjoy conversing with her as much as he had.

He could always come to another ball, he supposed, but people would take notice and distinguish whom he was hoping to see. Not that he cared what people thought. It would matter only to his mother.

He didn't care about that either. In fact, something about it tempted him.

James made another turn on the floor, and Miss Wilson followed him expertly. The corner of her full, pouty mouth curved up in a delicious little smile, and a base, male instinct sparked and flared instantly in his veins.

He wanted her. Every inch of her. There was no doubt about it. And being the highest-ranking peer in the room, he was very likely at the top of her peer-shopping list.

A small part of him felt a tremor of satisfaction at that—to know that if he desired to have her and all her bags of money, she would probably choose him above the rest.

It was highly uncharacteristic of him, he suddenly realized, to enjoy being the object of women's ambitions. He supposed he was looking at his match. With all her money, she was as much an object of ambition as he.

The music ended, and the dance was over. James stepped away from the heiress. She let her train drop to the floor. For a long moment they stood in the middle of the ballroom, looking at each other while other couples flowed around them like water past a rock. He should say good night to her now. Return her to her mother. . . .

"I should like to call on the Countess of Lansdowne

tomorrow afternoon," he heard himself saying, "if she is at home."

Calmly and coolly, Miss Wilson inclined her head. "I'm sure the countess would be honored, Your Grace."

Another few seconds dragged by before Miss Wilson gestured toward the edge of the dance floor, now almost cleared of guests. "I see my mother."

Her mother . . . yes. James offered his arm and escorted Miss Wilson off the floor.

"Thank you, Your Grace," the older woman said, smiling brightly.

James made a bow. "It was my pleasure, Mrs. Wilson. Do enjoy the rest of your evening." With that, he turned and took his leave.

During the carriage ride home from the ball, Sophia felt thoroughly dazed. Her mother and the countess sat together on the opposite seat, gloating and scheming, thrilled that Sophia had danced with the duke, not to mention the fact that he had kept her on the floor so long afterward, gazing at her.

Sophia barely heard a word they said. She was staring at the window, feeling weak and breathless and thunderstruck about tomorrow, for he had said he would call.

Lord! He had been such a magnificent dancer. The way he had held her about the waist—with such firm control and adept skill. It had been effortless to float along with him, following his strong lead about the room. It was as if she had possessed wings.

All at once, she remembered the disconcertingly erotic feel of her small hand inside his strong one, and here in the carriage, something fiery and startling swooped inside her belly. It was the same sensation she had experienced earlier, when she'd noticed the moist heat from his hand and reveled in it.

She'd never really felt anything like these swooping butterflies before. They were both physical and ethereal, for her pulse was racing, her skin tingling, while her mind was floating in a sea of emotional fascination.

She struggled, however, to remember that her mind must rule her emotions, and recalled what the young woman at the assembly had said. *A cruel lot, all of them.*

She had not forgotten it, nor had she forgotten the importance of being careful. She tossed her head, to throw a fallen lock of hair out of her eyes, and reminded herself of it again. *Choose with your head, Sophia. Be prudent. You are not only choosing a lover, you are choosing the practicalities of the rest of your life.*

Yet, her heart continued to tumble in her chest.

"I wonder when you'll see him again, Sophia," Florence said.

Sophia stared numbly at her mother and the countess. She saw the victory in their eyes. The aspirations. She heard the words *He's a duke!* bouncing off the walls inside the carriage, even though no one was actually saying it.

She tried to speak with indifference. "I don't know. Perhaps he will be at the Berkley assembly."

She was glad she'd lied, she decided, when the ladies turned back to their scheming and left her to gaze at the dark window again. Otherwise, they would question her all day tomorrow about when he would arrive. They would make her change her dress a dozen times, they would grill her on proper etiquette, and her mother would spend the whole day reminding her not to lean forward when she rose from her chair. She would most likely get caught up in the hoopla herself, and become even more tempted by a man she barely knew—a man who appeared to harbor a mysterious, dangerous darkness in his depths.

And oh, the certain uproar if he did not come. There would be questions about that. Conjecture. Reproach.

No, she would not put herself through that. They would be surprised when he arrived—*if* he arrived— and she would be surprised as well. Because under no circumstances was she going to spend another minute thinking about him.

"Is it common knowledge, here?" Sophia asked her mother over the breakfast table the next morning. "How much I am worth?"

Her mother set down her teacup and the fine china made a delicate clinking sound. She and the countess exchanged looks of concern. "Why do you ask, darling?"

Sophia wiped her mouth with her linen napkin. "I'm curious if there is an exact number floating around out there. Mind you, I'm not naive, I know there must be speculation, but do they know *exactly* how much Father is willing to pay?"

Mrs. Wilson cleared her throat. "I certainly haven't told anyone, except Florence, of course."

The countess didn't look up from her plate, and Sophia felt a ripple of mild anger. "Florence knows, but I don't?"

She glanced up at the footman standing behind the countess. Like a soldier on duty, he kept his gaze level, giving no hint that he was listening to the conversation, not even a hint that there was anything going on inside his head at all. Sophia knew there was, of course. The servants tried to act invisible, but they weren't. Not to her. They were human beings like everyone else, and they probably enjoyed the blue bloods' performance each day, like one big continuing opera—complete with costumes, glitter, and light.

Her mother reached for a roll and began to butter it vigorously. "There is no exact amount, Sophia."

"There must be a range." She looked up at the footman, and said, "Would you excuse us please? Just for a moment." He walked out.

Sophia pressed her mother further. "Well? Did Father give you some indication?"

"Oh, Sophia, why must you ask these questions?"

"Because I have a right to know how the world works, Mother. And certainly what my chances are of finding a man who will marry me not just for my money."

"No one will ever marry you *just* for your money, Sophia," Florence said. "You're a very beautiful woman. That will play a significant part in this."

"So it's my looks and my money. I don't mean to sound ungrateful, but don't my heart and soul and mind have any part to play?"

The two older women both reassured her at once. "Of course they do, darling! That goes without saying!"

Sophia ate a few more bites of her breakfast. "You still haven't told me how much Father is willing to pay."

After an uncertain hesitation, her mother replied, "He seemed to think five hundred thousand pounds was the going rate, darling, but there is of course room for negotiation, depending on who makes the proposal."

"It's quite standard," Florence added.

The going rate. Sophia sat in silence for a few moments, feeling her appetite drain away. "Thank you for telling me."

She said nothing more, and Florence rang her little bell for the footman to return and bring more tea. When he went to fetch it, Sophia made one quick request.

"Will you please not tell anyone, not even a gentleman who expresses interest? I know that there are of course presumptions that I will come with money, but I would prefer that it not be a certainty. That if a man wishes to propose to me, he would at least be willing to take the risk that my dowry might not be what he thinks or hopes it is."

Both women were quiet for a moment, looking at each other over the table. "If that will make you happy, Sophia, then yes, of course. Our lips will be sealed until you find a man you can love."

The word *love* uttered from her mother's lips was a surprise, one that made all the muscles in Sophia's back and shoulders relax. She let out a breath. "Thank you, Mother." Then she rose from her chair and kissed her on the cheek.

James stepped from his carriage, looked up at the front of Lansdowne House, and wondered uncomfortably if he was doing the right thing. It had been an impulse the night before, to say he would call, and he wasn't used to having impulses. He usually knew his reasons for doing things, but today, he was uncertain. Was he here because of the money? Was that the spark that had lit this little fire under him? Or was it Miss Wilson's uniqueness? He supposed it was a little bit of both—though he had never found uniqueness to be a desirable quality in a woman before. Quite the opposite, in fact.

He then considered getting back in his carriage and driving away. Something in him wanted to, but whatever it was, he rejected it. He decided to let this venture play out and see where it led, which would probably be nowhere. He would sit through dull talk about the weather, perhaps some gossip about the ball the night before, but nothing more consequential than that. With that supposition, he walked to the door and knocked.

A few minutes later, he was shown upstairs to the drawing room. The butler announced him, and James moved through the door. His gaze was drawn at once to Miss Wilson seated across the room, a teacup and saucer held in her delicate hands. She wore an ivory, tulle tea gown that complimented her complexion and gave her a look of sweetness—like some whipped cream confection. At the sight of her, he felt a ravenous, predatory rush.

It was the challenge of her, he supposed. She had disliked him on first impression.

There was a brief moment of stunned silence from the other women in the room—the countess and Miss Wilson's mother—then a sudden frazzled flurry of greetings. James moved all the way into the room, but stopped when he saw the dark image of another man to his left, seated by the fireplace. He glanced over to see Whitby.

"Whitby, good to see you," he said, keeping a calm,

cool tone while he shifted his walking stick from one hand to the other.

The earl rose from his chair. "Likewise."

An awkward silence ensued, until Whitby finally gave in to the rules of etiquette and leaned to pick up his hat and stick. It was appropriate that he, having already had a chance to pay his call, should politely bid his hostess *adieu*.

He bowed to the ladies. "I thank you for your society this afternoon, Lady Lansdowne. It was most pleasant. Mrs. Wilson, Miss Wilson? Enjoy your day."

He gave his card to the countess, then brushed by James on the way out. "Wentworth," he said, in a cool, hushed tone.

James swallowed the bitter taste of Whitby now considering him a competitor in the Marriage Mart. Bloody hell, it would probably be in the *Post* tomorrow.

"Won't you come in, Your Grace?" Lady Lansdowne said.

James nodded, trying to forget about Whitby and focus on Miss Wilson, but that wasn't so easy either, considering his own past with the countess. He'd never imagined he would ever call on Lady Lansdowne, not after the awkward circumstances that transpired three years earlier when she'd arrived in London for her first Season and had directed her ambitions toward him. Thank the Lord, the Earl of Lansdowne had proposed and prevented James from openly humiliating her.

"Please, make yourself comfortable," she said. Perhaps she did not even remember it.

Purposefully steering clear of the chair next to the countess, James took a seat beside Mrs. Wilson. A parlormaid poured him a cup of tea.

"It's a beautiful day, is it not, Your Grace?" Lady Lansdowne said. "I don't recall the month of May ever being so full of sunshine."

Ah, the predictable talk of weather.

"It is indeed a pleasant change from the wet spring we had in March," he replied.

"Is it usually this warm?" Mrs. Wilson asked.

The clock ticked on while they continued to make small talk about nothing of any relevance, and at the end of the obligatory fifteen minutes, James wondered why he had even bothered to come at all. Miss Wilson had not said one word.

While her mother went on about the Season in New York, James took the opportunity to study the quiet young woman across from him, sipping tea and contributing nothing to the conversation. Where was her fire from the night before?

"So you see," Mrs. Wilson continued, "it's quite the opposite in America. People tend to leave New York in the summer when it's warm, and retreat to their summer homes, where here, everyone leaves the country to come to the city."

"It is indeed a fascinating contrast," Lady Lansdowne said.

"I don't understand why you wouldn't prefer to be on your estates in the summer," Mrs. Wilson continued, "when the city can be so warm and . . ."

Could it be that Miss Wilson was disappointed that James had arrived and cut Whitby's visit short?

He glanced down at his walking stick, chiding himself. What did he care if she was disappointed or not? All he needed to care about was the simple fact that she was as flagrantly rich this morning as she was last night. Richer probably.

He gazed into her huge, unfathomable blue eyes. Lord, she was the most beautiful, exquisite creature he'd ever seen.

Perhaps he should leave.

At that precise moment, Miss Wilson interrupted. "It's because of Parliament, Mother."

The fact that it was the first time she had spoken was not lost on James. His desire to leave vanished abruptly, and he wondered with some interest if that had been Miss Wilson's intention just now—to keep him in the countess's drawing room a little longer. He felt his mood lift slightly, felt the hot, glowing embers of attraction smolder. He was back in the game.

"Well, of course I know that," Mrs. Wilson replied, but James suspected that she had not known.

Miss Wilson turned her attention to James. "Does Parliament take up a great deal of your time, Your Grace?"

He was thankful to have the opportunity to at last speak directly to her. Her eyes sparkled as she waited for his reply, and with pleasure he finally let himself imagine what it would be like to make love to her. Would she be as spirited in bed as she was in public, breaking etiquette rules in London ballrooms?

He felt a distinct tremor of desire as he studied the shape and line of her breasts and visualized her naked on his bed—with nothing upon her but *him*. Yes, it would give him great pleasure to make love to her.

For the next ten minutes, they talked about lighter Parliamentary matters. Miss Wilson's inquisitive nature and intelligent questions challenged him, and he managed to avoid thinking any more about taking her to bed. He considered more practical matters—like the obvious fact that she would be a fast learner, and a woman had to be such, in order to become a competent duchess.

A competent duchess. Perhaps he was getting ahead of himself.

When the time seemed right, James set down his cup and smiled at the countess. "I thank you, Lady Lansdowne, for the fine discourse this afternoon." He stood. She stood also, and walked him to the drawing room door. He handed her his card. "It was a pleasure, indeed."

He turned to take one last look at Miss Wilson, rising to her feet. "Thank you for coming, Your Grace," she said.

She watched him with some intensity, and again he wondered why she had been so quiet for most of his visit, for he had thought he'd made at least a little bit of progress with her the night before.

James inclined his head at her and walked out.

As soon as the duke left the room, Sophia turned to her mother. "I overheard you talking to the earl before I came in. You promised me you wouldn't tell anyone how much Father is willing to pay."

The color drained from her mother's face. "I'm sorry, darling. I wasn't going to say anything, but the earl expressed an interest in you, and it was my intention to tell him that to propose now would be a mistake—that you wish to truly *know* a gentleman before you can even consider a marriage proposal. I was only trying to do what you wished, but he pressed for more information. I couldn't lie to him. I tried to change the subject, didn't I, Florence?" She looked helplessly at the countess.

"Oh, yes, dear. She did. She was very discreet for as long as she could be, but the earl pressed."

Sophia suspected that wasn't the case. She tried to keep her voice steady. "So now everyone will know how rich we are—not to mention be shocked by the 'gauche Americans,' actually discussing money in drawing rooms."

"I told him in confidence, and he's a gentleman after all."

Sophia shook her head in disbelief. "I'm going to my bedchamber."

She was at the drawing room door when her mother called out, "But dear, aren't you happy about the duke?"

Sophia hesitated, then turned back to kiss her mother on the cheek, for she knew there was no point in punishing her further. She knew she had made a mistake and would probably lose sleep about it tonight. She was a good, kind woman and a loving mother. She simply lacked verbal discipline.

If that was the worst of her mother's character flaws, Sophia should think of her own mother's mother—who sold half her children to buy whiskey after her husband left her—and count herself lucky.

As for her being happy about the duke?

She wouldn't call it "happy." It was something else—something altogether different. Sophia had best be careful.

The liveried footman opened the coach door for James, then closed it when he was seated comfortably inside. Before the horses had a chance to move, however, a frantic knock sounded at the door. Whitby's face loomed in the window, his breath coming in rapid little puffs, fogging up the glass.

"Wait, driver!" James called out, then leaned forward to flick the latch.

"Give me a lift to Green Street?" Whitby asked.

James felt an unorthodox desire to hesitate, but swept it aside and invited his school chum in. Soon they were sitting opposite each other in silence while the carriage wheels rattled down the cobbled street.

"So you've changed your mind then?" Whitby asked.

"About what?" James replied coolly, though he knew exactly what Whitby was speaking of.

"About the heiress. You said you weren't interested."

James heard the animosity in Whitby's voice, saw it in the set of his jaw, but he kept his own voice calm and detached. "I don't recall having set my mind to anything at all."

"You said you weren't declaring anything."

"Precisely. So what are you getting at, Whitby?"

The coach bumped and Whitby shifted in his seat. "I would like you to know that I have declared to Mrs. Wilson an interest in her daughter, and she has given me some encouragement."

James squeezed the ivory handle of his walking stick. "Who has? Mrs. Wilson or her daughter?"

"*Mrs.* Wilson, of course," Whitby replied. "Though the young miss has been singularly forward and friendly and full of smiles on every occasion of our meeting during the past week."

"I believe that is the natural disposition of these American girls," James added with bite. Good God, he was sounding jealous. He quickly recovered his aplomb. "Have you proposed?"

"Well, not exactly. Mrs. Wilson informed me that a proposal at this stage would be a mistake, that Miss Wilson is determined to be courted properly before any disclosures of affection are made."

"Courted properly?" James raised an eyebrow. "How thoroughly American."

Whitby's shoulders rose and fell with frustration, and James guessed that his friend was working hard to control his rancor.

"I didn't think you wanted to get married," Whitby said.

Now he was sounding desperate. James hated this. He should just reassure Whitby that he had no intentions to propose to the girl and let it end at that.

"Did she tell you the amount?" Whitby asked.

The *amount*? Suddenly it was James's turn to feel agitated. "I'm not sure what you're referring to, Whitby."

"The amount of her dowry. Is that why you changed your mind?"

"I didn't change my mind about anything."

"But did Mrs. Wilson tell you?"

James took a deep breath. "Tell me about her daughter's dowry? Good Lord!" He laughed. "The call was not quite so engaging as that. All we talked about was the bloody weather."

"Oh, well . . . good then." Whitby was quiet a moment, staring out the window and looking quite full of relief.

James on the other hand, was beginning to feel tense.

"You actually discussed that? With Mrs. Wilson?" he said with disbelief. "The daughter wasn't present, was she?"

"Good heavens, no. She entered the room later. But I suppose you never know with these Americans."

They drove on a little farther, and James's damned irritating curiosity was beginning to poke at him. He found himself coming up with excuses for why Mrs. Wilson hadn't told *him* about the dowry. It couldn't be that she preferred Whitby. She was peer-hunting after all. She must understand how the aristocracy worked, and know that James was the highest-ranking peer. The countess would certainly know it.

On the other hand, perhaps it had nothing to do with what the mother wanted. Perhaps she knew that her daughter fancied Whitby over James—no matter that James was a duke—and she was aiming at a love match.

The degree of his annoyance at that prospect—that Miss Wilson fancied Whitby—was most unsettling.

"It's an odd business, really," Whitby said, gazing off into space, "that the father should have to pay five hundred thousand pounds to marry off such a beautiful daughter. If she'd been born as one of us with a face like that, it probably wouldn't cost him a bloody farthing. That's the price of being American, I suppose, and wanting to be part of the Old World. We live in strange times, don't you think, James?"

Five hundred thousand pounds? James digested the amount and slowly blinked.

The carriage pulled to a stop on Green Street, and Whitby waited for the footman to open the door. In those brief, floating seconds while James tried to conceive of five hundred thousand pounds in one lump sum, Whitby glared at him.

"James, I hope you don't intend to come between me and what *I* saw first. If you do, I assure you—you will live to regret it." His angry retort hardened his features.

James felt his blood begin to simmer. "You of all people, Whitby, should know I don't respond well to threats."

Whitby curtly thanked him for the ride and stepped out.

A moment later the carriage was on its way again, rolling down Green Street, and James had to work hard to control his fury, for he did not appreciate intimidation tactics. Not from a friend, not from anyone.

He felt the muscles in his jaw clench as he rationalized what had just happened. Just because the earl called on the countess a half hour earlier than James didn't give him any prior claim to anything. It could have been the damned traffic that let him get there first. Whitby knew that James was expected to take a wife— he had even tried to talk him into it—and the heiress, as yet, was unspoken for.

Five hundred thousand pounds! In light of the state of James's finances, he suddenly wondered if ignoring a sum like that would be bordering on negligence. Wouldn't it be a disservice to his family to resist the heiress because there was simply a *possibility* that he would become like his father? Surely he was stronger than that. He was capable of fighting whatever base instincts he might have in the future; he was sensible enough to see it coming and thwart it. Wasn't he? For pity's sake, he'd spent his whole life training himself to control his passions.

James decided to view the present situation with logic and rationale from now on. This opportunity was presenting itself almost shamelessly. One could even call it farcical. Fate was dangling the heiress in front of his nose like a solid gold carrot, baiting him with her beauty and her money. Yes, it was time James reached out and took a bite of that carrot. He was prepared for this. He'd learned to have self-control. He was disciplined. Passionless when he wanted to be.

Perhaps there was a reason for all that training after all. Now it would be tested by the beautiful, bewitching American heiress. For if he was going to secure that dowry, he was going to have to seduce her.

Chapter 4

Of course it was the money, James said to himself as his valet dressed him for the Berkley assembly. Learning that the heiress was worth five hundred thousand pounds had changed everything. He now had to think of the ducal estate and his tenants and Martin, who should study at Oxford when the time came, and Lily, who was out this year and would one day require a dowry of her own. At the moment, thanks to their father's careless living, there was nothing to offer a suitor—not a single farthing—and James knew that he had to turn this unpleasant idea of a wife into a business decision or risk losing more than just the French tapestries.

He also had to put aside his preference for the idea of a quiet, plain English wife, for one usually didn't come with five hundred thousand pounds in her trousseau.

His valet held out his black jacket and James slipped

his arms into it. Perhaps it was better this way, he thought. Knowing that the task was merely a matter of commerce eased his mind. He needn't worry that he was attending this assembly tonight because he was infatuated. Which he was not, and did not ever wish to be. Yes, he found Miss Wilson attractive—what man wouldn't?—but before he'd had that unpleasant conversation with Whitby, he hadn't the slightest intention of actually following through with a marriage proposal, to her or anyone else for that matter. For that reason, he could rest assured that he was still as levelheaded as ever.

An hour later, he was strolling into Berkley House. He walked into the crowded drawing room and conversed with the aging Marquess of Bretford. Perhaps this dowry-quest would turn out to be a bit of an adventure, he thought. Life had become monotonous lately, when all he ever thought about were bills and rising expenses and long lists of repairs.

It did not take him long to ascertain that she was here. She and her mother and the countess. All making their way around the room, flashing their jewels, charming the gentlemen and measuring said gentlemen's ranks, and planting their feminine seeds of success. What a transparent game it was. But who was he to criticize, when he was about to join in and outdo them all?

Sophia spotted the duke the exact moment he walked in the door, dressed in the appropriate black-and-white formal attire—the same as every other man, but looking ten times as imposing.

The black silk coat with tails emphasized his broad shoulders and narrow waist, and the contrast of his white shirt and white waistcoat against his midnight black hair sent her stomach into a heated, swift flip. She had not expected him to come. The countess had mentioned in the carriage that he never went out two nights in a row, let alone three. No doubt, this irregular appearance on his part would throw Florence and her mother into a wild frenzy of high hopes and calculations before the night was out.

To be honest, it had thrown Sophia herself into her own little frenzy of hopes. Hopes that she would speak to him tonight, if for no other reason than to reassure herself that she was still in control of her senses. Anything she might have felt for him in the past twenty-four hours was mostly about curiosity, for she had never in her life encountered anyone quite like the duke.

Was this imprudent of her? she wondered with some concern. To allow this curiosity to affect her so? She wouldn't get carried away by that charm, would she? She often heard that love was blind, and she could guess that this was how it started.

She watched the duke greet the other guests and meander around the room. With grace and confidence, he engaged in conversation and laughter. A few times, he glanced in Sophia's direction, and each time their eyes met, her heart quickened in response to his smoldering gaze, his darkly handsome face. He would smile briefly, then look away. She would do the same, wondering with some unease if he had somehow learned about her exact worth, as it must surely be all over fashionable London by now.

"Miss Wilson, what a pleasure it is to see you here this evening," the Earl of Whitby said, appearing beside her.

She turned to face him. "Hello, Lord Whitby. You're looking well."

"I believe it is the fresh spring air. It does wonders for the disposition."

They spoke of other things for a few minutes, nothing of any great importance, then the earl clasped his hands behind his back and gazed intently into Sophia's eyes. "Perhaps you would like to take a walk with me through Hyde Park one day this week? I would be pleased if your charming mother and the countess accompanied us, of course."

Sophia smiled. "I would be delighted, my lord."

"Wednesday?"

"Wednesday would be lovely," she replied. "Oh, I see Miss Hunt, of the Connecticut Hunts. Will you excuse me?"

He made a slight bow and stepped away, and Sophia spoke with a woman she had met at an assembly earlier that week. After a brief dialogue with her American acquaintance, Sophia caught the duke's eye, and as if with the common objective to speak to each other, she and the duke met in the middle of the room.

"Your Grace, what a pleasure."

His smile was seductive and heart-stopping, aimed at her and her alone, and she struggled to remember the necessity of caution.

"You look charming this evening, Miss Wilson. Exquisite, in fact." His gaze swept aggressively down the full length of her gown. She should have been insulted by such audacity, but instead, she was thrilled by it. Thrilled by the base wickedness.

"Thank you. You are most kind to say so. Have you been enjoying yourself this evening?"

"More and more with each passing minute. And yourself?"

There was a fluttering in the pit of her stomach. "Yes, more and more."

The way he was looking at her with such sexual intensity—it was almost frightening. Frightening because it made her feel weak and clumsy and deficient of sound reasoning. Those swooping butterflies were back. She wished she could control them.

"Have you had the pleasure of hearing Madame Dutetre since you've been in London?" he asked.

"No, I have not heard her perform. I will look forward to it. Will you stay?"

"Of course. It's why I came. Well, *one* of the reasons why I came."

With the riveting look he gave her, she couldn't miss his meaning—that he had come to see *her*.

She was feeling more and more alive by the minute.

"Would you care to look at the art in the gallery?" he asked. "I believe there has been a steady stream of admirers all evening."

He offered his arm and she accepted it. Together they proceeded through the adjoining drawing room and into the large, long gallery where couples slowly made their way down the length of it to admire the art. Because the room was so large, there was more space between guests and as a result more privacy. It was respectable of course, but intimately secluded at the same time.

Sophia and the duke moved at ease along the wall, looking up at the large family portraits and admiring the busts placed intermittently between chairs and potted palms. Farther down, they came to great works of art—a Titian, a Giorgione, a Correggio. His Grace was knowledgeable and full of information, and their conversation never faltered or grew forced or tedious. He was indeed an intelligent man beneath the mountain of physical allure.

"May I ask what you think of London so far?" the duke asked, stopping to pause in front of another family portrait.

"I am in awe. To be honest, I can barely believe I am here. I look around me, and I see centuries of life and love and war and art. You have so much history, and you place such a beautiful value on it. I would like to learn more about it—to see it from inside the very heart of it."

"That could be arranged."

She gazed into his eyes, searching for that devilish quality she'd been so wary of. Strangely, at this moment, she could see nothing but a genuine interest in her, and a sincere hope that she would enjoy London while she was here.

Was she being naive now, to allow herself to feel more comfortable with him because he was asking polite questions? Or had she misjudged him before and put too much faith in the drawing room gossip?

They strolled to another painting.

"What about the society?" he asked, studying her eyes as if fishing for something. "It must seem a great labyrinth for you."

She looked up at the top of the portrait—at the coronet upon the nobleman's head. "Rest assured, Your Grace, American society is equally as mystifying. We call ourselves a classless society, but we are far from it. In a country without titled nobility, people are ambitious. They want to better their situations and rise to the top, and rarely do their manners keep up with their wealth. Sometimes I think that certain rules of etiquette were invented just to make the barriers more visible and more difficult to circumvent, for we do not have aristocratic rank to make the lines clear."

"My apologies," he said, looking up at the coronet also. "I didn't mean to insinuate that society in your country is simple, on any account. I only meant to say that I, *myself,* find London society like a labyrinth on some occasions, and I had the benefit of being born and raised here."

She recognized what he was doing. He was trying to assure her that she was not an imbecile, that if she made the occasional social blunder, it was quite understandable. A tingle of appreciation moved through her.

They wandered along to the next work of art. "No offense taken," Sophia replied. "And I apologize for speaking so out of turn. I am grateful for your openness with me, Your Grace. It is the thing I find most difficult here."

"Openness?" He sounded surprised.

"Yes. Or the lack of it. I haven't been able to really talk to anyone or get to know them. The conversation is always so light, and I get my hand slapped for asking personal questions."

"Like Whitby the other night. I do apologize for that."

She smiled appreciatively and moved on. "I have two sisters." She knew she was leaping upon the very conversational topics she'd been instructed to avoid, but she didn't care. She wanted to show a little of herself to the duke. A little of the *real* Sophia Wilson. "I miss them very much. I long for our carefree talks and easy laughter. We tell each other everything."

"And what would you tell them if they were here now?" An appealing glint flickered in his eye, and she wondered what exactly he was expecting her to say. What he was hoping she would say?

She took her time before answering, thought carefully about what she was feeling. Was it contentment? A sense of adventure? She supposed with some surprise that it was a little bit of both. Her feelings about this man were changing, despite her resolve to be cautious.

Caution, as it happened, the very next instant took a holiday. Her reply came quickly, before she had a chance to heed it. "I would tell them that I prejudged someone that I should not have prejudged, and that I would like to start again with that person."

They stood in the gallery facing each other, staring. His expression revealed very little, but enough to tell her that she had done well with her reply.

"I am a great believer in new beginnings." He moved on, and she followed, feeling buoyant. "And I, too, have a sister I like to confide in, but I don't think I will say anything like that to her. She is eighteen and romantic and will have it all over London by teatime tomorrow, that I have met the love of my life." He grinned at Sophia. "And I don't appreciate being the subject of gossip. Even if it is true."

Sophia nearly swallowed her tongue. Had he just suggested that he had feelings for her? Or was it merely a hypothetical remark? She scrambled to fill the silence with a question while she recovered her equanimity. "You have a younger sister?"

"Three, actually. Two are married. One lives in Scotland and the other in Wales. Wonderful young women, all of them. I've even been blessed with two delightful nieces and a nephew."

Sophia could feel her eyes widening with every word he spoke. He was not devilish at all—at least not tonight.

"You like children, Your Grace?"

"I adore them. Every country house should be filled to the brim with laughter and the pitter-patter of little feet—to coin a tired old phrase."

If he was trying to impress her, he was doing an excellent job.

They began to talk about art again, discussing the latest trends and what the public galleries were displaying. They came to a Rembrandt, the *Young Woman Bathing,* and the duke reached out, as if he wanted to touch the canvas, but had to content himself with stroking the air in front of it. They admired the painting together for a moment.

"Notice the broad, creamy strokes there on the camisole," he said, his voice quiet—almost a whisper—for her ears only. "And the flat, opaque glaze of the pool. Such flawlessness in the reflection. And here . . . the directional shaping of the legs." The duke's large hand moved about, as if caressing the woman's bare skin.

Suddenly, a shiver coursed through Sophia's veins as she imagined what his long fingers would feel like, moving up under her skirts and over her own bare thighs. . . .

She suspected that most women would be shocked at what she was thinking and what he was saying, and by the seductive movement of his hand. She was a little shocked herself. Yet she could feel her body growing warm and relaxed. She imagined what it would be like to be free to melt into his arms here in the gallery. To be carried to that settee over in the dimly lit corner and be eased down upon it.

She worked hard not to sound breathless. "He is indeed a master."

Did the duke speak this way to everyone? she wondered. Or was he trying to seduce her? If he was, she would feel quite certain that he—with his own personal style of brushstrokes—was the true master this evening, for he knew exactly what he was doing. He was turning her into warm honey.

They moved on down the long room and started up the other side. "Would you like to take a stroll through Hyde Park one day this week?" he asked. "The weather has been splendid lately. Wednesday perhaps?"

She thought of Lord Whitby then, and wished he had not spoken to her first this evening, for she could not accept the duke's invitation when she already had a previous engagement. She began to feel a slight sense of panic, as if so much rested upon the outcome of this singular moment.

"Wednesday, Miss Wilson?" he pressed. "Or perhaps that is an inconvenient time." *Oh,* he was retreating.

"No, no. It's not that, or rather . . . yes, that is *all* it is. An inconvenient time. Another day, perhaps?"

"Thursday?"

"Thursday will be delightful." Her heart breathed a sigh of relief.

"Excellent. Shall we return to the drawing room? No doubt your mother is wondering what has become of you."

Sophia strolled into the room and met her mother. The duke exchanged pleasantries with her, then went to join a group of gentlemen on the other side of the room. Sophia watched him with an odd feeling of apprehension, realizing that with her unanticipated, fiery attraction to this man, her first, superficial impressions were becoming less and less a part of her idea of him. That worried her to no end, for she did not usually permit a fire in her blood to gain control over her intellect.

A few days later, hearing the clinking of plates in the dining room downstairs, Sophia took note of the time and realized how late it was. Her mother and Florence were having breakfast without her. With the help of her maid, Sophia quickly donned a late-morning gown of dark blue merino, rolled her hair up into a fashionable twist, and made her way downstairs to the parlor to join her mother and Florence for morning tea.

She stopped just inside the doorway. There on the table in the center of the room was a large bouquet of red roses.

She looked at her mother. "Heavens, where did these come from?"

Sophia walked slowly toward the bouquet, gently pulled a single flower to her nose, and inhaled the enchanting scent.

"Read the card and see for yourself," her mother replied in a joyful, slightly smug voice.

Sophia made her way around to the other side, where the card was lying on the marble tabletop. If they were from the duke, she would not go weak in the knees or simper like a lovesick fool. She would be wise and cautious. He would have to know that she was a sensible and stable young woman, and unlike these flowers, was not so easily plucked.

She read the card silently to herself: *Delicate roses for a delicate rose of a woman. Whitby.*

She read it again and blinked slowly up at her mother. She tried to mask the fracture in her pride, and not to look too disappointed, for they were not even *from* the duke. "They're from the Earl of Whitby."

Sophia flipped the card over and handed it to her mother, who was holding out her arm, wiggling her little fingers with impatience.

Her mother read it. With a squeal, she handed it to Florence. "Look what it says!"

The countess took her turn reading it, then stood up to hug Sophia. "Red roses. How deliciously aggressive of him. It is a clear message indeed. Congratulations, my dear. You've hooked an earl. Though was there ever any doubt you would be a success here?" The two ladies hugged each other.

Sophia tried to force a smile. She didn't want to dash their hopes just yet—for she had no intentions of marrying the Earl of Whitby, nor did she want them to know what was really going on inside her heart: that she was obsessing over a man she was still very uncertain about.

She felt it best to keep her cards close to her chest for now, until she could better evaluate the situation with the duke. She would know when the time was right to speak of it. Perhaps, if he did come today for the walk in the park as he said he would, Sophia herself could come to understand it enough to describe it.

"Well, what do you think of him?" Florence asked. "He's one of the best catches. He's already inherited his title, and he is handsome."

Sophia nodded dutifully. "Of course he's handsome, Florence. No one could argue that."

Whitby had fair hair and a strong jaw; he was slender and had beautiful white teeth, and not a hint of the duke's darker, more sardonic qualities. Perhaps she was wrong to discount the earl so quickly.

Just then, the butler appeared in the doorway. "Lady Lansdowne. There is a gentleman here to see Mrs. Wilson."

Florence looked at Beatrice uncertainly. "It's hardly the time for calls."

"The gentleman claims it is a matter of particular importance, and he did not wish to wait, my lady."

An unsettling silence hovered over them. "Who is it?" the countess asked.

"It is the Earl of Manderlin, my lady."

Another silence ensued while Florence decided what to do. "Show him in. Sophia? You and I will speak to the housekeeper about having Cook prepare those German sour cream twists you like so much."

Sophia and Florence left her mother in the parlor, to receive the Earl of Manderlin.

Not long after, the butler entered the kitchen to summon Sophia to the parlor, and she felt a sudden rush of uncomfortable dread. She followed the butler down the long front hall and into the room where her mother sat across from the earl. He rose when Sophia entered the room.

He was not a handsome man. He was small and slender, almost fragile in his appearance. Nor was he a warm man. He did not smile.

"Miss Wilson," he said, "thank you for seeing me this morning. I have something very particular I wish to discuss with you."

Her mother stood. "Perhaps I'll wait in the front hall." She walked out, looking a little pale. Sophia was beginning to feel a little pale, herself.

"Miss Wilson, I would like to ask for your hand in marriage," he said flatly.

That was it? No caveat? Not even a little bit of flattery to precede the offer? Good God, did these Brits know nothing?

She moved fully into the room and stood before him only a few feet away. He looked a little taken aback, nervous all of sudden, when he had not been nervous before.

Gently, she said, "I thank you, Lord Manderlin, for the generous proposal. It is most tempting, but I'm afraid I must decline." She was about to give him a polite reason why—to tell him that she wasn't ready to accept *any* offer of marriage quite yet—but he stopped her with a bow.

"I do thank you for your time on this lovely morning, Miss Wilson. You have been most kind to hear my offer." With that, he was out the door.

Sophia stood in the middle of the room, feeling utterly dumbfounded.

Her mother walked in. "What did you tell him?" she asked in a panic.

"I told him no, of course."

"It happened so fast. What did he say?"

Florence came dashing into the room to hear what was said as well. Sophia repeated it—it took all of two seconds—and the three of them sank into chairs in the parlor.

"I told him it would be a mistake," her mother said. "Truly, I tried to talk him out of it, but he would have none of that. He came here to propose to you, and he wasn't going to leave here until he had done just that!"

The weight of the shock lifted, and Sophia began to feel her heart sinking. "That was the most *un*romantic proposal I've ever heard of. He must know the amount of my dowry."

Her mother and Florence were quiet. The parlormaid brought in a large tray with a silver teapot, cups, and a plate of scones.

"Well, at least you have the Earl of Whitby to fall back on," Florence said, pouring a cup of tea and trying to change the subject. "A much handsomer man. And I daresay, if the flowers are any indication—a more romantic one. Don't you agree, Beatrice?"

Sophia, feeling a little uncomfortable at the reminder, accepted the teacup Florence handed to her.

"Let's not forget the duke," her mother said. "I haven't given up on him yet. Perhaps he just needs a few more opportunities to see Sophia. Then he'll be sending red roses, too."

Florence was strangely quiet for a moment. "I wouldn't get my hopes up about the duke." She sipped her tea.

Sophia sat forward. "What do you mean, Florence? What do you know about him?"

The countess shrugged. "Oh, nothing really. I just don't think he's the marrying kind, and there's no point wasting our efforts when they would be better spent elsewhere, in areas with more potential, so to speak."

"What makes you think that?" Beatrice asked. "He spent time alone with Sophia at the assembly the other night, and danced with her at the ball. He seemed the perfect gentleman, and very attentive to her."

Florence began to speak in hushed tones. "Yes, but he has been known to do that from time to time, with some of the more attractive ladies in the Set. Nothing ever comes of it, though." Florence lowered her voice even more and glanced over her shoulder at the door. "This is rather scandalous to speak of, but he has also been known to have brief affairs—discreetly of course—with married women. He's broken a few hearts, I assure you." Florence sipped her tea again. "He's quite a womanizer. Without compassion, they say. He's only interested in one thing and nothing beyond it. He's said to have a black heart."

Sophia felt sick.

"But who's to say he hasn't decided it's time to choose a wife?" Beatrice argued. "He's a duke after all, with a responsibility to carry on his line. Surely he must be thinking of that."

"His line. That's another thing. From what I've heard, the Wentworth Black Heart runs in the family. His father drank himself to death, and the duke before him—after a number of impossibly horrible scandals that some say involved his wife's death—took his own life. He shot himself in the head."

"Oh, good gracious," Beatrice said.

"Yes, I know, it's shocking, isn't it?"

Beatrice scrambled to grasp at straws. "But maybe the duke hasn't met a woman who has struck his fancy." She smiled at Sophia, who remained silent only because she didn't think she could move.

Florence poured herself more tea. "I still wouldn't get my hopes up, Beatrice. Even his mother, the duchess, is afraid to push potential brides on him."

"Afraid?" Sophia said, speaking up at last.

"Well, yes. You must have noticed that the duke can

sometimes be—how shall I say it?—*intimidating*. From what I understand, he and his mother are barely on speaking terms. He quite despises her, and she does her best to stay out of his way. This is all drawing room gossip, mind you."

Sophia sat in silence, staring. The duke despised his mother? "I'm sure he has his reasons," she said uneasily. "We should not presume to judge him without knowing all the facts, nor should we believe everything we hear." She wasn't sure why she was defending him, when all her instincts were telling her that the rumors could very well be true.

"You're right, dear. Of course, we should never judge a man's motivations. Who knows what secrets live in that vast country castle of his? I would wager quite a few." She reached for a biscuit and lightened her tone. "Oh, heavens, listen to me, spreading foolish gossip. It's probably all a bunch of silly stories anyway. Would you believe I once heard that his castle is haunted? That at night, you can hear the ghosts howling? Imagine that!"

Beatrice and Florence laughed for a moment, then began to discuss lighter matters, but Sophia could barely hear them above the roar of her blood like a beast in her ears. It was all she could do to sit still in her chair, sipping her tea and thinking about everything Florence had said, and wait uneasily for the duke's arrival.

Chapter 5

The Wentworth coach—polished shiny black, with liveried footmen and postilions—arrived with distinguished, clattering grandeur at Hyde Park, shortly after three o'clock in the afternoon. The horses whinnied and tossed their heads, while onlookers gaped in fascination at James, who stepped elegantly out of the coach, then turned to hold out his gloved hand to the Americans.

"Lovely day, Your Grace," the stout, little Mrs. Wilson said, struggling to sound British as she stepped onto the sidewalk.

"Ah, madam." He kissed her gloved hand. "It is all the more lovely by virtue of your delightful company this afternoon."

The small woman blushed at the flattery. He helped the countess down, then Mrs. Wilson's lovely daughter stepped out. He sensed all the gazes in the park converging upon her. People were quiet for a moment, then the whispering resumed.

The coach moved on, and James walked leisurely beside Miss Wilson. Today, she wore a cheerful, blue-and-white-striped walking dress with delicate chiffon ruffles. She carried a parasol and reticule, and upon her head, a straw hat had been pinned to her coiffure at a daring, forward angle. Just when he thought she could not possibly be more beautiful, she would appear in some new gown of the highest fashion and knock him to his knees.

He noted, however, that she was quieter than usual today.

They strolled down the park walk, along the water, and past numerous small gatherings of whispering ladies and gentlemen. He and Sophia conversed about art and books and the current opera that was playing at the Royal Opera House at Covent Garden. Miss Wilson was polite and civil to him, but not nearly as bright as she had been the other evening.

"When we spoke the other night at the assembly," he said, glancing over his shoulder to ensure that their chaperones were enough of a distance behind them to be out of hearing range, "I may have been too forward in my invitation to go walking today."

They strolled into the cool shade of towering oaks. The leafy branches stretched over the path like a canopy. James breathed in the fresh scent of damp earth and grass, and Miss Wilson lowered her parasol.

"Not at all, Your Grace. I hope I didn't give the impression that I did not wish you to ask."

"Of course not, but I must admit to being surprised to hear that you were out walking with Lord Whitby yesterday. And that Lord Manderlin paid you an important call this morning."

She gazed up at him with shock and horror.

"The English grapevine," he explained. "It's very active."

For a moment, she walked without saying anything, so he was forced to prod. He wanted to know why she was so quiet. "I heard that Lord Manderlin proposed. May I ask, what was your reply?"

She smiled up at him and at last gave a little laugh. "What do you think it was?"

He breathed a sigh of relief at the alleviating tension. "I would guess you refused, but very gently."

"I tried to be gentle, but I don't think it even mattered to him. I wouldn't talk about it if I felt there were any hurt feelings involved, but heavens, I think he thought I was a piece of commercial stock to be purchased."

James laughed, and was glad to fall into a more relaxed conversation. "He's not such a bad fellow. He just lacks social finesse."

"A lack of finesse I could live with. But not a lack of romance. I believe a man and a woman ought to marry for love. I'm afraid I cannot be moved on that point, even though my darling mother does her best to try."

Marry for love? A title-seeking heiress?

"But how do you define love, Miss Wilson? Is it passion you are looking for? Or simply sensible companionship?"

She thought about it. "Both. I want both."

"You are ambitious."

"I always thought it was my mother who was the ambitious one."

"Ah, but you are reaching for something much more difficult to attain than social position. I believe you are the most ambitious woman I have ever met."

She raised a delicate, arched brow. "You think love is difficult to attain, Your Grace?"

James stopped again on the promenade, stalling while he searched his mind for an answer. "What I mean to say is that true love is rare, and cannot be forced. 'Love sought is good, but given unsought is better.' And please, call me James."

"Shakespeare. That's very romantic, James." She put emphasis on his name. "Do you read much of Shakespeare's work?"

Thank the Lord she was changing the subject. "I read everything."

He recalled something else he had read by Plato—that love was a grave mental disease. Naturally, James refrained from quoting that one.

"So you've refused Lord Manderlin. But what about Whitby? He hasn't paid you any calls like that, has he? I try to keep abreast of these things, but—"

"I assure you, James, Whitby and I are acquaintances only."

"I see."

"He did send me flowers, though," she added, gazing mischievously up at the oak branches above them.

She was taunting him! He couldn't help but play along.

"What kind of flowers? And how many? I must know."

Miss Wilson laughed, albeit somewhat stiffly. "Red roses, and I would guess there were about three dozen of them."

James drew his hand to his chest and staggered sideways. "Oh, I've been bested already. Three dozen, and red, you say? How will I ever match that?"

She laughed again, a little more easily this time, and grabbed hold of his arm to pull him back onto the promenade. "You charm me, James, when you're not . . . puzzling me."

"Puzzling you?"

She glanced uneasily over her shoulder at their chaperones, then her eyes narrowed on him. "Yes. I may be a foreigner, but I do stumble upon good old-fashioned English gossip myself every once in a while, and there's no point dancing around that fact. From what I hear you have a scandalous reputation. It is said, among other things, that you are a womanizer."

She was certainly blunt. It was one of those American traits he couldn't help but admire. "I see." Squeezing his walking stick, he said nothing for a moment. "You told me once that you had a mind of your own, that you didn't believe every bit of idle chatter that came your way."

"Which is exactly why I am asking you about it myself."

James sighed deeply. She was commendably logical. "May I guess where you heard this gossip? It wasn't the countess, was it?"

Miss Wilson raised her parasol. "It was."

"She tried to warn you off me, no doubt."

"The countess is a very good friend to Mother and me. I won't have you insult her, if that's what you're about to do."

He raised his hands in surrender. "I have no intentions of insulting anyone. It's just that the countess and

I . . . well, we met under rather awkward circumstances."

"What kind of circumstances?"

He squinted in the other direction. "We met at a ball, I danced with her, and I believe she wanted to become my duchess. At least, that's what the gossips said."

Sophia dropped her parasol to her side. "Florence? And *you*?"

"Yes, though nothing came of it, I assure you. I merely danced with her a few times, sensed what she was after, then avoided society until someone else proposed, which I knew was sure to happen. She agreed to become Lord Lansdowne's bride."

"She said nothing to me about that."

"I wouldn't expect her to. She is happily married to the earl now." He looked directly into the heiress's eyes and spoke with conviction. "I am not a womanizer, Miss Wilson. I promise you."

I am many things, but not that. James had learned a long time ago how to identify women who wanted what he wanted—brief, superficial affairs. He never played games with the hearts of innocent, vulnerable women. Which was why, until now, he'd always avoided debutantes.

They walked on in silence, then Sophia began to recount another bit of drawing room gossip. Obviously, he'd been discussed in some detail. "She also told me that your father and grandfather both took their own lives."

God, he hated this, but he had to get through it. "That is somewhat true. My grandfather, yes, but that was a long time ago, and I never knew the man. My father, on the other hand, lived a life of debauchery which eventually led to his demise. Whether it was intentional or not, I'll never know. I'm not proud of the way he lived, Miss Wilson, you can be sure of that. I've done everything in my power to avoid becoming like him, and so far, I have succeeded. So please, do not judge me by his deeds."

It was true, all of it.

Sophia regarded him warmly, and he breathed a sigh of relief.

"I've always believed," she said, "that a man should be judged for himself and the person he is inside, not according to his past, or his class, or what others think or say. Rest assured, James, I will form my own opinion of you, based on our acquaintance. As I said before, I have a mind of my own."

He gazed at her with surprise and admiration, feeling an odd contentment from being with her. Part of him wanted to do anything to have her—for his body was presently reacting with blazing fervor—while something else in the deeper realms of his conscience wanted to warn her away. To tell her that the black truths of his existence were far worse than all the rumors, for the rumors were only stories.

Then he reminded himself that he shouldn't be concerned about those things. Miss Wilson was here in London to "purchase" a title, and he was in possession of a very good one and in need of what she offered in exchange. This was a business arrangement. She knew it. He knew it. He should not forget that.

Yet, his attraction to her was mounting at a shockingly brisk pace.

"Is that all?" he asked, steeling himself for more personal questions. Questions he was not accustomed to answering. Most people didn't dare.

Miss Wilson smiled. "Well, there was one other thing, and this is perhaps the most frightening of them all. I'm not even sure I should mention it."

He felt the muscles in his back stiffen.

Miss Wilson gave him a naughty little smirk. "I'm afraid there is a rumor that your castle is haunted, and that the ghosts howl all through the night. Please, James, you must assure me that this is not true."

He laughed out loud.

She continued to question him, sounding completely serious. "Because my parents convinced me when I was seven that ghosts weren't real, and to find out now that yes, they are indeed alive and well in Yorkshire . . . well, I just don't think I could live with that thought."

James could not keep from laughing. "I assure you, my dear, your parents were quite right. I've never heard a ghost howl at night, though the cook sometimes sobs over his fallen cream cakes early in the mornings."

They both laughed uproariously until there were tears coming out of their eyes.

"Good heavens," James said, "I hadn't heard that particular bit of gossip."

Sophia smiled. "Well, now you've heard it all. And please let me apologize for prying into all your secrets, where it was really none of my business. I just wanted to hear it from you."

He nodded. "Can we go back to what we were discussing before?"

She drew her pretty brows together. "I'm sorry, after all that, I can't even remember what we were discussing."

He let his expression go serious. "You told me that I charm you when I am not puzzling you. You charm me, too. Quite remarkably, in fact." It was the damned inconvenient truth. He hungered to touch her. So much so, it ached.

She stopped on the path and gazed up at him. "Please, call me Sophia. It would make me happy if you did."

"Sophia," he said, taking her gloved hand and holding it between both of his. "It's a beautiful name. I enjoy the sound of it."

He could sense her sudden unease. He was long past uneasiness himself. This was insane. He would never have permitted this kind of thing a month ago. Not even twenty-four hours ago.

"I enjoy the sound of it, too, James—when *you* say it." Her voice simmered with beguiling allure. "I would like it even more if you said it again."

All at once, he felt as if he were falling from a very high place. Apprehensions pierced through him, for none of this was going as he had planned. *"Sophia."*

He gazed down at her hand and turned it over. With his finger, he drew a little circle in her palm. He felt her body shudder, and her stimulation shivered through him as well.

Sophia gazed warily over her shoulder at their chaperones, who were slowly approaching.

"You're worried they'll see?" he said.

She nodded, so he eased her mind by taking a single step to the side. Now Sophia's body blocked their chaperone's view of her hand in his.

James unbuttoned her glove at her wrist and peeled it back. Sophia sucked in a little breath—a dainty gasp full of socially appropriate shock, as well as a less appropriate, spine-tingling delight, which roused him greatly.

He took a deep breath, pausing to glance up and ensure she was in agreement, then slowly traced a line from the center of her palm to her bare, luscious wrist, drawing tiny little circles over the delicate blue veins. He said nothing. He merely admired the softness of her skin, then lifted his gaze.

Her lips were mere inches from his own—deliciously full, precariously moist.

Her bosom was heaving.

His own heart was pounding.

God!

She spoke in a breathy little whisper. "That feels . . ."

"Yes?"

"Wonderful."

He smiled again, though inside, he felt like he was spinning.

"It tickles, James. I have gooseflesh."

James glanced over her shoulder at their chaperones, who were curiously slowing down, keeping their distance, then with a heavy dose of physical restraint, he pulled her glove back over her palm and labored to bring his mind around to focus on his objectives. He was not here to fall in love with Miss Wilson. He was here for the five hundred thousand pounds.

They faced forward and began to walk again. James took a moment to breathe while he fought to curb his vigorous and inopportune lust.

For a man of stringent control when it came to his passions, he was uncharacteristically flustered.

They came to the end of the path and emerged out into the sunny open air, where groups of ladies and gentlemen mingled on the green grass. Sophia opened her parasol again, and their conversation drifted into lighter matters.

Soon, Mrs. Wilson and Lady Lansdowne appeared,

and it was time to go. James escorted them to his
coach, and they returned to Lansdowne House.

He climbed out first to assist the ladies down, then
walked with Sophia to the front door to say good-bye.
Mrs. Wilson and the countess entered the house and
James was left alone with Sophia on the massive front
portico.

He took her gloved hand, raised it to his lips, and
placed a gentle kiss upon it. "No words can describe
how profoundly I enjoyed your companionship this afternoon, Sophia."

He let go of her hand and she gracefully lowered it
to her side. "I will never forget it, James. It was
most. . . . agreeable."

"Agreeable?" He laughed. "Is that all?"

"No, of course that is not all," she said in a low, sultry voice, then she gave him a flirtatious little grin and
turned away. She walked through the open doors to
where the other ladies were being greeted by the butler.

James stood motionless, astonished by Sophia's skill
and proficiency in this lovemaking game—a game he
had expected to belong principally to him. Judging by
the way his body was reacting to her now, however—
with an uncomfortable degree of peppery strain—there
was enough evidence to suggest she might be better at
it than he was. The title-seeking American heiress
had caught him and lured him in, and he hadn't even
realized—until this shaky, irrational moment as he
watched her disappear into the house—that he was on
such a huge, sharp hook.

Chapter 6

It was not James's habit to share the luncheon table with his mother, and today, as always, he had a plate sent up to his study so he could eat without the intrusion of tension-filled silences.

Today, however, the silence that came naturally from one's being completely alone was full of a different breed of tension—one that reeked of worry and regret for actions that he had perhaps not adequately thought out.

He had begun a courtship with a single lady openly seeking a husband—a single lady who was here in London to "hook" a peer. He had been seen walking with her in Hyde Park, and all of London must now be whispering his intentions. The English mothers were probably furious with him for allowing his gaze to wander away from English soil. He was a little bit furious with himself for becoming a thing he'd always despised—a fortune hunter. He was no better than she or Whitby was.

He supposed he should not be too hard on himself. Or Sophia. Aristocratic marriages were almost always based on matches that were in some form advantageous for both parties involved. Marriages were entered into responsibly rather than passionately, and he of all people should know that passion should not be sought after. It was not even an option. Not for him. It was far too dangerous. He had to look for other reasons to marry, and money was as good as any other. It was the utmost responsible choice, really, for he was doing this for his dukedom. He was doing it for Lily and Martin and the future heirs to the estate—whoever they might be.

So what was the problem then? Was it because she was American? Did he feel somehow disloyal?

Perhaps a little, but not enough to turn his head in another direction. He was determined now.

Then he realized it had nothing to do with what country she came from. His concerns were based solely on how she would not leave his mind, no matter how hard he tried to dislodge her from it. Nor would she give him a moment's peace regarding matters less to do with the mind and more to do with the body. All he wanted to do now was drive over to see her and cement this marriage proposal, so that he could move past all this indecision and proceed swiftly and without delay to the carnal pleasures of the wedding night.

He thought then of his father's nature—how the man lost his sense of reason when his passions took over. James did not want to become like him. Perhaps it was not possible to keep marriage inside the closed circle of a business arrangement. . . .

A knock sounded at his door then, and James jumped. An unexpected banging or slamming always startled him.

His butler appeared. "The Earl of Manderlin is here to see you, Your Grace."

A stiffness moved up James's spine. Had the earl heard that James had gone walking with Sophia yesterday, and was he here to discuss a battle he intended to fight?

"Send him up, Weldon."

James rose from his desk chair and went to the window. He moved the curtain aside with a finger to look down onto the street, where the earl's carriage waited out front.

Footsteps tapped up the stairs and shortly thereafter, the earl walked into James's study.

Weldon announced him: "The Earl of Manderlin." Then he backed out of the room and closed the door.

"Thank you for seeing me, Wentworth," the earl said. "I have a matter of particular importance I wish to speak to you about."

"Please, sit down."

The earl lowered his small, frail frame into a dark green upholstered chair. James wasn't sure what he was going to say if the man mentioned an affection for Sophia. He knew she would never even consider marriage to a man like Manderlin. Not because of his looks, mind you, but because the man had not the slightest clue how to stimulate her mind or rouse her interest. Sophia needed a man who could—

"I've come to seek your permission to speak to your sister, Lady Lily, about a possible . . ." He stumbled on his words at that point, then coughed into his fist and quickly recovered. "About a proposal of marriage."

*   *   *

Shortly after the earl left James's study, there was another knock at his door. This one was quick and anxious, and he knew it was not his butler. "Enter," James said from the chair at his desk.

The door swung open and his sister, Lily, swept in with an almost musical turn to close the door behind her. Sometimes she reminded him of a leaf floating in unpredictable directions on an invisible breeze.

"Oh, James, how can I ever thank you?" she blurted out, before he had a chance to even say good day to her. He rose from his chair, and she crossed the room and wrapped her slender arms around his waist.

"What's this about?" he asked.

"You know what it's about. You are the best brother in the whole entire world."

"I honestly don't know—"

"Lord Manderlin! You sent him away!"

James felt a slight tremor of unease. "Ah, the earl. You saw him arrive?"

"Yes, I was in the front parlor when he came to the door, then I hid in the servants' corridor! Mother would have a fit if she knew!"

"You didn't need to hide in any corridor, Lily. You are only eighteen, and I am not a proponent of child brides."

"But Mother will pressure me. She can't help it, and I don't want to tell her that I don't have to do what she says because you say so. That will only make her angry."

"It doesn't matter if she's angry, Lily. If she has a problem with it, she can speak to me."

"She never will."

"Precisely," he said. "Even if she did, I would tell her that you are too young."

Lily rolled her eyes heavenward. "I am not too young, James. I simply don't wish to marry a dull man like Lord Manderlin."

"You have some growing up to do, Lily. One day, you'll see that a dull man is often the better choice."

There was shock in her eyes as she stared at him. "Not you, too, James. I never thought you would turn out like Mother."

He moved to the window. "I'm not like Mother. I only want you to be safe. You of all people should understand that."

Lily sighed. "I don't want to be safe. I want to live. I want passion."

He gave her a look of warning, to remind her that the world was not always a kind place for people who were carried away by their passions. "No, you don't."

"I do. And I will have it."

Just then there was another knock at the door. "Come in," James said.

The hinges creaked and his mother entered and stood there, hands clasped tightly in front of her. The cold, hard lines of her face were deeply drawn.

What more today? he wondered, feeling tired all of a sudden.

Lily backed away from him. "Hello, Mother."

The duchess did not reply. She merely stood in the doorway, wringing her hands together, and James knew she could not hold in whatever was on her mind today.

He turned to his sister. "Lily, why don't you go and tell Cook that I will not be dining at home this evening. I have an appointment with my solicitor."

Lily, all smiles gone, nodded and walked slowly from the room.

James went to the window and looked out again. "What is it, Mother?"

The woman closed the door behind her and moved fully into the room. She gazed around her as if nothing were familiar, probably realizing, James thought, how long it had been since she'd been in this study.

"I came," she replied, "because I wish to make it known to you that I am not in agreement with what happened just now."

"Not in agreement?" he repeated, feeling almost amused by his mother's way of telling him that she was furious, and wildly so, that he had sent the Earl of Manderlin away.

Still, he supposed it was quite something that she was here to voice her opinion at all when she despised open confrontation of any kind. She usually got what she wanted through her intimidating manner—which was never more intimidating than when she said nothing. It was like she possessed an invisible hand that could clutch one around the neck and squeeze out one's resolve, without seeming to have been involved in the decision at all.

James faced her squarely. "You don't know what happened just now."

She shuffled her shoulders the way she always did when she felt she was being opposed. "I know that he came here to declare himself to Lily and you did not al-. low it."

They glared at one another for a moment. "I did not forbid it. I simply did not recommend it."

"The Earl of Manderlin would be an excellent match for Lily," she said. "His property is most auspicious, and his family name is respected at court. He may not run in your 'fast' set, but the Queen has a high regard for him."

James moved away from the window. "Lily is practically a child. She is not ready for marriage."

"What a young girl is ready for, or wishes for, is not always what is best for her. It is up to you as head of this family to see that the best decisions are made for her."

"Like they were made for you?"

His mother's lips pursed. "May I remind you that I am the Duchess of Wentworth, and we are one of the greatest families in England."

There was much he could have said to dispute that high opinion she'd always clung to, but he felt no need to repeat what he'd already said years ago, when he was young and full of fury and less able to control his impulses. His mother knew well enough what he thought of his family's greatness.

"The Season has only just begun, Mother, and Lily is young. She has time to look around. That's all I have to say on the matter."

The dowager was quiet for a moment, and James wondered why she was not leaving. Then: "I understand you went walking with the American yesterday."

"Ah, the American," he replied. "Is that what's really bothering you?" He strolled to his desk and picked up a letter at random. He glanced casually at the salutation.

The dowager took a few steps toward him, and he looked up to see a mixture of frustration and fear in her eyes. Fear of the unthinkable. "It's not serious, is it? You wouldn't actually consider . . ."

He did not reply to her inquiry. He merely watched

her until she was forced to continue what she had begun.

"She's American, James."

"I'm quite aware of that."

"From what I hear, her paternal grandfather was a bootmaker—a bootmaker!—and her maternal grandfather—oh, good gracious, I can barely even speak of it. He worked in a slaughterhouse. He butchered sows." She waved her arm through the air. "This appearance Miss Wilson has—the Paris gowns and the jewels and the charming smile—it does not cover up what she truly is beneath it all. She is nothing more than the daughter of a pauper and she is here as a . . . oh, what is that vulgar phrase? . . . a gold digger."

James had to laugh at that. "You forget, Mother, she is the one with the gold."

The Dowager Duchess shuffled her shoulders again.

"And her father is no pauper," James continued. "He is an enterprising man who built something from nothing, and I admire him for that."

"You're scaring me, James."

He laughed again. "You're frightened, are you? Well, don't expect me to make it all better."

It was cruel, he knew it, and for a fleeting instant he wished he could take it back. Then he saw his mother's eyes flare with that familiar cold fury—the disbelief that anyone could behave with such rebellion—and he did not regret what he had said.

Suddenly there was a ripple in his mind—like a stone had been tossed into his still waters. A vague memory of his mother walking into the schoolroom, finding him in tears on the floor at his governess's feet, meeting his pleading gaze, and in response—quietly backing out and closing the door. So many of those memories were vague—seen through mist and fog.

He was glad. Glad that he had been able to distance himself from them.

His mother wanted the world and everyone in it to quietly obey and do their duty without questioning it, even when it came down on one's hand with a painful, resounding crash.

She whirled around and left the room. When the door slammed shut behind her, James calmly lowered himself into his chair and returned to his correspondence.

Chapter 7

❦

The London Season, Sophia was coming to realize, was for her just one big assembly, with balls thrown in to mix things up. It was night after night of formal gowns and jewels and music and conversation. Of champagne and late suppers and plumed fans. Of dance cards dangling from slender gloved wrists and hostesses in great gaudy tiaras. To Sophia, it was a magical fairy tale, complete with the handsome prince who was, at this very moment, capturing her heart.

She walked with her mother and Florence along the red carpet that led to the front door of Stanton House, where an assembly was already in full swing. Her heart did anxious little flips as she glanced over the crowd moving up the wide staircase just inside. She was looking for the face of the man she hoped would be here tonight. Her prince.

Heavens, when had her opinion of him changed so drastically, and what in particular had caused it? It was a little bit of everything she supposed, and the past few days away from him had only intensified it. She'd done nothing but dream of him and quiver at the intoxicating memory of his finger brushing like a feather over her bare wrist when they'd gone walking in Hyde Park. Every fiber of her being had reacted with hunger and blistering yearning, and she had wanted—more than she'd ever wanted anything—to reach out and touch James.

She'd never experienced the desire to touch a man before.

It was more than a desire. It was a screaming, urgent need to be close to him, close enough to brush her lips over his skin and breathe in his masculine scent. It had become all she could think of the past few days. She wanted to taste him, to cling to him. She wanted to lie down on a bed and feel the weight of him on her body, while he kissed her open mouth and she drank in the drenching flavor of him.

She glanced around self-consciously, hoping her cheeks weren't flushing and giving away her shocking, indecent thoughts.

She entered the house and greeted the hosts, then marveled at how, against the odds, despite all the gossip, James had won her regard.

Yet, self-doubts continued to flood through her. She could not forget what people said about him, and she wasn't sure if she should follow her instincts about him and ignore the gossip, or *not* trust her instincts—for they were certainly being influenced by her feelings of attraction.

But her father had always told her to trust her instincts. *Trust your gut,* he would say, in his deep, Southern drawl.

They reached the withdrawing room upstairs. Florence whispered quietly, "This is largely a political party, so do try not to look bored if the conversation turns to whatever went on in Parliament this morning."

"I've been finding it all quite intriguing, actually," Sophia replied. "I've been following the speeches in the papers."

"That's fine, Sophia, but don't pretend to know too much about it."

Sophia was about to say she would never *pretend* anything, but Florence and her mother became distracted by a gown that a certain Miss Weatherbee was wearing—quite unlike anything she'd ever worn before, Florence said, with a very daring *decolletage* for an English girl who rarely spoke a word at these things, let alone came to them. It looked like the one Sophia had worn to the Weldon House ball, where she'd first danced with James.

Florence winked at Sophia. "You're setting trends, my dear. It was bound to happen. Soon, people will be looking for your picture in the shop windows with Lillie Langtry and the other English beauties."

They moved into the massive hall, brightly lit and adorned with ferns and leafy palms. For an hour or so, Sophia met gentleman after gentleman, peer after peer. There were politicians from the House of Commons as well as the House of Lords. There were newspapermen, bankers, wives and sisters and mothers and aunts. It was the largest assembly she had attended so far. She guessed the number of guests at an easy five hundred.

Not so easy to find her prince, however, when all the gentlemen were dressed the same—in black tails and white shirts and white waistcoats. Would he even come?

Then her mother said, "Look, there's the duke," as if they were wandering in Central Park, and she'd just spotted a partridge.

Sophia spoke as casually as she could. "Oh, yes."

Her mother's eyes grew wide. "*Oh, yes?* That's all you have to say?"

"That's all for now, Mother," she replied with a little grin as she snapped open her fan.

It was another half hour before Sophia found herself on the same side of the room as James. Every so often she glanced in his direction, admiring how his tall, dark figure towered over the other men, and how his facial features were both rugged and calmly somber. Even in a crowd, his presence was grand and imposing.

He was engaged in a conversation with someone, but as he took a sip of his champagne, he looked at Sophia over the rim of his glass. His green eyes flashed beneath the dark lashes.

She smiled daringly at him, and when he inclined his head in return with a sexy lift of his brow, she felt like her legs were going to give out beneath her. She longed to talk to him tonight. Just to be close enough to see the depths in his eyes and the smoothness of his lips. To hear the sound of his voice as he spoke her given name.

A few moments later he was there beside her, tall and suave, greeting her mother and the banker they'd been conversing with. After the appropriate light discourse, the duke said to Beatrice, "Would you permit me, madam, to steal your daughter away for a moment or two? I would like to introduce her to my younger sister, who is here this evening with my mother, the duchess. My sister wishes to make Sophia's acquaintance."

Beatrice's face lit up like an exploding gas lamp.

"Not at all, Your Grace. I'm sure Sophia would be delighted to meet your family."

He nodded and offered his arm, and Sophia slid hers around it. They began to cross the crowded room together.

"I'm glad you came," he said quietly to her. "I was hoping you would."

"I was hoping you would, too."

She could have said so much more: that she'd been unable to think of anything but him since they'd parted beneath the portico, and that she wished he would pull her into his arms and kiss her right here, and end this painful, frustrating feeling of "apartness."

They approached the young lady he had smiled at at the Weldon ball—the lovely dark-haired girl in the cream-colored dress. Tonight, she wore a becoming shade of blue. So she was his sister. A wave of relief moved through Sophia.

James touched his sister's arm. "Lily, may I present to you Miss Sophia Wilson, of New York. Miss Wilson, this is Lady Lily Langdon."

Sophia offered her hand. "It's an honor to meet you, Lady Langdon."

James leaned in very close and whispered so no one else could hear. "The correct form of address is Lady Lily."

The feel of his hot breath in her ear sent gooseflesh up her entire left side.

"Lady Lily," she amended, noticing that she did not feel the least bit patronized, or that James had been condescending. On the contrary, she felt rather grateful, as if he were on her side and wished only to help her.

"Please, call me Lily," the young woman said.

They both smiled, and Sophia suspected that if she

had the good fortune of becoming better acquainted with the duke's young sister, she would come to like her very much.

"I do love your gown," Lily mentioned, and they talked about some of the new fashions while James stood by, listening.

"Shall we all go out to the buffet table and see what is there?" Lily suggested. "I'm feeling quite famished suddenly."

"I'd like that," Sophia replied. She followed Lily and was pleased that James was coming, too.

They made their way through the crowd to the long table clothed in white linen and topped with decorative dishes and an Epicurean delight of finger foods. Scalloped oysters, pastry puffs filled with lobster salad, and fresh, colorful sliced fruit and grapes were carefully arranged on silver platters and spilling over the rims of huge china bowls. There were cakes and candies and fancy biscuits iced with butter cream, and sugar sculptures towering in the middle as immaculate centerpieces. Sophia, James, and Lily moved around the table, sampling and talking and laughing, and Sophia wished this night would never end.

They moved into a smaller drawing room that was less crowded, and Lily and Sophia sat down on a sofa at the far end. James chose a chair opposite them. Beyond them was the conservatory—visible on the other side of yet another hall—all lit up and looking like a great jungle of leafy greens.

The three of them sat and talked, and Sophia sensed a mild tension between Lily and James, a few looks of annoyance from Lily, the odd contradictory opinion. She wondered if they might have argued over something recently.

Two young ladies walked into the room and Lily recognized them. "Oh, look, it's Evelyn and Mary. I must go and say hello to them." She stood, crossed the room, and went to meet her friends.

Sophia was now sitting alone with James in front of the huge marble fireplace. There was no fire; the grate was clean.

"Lily is lovely," she said.

"She is indeed. Lovely and uncontrollably defiant."

Glancing over at James's sister, giggling with the two young ladies, Sophia was not surprised. "I sensed something was wrong. She seemed troubled."

James gazed at Lily, too. Candlelight glimmered over his classically handsome profile. "We had a disagreement recently. Over her marriage."

Sophia tried not to voice her shock. "Her marriage? But she's so young."

"Precisely what I said. Mother would marry her off tomorrow if she could, and when I told Lily that she didn't have to worry about that because she was too young, she didn't seem to realize that I was on her side. She accused me of underestimating her maturity as far as 'passions' were concerned."

Sophia smiled sympathetically. "She'll come around. I'm sure she'll meet someone respectable who will suit her well."

James leaned his temple on a finger and gazed at Sophia. The lines around his eyes softened, and he smiled lazily. "How is it possible that we found a way to be alone in this crush?"

Sophia smiled. "I'm not complaining."

"Nor am I," he replied, uncrossing one long leg and crossing the other over it. At the sight of his powerful, muscular thighs, she felt a tingle of desire move through her and had to pull her gaze away and try to focus on her gloved hands instead. "I recall admiring art with you a few nights ago," he continued. "We were alone, then, too."

"Yes. I've been thinking of those paintings we looked at. Especially the Rembrandt—the *Young Woman Bathing*. It was like peering into someone's private moment. I've wondered what she was thinking about." Sophia paused and gazed off into space.

James stared intently at her. She supposed he was witnessing her own private moment.

"I believe there is another Rembrandt out in this hall." He gestured toward it. "A self-portrait."

Sophia looked at the doorway that led out into the hall, and back at Lily, who was still conversing with her friends on the other side of the drawing room.

Could Sophia go alone with James into another room that seemed currently uninhabited?

Could she *not*?

Even here, sitting across from him in this drawing room, she was too far. She felt that "apartness" again and wanted more than anything to bridge it. Perhaps it was a physical thing; she wasn't sure. She only knew that flame-hot desire was pulling at her, wrenching her away from her common sense.

Sophia stood up. "I would very much like to see the painting. Lily will see where we are going."

Lily did, at that instant, lean out to watch them walk together out of the drawing room and into the hall.

Sophia and James crossed the quiet room. Her heels clicked over the marble floor and echoed over their heads; she looked up at the high cathedral ceiling. Even though she'd always considered herself a liberal girl, she nevertheless felt uncomfortable with what they were doing.

"Over here." James led the way to a painting at the bottom of a wide staircase.

Sophia stood before it and let her mind relax about where she was and who she was with. She stared for a few minutes at the portrait. "He looks dignified."

"Yes. Self-assured."

"But sad, too. Look at his eyes. I wonder what he was thinking when he painted this."

As she stared up at the work of art, she felt James studying her profile. "You often seem to wonder what people are thinking."

She shrugged. "I suppose so. People are a mystery, are they not? You never know what is going on in a person's mind or heart, and even if they tell you, how do you know they are telling you everything?"

He continued to stare at her profile. "I believe you are the most beautiful woman I have ever seen."

Sophia's heart lurched in her breast. She met his gaze and tried to fight the aching need to reach out and touch him. James looked over his shoulder. They were still completely alone, though Sophia could hear the hum of the crowd and the laughter of Lily and her friends not far from where they stood.

His fingers came up to touch her cheek, and she felt like she was going to melt into a puddle of desire right there in the hall. "I want to kiss you, Sophia."

Her knees turned to liquid. She wanted to say, "We shouldn't be here." She *should* have said it, but something else spilled out before she could stop it. "I truly wish you would."

His hand found hers; his was large and warm and

strong as his fingers weaved through her own. He led her around a corner into an alcove.

She knew she was doing something unthinkable, but this man—this beautiful man—brought out a riotous fire within her, the kind of heat she had longed to feel in all those dull, stuffy New York drawing rooms, when she'd resigned herself to the fact that her life was going to be one colorless, tedious meaningless soiree after another. With James, for the first time in her life, she felt potent and indulgent. Alive.

God help me, she thought, as he slowly lowered his lips to hers.

All her life's experience could not have prepared her for that moment—for the echoing sweetness of his kiss and the spinning sensations that came from the mere feel of his moist lips upon hers. For the tickling of his thumb as it gently caressed her cheek. For the naughty impropriety of kissing a man in a secluded corner of a London assembly. She knew it was wrong, but she could not stop herself, and the sweeping power of it all was more electrifying to her than anything she'd ever seen or done before.

She parted her lips to taste the flavor of his tongue, and then he was taking another step closer and gathering her into his arms. The apartness faded away, and there she was, floating in his embrace, holding on to him with a desperation that was almost frightening. A whimper escaped her. He, too, made a quiet breathy noise from somewhere deep in his throat, and she knew that he was as dizzy as she, with this fierce passion and longing.

Before she knew what was happening, he had taken her hand and was leading her across the hall. She looked over her shoulder to see if anyone was watching them. There was no one, so she followed him willingly into the conservatory, which was unconditionally off-limits to a young lady and a single man, but she had no common sense left—only the desire to feel James's hands on her body again, to feel his mouth upon hers and to hold him close, pressed hard against her breasts.

He led her down the stone steps and around a wall of ferns and palms and flowering shrubs and bushes, into a back corner where no one who might walk in could see them. Sophia would have followed him anywhere at that moment. She would have followed him upstairs to some unknown bedchamber and let him lock the door behind them if he'd gone that direction. Thank God he had not. There was still a chance they could sneak out of here unnoticed when they finished whatever it was they were about to do.

He leaned back against a wall and pulled her by the hand, firmly up against his hard body. "You taste like wine," he said in a sensual whisper, "only better."

"And you taste like nothing I've ever tasted before."

Then she was kissing him again, running her hands through his beautiful, thick black hair and feeling his fingers tickle her shoulders and neck. It was too much for her to take—she didn't know what to do, how to think, how to touch him. She'd never kissed a man like this. Had she been asleep her whole life? Was she waking up only now?

The next thing she knew, she was tossing back her head and he was kissing her neck and her breasts along the neckline of her gown. God, how she wanted him to be able to kiss beneath it, for his lips to penetrate the fabric and the firm wall of her corset.

"I wish we were alone," she said breathlessly. "Truly alone."

His eyes devoured her, his mouth melted her with a sexy, naughty grin that worked over her like magic. "That would be dangerous, my dear. I may be a gentleman, but I do have my limits, and if I had you alone, I would taste you, then fill every inch of you, and mark my words, you would walk away quite without your virtue. So perhaps it is best that we are here—at risk."

She bent a knee to stroke the outside of his leg with hers. "I don't want to think about that . . . about the risk."

Although she knew she should.

He slid his hand around her thigh and raised her leg even higher. She could feel the firmness of his sex beneath his pants.

What in God's name was she doing?

She'd never known what a man's sex felt like, that it could grow and become so large and hard. She found herself pressing up against him, thrusting her hips through all their clothing and feeling drawn into some fiery, burning flame. She could not back out of it. She felt lust mounting in her like the hottest blaze, clouding all sense of reason.

Then she felt his hand lifting her skirt, sliding up under it to stroke her bare thigh above her stocking. She moaned softly, and he turned them around so that she was now up against the wall and he was pressed against her, his hips thrusting into hers.

"Oh, James," she managed to whisper. But she did not know what to say after that. She couldn't think.

Then there was a noise. Laughter echoing in the hall outside the conservatory.

James dragged his mouth from hers and lifted his index finger to his lips. She gazed into his sizzling eyes, only inches away, and felt his breath beating against her face. Her heart was pounding out a breakneck rhythm in her chest. They stared at each other for a moment, then he kissed her again and she kissed him back with abandon and raked her fingers through his glorious black hair.

They heard the laughter again. James pulled his mouth away from hers. "This is insane," he whispered.

It was.

It was insane.

What had she been thinking, behaving this way? The duke probably thought she did this with every gentleman who suggested it. Surely he had lost all respect for her now.

Horror and regret coursed through her. Had she spoiled everything?

What could she do? How could she reverse it? She couldn't.

"Let me go, this is wrong," she whispered, in an instant of panic.

She pulled out of his arms and hurried along the leafy enclosure to peer out into the hall. The group of assembly guests—whoever they were—were out of sight, so she hurried from the conservatory and somehow found her way back to the buffet table, feeling breathless and bewildered and dazed with passion, which was not yet receding.

She touched a hand to her warm cheek. How could she have behaved with such a lack of restraint, when she continuously willed herself to act according to what her head told her to do, not her passions? What had happened to her logic and clearheadedness?

* * *

James closed his eyes and leaned his head back against the wall in the conservatory. He tapped it a few times. Hard. He felt disheveled and shaky and out of breath, and wondered how—in a few singular passion-filled minutes—he could have lost all control of his senses. It was something his father would have done.

Sickened by that thought, he cupped his forehead in his hand and tried to gain back a semblance of calm.

"Dammit." He could not possibly have handled this in a worse way. Yes, he'd kissed women in conservatory corners before, but experience had taught him never to kiss unmarried women in search of husbands. What had just occurred was proof that he was less in control than he had thought, and if he had any brains left in his head, he would recognize his failing and retreat from the path he'd set out upon.

But he could not. Not now, for he had just started a very heavy ball rolling with a momentum he could not stop. There could be no more thinking about things, no more considering the *possibility* of proposing. After what happened tonight, it was inevitable. There was no turning back, no way to get out of it, at least not honorably. He would have to ask for Sophia's hand immediately before word of this got out, for surely someone must have seen them. Lily certainly had. Her friends were young; they did not know the importance of discretion.

God, the American heiress. Perhaps the strangest thing was that despite all his staggering misgivings, it was marvelously fantastic to know that he would have her.

His mother was going to cough up her lunch.

Chapter 8

The next morning, Sophia awoke early after a restless sleep. She ate a light breakfast and ventured outside to wander in the gardens. Lansdowne House—one of the few private London mansions to have its own gardens—was shrouded in a thick, yellow fog, as was the rest of the city. She felt the damp coolness of the air on her skin, imagined that her hair was turning a bit frizzy, but what did it matter? she thought, as she stepped over the flat stones that traced a path through a grove of towering elms. She was alone finally, thank goodness, away from the questioning looks of Florence and her mother.

They had left the assembly early the night before because she had told them she felt unwell. They were unconvinced.

She was not quite sure what else to say about it now. She was thoroughly ashamed of her behavior and could not bear to think of her mother knowing about it. Or her father. He would be so disappointed in her.

Just then, the clatter of hooves alerted Sophia to a visitor. The iron gates to the house swung open in the distance, and a large coach entered the courtyard, a coat of arms emblazoned upon its doors. There was a flurry of activity—groomsmen running out of the stables to tend to the horses, a footman in everyday livery scooting down the front steps to greet the guest.

Sophia watched from the garden as James—wearing a sleek black greatcoat and top hat—stepped gracefully down and looked up at the house.

What is he doing here? she wondered in a panic. It was not the proper time of day for a social call. If he was here, it was an important matter of business.

Ten minutes later, Sophia, perched nervously on a bench under a tree, watched James exit the house and settle his black hat upon his head.

He crossed the courtyard toward the gardens. He knew exactly where he was going—straight toward *her*.

Sophia's heart began to pound against her ribs. He looked like some dark, seductive creature against the grayness all around him—the stone mansion, the gravel courtyard, the fog, the mist. She could barely move from her place on the cold bench. All she could do was watch him walk toward her, growing closer and closer with each sure stride.

He stopped a distance away, fifteen feet perhaps. He removed his hat and held it at his side. "Are you not cold out here, Sophia?"

She swallowed hard. "It's quite refreshing actually."

Heavens, what did a girl say to a beautiful duke dressed in black the morning after she'd behaved like a trollop in his arms?

He took a few steps closer. "You're not punishing

yourself, I hope." When she said nothing, he took a few more steps closer. "Because if anyone deserves to be punished, it is I."

He sat down beside her, and his nearness made her whole body turn to sticky honey. She couldn't seem to find a single word to say.

"I've spoken to your mother," he said matter-of-factly. "She was kind enough to tell me where you were. She also gave me permission to speak to you about something rather consequential." He laid his hat down on the bench and reached for her hands, which were like ice. He rubbed them and warmed them between his.

After a moment or two, he kissed them. All Sophia's senses leaped to life. The feel of his warm lips upon her skin made her tremble with longing—longing to be in his arms again, to be swept away by the enormous, powerful lust she felt every time she looked at him.

He gazed into her eyes. "You must know why I have come."

Speechless, she waited for him to continue.

"I've come, Sophia, because I wish to ask you to be my wife. To be my duchess." He lowered his head to her hands and kissed them again—a long and lingering kiss.

Sophia wasn't sure she could breathe, let alone speak. She had dreamed of this moment, but not quite like this. "Is this because of what happened last night?" she asked. "Because I don't wish to be a wife you were forced to marry."

He gave her a compassionate look that told her he had expected such a response. "I would be lying if I said last night had nothing to do with this. It has a great deal to do with it—but only because I realized that I could not bear another moment thinking that you might return to America, or that you might marry some other man, or that I would never have the chance to hold you in my arms again. I was bewitched last night, Sophia. Bewitched. I could no more have stopped kissing you than I could have stopped breathing. You are the most intriguing woman I have ever known, and I need, more than anything, to know that you will belong to me and no other."

She gazed unblinking at his face. Had she heard him correctly? Had he said he was bewitched?

Of course the doubts came hurling at her all at once. "Did you speak to my mother about a settlement?"

He stared at her a moment, then cupped her chin in his hand. The intimacy of the gesture made her head spin with desires.

"Is that what you think? That I want you for your money?"

She gazed into his eyes, searching for truth. Was all this planned? Had he seduced her the night before to ensure her acceptance of his proposal? She did not know him well. Perhaps he was like all the rest—pretending to be interested in her when all he really wanted was her dowry. She could see it in their eyes.

But James . . . what did she see in his eyes? She wasn't sure. She thought she saw desire, but was she seeing only what she wanted to see? Was she blinded by her attraction, which perhaps was only physical?

If only she had more experience in these matters. She'd never felt such lust before. She was not capable of judging its integrity. What if it passed in a week's time? What if she later discovered he really was as devilish as all the gossips claimed—an accomplished rake who knew exactly how to seduce a young, innocent woman with money?

"I don't know," she replied at last. "Surely all of London must know what I am worth. Whitby knows."

"Ah, Whitby." He lowered his hand to his side and looked away, toward the house. "Are you thinking of him now?"

"No!" she blurted out. "It's not that. It's just that I thought because Mother told him, everyone must know."

His chest rose and fell with a deep breath. "I am here because I can't comprehend the idea of not having you." He met her gaze directly. "And that is the truest thing I have ever said to you."

Can't comprehend the idea of not having you.

Nor could she comprehend the idea of not having him.

Having. What did that mean exactly?

To have and to hold. . . .

What she wouldn't give to have him hold her now.

"James, I'm not sure. This seems sudden."

He took her hand again and kissed it many times. "Please, Sophia. Marry me and make me the happiest man alive. Come to my castle and be the greatest duchess my family has ever known. You told me once that you were in awe of England for its history. Come and be part of it—live it, become it. You wanted to see it from inside the very heart of it. You can, if only you will be my wife."

Sophia sucked in tiny little breaths between parted lips. Was this real? Could she actually walk into a fairy tale and marry her prince charming?

Then, with no further contemplation, a response

spilled out of her mouth. "Yes, James, I will be your wife."

The whole world disappeared, just for a second, then it returned with the blissful awareness that he was going to kiss her. He pulled her into his arms and pressed his lips to hers, and she felt transported as if on a cloud. She was going to be his wife! They would spend the rest of their days loving each other, living happily ever after!

She glanced up at the house and smiled, for her mother was watching from an upstairs window, jumping with joy.

Chapter 9

It was done. He was betrothed to an heiress.

James returned to his carriage. He sat alone, listening to the horses' hooves clopping over the cobblestones as they drove slowly through Piccadilly, clogged with traffic.

Why did he not feel more satisfied? he wondered with some apprehension. He had been determined to win the race, to acquire the dowry every other man in London was coveting, and this morning he had triumphed. He had secured the prize. Yet still, he felt displeased with himself when there was no logical reason to feel displeased. Why?

Perhaps it was because everything he had said to Sophia that morning was true. In all honesty, his proposal had not been about the money. Not when he was looking into her eyes and telling her he wanted to make her his duchess, that if she said yes, she would make him the happiest man alive.

Imagine that. Him, the happiest man alive. Good God, he had been carried off on a huge wave. He had blathered on and on to her about how much he adored her—he'd sounded like a damned schoolboy. He had never intended to be so romantic about it. It was supposed to be a business arrangement.

But she was the most beautiful woman he had ever known, and it was exactly as he had said—he simply had to have her. Bloody hell, he wanted her now. He wanted her here in the carriage beside him. In his arms.

Perhaps that's why he felt a lack of satisfaction. He knew deep down that he had not really triumphed. In truth, he had lost the fight against his impulsiveness, given in to his desires, and there was nothing he could do about it now except live with what had suddenly become his future and somehow survive it without descending into hell.

What a morning. And he still had to break the news of his engagement to his mother.

James squeezed the ivory handle of his walking stick while the carriage continued to clatter through the noisy London streets.

A half hour later, he was entering his own London house.

Her Grace, his mother, was sitting in the morning room, sipping tea. Her harsh gaze lifted when she sensed his presence in the doorway. "James," she said, somewhat startled.

He moved into the room and took a seat on the chintz sofa, deciding that there was no point putting off the inevitable. No need for idle chatter. He would be direct.

"I have news, and I thought you should be the first to know before you read about it in tomorrow's paper."

"Tomorrow's paper. Oh, good gracious." His mother leaned back and rested a hand on her heart as if she had been shot. "Don't tell me . . . not the American."

James crossed one long leg over the other. "As a matter of fact, yes. The American."

She rolled her gaze heavenward. "Oh, my dear." She stood up and walked to the fireplace. "No, no, I don't understand. You've been so difficult to move on the matter of marriage. Wait . . ." She faced him. "Is this some kind of childish rebellion against me? To hurt me? Because if it is, you have succeeded."

"It's not rebellion."

"What is it, then? How in the world did this happen? This girl—in barely more than a fortnight—lured you away from any number of lovely English girls from excellent families. There must be a reason. If it's not to hurt me . . ." She glared at him. "Surely James, you have not given it adequate thought."

"I have given it more than adequate thought, and even if I hadn't, the machine is in motion. There is no turning back now. I've already placed the formal announcement in the newspaper."

He'd never imagined he would receive such perverse pleasure from this moment, but there it was.

"Good heavens." She sank into a chair. "She's not in the family way, is she?"

"Now you're being ridiculous, Mother."

"Well . . ." She waved a frivolous hand about, as if to say, "You never know with these Americans."

"I told you her grandfather was a bootmaker, didn't I?" she said.

"Yes, you told me."

"And her other grandfather slaughtered pigs."

James stood. "I beg your pardon, Mother, but there is business to attend to this morning. I must go."

He started toward the door, but she stopped him with another question. "Have you set a date?"

He turned to face her. "August 25."

"*This* year?"

"Yes, there's no point prolonging the engagement. Sophia's parents will be returning to New York after the Season. Rather than send her back with them, I would prefer that she accompany me to Yorkshire."

His mother laid a hand on her chest again. "I can't bear to imagine the gossip when the servants see her. She dresses like an actress, James."

"She has style, Mother, and that is the last time you will insult her. She is the next Duchess of Wentworth." With that, he left the room.

He went upstairs to write to his agent, Mr. Wells, to instruct him to at once make the arrangements to have the roof over the state room fixed, and while he was at it, to at long last have the lake dredged.

"You bastard," Whitby said, stopping halfway up the stairs at Parliament to grab James's arm.

James turned to look down at his old school chum, who stood on a lower step. He yanked his arm out of Whitby's grasp. "Get ahold of yourself, man."

"Ahold of myself? I think you are the one who should have gotten ahold of something. You forced your hand on her, and you know it."

James straightened his tie and resumed his ascent up the stairs. "I know no such thing."

Whitby followed beside him. "Where were you at the assembly the other night? You disappeared with her for half an hour."

"We were with Lily."

"Not the entire time. I saw Lily later, and you weren't with her."

"I returned Sophia to her mother." He stopped at the top of the stairs and met Whitby's heated gaze. "Why am I even explaining myself to you?"

"Maybe because you fancy that you are an old friend of mine, and you feel guilty for stepping in on a woman I was openly pursuing."

James pointed a finger at Whitby. "She was not spoken for."

"I had spoken! Privately to you, of course, but I had thought we were friends. I thought you understood that I was asking you to back off."

James shook his head at the ridiculousness of this conversation. He started walking again, down the long Gothic corridor of the building. Their angry footfalls echoed off the arched ceiling. "You had no right to ask that."

"But you had assured me at the Bradley assembly that you were not looking to marry. That you would never marry. How did that change completely in a matter of weeks?"

"I had simply not met the right woman."

"You mean you hadn't met a rich enough woman."

James stopped. He stabbed a finger on Whitby's chest. "You're crossing the line."

"I think it is you who has crossed the line." Whitby lowered his voice. "You don't love her. You've never loved any woman, not even any of the ones you've bedded."

"I would oblige you to make your point."

"You're a cruel man, James, if you think you can

take her to Yorkshire and toss her to your mother to look after. That woman will have her for breakfast."

"Sophia can take care of herself."

"And that's why you proposed to her, I suppose. So she can take care of herself, and you can forget you've ever been married. You said it yourself. That's what you wanted."

James started walking again. He had the distinct feeling Whitby was looking for a fistfight, but he would not get one. Those days were over. If not for Whitby, at least for James.

"I would have loved her!" Whitby called out after him, his voice full of fury, and James felt the words like a knife sailing through the air and puncturing his back.

Nothing less than a wedding gown by Worth would do for England's newest duchess—for Monsieur Worth didn't just sew a dress for a woman, he created a whole new look—so Sophia and her mother packed up and left for Paris. They met her sisters there, accompanied by an aunt, for they, too—being Sophia's bridesmaids—required Worth gowns for the ceremony.

Clara and Adele were astute enough to bring stacks of New York newspapers with them in their trunks, for news of the upcoming nuptials had hit the headlines in America, and Sophia and her mother were anxious to read them.

The stories dripped with delicious details of the couple's romantic first encounters at London assemblies and balls. The Wentworth family tree, illustrated with coats of arms and portraits, and augmented with sketches of the castle in Yorkshire, filled column after column of every society page. As well as flattering mis-information about the bride's family history.

Even in Paris, journalists scurried out from behind shrubbery and parked carriages outside Sophia's hotel, hoping for a chance to ask her questions and have her pose for a picture. She had become an overnight sensation in the papers, and she could still barely believe any of it was happening. She found it all quite distressing and tried to remind herself that life would soon settle down once the wedding was over, and she and James retired to his country estate for the winter, where they could finally be alone together as man and wife.

Late one evening, Sophia sat up in her bed in the Paris hotel, wearing a white nightdress and reading the inside pages of a New York paper by the light of a gas lamp. She rose from the bed, however, when she came across a disturbing editorial piece.

"Clara, Adele, listen to this." She began to read aloud: "It is an affront to our flag that so many hard-earned American dollars are leaving our country to fill the bare bank accounts of British nobles, who know nothing of proper work ethics or proper morality for that matter. Our wealthy American brides are victims of greed and laziness; the girl's value is appraised only by how much she can do to restore the decaying castles of a decaying England. It is no secret that the English nobles squander their rent-roll money in the gambling houses of London with careless abandon, for they have never had to lift a finger to earn it."

Feeling a lump form in her belly, Sophia lowered the paper. She looked beseechingly at her sisters, who had been combing each other's hair. They were staring blankly at her now. "Have you heard this sort of thing before?" she asked them. "Is this what they're saying in New York?"

Clara rose from her chair to take Sophia's hands and reassure her. Clara had always been sensitive to everyone's feelings. She was an emotional girl who understood mental torment. In all honesty, sometimes Sophia suspected her sister of actually enjoying it. She liked melodrama in any form.

"Oh, no, Sophia," Clara said. "Everyone's thrilled for you. It's like a fairy tale. You've read the headlines."

"Yes, but this person seems to think James is some kind of lowly scoundrel, when in actuality, he's a responsible landlord of a huge estate. He's a successful, well-respected man!"

"Of course he is," Clara said. "He's an English nobleman! This writer, whoever he is, is just jealous. Some people are always looking for things to complain about, and they hate seeing anyone else happy. They have to spoil it somehow. Don't they, Adele?"

It seemed a simple way to cheer her up, but Sophia appreciated the attempt.

Her other sister nodded. Adele, unlike Clara, despised anything melodramatic or scandalous or the least bit out of the ordinary. Clara sometimes called Adele a prude, but Sophia knew Adele was just a proper young lady who wished to please her parents and follow the rules. There was nothing wrong with that. Probably, when she was out, she would marry a Mr. Peabody. Someone acceptable. Someone who wouldn't surprise anyone or cause any friction or gossip.

Clara smiled and strolled back to the dressing table. She picked up her brush and ran it through her thick hair. "If we had noticed that article, we would have pulled it out and burned it before we gave the paper to you. Like Auntie made us do with the other one." She gave Sophia a mischievous little grin.

"What other one?" Sophia asked.

Adele gritted her teeth with a good-natured warning. "Clara . . ."

"Tell me!" Sophia demanded, laughing and grabbing the brush from her sister.

Clara turned to face her. "Oh, all right," she said, sounding pleased to have something juicy to relate. The three of them in their nightdresses leaped onto the bed.

Clara started giggling. "Poor Auntie nearly swooned on the train when she read it."

"Read what?" Sophia demanded.

"There were illustrations and everything. I don't know where they found such sordid details."

Sophia grabbed her sister's arm. "Tell me!"

Clara paused for a moment to draw out the suspense, then said, "There was an entire column all about your wedding day underclothes!"

"What?"

"Which, of course," Clara added, "only the duke will ever see in real life."

"Clara!" Adele scolded. "You needn't be so vulgar about it!"

"They said the ribbon on your chemise came from Queen Anne's own trousseau, and that your corset hooks were made of gold."

"And there were illustrations?" Sophia asked in dismay.

"Yes!" Clara laughed and flopped down onto the bed. "You should have seen Auntie's face! She looked beastly!"

Sophia stood up and went to the dressing table to

look at her reflection in the mirror. "I hope James doesn't hear of it. Imagine. Corset hooks made of gold. As if any of that mattered."

Meanwhile, back in London, James's mother—claiming she was unwell—packed up in a huff and left for the country, while his solicitor and the Wilson family lawyers haggled over the finer points of what was to become the largest marriage settlement in English history.

Chapter 10

〜⌒∽⌒〜

"I wasn't sure you'd come."

The sound of her fiancé's deep, seductive voice from behind, his breath hot and moist in her ear, sent gooseflesh dancing down Sophia's spine. Standing next to her mother in a stuffy, overcrowded ballroom at a country estate not far out of London, she smiled and turned to face him.

God, but he was gorgeous. It was excruciating just to look at him. He wore his usual black suit with tails, white shirt, white bow tie and waistcoat, and it contrasted so sharply with his midnight black hair, the effect was devastating.

James took her gloved hand, raised it to his lips, and laid a warm kiss upon her knuckles, never taking his fiery gaze off her as he did so. "A walk on the terrace, perhaps?" he suggested.

"That would be delightful."

He greeted her mother and the other ladies in the

group, then offered his arm. He and Sophia headed toward the large, open doors on the opposite side of the ballroom.

Everyone was watching them, whispering with curiosity and fascination. Sophia didn't mind. She was proud to be the woman James had finally chosen as his wife. Proud to show them all how gloriously infatuated with each other they were. And how wrong the gossips were about him.

"You look ravishing tonight," James said. "You make it difficult for a man to wait for his wedding day. It's painful, actually."

She laughed and rubbed her shoulder up against his. They reached the cement balustrade and faced each other under the stars. A breeze swept through the leafy oak trees and swooped down over the grass, like a whisper in the night.

"Have you been enjoying all the attention?" he asked. "I imagine your social calendar has filled up considerably."

"Yes, it's astonishing. I can't get over it."

"Everyone wants to get a look at us together, be the first to congratulate us. They are in awe of you, my dear."

Sophia lowered her gaze. "You know I don't care about any of that, James. I just want to be your wife."

"I want that, too." He surveyed the couples around them as if to determine what social rules currently applied, then reached a hand out to touch her cheek.

His thumb feathered over her skin, then moved lightly over her lips. The sensation was tantalizing. Sophia closed her eyes briefly, took his hand in hers, and pressed it to her open mouth. She boldly tasted his palm with her tongue.

"You're killing me, you know," he said, taking a step closer to her.

She met his wicked gaze. "It's not my intention."

"No? Our wedding is not for two months. I don't think I can withstand this kind of thing until then."

"I want to be alone with you, James. Every minute of the day, it's all I can think about. I had no idea it would be like this."

With an experienced eye, he glanced around the terrace again, then reached for her hand. "Perhaps a walk in the garden."

"Yes," she replied breathlessly. *Yes to anything. To everything.*

"I am a well-bred gentleman," he said, leaning close, "so I will offer you my arm and politely escort you down the stairs, when what I really want to do is grab your hand and run."

She laughed and took his arm. They descended the stairs and stepped onto the soft, cool grass. The moon was full. The sweet scent of roses drifted languidly upon the clean, night air. It was a perfect, perfect evening.

"Have you picked out your wedding dress?" he asked, resting his hand upon hers.

"Yes, but I'll tell you nothing about it, nor will I say anything about the flowers I'll be carrying or the color of my sisters' gowns or the fabric of their sashes."

His voice was tinted with amusement. "You seem to enjoy torturing me with suspense. Just a little hint?"

"Absolutely not!"

"Please?"

"No!" she said, laughing.

"I give up. You are a rock. You'll make an excellent duchess."

She rested her head upon his shoulder. "I hope so. I want to make you proud."

"You've already made me proud. Every man in London envies me."

"You're just trying to flatter me."

"Indeed I am, but it's God's honest truth."

They strolled around the garden to the other side, where the trees grew tall and full.

"I'm glad you're wearing a dark gown this evening," James said.

"Why?"

Guiding her by the hand, he began to back away, into the wispy branches of a weeping willow. They draped like a beaded curtain, and he passed through, lifting the boughs for Sophia. His voice was quiet and searing with tempting allure. "So no one will notice when I lure you into the shadows."

Sophia smiled and bent forward to pass under the leaves, then straightened beneath the thick canopy. Though the moon was full, it was almost pitch-black beneath the tree.

"What are we doing?" she asked in a sultry voice.

"We're stealing privacy."

"This is dangerous, James. If anyone sees us . . ."

He backed up against the huge trunk of the tree and gently pulled her toward him. "They won't. Come closer."

"Why?" she asked wickedly.

"Because I want your lips, Sophia."

She could barely see his face in the darkness, only sensed where he was and where his mouth was. The thrill of touching him without really seeing him sent a flurry of titillating tremors through her body.

"Then take them." She sighed, pressing her lips to

his and giving in to the lusty hunger that had been assaulting her senses for weeks.

The kiss was deep and hot. Knees melting into a syrupy liquid, she whimpered at the feel of his tongue mingling with hers, the exquisite, spicy, soul-blazing taste of him. She clutched at his strong, broad shoulders for support. Leaned into his hard body.

She felt an instinctive need to push her hips into his pelvis, and he moaned and grabbed onto her bottom when she gave in to it. His firm arousal, pressing against her pelvic bone, caused a torrent of drenching heat to escape her feminine center.

He tilted his head one way, then the other, eating at her mouth as if he were starving for her. She pulled off her long gloves and let them drop to the ground. Shamelessly, she moved her hands over his chest and into the warmth of his suit jacket, around his hips and under the waistband of his trousers. She tried to unfasten a button—doing everything by feeling for it— wanting to slide her fingers in and touch him, but he took hold of her hand and shook his head.

"You're entering dangerous territory, darling. Perhaps, not yet."

An owl hooted somewhere in the distance. "But the waiting . . . it's impossible, James. I've been able to think of nothing but this. I want to know what you feel like."

He closed his eyes, went still for a moment. "When you say things like that, it becomes a painful exertion to behave like a gentleman."

He was struggling to pull back on the reins. For some unknown reason, his need to do so, and the fact that it was difficult for him, aroused Sophia even more. She opened her mouth and kissed him again, finding a perverse pleasure in this power that she seemed to have over him—in knowing that she pushed him to his limits.

He responded passionately, cupping her head in his big hands and thrusting his tongue into her mouth. "I should take you back," he whispered against her cheek as he left a trail of kisses to her neck.

Sophia let her head fall to the side. "Not yet. Please."

"You mustn't plead with me, darling, it makes me insane."

"Then I'll beg. Please, James, please . . ."

She felt him smile against her neck, then nibble at her ear. "You have no mercy, do you?"

"I don't know. I don't seem to care about anything right now except the feel of your hands on me in this delicious darkness. This is all so new to me, James. I've never felt anything like it. Everything seemed to happen so fast between us, but now, the time is passing so slowly. I want to marry you now. This minute. I want to be your wife."

He dragged his lips from her neck and glanced up at the house. A Strauss waltz was playing inside the ballroom; the sounds of the orchestra were faint but discernible. "We've been gone a while."

He was right, and she knew it, but that didn't make it any easier to take even one small step away from him.

"I know," she said. "We should return, but I don't want to."

"I don't either, but this is torture. You are an extraordinary woman, Sophia."

She smiled at the compliment and backed away from him, picking up her gloves and smoothing out her gown. "All right then, since you put it that way."

"Mercy at last."

He moved away from the tree and straightened his tie, then graciously offered his arm. They strolled back to the ballroom.

James danced with his future wife, laughed with her and openly flirted with her, and realized with profound turmoil that tonight he had relinquished any futile attempts to exercise his self-control. Out there in the darkness, he'd been entranced by her. Enthralled by the hot, wet texture of her mouth, shaken by his own body's response to the way she'd touched him with those eager, searching hands.

She now stood beside him, talking to a gentleman in their group. God, he wanted to touch those hands— peel off her gloves and take each of her slender fingers into his mouth and suck on them for an eternity.

It was as if the flood gates had opened, and he'd completely given in to this mad, ravenous desire for his betrothed.

He glanced around for a tray of champagne and took a glass from a passing footman.

This was not at all how he'd imagined things would be, he thought, as he took the first sip, nodding politely as if he were listening to the conversations around him. He'd intended this marriage to be a business matter, dammit. As Sophia said—*a fair exchange*.

Perhaps it was simply the lure of the forbidden and the strain of constantly suppressing a damned inconvenient number of persistent, aching erections. He tried to tell himself that after he made love to Sophia properly on the wedding night and on their honeymoon, the pressure would ease off.

But for now, what to do. He wanted her, there was

no getting around that, and she wanted him. Fortunately, they would have each other soon. The wedding day was approaching, and he would finally be able to quench this massive fire in his sexual core. Sophia would satisfy her curiosity. He would have the honeymoon to enjoy her, as she would enjoy him. They would travel to Italy, spend a few magical weeks with each other. Perhaps it would be best to hold nothing back, he thought. Perhaps he needed to release this pent-up lust. He had been suppressing his passions for what felt like forever.

After the honeymoon, they would return to England and travel north to his house in the country, where his mother was now, where the reality of his life existed. He would curtail what was left of his passions and settle into a more tranquil life with a beautiful duchess at his side. They would produce an heir or two or three.

Feeling his shoulders relax somewhat, James swallowed the last of his champagne. *This shall pass,* he told himself. For the good of everyone, this madness—as enjoyable as it was—was only temporary.

Chapter 11

A ugust closed in and London cleared out. The lords and ladies and sirs and honorable misses skipped off to their country estates, for everyone knew that it was better to be seen in one's underclothes than wandering about the streets of London in August.

Unless, of course, you were planning a wedding and you were marrying the Duke of Wentworth. Or any duke for that matter. Then you could set your own rules and do whatever you liked—anything short of wandering about in your underclothes, of course.

August passed, the wedding day arrived, and that very morning a package arrived from New York—a wedding gift from *the* Mrs. Astor—the matriarch of the Knickerbockers, who before that day had refused to acknowledge the Wilsons' existence. She had sent an exquisite string of pearls for England's newest duchess, and Sophia's mother wept with perfect joy as she ripped and tore at the tissue paper. "Now," she said between deep, resounding sobs, "Clara's and Adele's futures will be assured."

Shortly after that, a gift arrived from Buckingham Palace—a magnificent gilded clock, and her mother wept again.

The horses that were hired to bring the bridal carriage to the church were matched grays—a time-honored tradition—and the streets were lined with crowds of enthusiastic spectators wanting to get a look at the famed American heiress. Held back by rows of uniformed London constables, the throng cheered and waved and threw flowers. Sophia squeezed her father's hand as they rode in an open carriage behind another carrying her bridesmaids, Clara, Adele, and Lily. She raised the other gloved hand to wave nervously to the crushing mob.

The carriage arrived at St. George's Church in Hanover Square, and with a trembling heart, Sophia stepped out of the carriage. She followed her bridesmaids up to the door of the church. She heard the peal of the pipe organ and caught a glance of the guests seated inside. There were over a thousand of them, from both sides of the Atlantic.

The bridesmaids—dressed in gowns of white satin with pink sashes—embarked upon the long walk up the aisle to the music of Mendelssohn, then at last Sophia reached the altar. The bishop, with a deep, resounding voice, asked, "Who giveth this woman to be married to this man?"

Her father replied in his deep American accent, "I do," then the bishop took Sophia's hand and placed it in James's. She gazed up at him and saw the man of all her dreams. Handsome, strong, intelligent, and professedly enamored with her.

He smiled with encouragement—his blue eyes warm and true—and all the madness of the morning melted away inside her body. There was only herself and her elegant groom, here to pledge their undying love to one another.

God. He hoped he would not become like his father.

James and Sophia spoke their vows, then knelt on the red velvet cushions for the blessing. The bishop prayed.

What would happen when the novelty of their new life together was no longer novel? James wondered suddenly, feeling a sense of panic he was wholly unaccustomed to. When expectations were not met by one or the other? What if Sophia took a lover, as James's own grandmother had done all those years ago? Would he be able to restrain himself from becoming the man his grandfather had become, full of jealousy and rage?

"What God hath joined together, let no man put asunder."

James and Sophia rose from their cushions. He studied his bride's face and saw the exuberance in her eyes. She was born to be a duchess, there was no doubt about that. Her portrait would hang in the gallery, and no one would ever think she did not fit the part. Life as an aristocrat was what she had come to London seeking, after all.

A deeper tension found its way into his gut. He hoped she would conceive on their honeymoon, so the initial obligation would be fulfilled sooner rather than later. Then they could each settle into their individual roles as duke and duchess. She would make a home for herself in her own private rooms—as all the duchesses had before her—and he would continue as he always had in his. Dinner each evening would be a pleasant time for conversation. He would hear about her undertakings for that day, and she would hear about his.

He slid the ring onto her slender finger, and tried to assure himself that everything would work out—that his self-control would not be lost.

James and Sophia rushed out to the carriage that was waiting to take them to their private wedding breakfast at James's London residence. First, however, they were driven ceremonially through the streets of London, lined with crowds of screaming onlookers.

Sophia waved at the people on her side of the street, and James did the same for those on his. Here they were, alone for the first time as man and wife, and they were too busy waving to strangers in opposite directions even to look at each other. Sophia tried to remind herself to be patient. Life would settle down soon enough.

The wind had gained force while they were inside the church, and though it was warm, it blew hard against her veil and loosened the Greek twist in her hair. She raised a hand to keep the veil in place, which caught James's attention. He finally turned toward her.

"You look beautiful," he said.

She gazed appreciatively into his eyes. "Thank you, James."

"You're a duchess now."

Sophia smiled. "Funny, I don't feel any different."

"You will. Just wait until you arrive at Wentworth. Life will be very different from what it is here."

She wasn't quite sure what he was referring to, exactly, but she did know one thing. They would be man and wife, and sharing a bed. Making love.

A ripple of anticipation—both frightening and exciting—shimmied up her spine. She remembered their singular night in the conservatory and gloried in the fact that no one would interrupt them next time, when they were alone in their bedchamber. Whatever desires they experienced together, they would be free to explore.

There was so much she did not know about that side of marriage—what took place in the bed at night. So many wondrous moments lay ahead of her. . . .

"Will we be leaving for our honeymoon first thing in the morning?" she asked.

Like a wolf picking up a scent, he seemed to detect her meaning. He smiled. "Are you anxious to see Rome? Or just anxious to be a wife, my dear?"

Sophia met his gaze boldly, her eyes glimmering with heat and daring. Here they were, in an open carriage, rolling through London on parade for all the world to see, and she wanted to put her hands on him.

She glanced up at their driver in front. Steering the team of grays, he was oblivious to what was going on anywhere but in front of him.

They were on a wide street now; the people waving at them were a distance away.

Sophia felt a rush of impatience where her husband was concerned. Her heart pounded a wild rhythm. Intimacy with the man beside her was all that mattered, so absorbed in his gaze was she.

Her world seemed like a fairy tale all of a sudden—full of magic and grandeur. The magic seeped through her gown and tingled over her skin. Her wedding day had been as enchanting as she'd ever imagined it would be, and she wanted to leap with all her heart and soul into this glorious marriage.

She slid her fingers along the crimson leather seat

and let them find their way to James's muscular thigh beside her. All the while, she smiled and waved at the crowd with her other hand.

"I suppose we could begin the honeymoon, now," he said, still waving at the crowd on his side, "even though we don't leave for Rome until tomorrow."

"Perhaps a kiss would give everyone something to talk about," Sophia suggested.

With a lazy grin, he leaned into her. "I'm eager, if a little shocked."

Sophia's heart trembled at his nearness. She wanted all of him. More than just his mouth.

The kiss was neither tentative nor sweet—it was wet and open and deep, and her blood quickened as his lips brushed hers. The crowd cheered even louder, then seemed to disappear. Sophia let her hand slide over his thigh and down between his legs, discreetly feeling the arousal that was pressing against his trousers.

"Do you think anyone can see this?" she whispered into his mouth.

He cupped her head in his hand. "No one would believe it if they did." He deepened the kiss, while she stroked the firm proof of his arousal.

"You are a very naughty duchess," he said, and she gloried in the sound of his approval and the lusty glint in his eye. "But you best be careful, or you'll find yourself flat on your back in a moment, and I don't think your mother would appreciate a photograph of your legs in the air as the carriage passed by, on the front page of the *New York Times*."

Sophia laughed and turned to the crowd. She couldn't wait for darkness to fall.

"I'm looking forward to spending the days alone

with you, James, so we may get to know each other better."

"You don't feel you know me?" He faced the other direction.

"Well, as much as a person can know another person, having spent so little time together," she replied.

"A good point with much validity." For a long time he was quiet, and when he finally spoke, the flirtatious tone was gone. Sophia gazed curiously at him.

"It's only natural," he said, "that as the years go by, there will be an increased sense of . . . familiarity."

"Familiarity?" Something tensed inside of her. Had James just cooled toward her? A second ago he was on fire, now he wouldn't look at her. It seemed strange.

She watched him for another moment, then swept the foolish notion away. She was just nervous because it was her wedding day. She was imagining things. He wasn't cooling toward her. He was playing with her.

She laughed and spoke with amusement. "James, sometimes you are so very British. It's why I love you."

James turned back toward her again, just as she turned the opposite way to resume waving at the Londoners. Her words resounded in his brain. *Why I love you? Love?*

Feeling numb all of a sudden, James watched his wife. Good God, she was his wife, wasn't she, and she was laughing at his heritage and tossing the word *love* around like it was something commonplace.

No one had ever used the word with him before, and he wondered if it was an American thing—to say it so lightly, with such innocuous ease.

"Did your mother come?" Sophia asked without

looking at him. "I was too nervous to look and see who was sitting in the front pews."

James searched his mind for an excuse. "She is still unwell. Of course, she sends her regrets and is anticipating your arrival at Wentworth with much eagerness."

"I'm looking forward to meeting her. She won't mind, will she? Handing her duties and responsibilities over to me? Or having to vacate her rooms?"

"Why do you ask? You aren't nervous about meeting her, are you?"

"No, I just . . . I always expected to know a man's family before I married into it. As it stands, I will only meet your siblings for the first time today."

"You've met Lily."

"Yes, and I like her very much."

He took her gloved hand. "Then do not worry yourself. You are the new Duchess of Wentworth, and Mother knows well enough what her duty is—and that is to step aside. You shall have no problems there. Believe me, she will know her boundaries."

Sophia's eyes met his directly. "Please, I beg your pardon, James. I wasn't suggesting that there should be boundaries. I merely worry that she might feel left out, or feel as if she has no more purpose. That won't be the case, of course. I am sure I will rely on your mother for everything. To show me what to do. To share my joys and disappointments as I share them with my own mother. I hope we will be close, James. I hope she will love me like a true daughter."

There was that word again—*love*—carelessly flung about. It was one thing to say it with him, in the privacy of their carriage, but he hoped Sophia would know enough to be a little less candid when she met her mother-in-law. James doubted his mother would know what to make of such sentiments, especially considering how she felt about her new daughter-in-law.

If Sophia was ever going to be accepted by the woman, she would have to learn to behave with a little more . . . Englishness.

"Let us think of ourselves today, Sophia, and not worry about the future. Everything will work out."

"I do apologize, James. There have just been so many changes these past few weeks. I suppose I'm a little overwhelmed."

"As any bride would be on her wedding day, when crowds of strangers are cheering and shouting her name." They both waved simultaneously in the same direction. "Do not feel anxious, my dear. Tonight, it will be just the two of us, and we will celebrate in our own, private way."

James stroked Sophia's cheek with a finger, and with one single kiss, knew he had successfully melted away her concerns just in time for their arrival at Wentworth House.

Late in the afternoon, after Sophia had spent a pleasant few minutes conversing with James's younger brother Martin—who was a handsome young man at sixteen—her father took her by the arm and led her to a settee. She gazed lovingly at his bushy gray sideburns and mustache, his wild mane of gray hair. He looked so handsome in his wedding attire.

"My darling girl," he said with his booming, Southern drawl, "I haven't had a minute alone with you—such a beautiful bride—to really congratulate you. You know how proud I am?"

Sophia wrapped her arms around her father's big shoulders and hugged him tightly. "I'm going to miss you all so much."

"Now, now, don't fret, we're only a steamship ride away, and I'm sure your sisters will be writing to you constantly. I don't doubt, after the pageantry they've witnessed today, they'll be wanting to come back in a year or two and snare English husbands for themselves."

Sophia grabbed his nose and wiggled it. "Oh, Papa, I didn't snare anyone. James and I are in love."

His voice became more serious. "I know you love him. I can see it in your eyes. But do remember, this is a different world, Sophia, and if you ever need me to come and fetch you . . . I know your mother wouldn't like it but—"

"I'll be fine, Papa," she replied, uncomfortable with the direction this conversation was taking. "You needn't worry. I'll be the happiest woman on earth."

He hugged her again. "Ah, my young girls. You're a horde of hopeless romantics." He withdrew from the hug and took her hand. "I know this is your wedding day, but I do have to speak to you about the marriage settlement. I want you to know what your situation will be, before you go off and become known to the world as the new Duchess of Wentworth."

"Of course," she replied, feeling her smile slowly drain away.

"The amount of the dowry was settled at one million pounds, five hundred thousand as a lump sum and the balance paid in installments for the first two years of your marriage, as well as two hundred thousand pounds worth of my railway stock, the yield payable annually. I've also agreed to pay all the country estate debts outstanding as of the date of the settlement; otherwise, half your dowry would have been gone before you'd even reached Wentworth."

Sophia snapped her mouth shut. A huge surge of nausea flowed like a river into her stomach. "I had no idea the settlement would be so large."

Nor had she known that James's estate was so deeply in debt.

Her father seemed to notice something change in her expression. He began to ramble with some explanations. "James wasn't present for the negotiations, of course, nor was I. Our lawyers hammered it out, and you know how cutthroat those people can be."

She nodded, but inside, there was a painful, squeezing despair. It was like having her fairy-tale wedding bubble pricked with a gigantic knitting needle.

"In addition to that," he said, rubbing his hand over the back of hers, "I've arranged for you to have your own bank account and an annuity of fifty thousand pounds per year, payable quarterly."

"Papa, that really wasn't necessary."

"Well, well, maybe not for you, but it's more for my own peace of mind. I need to know that my little girl will never want for anything. Things are different here, darling. Married women, according to law, have no control over their money. Dowries are absorbed into the husband's estate, and wives are given an allowance, which depends solely on their husbands' generosity. I'll not have you going to James every time you want to buy something. That was the deal, and I said 'it's the American way, so take it or leave it,' and naturally the Langdon lawyers took it." Then as an afterthought, he added, "Because, of course, James would never have allowed anything to keep him from marrying you."

Sophia swallowed over the painful lump in her throat and hugged her father again. "Thank you, Papa, for everything you've done. You've made me very happy." She rested her cheek on his broad shoulder and squeezed her eyes shut to keep him from seeing the single tear that was spilling from her eye.

"Congratulations, Duchess," Lord Whitby said, appearing beside Sophia after the German soloist finished his set. "I do believe you are the most dazzling bride London has ever seen." He raised his champagne glass to toast her before taking a sip.

"Thank you, Lord Whitby."

"Lord Whitby! Please, you must call me Edward."

Sophia smiled. "Edward, then. You are enjoying yourself, I hope?"

"Immensely. And I am a big enough man to admit that I am envious of your husband—the lucky devil." He glanced around the room over the rim of his glass, his gaze searching for James. "I have accepted that the better man won. He is a duke, after all. I shouldn't take it too personally."

Sophia would have liked to correct him on that—that he should indeed take it very personally, for there was no other way to take it—but of course, she held her tongue.

"So you're off to Rome tomorrow," he said, and she was thankful he was changing the subject.

"Yes, we'll spend a fortnight there, then return to Yorkshire."

"You've not been there yet?"

"No, but I'm looking forward to seeing the house and the countryside. I hear it's lovely in the north."

"Yes, there is a certain 'oldness' to the place. Lots of

fog. It's very damp; I hope you have a warm cloak." He took another sip of champagne.

"I do, Edward, thank you." She sipped from her own glass and gazed across the room to where James was conversing with a man she did not know. *Please, come and rescue me,* she thought.

At that precise moment, their gazes locked and her husband noticed the earl beside her. Without a second's hesitation, he tapped the man he was talking to and left him. It was as if her husband had read her mind.

She felt a sudden buoyant euphoria—that her belief in their soulful connection had just been validated.

He crossed the room toward her, looking so handsome that she feared she might forget decorum and drag him upstairs that very minute. The anticipation for the night ahead was almost painful.

"Whitby," James said, reaching them, "you're not trying to charm my wife away from me, I hope."

The two gentlemen laughed, but Sophia sensed tension between them. Had her marriage to James caused a rift in their friendship? she wondered, for she knew that Lord Whitby had wanted her. He had sent those beautiful roses . . .

After a few minutes of awkward conversation, the earl politely took his leave, and Sophia was left alone with James in the crowded reception hall. He touched her under the chin.

"It seems as if I've married a heartbreaker," he said with some humor.

Sophia smiled guiltily. "I hope Edward had not held any unrealistic hopes that there might have been a match between us."

"How could any man refrain from hoping where you are concerned?"

She felt a curious whirling sensation in her belly and farther down. How was it possible she could have matured into a grown woman and never known how desire could eclipse one's ability to think rationally? How it could make her tremble with such need, that all she could comprehend was her body's sensation, with little care about anything else? If she hadn't had such a firm head on her shoulders, she would have kissed him right there in front of everyone. Passionately.

Sophia gazed into her husband's eyes. "I've never known a man more charming and handsome than you."

"Nor I a more fascinating woman. We are a good match, then."

"We are, James." She tasted another sip of the pleasantly intoxicating champagne, and anticipated the night ahead with indulgent, naughty expectation.

Chapter 12

James dismissed his valet early, and still in his wedding clothes, picked up a candelabra and left his room. He'd been anticipating this moment all day long—all season long if he was honest with himself—and a firm urge for hastiness overcame him. He'd done enough waiting. It was time to enjoy his enthusiastic bride.

He walked down the dimly lit corridor of his London house. Already, he was feeling a tremor of arousal for what lay ahead in the next few hours. Best, however, to curtail those thoughts until he was at least in her room, preferably in her bed.

He reached his wife's boudoir and knocked. He hoped he had given her enough time to undress and settle in. Surely Mildred, her new maid, had taken good care of her.

"Come in," he heard, from inside.

He opened the door and stepped over the threshold.

Sophia wore a white nightdress. She was sitting up in her huge, canopied bed, her legs crossed at the ankles on top of the covers. Waiting for him, apparently.

He gazed at her small bare feet and saw the wicked smile on her face, and congratulated himself upon being right about one thing. She was ardent about her duties—at least this particular one, to produce an heir. He had chosen well, for this aspect of their marriage—the carnal pleasure that would result while they both did their "duty"—was in all likelihood the only thing he would permit himself to enjoy over the long term.

He moved calmly into the room and set the candles on her dressing table. "You're not too tired, I hope, after such a long day."

She shook her head quickly to say no, so he sauntered toward the big bed, tugging his neckcloth from side to side.

"Well, then," he said with a smile, "perhaps we can make use of this private time together to get to know each other in a more intimate manner."

"I would like that, James. More than anything."

He shrugged out of his white waistcoat and began to unbutton his shirt. "You met Mildred?" He thought it might be good to make some light conversation in an attempt to lighten his bride's nerves.

"I did, and I sent her out. I hope that was not too wrong of me."

He paused at the bottom button. "You sent her out? What do you mean?"

"She wanted to bathe me, James." She said it as if it were something strange.

"You weren't comfortable with that?"

"No. I haven't had anyone bathe me since I was a child."

He pulled off his shirt and climbed onto the bed beside Sophia. "But duchesses are always bathed by their maids."

"That's exactly what Mildred said." She lowered her long-lashed gaze to her hands on her lap. She was fiddling with her wedding band, turning it around and around on her finger.

He covered her hands with his own. "You'll become accustomed to things in time."

His touch seemed to appease her. "I suppose. I'm glad you're here."

"I'm glad, too. Would you like me to put out the candles?"

She gave him a mischievous smile. "No, I would like to leave them burning. I would like to be able to look at your face tonight."

He had the distinct impression, however, she wanted to see something beyond just his face.

The comment shook him, perhaps because she was his wife and there were certain expectations—expectations that were different from what he was used to in a bed partner.

He felt a great weight upon his chest suddenly, knowing that it would not be easy to resist the emotional involvement that would—or should—come from this marriage. This was new territory.

"We shall let them burn all night, then," he said nonetheless, because he was an expert lover, and his desire to pleasure his wife outweighed his misgivings.

He leaned toward her and touched his mouth to hers, easing her full lips apart. The inside of her mouth tasted like paradise as her sweet tongue twirled enticingly around his. Like his courtship and proposal, he was being carried away again on that unmanageable wave, forgetting his objectives, and instead, enjoying the journey to wherever the current took him. He was now completely immersed in the pure enjoyment of this provocative woman, in the texture of her soft skin and the rapturous scent of her perfume.

Her hands clutched at his shoulders, a whimper escaped her, and he realized he was rock-hard already—painfully so, in fact. He eased her back onto the soft pillows, his hands sliding down her belly, over the soft linen of her nightgown, while the taste of her mouth quickened his blood and washed his senses in hot, mellifluous desire. He kissed her deeply, devouring her mouth with his own, then suckled the soft skin along her warm, slender neck.

Sophia inched down to lie back on the bed. "I've dreamed of this moment ever since that night in the conservatory. I didn't know the meaning of passion before then."

God, his head was swimming. Searching for patience to resist taking her here and now, he leaned on one elbow to gaze down at her face in the dim light. "You've been looking forward to this, then?"

"Yes. I want to do everything with you, James. I want you to show me how to make you happy."

"It would indeed be my pleasure, Duchess."

She began to unbutton her nightdress, then sat up and pulled it off over her head. Leaning back to make way, James realized he'd married an uncommonly assertive woman. Assertive, at least, in the bedroom, and he was not sorry for that, no.

She was naked now, cupping his face in her hands. She pulled him down for another openmouthed kiss. His own passions bucked wildly again, and he rolled on top of her and thrust his hips against hers, let his hand glide over her bare breasts and down to her long, slender legs, which she wrapped around him.

He began to suckle her breasts, feeling dangerously out of control with need. She moaned and buried her fingers in his hair as he licked and teased her taut nipples like a starving man.

"That feels so good, James." Her voice was breathy and feverish. "How do you know what feels so good?"

"Because it feels just as good to me."

"Oh, I suppose men and women are designed for this, aren't they?" She writhed with pleasure beneath him. "Like a round peg and a perfectly sized hole."

He couldn't have said it better himself.

His hand worked its way down her adorable flat belly to the cleft of soft hair at its base. She instinctively spread her legs apart and he slid a finger into the creamy, liquid heat of her womanly flesh. Sexual intoxication swirled inside his head. He shut his eyes and pleasured her, at the same time preparing her for what was to come.

"What are you doing to me?" she asked him in a way that revealed her surprise that such delights were possible.

He watched her face intently, his own body hot with urgent need. "I thought we'd start small and work our way up."

"To what? This doesn't feel small to me. It's overwhelming, James."

He smiled wickedly. "There will be more, I quite assure you."

With the barrier of her virginity loosening around his finger, a flaming heat began to ignite deep in his loins. She was drenched, and he wanted to feel that damp heat around his own center of desire. He withdrew his finger and reached down to unbutton his trousers.

Sophia opened her eyes and rolled to her side. She was wet and tingling between her legs. She could only assume this was normal, for James seemed at ease with it. A slow, lazy grin moved across his lips as he slid his pants down over his hips. Sophia trembled at the fire racing through her veins—then the shock and fever that exploded at the sight of his tremendous arousal. Too late, she realized her eyebrows had lifted in shock.

"I've frightened you," he said, tossing his trousers to the floor and rolling onto his side to reassure her. "Perhaps we should have snuffed out the candles after all."

"No," she lied, trying to keep her gaze fixed on his eyes when all she wanted to do was look down at what she'd never in her life imagined was possible.

He reached for her hand and gently wrapped it around him. He was rigid there, yet the skin was warm and silky-smooth to her touch. He showed her how to stroke him. She enjoyed watching how the pleasure carried him away, as it had carried her earlier.

Then he slid his hand between her thighs again. Sophia spread her legs and grew short of breath as her belly quivered with a delicious, pulsing need. He stroked her until she grew gloriously numb in certain places, wildly sensitive in others. All the while, he kissed her breasts, flicked his tongue over her nipples, and drove her mad with exotic desires.

He left a trail of kisses down her belly, then slid his shoulders between her legs and kissed her lower, where the creamy, hot pleasure was centered. She raised her knees and clutched at his head, feeling drunk with lust and disbelief as she murmured his name.

For a long while, he pleasured her that way, then climbed catlike over her.

"I can't wait much longer," he said, touching the hot skin of his torso to hers. He gazed down at her for a moment, his expression tender and blissful.

Sophia's heart quickened with both fear and eager anticipation. The silky tip of his erection touched her most intimate place, and she knew he was about to thrust himself inside. Her husband, her mate, the man of her dreams . . . they were about to be joined forever, in both body and spirit. She clutched at his broad shoulders and braced herself, for she could not imagine the hugeness of him penetrating what had been difficult for his finger to penetrate only moments ago.

"Try to relax," he whispered in her ear.

She nodded. "I will."

He reached down with his hand to guide himself to her opening, then slowly thrust forward.

The pressure made her inch away from him. She bumped her own head against the headboard.

James retreated.

She swallowed nervously and realized she would have to stay in one place if he was going to gain entry. "I'm sorry, I couldn't help it. You're just so very . . . large."

She inched her way back down so her head was on the pillow again.

"I'll take that as a compliment."

"Try again, James. I want to feel you inside me."

He kissed her then, and she parted her lips for him and felt the heat of his tongue and the heat of her own desire—a wave of moisture down below where he was poised, waiting. God, she wanted him with such fury, her body was pulsing with it. "Please, James . . . now . . ."

He thrust ever so gently, and she forced herself to relax as he drove forward and broke through her maidenhead.

Sophia cried out and held tightly on to him. He went still.

"We're not there yet, darling." He pushed again and drove more deeply into her. She cried out again.

"It won't hurt after this," he whispered in her ear, dropping apologetic, affectionate kisses on her cheeks and nose and eyelids. "My darling Sophia."

She felt a lump form in her throat with the urge to cry from the pain, but another part of her felt the most extraordinary, dreamlike joy and yearning. She longed for him to push again.

He slid all the way out—at least it felt like it, she couldn't be sure, he was so huge inside her—then slid back in and repeated the rhythm until all the pain was gone and she was slick with moisture, feeling dazed with hot-blooded delight as he drove into her again and again.

She cried out differently this time and clung to his shoulders as he worked inside her, his hard, muscular body now growing damp with perspiration. Squeezing her eyes shut, she felt like she was touching heaven. James—her mate for all her life—had taken her there.

James felt the heat of his own orgasm approaching, centering deep in his core and dimming his sense of rational awareness. Then he climaxed and experienced an ecstasy so electrifying, so rich and new, he felt like a virgin himself. A low groan escaped him. He poured into his wife and could not for the life of him fathom the jubilation that came at him from all directions. She was so hot and tight and glorious, and she was his.

Sophia hugged him. "Oh, James."

He realized with some uneasiness that a part of him relished the sound of his name spoken so lovingly on her lips, while another part of him tensed at her emotional abandon.

His breathing slowed and he carefully rolled off her. Sophia lay there with her head on his shoulder, sighing with contentment, rubbing her fingers over his bare chest. Then she fell asleep.

James lay still, trying not to think, trying only to sleep like he did every other night of his life, but this was not, unfortunately, every other night, and he did not want to sleep. He wanted to do one of two things—make love to his wife again and experience another brilliant, soul-blazing pinnacle, or make haste to leave her bed.

He opened his eyes to watch her resting peacefully beside him, then sat up to reach for his trousers.

Chapter 13

James had just fastened his trousers and was reaching for his shirt on the chair when he heard the bed creak and knew Sophia had awakened. Dread flooded through him. He had hoped to sneak away unnoticed.

"Where are you going?" she asked, sounding genuinely puzzled.

With his back to her, he breathed deeply to allay the frustration at having not been able to leave quietly, then he turned around and faced her with a smile. She was naked on the bed, lying on her side and resting her cheek on her hand, and she looked like an ancient goddess in the dim golden firelight. The curvaceous line of her waist and hips and legs and the triangular mass of curls at their apex distracted him for a second or two, but he quickly regained control of his thoughts. "I'm going back to my bedchamber, of course," he explained.

"Your bedchamber? I thought this was your bedchamber. Our bedchamber."

James stared at her wordlessly in disbelief. Perhaps, in his mad rush to marry Sophia, he had not realized the full extent of her innocence. He had known of course that she would have much to learn regarding the running of his house in Yorkshire, but this—not knowing they would have separate rooms—this was a surprise.

He buttoned his shirt as he spoke. "The duke and duchess have always had separate rooms. Did no one tell you that?"

She continued to gaze up at him with confusion. She didn't seem to want to believe what he was telling her. "But we're man and wife. I thought . . ." She hesitated for a moment, as if considering this. "But you'll sleep here with me, won't you? I mean, after our servants have retired."

"You mean Mildred and Thompson."

"Is Thompson your . . . ?"

"My valet, yes." She seemed to find it unsettling that she had not known the man's name.

"All right then, after Mildred and Thompson have retired," she repeated for clarification. "You will be sleeping with me, won't you?" She sat up and swung her legs over the side of the bed.

James took in the graceful way she moved, the beguiling length of her legs, the perfect fullness of her breasts now that she was no longer lying down. He noticed with a resounding report of desire that her pink nipples were soft, and he remembered how they had tasted when they were hard, how he had enjoyed flicking his tongue back and forth over them and feeling her soft, warm body melt and wiggle beneath him.

A violent compulsion to touch her again and bend

to all her whims overpowered him as he gazed at her, as if he wished to adapt himself to her customs and expectations instead of the other way around. For a moment, the very common idea of sharing a bed with his wife night after night seemed intriguing. What a curious thought it was. Imagine how comfortable two people would become with each other. There would be no pretenses, no secrets—only an intimate connection that would surely deepen through the years, and a coinciding confidence in the other person's affections.

He forced himself to tear his gaze away from her and button the last button on his shirt. He was suddenly thankful for this particular custom of his class—separate rooms. He was not sure he could handle that kind of intimacy too often. Perhaps, he thought with some curiosity, becoming too intimate and presumptuous had been his father's downfall.

"I'll come to see you of course," he said in reply to her question.

"Come to see me? Then you'll leave like this every night?"

He chose not to answer her on that, for he wasn't even certain he would come to see her every night. He wanted to produce an heir, not become besotted with his wife, and he surely would become besotted if he made love to her constantly. He reached for his waistcoat and pulled it on.

Sophia stood. She crossed toward him, her bare feet padding soundlessly over the rug. All at once, she was standing naked in front of him, and he could smell her perfume. Her thick, wavy hair spilled down over her shoulders and covered her breasts; her turquoise eyes were wide and worried and brimming with anxiety.

She took hold of his waistcoat to prevent him from buttoning it, and used it to pull him forward a step.

"Tonight's our wedding night, James. Can't you stay a little longer?" Her voice quivered a little, then she rose up on her toes to press her lips to his.

While he kissed her in the flickering candlelight, an involuntary tremor of arousal began. He searched his frazzled mind for a reply to what she had just said—if he could even remember—and succeeded, thank God, in dragging his lips from hers. "Yes, exactly—it is our wedding night. I thought you might be sore."

"I don't care if I'm sore," she said. Was she afraid to be alone? "I didn't mind the pain the last time. In fact, in the end, I quite liked it."

Her words were somewhat shocking for a duchess—at least any duchess he had ever imagined himself being married to—and the shock pummeled his restraint. With a deep shudder of erotic exhilaration, he found himself gathering this gloriously naked woman—who seemed to have no inhibitions sexually like most of the peeresses he knew—into his arms and covering her mouth with his own. His blood quickened in his throbbing veins. He let his hands cup her beautiful bottom, warm and fleshy to his touch. She let out a little moan of pleasure and buried her fingers in the hair at his nape, and the next thing he knew, he was tumbling her onto the soft mattress and coming down, heavy upon her, unfastening his trousers for the second time that night. He pushed them down enough to free his pulsing erection.

"Are you sure?" he asked her, as his hand traced a path down her belly to the damp center of her desire.

"Yes, if you'll only stay . . ."

He realized then that this was some kind of bargaining, and his wife was a very skilled negotiator. For him, there was no backing out now, even if he wanted to. "Of course I'll stay," he replied, suckling her smooth chin.

Adjusting her body to fit perfectly beneath his own, he entered her just as her thighs spread wide and her long, luscious legs wrapped around his hips.

The tight heat of her womanhood took his breath, and sensation overpowered reason. He let himself enjoy all of it until he felt the oncoming white-hot flooding of his sex.

He matched her gasping climax with his own potent release, then hugged her and squeezed her beneath him in a strangely delirious state of being. For a long time, he could not think of his past or his present; it was as if he forgot who he was. He could have been a simple American merchant or a poor blacksmith in bed with his wife for all he knew.

He lifted his head to gaze into the depths of her long-lashed blue eyes. "Did you really think this was our bedchamber?" he asked her, suddenly realizing the charming, adorable sweetness of such a notion.

She smiled up at him. "I did. And it is."

He stared at her for a startling moment, wondering what would happen if he did let himself love her. Really love her. Was there a chance everything would work out all right? That he would never become like his father or his grandfather or the great-grandfather before him. Could James actually end what was in his bloodline by simply loving her?

It was too soon to tell, so for now, he decided, the best thing for everyone was to play it safe and continue to keep his emotions in check.

* * *

Marion Langdon, the Dowager Duchess of Wentworth, sat down on a chintz chair in her boudoir at Wentworth Castle in Yorkshire. She gazed numbly at the pale blue walls framed in dark oak, the imposing family portraits hanging in precise balance upon them, and the bulky chest of drawers supporting a malachite vase that she hadn't really looked at in years. It had a chip near the bottom. Why had she not noticed the chip before, and taken steps to have it repaired? she wondered with some irritation.

She supposed she'd become too comfortable in this room and had not noticed a great many things, and it was only a silly sentimental weakness that made her take note of them now, for as of yesterday, her fate had become a certainty: her son had taken a wife and she herself would be cast out to the east wing, where all the dowagers before her had always been cast when the new, younger duchess arrived.

She had been a new, younger duchess herself once, she recalled with some melancholy. Many, many years ago. She still remembered the day she walked into the house with Henry—proud and regal for he enjoyed the pomp of his position—and was introduced to the servants as the new mistress of the house. She recalled how her frail mother-in-law had curtsied before her. How the servants had looked upon her with uncertainty, not knowing what to expect.

She, of course, had come from a great English family of her own, and had possessed every skill necessary to manage the household of Wentworth Castle. Surely her late mother-in-law, the former dowager, had relinquished her position with confidence. She must have felt some relief to know that her son had selected a worthy successor. Though, naturally, they had never discussed such things.

She herself was not so fortunate. Off on a honeymoon in Rome—no doubt corrupting her eldest son—was a little American upstart with the manners of a savage and the surface gush to make a proper Englishwoman's toes curl. Her American dollars—substantial as they were—were her only recommendation.

What will the servants think when she walks into the house for the first time? Marion wondered, almost wincing at the thought of it. How in heaven's name will the girl ever learn all she needs to know, to perform the duties of her position with dignity and grace?

She will come to me for help, Marion reasoned with a hint of cruel anticipation, for James will offer no support to her.

It was a miracle he'd even gone through with the wedding. Marion had begun to believe the dukedom might pass to her younger son, Martin. Not that that would have been the end of the world, but Martin was not reliable. He was too impulsive and quick to follow his heart. He could not be depended upon to do what sometimes needed to be done.

James, however, was nothing of the sort. Sometimes Marion wondered with a hateful feeling if he even possessed a heart at all. Then again, he was his father's son . . .

A knock sounded at her door. A footman entered. He presented a silver tray to her, and she reached for the letter upon it, which was sealed with silver-gray wax. The paper smelled strongly of cheap perfume—a vaguely familiar scent that caused a tightness to squeeze around Marion's chest. She turned the letter over a few times before breaking the seal, barely noticing the footman exiting the room.

Carefully unfolding it, she glanced at the fancy penmanship. Her anxious eyes fell to the bottom, to ascertain the name of the sender. Recognizing the signature, she felt as if her lungs were going to fail. A sick feeling moved through her body.

The letter had come from Paris. From Madame Genevieve La Roux.

Before the dowager could comprehend the idea of having to again protect her exalted place in the world—and the place of her son—she cursed her late husband with foul, loathsome words in her head, then fainted dead away in her chintz chair.

After a fortnight's honeymoon in Rome, where they spent their days touring the city and viewing the antiquities, and their nights tangled in sheets and poetry and each other's arms, the Duke and Duchess of Wentworth prepared to return to England. They did not make love that final night, however, for Sophia's monthly had begun.

On this misty, cold, overcast day, they arrived at the Yorkshire train station to find it adorned with flags fluttering in the wind and triumphal arches of white carnations and English ivy shivering in the cold.

Sophia stepped off the train just as the whistle blew three times and a burst of steam hissed from the engine. A sudden gale came out of nowhere and she had to hold on to her hat.

James assisted her down to the red-carpeted platform, where a welcoming committee of local dignitaries had been awaiting their arrival. Included among them was the local mayor, dressed in his formal regalia.

Not knowing quite what to do or where to step, Sophia held tight to James's steady arm.

They stood by the mayor, who gave a brief speech about history and tradition. A young girl, no more than four years old, brought a heavy bouquet of roses to Sophia, and curtsied.

A short time later, they stepped into their waiting coach. They drove through the village, waving at the tenants who had turned out with their pitchforks along the cobbled market square, to cheer and wave flags and welcome her and James home. Church bells pealed as they drove through. They began the journey to the castle.

The coach bumped and rattled along a muddy road. They drove into a cold damp fog and traveled over rolling moors and dales and past meandering stone walls. There was a bleak emptiness to the land, Sophia thought as she peered out the window into the mist. It was as if she were being driven to the farthest reaches of the earth.

Soon, they rounded a curve. James—who had been strangely quiet since they'd arrived in Yorkshire—leaned forward in his seat. He pointed to the north. "There it is."

A rush of anticipation burst forth in Sophia's heart as she stretched to see her new home. It would be the core and haven of her existence, where she would raise her children and be a loving wife to the man she adored. She promised herself she would be a charitable and devoted duchess for the good people of Yorkshire.

At last she ascertained a clear view of the estate. The castle loomed like a fortress at the top of a steep hill, beyond iron gates and a stout stone wall. What a giant dragon it was in the distance, with crenellated parapets, battlement walks, and hexagonal belvedere towers. She reached nervously for James's hand and squeezed it.

He squeezed hers in return, gave her a smile of encouragement, then turned his face the other way to look out the window.

A short time later, they reached the gates, which had already been cast open for them. At the gatehouse their coach came to a halt.

"Why are we stopping?" Sophia asked, watching a dozen or so men come darting toward them to unharness the team. It was all done in a matter of seconds, the gray horses were led away, and the men took hold of the poles to haul them the rest of the way. Sophia heard them grunt in unison as they pulled for the first time, to set the carriage in motion.

She laid a gloved hand upon her breast. "Goodness, James, is this really necessary? You needn't do this to impress me. I'm quite impressed already."

"It's not to impress you, my dear. It's tradition."

Tradition. She'd heard that word a great many times today.

They embarked upon the final leg of the journey—a steep, bumpy hill up to the house—and Sophia felt her muscles tense in sympathy for these men who were dragging the carriage like mules!

She glanced at James, who was looking in the other direction, unaffected by any of this, it seemed.

They finally reached the front door of the massive stone castle—solid and imposing—and upon a closer look, stained black in places where the weather had been unforgiving over the years. Sophia's sense of wonder and awe began to recede. Apprehension took its place. London balls and drawing rooms and lace-trimmed parasols suddenly seemed a thousand miles away from here. Not that she wasn't happy to be married to James, but the castle suddenly seemed less like a home and more like an old, Gothic museum—massive and sprawling and daunting. She suddenly understood the gossip about ghosts.

Would there be a cozy corner somewhere, for her and James? A place to be a close-knit family when their children were born?

The servants were lined up on the front steps, steely-faced and silent as the wind tugged at the girls' caps and the men's lapels. They were all dressed the same: black uniforms and white aprons for the women, everyday black-and-white livery for the men. There was no cheering or flag-waving here. No generous, heartfelt gushing of welcomes or giggling chatter or warm hugs. Sophia felt very alone all of a sudden and out of her range of experience. She wished her sisters were with her.

They were not, however, and she would have to learn to get along without them. Without her mother. Without her father, who used to snap his fingers and with a laugh and a smile and a big bear hug make everything better.

James helped her down from the carriage, and she walked past the men who had hauled them up the hill. Discreetly, she glanced at one of them. His eyes were lowered, his chest was heaving—for he was out of breath for good reason. His face was covered in a shiny film of perspiration. Sophia wanted to thank him, but he would not meet her gaze, and her instincts warned her that it would not be appropriate. She felt another wave of wariness spread through her.

You're just nervous, she told herself. *You are about to meet your mother-in-law and see your new home, and you're worried they won't approve of you, and surely everyone else is nervous, too.*

James led her up the stone steps, between the rows of servants, none of whom offered the smallest welcoming smile. Even James seemed distant at this moment, avoiding her gaze, his expression serious. Sophia cleared her throat and stepped over the threshold.

Inside, more servants stood like soldiers in a straight line, to greet their new duchess. Sophia smiled at them, then her attention was arrested by the great hall around her. Her gaze traveled up giant Corinthian columns to a towering cathedral ceiling, the walls made of enormous blocks of gray stone. There was a chill in the air as her heels clicked over the stone floor. She took a breath and hesitated. Still holding her hand, James stopped to look back at her questioningly.

Just then, Sophia noticed a woman emerge from the shadows at the base of the staircase. She was clearly not a servant, for she was dressed differently, but the drab color of her gown and the lack of jewels made Sophia wonder if perhaps she was the housekeeper. Her face was thin and the angle of her jaw, hard.

The woman walked straight toward Sophia and curtsied before her. James said matter-of-factly, "May I present my mother, Her Grace, the Dowager Duchess of Wentworth."

Sophia's eyes widened. "Oh!" she said with a smile, offering her hand. "Yes! It's so nice to meet you at last! I hope you are feeling better."

The woman rose from her curtsy, her expression edged with steel. Without responding to Sophia's effervescent greeting, she simply said, "Welcome."

James let go of Sophia's hand and crossed the hall to stand beside an empty suit of armor.

A dark tension closed around Sophia's heart, coupled with a sudden fear that she had made a terrible mistake. Poor sweet Cinderella came to mind. What was Sophia doing here in this spooky old castle with these unsmiling strangers? Where were her sisters and her mother now? Had they left the country? Were they on a ship bound for America yet?

She turned her head then, toward the other side of the hall, and saw James, standing beside that shiny suit of armor. Her prince. How handsome he was. She told herself that *he* was her hearth and home, and no matter what kind of house they lived in—whether they were rich or poor—her heart would forever be full of cheer because they were together.

Just then, Sophia heard the fast clicking of heels down the staircase, and she turned to see Lily scurrying down in a blue-and-white-striped dress. As soon as she reached the ground floor, she slowed to a more ladylike pace and approached Sophia.

Lily curtsied. "Welcome, Duchess." She gifted Sophia with an extravagant, twinkling smile that sent a much-needed surge of relief through her. Lily wiped the smile away, however, as soon as she stepped back in view of her mother.

Sophia then understood the family dynamics at work here. All this cool detachment was for ceremony; her mother-in-law was a strict woman, but behind closed doors, perhaps she would be more relaxed. Perhaps everyone would. Surely, their true personalities would surface then, and Sophia over time would come to know and care for them in a deeper, more intimate way.

She was handed over to Mildred then, who was there at the front of the line, and the stout little woman escorted Sophia up the stairs to the ducal rooms.

When she reached the top, she glanced down over the railing to where James had been standing for one last look at his handsome face before she retired for the afternoon. She felt a ripple of disappointment, however, to discover that he was gone.

Chapter 14

Mere minutes after Sophia was shown to her rooms, the household—like a well-oiled machine—returned to its crank and turn, and she was left alone to take a much-needed and well-deserved nap. She had not been awake long, however, when the loud dinner gong sent its pompous call echoing off the stone walls of Wentworth Castle. Mildred had at least prepared her for it with a few simple words: "The family dresses formally for dinner, Your Grace. The dressing bell will ring at seven for dinner at eight."

Sophia, dressed in one of her spectacular Worth gowns and the sparkling jewels her parents had given her as a wedding gift, pulled on her long gloves and ventured out into the hall behind Mildred who—just for today—would show Sophia to the drawing room, where the family would gather before entry to the dining room.

Sophia wished that James could have come to fetch

her, but she supposed he must have had many duties to attend to, his first day back.

She entered the drawing room, and like a ghost, Mildred quietly disappeared. Sophia stood alone inside the great arched entry, staring at her mother-in-law, who wore a modest dark gown—long-sleeved and buttoned at the neck—without jewels. Sophia touched the large emerald displayed at her low, satin neckline embroidered with pearls, and felt suddenly that everything about her attire was all wrong. "Good evening, Your Grace," she said.

Her mother-in-law fired a shocked gaze at Sophia. "No, no, no. You are not to address me that way."

Sophia felt a whoosh of nervous butterflies in her belly at having blundered before she had even fully entered the room. "I do apologize. How shall I address you?"

"You are the duchess now. You are no longer a social inferior. You may address me by my Christian name."

Sophia cleared her throat. Should she say, *Good evening, Marion*, now? Or would that be redundant?

Marion turned away from her to the fireplace mantel, to move a small statue an inch to the left. Sophia decided it would be best to keep quiet.

Much to her relief, Lily entered the room. "Oh, Sophia, what a stunning gown." Lily wore a dress not unlike her mother's. "I do so admire your sense of style."

"Thank you, Lily."

"Are you well rested? I peeked in on you a couple of hours ago, but you looked so peaceful, I didn't want to wake you."

If Lily could only have known how much her caring meant to Sophia.

She felt Marion's hovering stare—looking on, judging. Sophia tried to tell herself that she was being overly sensitive. She felt inadequate only because she was not fully settled in or aware of her duties and responsibilities yet.

She considered what Marion had just said—*You are the duchess now.*

Perhaps there *was* some ill feeling, as she had feared there would be.

Awkwardly, Sophia cleared her throat again; she could feel her confidence draining away into the cracks in the stone floor, as if there were a great big leaking hole in her shoe. She watched her mother-in-law sit down regally on the sofa and gaze out the window, then tried to tell herself that this would get easier in time.

She realized suddenly that if she had a farthing for every time she'd told herself that, she'd be able to put central heating in this cold stone house before the first snowfall.

James entered. Sophia's whole being perked up at his arrival; her body returned to its natural rhythm, and her reason for being here suddenly made sense again. What power he had to make everything worthwhile.

He took her hand in his and kissed it. A titillating arousal sparked and exploded in Sophia's veins.

"You are comfortable, I hope?" was all he said, and she nodded, then eagerly anticipated their lovemaking later, after the rest of the household retired.

At precisely eight o'clock, they all moved into the grand dining room and sat down at a massive oak table clothed in white. James sat at one end of the table; Sophia was instructed to sit at the other. She doubted she would be able to hear him if he called out for her to pass the salt.

Not that he would ask that—there were half a dozen servants here at his beck and call to do whatever he wished.

Then she noticed that she had her own silver salt and pepper shaker in front of her, and so did everyone else. How convenient: a self-contained place setting for each and every one. No one needed to ask anything of anyone else—except the nameless servants, of course.

Formally dressed footmen served them in the German fashion, *à la Russe,* and though the food was delicious, the conversation was nothing of the sort. Sophia quietly ate her soup, trying to fit in and do what everyone else did, but to do that was to not talk. She had to wrestle with her tongue to keep herself from asking all the questions she wanted to ask—like why Mildred had shaken her head disapprovingly when Sophia had asked the footman to light a fire, and why she could not have tea at five o'clock tonight when she'd asked, after having slept through the usual teatime at four.

She held her tongue and decided to ask James all these questions tonight, when they were alone.

How grateful she was for the pleasant anticipation of her private time with him later when the lights were out.

After dinner, when James rose from his chair to retire to his own rooms for the night, his mother requested a private meeting in his study. He instructed a servant to go and light the lamps, and a few minutes later, he and his mother were standing on opposite sides of his ancient, monstrous desk, facing each other.

"What is it, Mother?" he asked without ceremony.

The dowager cleared her throat. "I understand that the marriage settlement was quite substantial, and I would like to ask if I may have an increase in what has traditionally been the amount of my allowance."

James knew his mother, and he knew this could not have been easy for her, for she did not like to ask anyone for anything.

"Of course. How much would you like?" He knew it was cruel to ask the amount, but at least he was agreeing.

She cleared her throat again. "Well, I would like to have a large lump sum I could draw from, rather than a number of smaller monthly sums. That would give me more freedom to spend—"

"Freedom. There's a word I've never heard you use before. Has some of Sophia's democratic fragrance rubbed off on you?"

It was cruel, he knew it, but he didn't let himself regret it. If anyone should feel regret in this room, it was not he.

"How much?" he asked again.

"A thousand pounds would be very generous of you, James."

For a long moment he stared at his mother. He hadn't expected her to be quite so eager to spend their American riches. In fact, he'd had some doubt as to whether or not she would dare to soil her hands touching any of it.

"A thousand pounds? Martin's not in trouble again, is he?" James asked, thinking of his younger brother, who had just returned to Eton.

"Of course not."

Neither of them spoke for a few seconds. "What does this concern, exactly?" he asked, probing.

"It is just the total of some unfortunate debts I have incurred over the past few years. Things, as you know, have been tight, and I did not want Lily to suffer."

"I see." James moved around the desk. He could tell by the pale color of his mother's cheeks that this was extremely trying for her. He decided he'd tormented her enough. He moved behind the desk again and sat down. "All right, you have your thousand pounds." He wrote out a note to her. She took it and stuffed it into her skirt pocket, then turned and left him alone to wonder what cause that money would serve.

Like most things, it would probably reveal itself to him in its own convenient time.

Sophia sat up in bed, waiting for her husband. It was eleven-thirty. Her candles were still burning on her dressing table, but her fire had gone out.

The room was getting chillier and chillier, so she decided to snuggle down under the covers to wait, rather than sit on top of them.

She pulled the coverlet up to her ears and realized her feet were like ice. She leaped out of bed to retrieve a pair of stockings from her dressing table and pulled them on, then leaped back into the bed. She wished James would hurry. Once he was here with her, he would certainly keep her warm.

It seemed like forever that she lay there, watching the door, sitting up whenever the house made knocking sounds or the wind rattled the window panes. Still, he did not come, and she was beginning to feel a bit frustrated. There was so much she wanted to tell him and ask him.

She closed her eyes briefly, and when she opened them again, it was two o'clock. He still had not come, and she began to think that perhaps he had accidentally fallen asleep, as she had just now. They'd had a busy day, after all, with their official arrival in the county, and who knew what other kinds of problems he'd come home to, after a fortnight away? Perhaps she could go to him instead.

She slipped out of bed, pulled a huge woolen shawl around her shoulders, and picked up the candelabra. She opened her door to find the corridor cloaked in darkness. There was no sign of anyone anywhere.

She padded down the hall. Mildred had pointed out James's door to her when she'd first brought her upstairs, and Sophia was certain she would be able to find it again. It was down this hall, she thought, and then at the end, she would turn left and it would be at the end of the next hall, beyond the red saloon.

Good heavens, it was chilly out here in the corridor! Her candles were the only source of light, and as she moved quickly she heard the flames flicker and hiss against the air; she smelled the dripping candlewax. It all seemed so spooky and primitive. Like she'd stepped back into another century. Her own home in New York had all the modern conveniences—gaslights and very recently, electricity. She had central hot water heating and hot running water in a porcelain tub in her own private bathroom. Tonight, frail little maids had lugged jug after jug of water up from the kitchen to her room, and had spread towels on the floor around a tin tub they had dragged in. At that moment, the grandeur of her elevated rank hadn't seemed quite so grand.

But that was not why she was here, she reminded herself. She was here because she loved James. If she could only find his room.

She turned left where she thought she should, then found herself stopping in yet another unfamiliar corridor, feeling quite decidedly lost.

Sophia gathered her shawl around her shoulders and turned around to face the other way. This particular corridor was lined with massive portraits framed in fancy gilt. She tiptoed closer to one of them and held up her candles. The gold marker at the bottom labeled the man as the second Duke of Wentworth—a frightening-looking person who looked more like a warlord than an aristocrat. His eyes were dark, full of menace and rage and ugly hatred. She gazed uncomfortably at those eyes, remembering the night she had seen James for the first time . . .

She shook that memory away and turned back to her task of finding her way to his rooms, but passing a number of doors made her realize that she had no hope in heaven of knowing which one was his. They all looked alike. She would have to return to her own bedchamber.

A short time later, she was still wandering up and down corridors, searching for her rooms. She had never had a particularly impressive sense of direction, and she had obviously underestimated the size and complexity of this house—if one could call it that. James had once described London society as a labyrinth, but that was nothing compared to this.

Feeling defeated, she knew she was going to have to knock on someone's door and ask for assistance. Every door she knocked on, however, found no reply, and when she tried to open them to see what was inside, they were all locked. They must be guest rooms, she surmised. The servants likely kept them closed off when they weren't in use, to prevent having to clean them.

Sophia came to a baize door studded with brass nails at the end of a hall, and pushed through it. She entered into a much narrower hall that smelled of stale cabbage and creaked from squeaky floors. The servants' wing. Thank goodness. She had dreaded the thought of waking her mother-in-law to tell her that she was lost. Sophia would have preferred wandering all night to the humiliation of that.

She quickly discovered, however, that the servants' wing was as vast and complicated as the rest of the house. She walked past a number of separate storage rooms.

She entered the servants' hall—a large common room. Two massive tables filled its center, and she went to put her hand upon one of them, to touch the gouges and markings that came from years and years of use; these tables were probably more than a century old. She felt the fascination of the history all around her then, and remembered what James had said when he'd proposed—*You wanted to see it from inside the very heart of it. Come and be part of it.* Well, here she was, part of it, and all she felt was lonely detachment, as if she were still on the outside, an interloper who was not even able to find her way around it when she tried.

She felt a lump form in her throat, but refused to give in to it. She would not cry. She would go back to her room, forget about seeing James tonight, get a good night's sleep, and start again tomorrow. She turned to leave, but bumped into a young maid who was hurrying into the room in her nightdress. Their

candles clicked together, and both Sophia and the girl
stepped back with gasps of surprise.

The girl curtsied. "Begging your pardon, Your
Grace!"

Sophia tried to catch her breath. "It's all right. I
didn't see you either. I'm just glad to have met someone."

The girl's lips were trembling as she backed up
against the wall, as if to clear a path and make herself
invisible. Sheer terror seemed to fix her to her spot.

Sophia took another step closer. "I'm wondering if
you could help me."

"Help you, Your Grace?"

"Yes, I'm lost."

"Lost?" She contemplated that for a moment. "I
should go and fetch the housekeeper." She made a
move to venture deeper into the servants' wing.

Sophia stopped her. "No, please, don't. I would prefer it if you would take me back to my room. There is
no need to wake anyone."

"But I'm a scullery maid."

Sophia laughed. "That's fine. All I need is someone
who knows this house better than I do."

The girl glanced up and down the hall. "I don't
want to lose my position, Your Grace. There are rules
about—"

"You won't lose your position. What is your
name?"

"Lucy." She curtsied again.

Sophia offered her hand. "It's a pleasure to meet
you, Lucy."

The girl stared at Sophia's proffered hand like it was
some foreign object, then finally offered her own with

visible uncertainty. Sophia clasped it in hers; it was rough and scabbed.

"Good gracious," Sophia said, bringing the candlelight closer so she could look at the girl's chafed, red palm. "Your hand . . ."

The girl withdrew it. "It's fine, Your Grace."

"No, it's not fine. How did this happen?"

"I scrub."

"But . . ." Sophia did not know what to say. She still felt like a guest here and was inclined not to say anything, then she reminded herself that she was not a guest. She was in charge of this house, and if she felt that a servant was being treated unfairly, she would see to the situation.

"Where is your home, Lucy?"

"I live here, Your Grace."

"No, I mean, where does your family live?"

"In the village."

"Would you like to go and stay with them for a while?"

To Sophia's dismay, Lucy began to cry. "I'm very sorry, Your Grace. I know I'm not supposed to be down here, but I forgot to clean something that Mrs. Dalrymple asked me to clean, and I only wanted to do my job the best I could. If you'll only reconsider, I promise I won't—"

"Oh, no, dear Lucy! I'm not dismissing you. I only wish to give you a holiday so that your hands have a chance to heal. You can think about it." She guided Lucy toward the baize door. "Now, if you'll just help me get back to my room, no one even has to know we bumped into each other tonight."

Looking doubtful, Lucy went with her. As soon as

they set foot in the main house, the young maid scurried along like a fast little mouse, as if she wanted to get back to her own room before she was caught doing something she shouldn't be doing.

She found the correct door and opened it. Relieved, Sophia entered the room. Lucy stood in the open doorway. "Is there anything else, Your Grace?"

"No, Lucy, that's all. Thank you."

Lucy curtsied and hurried away, and Sophia crawled into her cold bed, feeling not only displaced, but rejected. This was the first night since their wedding that she and James had not made love. She'd been forced to go searching for him in the dark, she had failed, and here she was—alone again in this ridiculously cold room.

Why had he not come? she wondered, snuggling down under the sheets embroidered with coronets, trying hard not to read too much into his absence, and more importantly, not to cry.

Chapter 15

Sophia said good morning to Marion and Lily, and sat down at the breakfast table. A footman set a boiled egg in front of her. "Thank you," she said without thinking, then felt Marion's gaze bore into her.

"There is no need for that here," the woman said.

Sophia picked up her knife and tapped it against the eggshell. It was early and she'd barely slept a wink, her feet were still numb from being cold all night, and she was suddenly feeling quite depleted of patience when it came to being corrected at every turn. Marion had not said one nice thing to her yet, nor had she offered a smile or any kind of encouragement.

"No need for politeness?" she replied with a somewhat terse edge to her voice. She knew she would regret it later.

But oh, if felt good now.

Lily kept her gaze lowered the whole time.

Marion showed no reaction. She smoothed the table

179

cloth beside her plate. "We have never thanked servants here."

Sophia wanted to say, "Well maybe you should," but held her tongue. She'd said enough. Her passions sometimes got away from her, and she could not afford to displease her mother-in-law, who was clearly having some trouble with this transition. Sophia was certain of it now. She would have to try harder to be understanding, and hope that things would soon get easier.

"Has James eaten yet?" she asked, trying to keep her voice light and not show how heartbroken she had been over his failure to come to her the night before.

"James does not take breakfast with the rest of the family."

Sophia swallowed a bite of her egg, hating that she had to press her mother-in-law for more information about the man who was supposed to be her life's partner. "Where does he take it?"

After a long hesitation seemingly intended to torture Sophia, Marion replied, "In his own rooms."

"He doesn't usually share the luncheon table with us either," Lily added helpfully.

Sophia continued to eat her breakfast, not wanting to ask any more questions, but she couldn't help herself. "Will he be in his rooms now, do you think?"

Lily gave her a look of sympathy. "He's not here. He left early and said he wouldn't be back until dinner."

Sophia dabbed the corners of her mouth with her napkin and forced herself to sweep away all hopes of seeing James before then, for she did not think she could handle any more disappointments.

"Perhaps then, after breakfast, Lily, you could give me a tour of the house?"

"I would be delighted to."

They finished eating in silence.

James mounted his horse and trotted out of the courtyard, listening to the pleasantly predictable sound of hooves crunching over gravel. Beyond the gate, a chilly mist hung in the air and floated motion-lessly over the moors. It was just like the fog of incom-prehension inside his head. He urged his horse into a gallop.

He needed to decide how he was going to handle this marriage, for last night had been troublesome. No, not troublesome. It had been utterly chaotic—and he loathed chaos. He had climbed out of his bed at least a dozen times to go and see Sophia, gone to his door and opened it, then each time, he'd halted and stuffed him-self back into his own bed, determined not to get out of it again. For fear had held him back.

Fear of what? he asked himself with some irritation, urging his horse to gallop faster.

He despised fear.

He was not accustomed to it.

Well, he had been once. A lifetime ago.

The animal jumped a low stone wall and landed smoothly.

Was it fear of his wife? No, that was not it. It was fear of the inevitable—that he would fall so deeply in love with her, he would lose his sense of reason. Per-haps he had already lost it. He'd certainly felt like it in Italy. He'd become obsessed with seeking pleasure with his new wife, whether they were making love or merely laughing and throwing pillows at each other in the nude.

She had satisfied his every desire, entertained him,

soothed him, and he'd let himself enjoy her, for it did not seem like his real life. He'd felt like a different person in a foreign country with a foreign bride.

Now they were back on the foggy moors of Yorkshire.

People's accents were familiar again.

His bed felt the same as it always had.

The honeymoon was over, and this was reality. It was time to remember who he was and what his intentions had been when he'd decided to marry Sophia— for they had been humane, responsible intentions, he reminded himself. Well thought out for the good of everyone involved, including his wife and his unborn children.

When he'd proposed, he had been confident in his ability to resist his base nature and see that any child born of this marriage never witnessed or suffered what he had witnessed and suffered as a child. In order to create the kind of tame, peaceable environment that had been absent from Wentworth for centuries, he knew he would have to keep his distance. He could not act selfishly and risk falling back into the pattern his forebears had set, merely to fulfill his own personal avaricious lust for his duchess.

He steered his mount across a sloping dale and decided that he would limit his visits to her room—at least for a while until he could curb the passion between them and establish a more practical arrangement. He would try to focus more on his duty and his dukedom, for those were his reasons for marrying Sophia in the first place.

For the sake of his future children, he could not afford to forget that.

*   *   *

James had not returned home in time for dinner. Sophia was forced to sit through yet another agonizing meal in an ice-cold dining room where no one said a word, and even the clinking of silverware seemed to be a *faux pas*—for it echoed off the stone walls, high up into the ceiling.

Now, Sophia was again climbing into her cold, empty bed, feeling unpleasantly skeptical about whether or not she would see her husband tonight either. And she really needed to see him.

She waited for a little while, and when there was no knock at her door, her hurt transformed to anger.

Surely James must know that this was a difficult time for her. That his mother was not the warmest of individuals. Surely he must know that his new wife would need some support and guidance, and that she would be missing her own beloved family and might benefit from a simple word of affection.

Her dander was flying now. Even if he didn't realize these things, wasn't he at least longing for her sexually as she was longing for him? Was he not counting the minutes until they could make love again? Her body was positively burning for him. All day long she had not been certain she could survive another minute of it.

Well, tonight, she would know the way to his rooms. Lily had given her a thorough tour, and Sophia had made sure she took note of everything.

She scrambled out of bed, pulled on her shawl, and picked up her candles.

A few minutes later, she was knocking at her husband's door. "Enter," she heard from inside.

So, you're here.

She pushed the door open to find him sitting in front

of a roaring fire, an oil lamp shining brightly onto a book on his lap. The sight of him there sent a painful surge of heartache through her. Did he prefer reading that book over a night of fun and games with his wife?

"You're here," she said, with every intention of sounding surprised.

"Of course I'm here. Where else would I be?"

She moved into the room, taking note of the fact that he had not invited her here, nor had he risen from his chair to greet her or even closed his book, for that matter.

"I don't know. You didn't join us for dinner. I thought you must have had duties to attend to somewhere."

Finally, he did close his book. "Yes, there are always duties."

He said no more than that, and it pained her that he was being so vague and dispassionate with her. She had expected—after their time apart in the last twenty-four hours—that there would be an ardent dash into each other's arms. She had expected him to pick her up and twirl her and kiss her deeply and tell her he couldn't bear another moment away from her.

Sophia swallowed nervously and tried to communicate to him what was bothering her. "I thought you might come to my room last night."

He was quiet a moment. "It was a busy day."

"I know that, but I would have liked to see you. I had so many questions to ask."

"You wish to know something? Feel free." He spread his hands wide. "Ask away."

For the life of her, she couldn't remember any of the questions she'd had during the day. All she could think of now was her heartbreaking confusion over his conspicuous emotional retreat.

When she asked no question, he set his book down and stood. "Perhaps you could ask Mildred if you need to know something. She is your maid, after all."

"Mildred's not the most talkative woman in the world." Sophia did her best to keep her tone light.

"Maybe not, but it is her duty to meet all your personal needs. If you ask her a question, she is required to give you a straight answer."

"I don't want straight answers," she told him directly. "I want you to come to my room and make love to me."

He slowly blinked.

Sophia suddenly remembered where she was, and what she was supposed to be—an English duchess. "I don't mean to be quite so forward. I know it's not how a duchess should speak."

James's eyes grew steely. "You seem to be referring to your marital duties. I thought we discussed this on the way back from Rome."

"Discussed what?"

"You told me that your monthly had arrived, and according to that, you would not conceive now anyway. There is no point in my coming to see you for at least a week, and certainly no point in making love."

His shocking assertion hit her full force. She crossed the room to stand before him. "You're not serious."

"You seem surprised."

"What are you telling me? That you don't even want to see me? That you didn't enjoy making love to me? That you only did it to produce a child?"

A muscle twitched at his jaw. "Of course I enjoyed

it. You've been perfectly dutiful, Sophia. I am more than pleased. You can have some time to yourself now. It might be a good thing, for both of us."

"I don't need time to myself. I'm already alone enough as it is, even when I'm sitting in a room with Mildred or your mother or ten footmen!"

"Lower your voice."

Sophia took a deep breath to calm herself, then continued. "James, you must know I want to share a bed with you. Perhaps it is not very ladylike or very English of me, but I am not an English lady. I spent my childhood in a one-room shack in Wisconsin, where manners were a little more lax to say the least, and we all slept together and woke up together and ate together. I have some deep-rooted values that are not so easy to abandon."

"You're in England now," he reminded her, "and you are a duchess. You can't expect us to adapt to your ways and all share the same room."

"I don't expect that."

"Then what do you expect? You must realize that we, too, have deep-rooted traditions that are not so easy to abandon."

Feeling defeated, she dropped her forehead into her hand. "I don't expect you to change everything for me." She looked him in the eye again. "There are only a few things that I feel are important."

"Sharing a bed is one of them."

"Yes. And . . ." She hesitated, hating the fact that she had to request this. "And I need to know that you care about my welfare."

"Of course I care about your welfare. You're my duchess, the mother of my future children. Do you not feel taken care of here? You are mistress of this house. You have over fifty servants at your disposal."

"I'm not talking about servants. I'm talking about *you*. I need to know that you care."

"I do care," he said matter-of-factly. Dutifully.

Where was the passionate man she'd come to know on their honeymoon? Sophia wondered. Who was this person and why had he changed? Was he afraid of something? Did he not know how much she loved him?

"I have enough money of my own. I could have married whomever I wished—rich or poor—and I chose *you*, James. I came here to live in your house because I love you, and I want to be with you."

He considered her words, then turned his back on her. "It was my understanding you came to London in search of a title."

She felt the air flee her lungs. He might as well have hauled back and punched her in the stomach. Where was all this coming from? "Don't you remember what I said to you that day when we went walking together? That I believed marriage must be based on love?"

"You said what you had to say to—"

"You thought I was lying?"

"No, not lying. . . ." He paced around the room. "Sophia, we are both rare individuals with duties and many different qualities to recommend us besides our . . . lovability, for lack of a better word. I am a duke, and you are an heiress."

"What are you trying to tell me?" A sick feeling began to spread through her.

"I'm trying to tell you that marriages between people like you and me are not like marriages between more common people. In my family, there are too many other factors to complicate matters and—"

"What do you mean, in your family? Why? Because by mere accident of birth you were born into a title? That doesn't make you any different from me or the servants or the people who work their fingers to the bone on your land. You are still a man, and I am a woman, and it is in our nature to *want* to love and be loved in return." She took a step forward.

His brow furrowed with anger, as if she had overstepped some invisible boundary. She halted where she was.

"Why did you come here?" he asked. "What do you want, exactly?"

Cold-hearted veracity blazed in his eyes. It was the same angry bitterness she had seen in the portrait of his ancestor.

Alarmed, she gazed at James in the lamplight. No, she could not have made such a ghastly mistake, and been so wrong about what she had seen in his eyes in all the minutes and days leading up to this one. He was her prince . . .

"What I want is for you to love me." She hoped she would not live to regret saying it.

For a long moment he stared at her, his chest heaving with deep, furious breaths, then he shook his head. "You do not know what you're asking."

"I do. I want you in my bed."

"Your bed." He contemplated that, then crossed the room toward her. She took an instinctive step back.

"You want me to make love to you, like I made love to you in Rome?" His voice became a dark, menacing seduction. "Is that it?"

"Yes," she replied breathlessly.

"Is that all? Because I have no reservations about making love to you for the sake of *enjoyment*, Sophia."

For the life of her, she did not recognize the man before her. He was a complete stranger. "I don't understand. Why are you acting like this?"

"I'm not acting like anything. You came here for sex, and I'm willing."

"I didn't come just for sex."

"Well, I can't make any promises beyond that, because I never intended to love you."

Shock and disbelief forced the air out of her lungs. She felt as if he had slapped her. "I beg your pardon?"

He said nothing more.

Her voice broke as she stumbled over words. "Are you telling me you only married me for my money?"

"It wasn't quite as mercenary as that. I wanted you when I proposed, Sophia, and I want you now."

With a choking cry, she moved away from him. "I can't believe you're saying this."

He followed her with his eyes. "You pushed."

"I didn't push. I just wanted to be with you." Her shock erupted into anger.

"There's nothing wrong with enjoying each other, as long as it doesn't give you unrealistic expectations."

"You tricked me. I thought you loved me."

"I never said I did. Besides, how could I love you? I barely knew you. And what did you expect, coming to London and offering a colossal marriage settlement? You must have known you'd be snatched up for your money."

"But not by *you*! The way you spoke to me . . . the way you looked at me . . ."

"I was courting you for your dowry, just like all the rest."

She could not restrain the fury that was cutting her from the inside out. Her gaze clouded with tears; she had to fight for a breath.

To her surprise, James moved closer, pulled her into his arms, and held her. He raised her chin with a finger and kissed the tears on her cheeks, then laid his soft lips upon hers. She drank in the comfort he was offering, for it was all she had. *He* was all she had, and this seemed to be all he could give.

Then something stopped her. She turned her face away. "No."

"We can still enjoy each other, Sophia, as long as you don't expect too much from me."

Her anger swung around again. All she could do was pull away and wipe his kiss from her mouth.

"I don't want to *enjoy* you. Not like this. I would rather hate you."

"You don't know me well enough to hate me. You married a fantasy. Now it's time to settle down to real life."

"You think love is a fantasy?"

"Most definitely." He spoke with unwavering certainty.

"But I've known real love," she told him. "The love of my family. A family I am missing very much."

"Maybe you should have considered that before you steamed across the ocean in search of a husband."

"I gave everything up for you, because I loved you."

He stiffened at her candor, and his brows drew together in stupefaction—as if her belief in loving him was as ridiculous as a belief in leprechauns.

"Maybe you will rethink how you feel about me."

Sophia's body went completely numb at the realization that in falling in love with this man, she had made the worst mistake of her life. There was nothing more to say. She turned from him and walked out.

James stood in the center of his bedchamber, staring at the door for minutes that seemed more like hours, then he collapsed into his chair by the fire and downed his brandy.

He pinched the bridge of his nose. God, his heart was aching! He should have known marrying Sophia would be a mistake, and giving in to his desires on their honeymoon had been an even bigger mistake. He should have known he would not be capable of meeting her needs for intimacy and love. He could not love. There had been no seeds for it sown into his heart as a child, nor had he ever come to understand it through experience as a man.

All he knew was cruelty, and he had been cruel tonight. Just as he had always suspected he would be someday. The irony of it was that he had been cruel in some deranged effort to be kind. His life made no sense.

Kind was what he wanted to be. He had thought that by pushing Sophia away, by forcing her to give up the idea of a true bond between them, he would be protecting her. Protecting them all. If only it was not so complicated. If only she did not want so much from him.

He poured another glass of brandy and took a long sip, then settled back in his chair, praying that its numbing effect would come quickly, for he could not bear to think of Sophia in her room. Alone, and no doubt crying. Another fierce ache squeezed inside his chest. James shut his eyes in an attempt to overcome it.

He could not give in to the temptation to go to his wife and hold her and plead for her forgiveness.

For if he gave in to such feelings, hell would surely follow.

Chapter 16

~~~

Sophia climbed into her cold, mammoth bed, wishing she had dreamed or merely imagined all the shocking, hurtful things James had said to her. She had left her beloved family, given up her home and country for him. Hadn't he believed the sincerity of her feelings on their honeymoon? Surely he must have felt it in his bones every time she cried out his name or told him that she loved him. Did he not want to be loved? Was that it? How could anyone not want that? It was the only thing in life that mattered.

Why had he changed so drastically upon their arrival here? Was it this house? Was it a need to be what everyone expected him to be? A duke, not a man?

The idea of such a thing made her squirm in her bed with fist-clenching fury. This world of titles and crests and coronets had such power, it crushed and smothered the passions of the people who were born into it.

Or those who married into it.

Her spine prickled. Would she become like them someday? With a heart made of stone? Would her spirit and ideals and optimism be beaten down and sucked out of her? Would she feel dead inside and disillusioned and finally become too weak to cling to the person she once was?

Feeling as if she had been cast adrift in a stormy sea, Sophia clambered out of bed and went to her desk, where her candles still burned. She pulled out a single sheet of stationery, picked up her pen, and dipped it in ink. She wanted to write to her mother and tell her how miserable she was. She wanted to pour out all her woes. She wanted her father to make it all better like he always did. He had even said he would come and fetch her if she wanted him to.

Sophia held the pen over the paper. Her hand trembled; she shut her eyes.

She was a grown woman now, a married woman. She couldn't go sobbing home to her parents at every disappointment, no matter how enormous that disappointment was or how desperate she felt.

She searched inside herself for the strength she knew she still possessed, and reminded herself that she had only been here a few days. Perhaps all she needed was more time to adjust. James had admitted that he wanted her. Maybe that was the way it was with men. Maybe they simply required more time to develop their deeper feelings.

But he had not just said that he didn't love her. He'd said he didn't *intend* to love her. Ever.

Sophia dropped her pen and covered her face with her hands. The memory of his cruelty pierced her heart again and again. If only there was someone she could talk to.

Sophia wiped the tears from her face. Florence! Who better to understand what this was all about? Florence, too, had left her home and country to marry an English aristocrat—a man who was kind, but very reserved.

Sophia penned a short note to Florence: *Please come. I must speak with you.* She signed it simply, *A fellow countrywoman.* She sealed the note and set it on her desk to send first thing in the morning, then climbed back into bed.

Despite her letter to Florence and the tiny grain of hope it rendered, her insides continued to pitch and roll, and she did not know how to make the sick feeling go away. The only thing she knew was that she would not allow herself to lose her dignity and self-respect. It was the only thing she had left. No matter what Florence had to say, if Sophia's husband did not truly love her, she would not go begging for his attentions again. He would be the one to come to her.

For an entire fortnight, Sophia did not see or hear from James. He had gone to London allegedly for Parliamentary business, without even informing Sophia that he was leaving. His drawn-out absence without a single letter to his wife only served to stoke the flames of her anger and discontent.

Day after difficult day, she ate breakfast, lunch, and dinner with her mother-in-law, who continued to criticize Sophia's manners and her lack of knowledge about her duties. The dowager offered no help or encouragement, and tormented Sophia with a "you-are-so-hopeless" tone whenever Sophia was forced, out of sheer desperation, to ask for guidance.

It was all she could do to keep up with her daily duties: the ceremony of her attendance at the morning prayers in the chapel, consulting with Cook about meals, learning the way things were done and keeping up with all the little traditions Marion had always adhered to. All this, between trying to learn proper forms of address and study *Burke's Peerage,* which Marion had insisted was a top priority.

Sophia did not even have her more congenial sister-in-law, Lily, to turn to, for Marion had sent her away to visit an elderly aunt in Exeter. Sophia was beginning to think that the dowager had sent her daughter away for the express purpose of removing the one person who would offer some cheer to Sophia and make her life even slightly, momentarily enjoyable.

Sophia was hanging on to her grand ideals by her fingernails, and she knew it. She had wanted to be a devoted wife and a great duchess and make a difference in people's lives. She'd wanted to help those in need.

Now, all she wanted to do was survive.

Sophia opened the door of the coach just as Florence Kent, the Countess of Lansdowne, stepped off the train into a harsh downpour of rain. A footman greeted her and escorted her to the carriage, where she hugged Sophia. "I left home in a beastly state of panic. What is it, my dear? Your note sounded urgent."

The footman attended to her bags and assisted them both into the shelter of the coach, then leaped up onto the page-board as the vehicle lurched forward.

"It felt urgent at the time," Sophia replied, recalling how desperate she had felt the night James had rejected her. She had needed to talk to someone, someone who would understand. Someone who would be able to shed light on the situation. Florence was an American, and she'd been through all this a few years ago, marrying an earl. Surely she would have some words of wisdom for Sophia.

"Thank you for coming, Florence. It does me good to see a familiar face, to hear the sound of your voice."

"Is everything all right? Where is James?"

"He's in London attending to some Parliamentary business. He left two weeks ago." Sophia neglected to mention that he had not even informed her that he was leaving, nor had he contacted her since.

"Why didn't you go with him?" Florence asked. "We could have met there instead of here." She tried to peer through the rain-soaked window. "Heavens. I've never been this far north before."

Sophia peered out, too, at the mist and moors in the distance, at the stony grayness of it all. "It's not exactly how I pictured it either."

Florence squeezed her hand. "You sound disappointed."

Oh, she hoped she had done the right thing, bringing Florence here. "It's just not what I expected, that's all."

"Is it the countryside that has not met your expectations? Or the house?"

Sophia shook her head. "It's all of it."

"All of it. Oh dear." Florence pulled off her gloves. "You must tell me what has happened. Nothing could be as bad as all that."

The coach rattled and bumped over the road; the narrow wheels washed through deep puddles. Sophia gave in to the motion and let everything spill out in one simple verdict. "I've discovered that James married me for my money."

Florence rubbed a finger over Sophia's cheek. "Oh, my dear, sweet Sophia. *That* is what's bothering you? But you knew your dowry was a part of this. You knew how much your father was offering, and you came here to raise your family in society. Don't tell me you thought that you were marrying for love." Her face went pale. "You *did* think that?"

Sophia gazed at Florence with surprise. "Of course I thought it. Couldn't you tell how I felt about James?"

Florence hesitated before she answered. "I knew you wanted him."

"Of course I wanted him. I was in love with him. Madly in love. I thought he loved me, too. He made me believe he did. The way he looked at me and spoke to me . . . there was such passion between us. Or so I thought."

Florence grimaced. "Passion is easy for men. You're a beautiful woman, Sophia, and it would be impossible for a man *not* to feel desire when he looks at you. The important thing is that James did marry you. He could have had any woman he wanted, and he chose you. He made you a duchess. You don't realize how lucky you are."

The coach swayed beneath them. "I don't care anything about being a duchess."

"You don't mean that."

Sophia gazed resolutely into Florence's blue eyes. There was a question that had niggled at Sophia since the moment Florence tried to discourage them from hoping for a proposal from James. Then, when Sophia began to fall in love with him, she had shut her eyes to anything that might have been a cause to dismiss him.

For some reason, that question was niggling at her again. "Did you tell me everything about how you first met James?"

Florence's shoulders lifted as she took in a deep breath. "Why must you ask me that?"

The reply sent a stabbing dread through Sophia. "You have kept something from me. Please, tell me what it is."

A tension closed around them. "It's nothing. It doesn't matter now."

"It matters to me, Florence. You must tell me."

"I don't see what—"

"*Please.*"

She sighed in defeat. "All right. Something happened between us, but as I said, nothing came of it. I met James at a ball, my first week in London, when I was still in awe of everything. He walked into the room looking so beautiful and elegant, and I wanted him, then and there, more than I ever wanted any man in my life."

Sophia felt a sudden chill move over her.

Florence continued. "I was presented to him and we danced, and we met a few more times at assemblies and such, until one night, I was determined to make him mine, and I went off with him, alone. We found a private library that was closed off to everyone, and we remained there for . . . a while."

Sophia's heart was ramming against her chest as she

listened. She felt like she was going to be ill there in the coach.

"I could have been ruined," Florence said.

"*Were* you?"

The countess shook her head. "No, but I came very close. Thank goodness I came to my senses and put a stop to things, not a moment too soon I must say. Miraculously we were not caught, but he never spoke another word to me. I even wrote letters to him, hoping he would request my hand, but he never replied. He was as silent as a grave, and as cold. A heart made of stone, I soon came to see. I hated him after that. I still hate him now." She stared out the window for a long time, then spoke softly. "I'm sorry. I shouldn't say that. He's your husband."

Sophia swallowed over the sickening lump in her throat. "Why didn't you tell me any of this?"

"I did try to. I told you about his reputation."

"But you made it all seem like idle drawing room gossip."

Florence clenched her jaw. "Most of it was. Even so, you and your mother wanted him so badly, nothing I said would have made any difference. And then—every time I thought about the time when fashionable New York wouldn't touch us—I couldn't help but cheer you on. I wanted to be part of that."

Sophia tried to keep the shock and anger from her voice. "You kept those things from me because you wanted revenge on the Knickerbockers?"

Florence sat forward on the seat. "It wasn't just that. It was the thrill of the hunt! He was the best, Sophia, and I knew you and your mother wanted him. I wanted you both to succeed and be happy."

For a long moment, Sophia sat and listened to the blood rushing hotly through her brain. Wishing she had been wiser. Wishing she had not been blinded by a fairy tale. "Please tell me that you are happy now in your own marriage, Florence."

Florence shrugged. "I'm not sure anyone really knows what happiness truly is. The point is, I married *very* well."

Tears began to fill Sophia's eyes. "But you and your husband have grown to love each other, haven't you?"

Florence kept her eyes downcast as she smoothed a gloved hand over her skirt. "Of course. Just as you and James will, too."

With all her might, Sophia smothered the urge to cry.

There was an uncomfortable silence in the coach. It was as if the air had suddenly become too thick to breathe.

Florence covered Sophia's hand with her own. "You should be proud, Sophia. The Duke of Wentworth married you, after he vowed never to marry anyone. You accomplished a great feat. And you, an American. No one ever thought you would actually pull it off. You cannot possibly be anything less than ecstatic over your victory."

Staring bewildered at Florence in the dim, dusky light, Sophia realized that the woman had no words of wisdom to offer. Sophia had hoped Florence would be a kindred spirit in this matter, but she was far from it. She did not understand, nor did she care to. She had come to England in search of a title, she had found it, and nothing else mattered.

Or perhaps she did not wish to be reminded of what she had *not* found.

Sophia gazed out the window, feeling more displaced and alone than ever, wondering if in a few years, she would become like Florence, and not want to face the idea that she had made a mistake. Would she ever be able to do that? To paste a pretty smile on her face, pretend that she was happy, and eventually forget that she'd ever known what real happiness was in the first place?

The carriage bumped, and her head began to throb. Florence's attempt to appease her meant nothing, for she now knew that both James and her mother's dearest friend had kept a secret from her. They had both ushered Sophia into a world that they must have known would suffocate her.

Sophia suddenly felt as if her soul was being annihilated. She had been stuffed and sealed in a gilded tomb with nothing but a coronet on her head to keep her happy, and no one wanted to hear her complain about it.

A few days after Florence left, the dowager announced over breakfast that it was tradition in late October for the Duke and Duchess of Wentworth to host a shooting party. Sophia would therefore be required to send out invitations to the usual people.

Who the "usual people" were was left for Sophia to guess at, until the time came to actually prepare the invitations. Sophia had to go to the dowager and request a guest list.

She raised her hand to knock on Marion's door, but heard a loud, gut-wrenching sob from inside. Startled, she hesitated and listened for a few seconds, then gathered her resolve and knocked.

Something dropped on the floor inside the room,

and it was a few more seconds before Marion said, "Come in."

Sophia entered.

If Marion had been crying, it was over now. Her face was as cold and unfeeling as ever. "What do you want? I'm busy."

Sophia gazed down at the scarf Marion was knitting. "I need a guest list for the party."

Should she ask Marion if she was all right?

Marion huffed as she rose from her chair. "I don't have the time or the energy to do your duties for you, Sophia. You must learn to do them on your own."

Sophia decided not to pry into Marion's business. She just wasn't up to being shouted at today. "Believe me, Marion, I want that more than you do."

The dowager gave her a sidelong glance, then went to her desk and retrieved a book. She handed it over. "This is my record of last year's party. It includes the menus and the guest list as well as my notes about each guest's tastes and preferences regarding food and rooms. Viscount Irvine, who is quite elderly, found the bed in the green guest chamber too hard, if I recall. You'll have to put him elsewhere this year."

"Thank you, Marion, this is exactly what I need." Sophia accepted the book, then turned to leave.

She had just stepped over the threshold when the door slammed behind her and almost caught the hem of her dress in the doorjamb.

Forcing herself to ignore her mother-in-law's contempt—for if she lost her temper, there would be no turning back—Sophia returned to her own boudoir and sat down at her desk, dipped her pen in the ink, and began her letters. Three hours later, she leaned back in her chair, and with a sigh of fatigue, marveled at the huge stack of invitations on her crested writing paper, sealed with red wax, impressed with the ducal coat of arms.

A knock rapped at her door. "Come in."

The door slowly opened, creaking all the way. Her mother-in-law walked in.

Sophia sat up straight again. "Hello, Marion."

"You've been working on the invitations?"

A sudden and surprising desire to please this woman—whose approval should not matter to her—inched up Sophia's spine. She gestured with her hand toward the huge pile in front of her. "Yes, I finished all of them. I invited everyone who came last year."

"Not Lady Colchester, I hope."

"Yes . . . I believe I did invite her, with her husband."

Marion shook her head in that slow, eyes-toward-the-ceiling manner. "No, no, no! Lady Colchester passed away last winter. You must redo that one. It will be Lord Colchester only."

"I see." With hands stiff from all the writing, Sophia began to sort through the pile of invitations on the desk, searching for the one she'd written to the Colchesters. They slid off each other and a few fell to the floor. Marion approached and began searching, too, squinting to read the names on the outsides of the invitations, and scrutinize the quality of Sophia's penmanship, no doubt.

"I can find it," Sophia said, bending down to pick up the ones she'd dropped. Oh, how she disliked the feel of her mother-in-law leaning over her shoulder, breathing down her neck, as if Sophia were incapable of finding one simple invitation.

"Here it is," Marion said, her blue-veined hand

scooping it up from near the bottom. She broke the seal and opened it. "Oh, good gracious!" she bellowed, as if Sophia's letters were lists of profanities.

"What's wrong?" Sophia asked, not quite sure she wanted to know.

"You do not sign your name as Sophia Langdon! Your signature must read Sophia Wentworth! Wentworth!" Marion threw the letter down onto the desk and picked up another and ripped it open. "This one is the same." She ripped open another. "And this! They're all wrong! You must redo them all! All that paper wasted. You will have to burn it."

She walked out, slammed the door behind her, and Sophia swallowed hard over the rage rising up in her chest. She felt like a child, back in the one-room schoolhouse with Mrs. Trilling as her teacher. Sophia could still hear that ruler smacking the desks.

Well, she would not let the dowager break her. She would not let a hateful woman crush what was left of Sophia's old self nor the dream of what she had wanted to become.

Sophia picked up her skirts and hurried to the door. She would not look at her mother-in-law the way the pitiable servants looked at members of this family— with lowered eyes and fear and subjugation. She was tired of seeing them look at *her* that way! She would not let the dowager break her spirit like she'd broken everyone else's. No wonder James didn't know how to love!

Sophia pulled open her door and swept out into the corridor. Marion was just disappearing around a corner. Sophia ran after her. She reached her at the top of the wide staircase in the main hall.

"Wait!" she called out. Marion stopped and turned.

Heart racing in her chest, Sophia approached. "I've had enough of this."

"I beg your pardon?" Marion replied indignantly.

"I've had enough of your critical, disdainful tone. If you don't like me, that is your choice, but your son married me, and I'm here to stay. I am the mistress of this house and I expect from now on to be treated—at the very least!—with civility."

Marion glared in dumbfounded shock, then without one retaliating word, turned to hurry down the stairs. *Typical,* Sophia thought. *Raise your nose in the air and ignore the lowly unpleasantness of emotion.*

Sophia stood at the top of the staircase, feeling triumphant at last. For days she had been struggling to hang on to her self-confidence and fit in here with these cold, unfeeling people. Agonizing over her husband's cruel withdrawal, endlessly analyzing why he didn't want to love her, and wishing for answers that were simply not going to come. Not if she continued to feel like a victim.

No more. Starting this minute, she would seize the reins. She would live here as duchess on her own terms. She would never again allow her mother-in-law to intimidate her, nor would she allow her husband to think that she was going to be a simpering, emotional burden, pining away for him. When he returned from London, he was going to learn that his wife was stronger than that. He was going to learn that *he* would have to do some fancy footwork to gain back her regard.

With a mental "so there," she returned to her boudoir to redo the invitations. After that, she would take a buggy out to visit some of her husband's tenants, and see what she could do to give something of herself to those who needed her, and those who would welcome her.

Two weeks later, James returned. He had been gone for a month. It was late in the evening—past eleven. He entered his rooms to find the fire already burning and Thompson waiting dutifully with a glass of brandy on a tray.

"Ah, just what I need." James picked up the glass and took a deep draught. He tugged at his neckcloth and sat down.

"Welcome home, Your Grace."

"Thank you, Thompson. It was a tiring journey this time around, don't you agree? It seemed so much longer than usual."

Probably because he'd had to deal with more problems concerning Martin. The boy had been suspended from Eton again, and James had been forced to make arrangements for him to go and stay with their aunt Caroline.

Just then, a knock tapped at the door. "Enter," James called out.

The door swung open, and his wife stood there in the threshold wearing a white dressing gown with a shawl around her shoulders. She held a large brass candelabra. Her hair spilled down over her shoulders in thick, wavy locks, and the candlelight glimmered in the deep blue of her eyes.

Feeling a sharp surge of arousal at his wife's incredible beauty, James stood up.

Without ever taking his eyes off Sophia, he said to Thompson, "That will be all." The valet obediently took his leave.

Sophia walked in and closed the door behind her,

then set her candles on a desk. "You never told me you were leaving to go to London."

James let his gaze sweep down the full length of his wife's slender body. His eyes fixed for a second on her tiny bare feet, then rose again so that he could look her in the eye when he answered her question.

Words, however, seemed elusive to him, like fluffy feathers on a breeze that he was clumsily trying to grab at.

He tried not to concern himself too much about it. Their separation—though unpleasant at times—had provided the much-needed proof to him that everything was normal. That he was still in control. He'd managed to justify all the cruel things he'd said to her the last time they spoke, and he'd even managed to forget about her completely for certain extended periods of time during the days.

But not at night. Never at night.

That, however, was manageable, he told himself now, for it was only lust. He'd felt lust for women before and he'd never lost his head over it, and he would not lose his head over Sophia.

He tipped his glass and downed all of his brandy. "The decision was a sudden one."

"I would prefer it," she said flatly, "if from now on you would inform me of any overnight trips and kiss me good-bye."

He studied her expression—austere with a hint of arrogance.

He had expected wrath—she certainly had good reason—and had even braced himself for it.

If not wrath, then tears.

At the very least, some form of pleading.

"Agreed," he said, gazing at her ivory face and the rigid set of her jaw.

"Good." She padded across the floor toward him with a determined look in her eyes, and his trousers tightened around an arousal he did not even consider resisting. He had been a whole month away from his wife, and seeing this self-assured air of hers without any of the tears he had expected to come home to, he was pleasantly surprised.

He was all of a sudden hotly in the mood for sex.

She stood before him, her full lips moist and inviting, her perfume like a potent aphrodisiac to his senses. He laid his palm on her cheek and stroked her bottom lip. She closed her eyes and kissed his thumb, then took it into her mouth and sucked on it. The intense wet heat of her mouth sent a wild yearning through him.

He took her whole face in his hands and lowered his lips to hers, but she gently pulled back. Momentarily stalled, he opened his eyes.

Sophia stepped away from him. "I'm sorry, James, I won't be performing my duty tonight."

Her perfunctory statement was like a bucket of cold water dumped over his head.

"My monthly began yesterday, so there's really no duty to perform." Without the slightest hint of disappointment, she turned from him and picked up her candles. "I'll see you in my room when I'm ripe to conceive in about a week?"

He stood motionless, not entirely sure this woman—speaking with such casual indifference—was his spirited American wife. She almost sounded. . . . British.

She opened the door to leave, but faced him for one

more thing. "By the way, Florence was here while you were gone. We had a lovely visit. Talked about all kinds of interesting things."

Feeling stuck to the floor, James blinked slowly at her.

"Good night," she said.

James took an anxious step forward. "Sophia—"

She stopped.

"I . . . I'm sorry." The words spilled over his lips before he even knew they were on his tongue. Shaken by the sound and feel of them—for he had never in his life apologized to anyone for anything—he stood unsteadily in the middle of the room with no idea what to do or say next.

For a long time his wife stared at him, and he thought he saw her cheeks flush, but he couldn't be sure in the candlelight. There was something in her eyes, though. Something that looked perhaps like longing. Maybe she wasn't as confident as she appeared.

"Sorry for what?" she asked.

He thought long and hard about how he should answer that, for what he really regretted was taking her away from the home and country she knew and a family she loved. He had lied to her about Florence and so many other things. He had brought her here to this godforsaken purgatory—where the echoes off the walls resonated with the ghostly howls of an unthinkable past. Then, after all that, he had been cruel to her and had left her here to face all of it alone.

That's what he was sorry for, and it pressed upon him. He could feel it squeezing around his chest.

"I'm sorry we haven't been successful yet," he replied.

"In conceiving a child, you mean?" she asked, searching for perhaps another deeper clarification he wasn't ready to give.

"Yes."

She nodded, as if that was the answer she had expected, then left him alone.

Chapter 17

James leaned forward in the saddle, his grip tight on the reins as he galloped across the moors on his return from an inspection of the east drainage ditches. He'd worked hard to keep himself occupied the past week, to forget his worries over Sophia. He accomplished that feat simply by not thinking of her. There were moments when he hadn't been sure that he could not think of her, but he realized now that he'd always been very skilled at shutting out the world, for there was a time when his sanity required it—when he, as a boy, had had no control over his environment.

James urged his mount over a low, stone wall and landed on the damp grass. He slowed his horse to a walk, however, when he spotted his own cabriolet parked outside a tenant's cottage, with the top down. He drew closer and found the coachman lying down in the seat, sleeping.

James cleared his throat. The man, who had pulled

his top hat down to shade his eyes from the sun, waved at a fly buzzing around his head. James cleared his throat again.

The man raised his hat, saw James, and leaped out of the carriage. There was a flurry of chickens clucking and flapping their feathered wings in the yard. "Your Grace!"

From high up on his horse, James gazed down at the man. "May I ask what you're doing here with my vehicle? Sleeping in it?"

"I'm here with the duchess, Your Grace. And she told me to sleep. She said I looked tired, and she wouldn't take no for an answer. She *made* me get in the back."

James pondered that. It was one of those moments he felt the differences between himself and his wife like a deep, impossible chasm. Not that he didn't feel a man deserved his sleep, but there were rules to consider, especially when servants were on duty.

James glanced at the front door of the little stone cottage. He knew the farmer who lived here. He was a young, stalwart man. Respectable and dependable. Then again, James spoke with him so rarely. It was difficult to judge a man.

"The duchess is inside?"

"Yes, Your Grace."

James hadn't known his wife was out visiting today, but he had made a point to avoid any and all contact with her since their last encounter. She had not voiced any complaints, and the schedule of her courses had freed him of any expectations he or she might have regarding their more intimate relations. At least for a few more days.

Still, a ripple of curiosity moved through him.

"Is her maid here as well?"

"She didn't want to bring anyone, Your Grace. She wanted to come alone."

"Alone," he repeated. Was she doing something she didn't want anyone to know about? Or was this just another of her errors in protocol?

He would have liked to ask the coachman exactly what Sophia was doing here on this sunny afternoon, but decided against it, for he did not wish to draw attention to the fact that his servants knew more about his wife's comings and goings than he did.

"How long have you been here?" James asked.

"An hour, Your Grace. She usually stays for an hour."

"Usually? You've been here before?"

The man nodded. "Three times this week."

"I see." James looked at the front door of the cottage again and found himself quite unable to be on his way.

He dismounted and tethered his horse to the others in the harness. Carrying his riding crop, he stepped up to the front door and knocked.

A young woman answered. He was quite certain it was the farmer's wife. He was relieved.

The woman wore a lace cap and a white apron, and she held a small child on her hip. Her eyes widened when she recognized James, and, looking a little flustered, she curtsied. "Good afternoon, Your Grace."

"Good afternoon," he replied. "Is the duchess here?"

The young woman stepped aside and held open the door. "She is."

James removed his hat as he entered the small house. A fire blazed in the hearth, and he could smell food cooking—turnip or something of that sort. His gaze followed a deep crack up the wall to the thick, exposed beams across the low ceiling.

"She's through here," the girl said, leading the way to a room at the back of the house. The floorboards creaked beneath the soles of James's shiny riding boots as he followed.

They pushed through a door, and there he saw his wife with an open book in her hands, reading to an old woman in a rocking chair. The woman wore black. Thin, coarse-looking gray hair fell loose over her shoulders.

Sophia's gaze lifted as the door opened, and when she saw James, she stopped reading. They stared at each other wordlessly for a moment. James found himself gazing at her in her plain afternoon dress, and imagining her in America—in a wheatfield or something. She'd never looked less like a duchess.

"Who's there?" the old woman said, and James knew at once that she was blind.

"It's the duke," Sophia replied.

"The duke. My word." The frail woman tried to get up.

Sophia covered the woman's craggy hand with her own. "It's all right, Catherine. There's no need to get up. James, this is Mrs. Catherine Jenson."

The informal introduction would have exasperated James's mother, but contrarily, James felt nothing but relief at having, for once, been spared ceremony.

"What are you doing here?" Sophia asked him. "Am I needed at the house?"

"No, I was simply passing by and I noticed the carriage out front."

"I see," she said, seeming a little puzzled by his reply. He was puzzled by it himself, because he didn't know what the bloody hell he was doing here.

The farmer's wife behind him excused herself to the kitchen.

"Would you like to sit down?" Sophia asked, as if she were completely at home here. "I'm almost finished our reading. Would that be all right, Catherine?"

"It would be an honor, Your Grace."

"The honor is mine, madam," James said. "Though I do not wish to intrude."

"You won't," Sophia answered.

He sat down on a wooden bench by the wall.

Sophia continued to read from where she had left off—the Book of Revelation. *"Behold I stand at the door, and knock: if any man hear my voice, and open the door, I will come in to him, and will sup with him, and he with me."*

James listened to his wife's melodic voice and thought about what she read, and the person she was.

A quiet feeling moved over him. He imagined life in America with no aristocracy, where the class structure was based on wealth rather than accident of birth. He imagined Sophia in that one-room house she had told him about, and wondered with an odd sense of amusement what she must think of this very different world she'd married into. She hadn't really questioned it in London or on their honeymoon, for there hadn't been time to contemplate it, he supposed. Nor had she yet at that time experienced the reality of being a peeress. Was it settling in on her now? Would she even be able to adapt to it? Was that why she was here? To escape it for a few hours?

He felt a tremendous responsibility suddenly, to see

that she was taken care of and eased into this new life, especially after the way he'd treated her before he'd left for London. The way he'd crushed her fantasies, even though he'd done it for her own good.

It was a novel thought for James, who had never intended to care one way or the other if any wife of his was "settling in." He had always expected to leave her to his mother to mold and train, and to leave any future children to nannies and nurses to educate. But Sophia was turning out to be a rather formidable substance. She was—unfortunately for his mother—not very "moldable."

Perhaps if his upbringing had been more nurturing, he might have in the past been more inclined to concern himself with his duchess's need for assistance and support. What was it about Sophia that was raising this response in him today? A greater sense of familiarity, perhaps? Or was it simply her overwhelming kindness toward this woman?

James watched Mrs. Jenson nod in response to the readings. Sophia finished and closed the Bible.

"That was beautiful, Your Grace," Mrs. Jenson said.

Sophia knelt on one knee in front of the woman, and took her hand. "Thank you for letting me come. I'll be back on Monday to see you again."

"May God bless you," the woman replied, pulling Sophia's hand to her cheek. Sophia stroked the woman's hair, kissed the top of her head lovingly, and gave the Bible back to her.

With an almost crippling sense of awe, James watched Sophia rise to her feet.

A few minutes later, they were saying good-bye to the farmer's young wife at the front door. She curtsied

and smiled exuberantly at Sophia, but seemed afraid
even to glance at James. Another man might have been
unsettled by it. He was accustomed to it. The local vil-
lagers couldn't help but know certain things about his
family's bleak history.

When the door closed, he and Sophia faced each
other in the sunlight.

"You hadn't told me you started visiting the tenants," James said.

She pulled on her gloves and walked to the carriage.
"You didn't ask." The coachman helped her into her
seat and she adjusted her skirts. "I want to get to know
our neighbors."

Neighbors. He had never thought of the tenants as
neighbors. He glanced back at the cottage door and
found himself wondering the Christian name of the
farmer's wife, and the name of their child. He wondered how long ago Mrs. Jenson had lost her sight, and
why he hadn't heard about it, for they did not live far
from the castle.

"And it does me good to come here," Sophia continued. "When I look at dear Mrs. Jenson's face, listening
intently to what I'm reading and finding such joy in the
words she cannot read for herself, I feel the peace of
God descending upon me. I'm happy to come here and
do something for her, James, for the strength and tranquillity it gives me."

Gazing into Sophia's clear blue eyes, James began to
feel a similar sort of peace and tranquillity descending
upon himself. He had never felt anything like it before,
and it shook him deeply, from the inside out.

"You really should bring your maid with you," he
said, for he didn't know what else to say.

"Actually, James, I am considering replacing Mildred."

He rested his hands on the side of the cabriolet. "Replacing her? But she is very experienced and came highly recommended. She has *always* been—"

"*Always*. Yes, I know. But that's just it, you see. She is your mother's choice, not mine, and I am nothing like your mother."

That was becoming more and more clear to him every day.

"I wish to choose for myself," she continued. "I want someone I can feel comfortable with. Perhaps then I wouldn't mind my maid doing all the things a maid is supposed to do for me."

Comfortable. "All right then. Why don't you see the housekeeper about it? I'm sure she'll be able to look into—"

"I already did. I explained everything to Mildred last night, and she agreed to accept her pension early. She was quite relieved, actually. I think I might have . . . how shall I say it? . . . put her off more than once."

James couldn't help smiling at the thought of Sophia putting Mildred "off." "Somehow I'm not surprised."

Sophia returned his smile. "You don't mind, then?"

"Of course not. If it will make your adjustment easier."

James realized with an unaccustomed sense of easiness that they were having an orderly, casual discussion about the household. Perhaps it was possible for them to abandon what they had been to each other on their honeymoon—when they'd touched and kissed constantly, held hands, locked ankles under clothed tables.

There was some aloofness on Sophia's part today, as if she was willing to operate in this marriage without wanting his affections. As if she was getting over the anger she felt toward him. She seemed stronger.

Perhaps he had not made such a terrible mistake after all.

He slapped the side of the carriage to signal the driver and watched until they grew distant down the rocky, winding road toward the house.

Sophia did not permit herself to turn around in the carriage and look back at James at the Jenson cottage. He was too handsome, today, too charming, and she was afraid that if she did, she would slip back into that hopeless obsession, for she still loved him far more than she should. Instead, she violently suppressed the urge and forced herself to gaze up at the clear blue sky.

Lord, she'd had so many moments of flip-flopping emotions over the past month. One minute she wanted to pitch a vase at her husband, who had been inconceivably cruel to her on that horrible night—still with no explanation that made any sense to her. On top of that, he'd thrown her into this new life with a cavalier "sink or swim" approach, and had offered no support.

Other times, on those rare occasions like today when he spoke to her and flashed a smile, she wanted him back. More than she'd ever wanted anything. The knowledge that he would make love to her again when her body was ripe to produce an heir was, quite frankly, the only thing that kept her going. She could not let go of the hope that they would rekindle something of what they'd had, for she needed intimacy in her life, a deep soulful connection with another human being. She could not live without it. Her visits to the tenants were filling a small part of that need, but it was not the same thing as the spiritual and physical connection she'd thought she'd had with her husband.

She pulled off her gloves and felt a sting at the realization that she had given up all her previous intimacies for him—her sisters, her mother, her father. She had been so sure that he would be there for her.

With a heavy, melancholy sigh, she prayed that one day they would come to a livable arrangement that would suit them both and that she would understand the real reason why he had rejected her.

Chapter 18

Exhausted, hoping sleep would come swiftly, Sophia climbed into bed after an evening of interviews with possible new maids. Sophia required a woman with experience—for she needed to rely on her maid to understand and teach her aristocratic protocol. Yet at the same time, Sophia did not want anyone quite as "experienced" as Mildred.

She turned the key in her crystal lamp and snuggled down into the ducal sheets.

A gentle knock sounded at her door. Sophia sat up in the darkness. "Come in."

The door opened and there stood her husband in his black silk night robe, holding a candelabra. The robe was open in front, and Sophia could see the smooth, muscular curves of his chest and stomach. His jet-black hair tumbled loose and wavy about his shoulders.

A quiver coursed through her veins. She wiggled on the bed and pushed a lock of hair behind her ear. He was the most magnificent specimen of a man she'd ever encountered in her life. She could not even imagine that anyone on the planet could be more visually impressive.

"Did I wake you?" he asked.

She struggled to sound casual and at ease. "No, I just put the light out a moment ago. Come in."

Was he here for what she thought he was here for? To make love to her again, after all this time without so much as a smile or gesture of affection? Had the time finally come?

A hot lightning bolt of desire slammed into her, for despite all her anger and determination not to think of him these past weeks, she *had* thought of him. She'd dreamed of making love to him again, imagined the feel of his hands under her gown, the heavy warmth of his naked body on top of hers, the mind-numbing sensation of his erection sliding into her.

He moved into the room and set his candles on a chest of drawers. Like Sophia, he must have been counting the days until the time was about right to conceive a child.

A more rational part of her felt some indignation at that, for he was making it clear that their lovemaking was still about duty, nothing more, just like he'd said it would be that dreadful night before he left for London.

Another part of her—the more hedonistic part she could not seem to deny no matter how hard she tried—couldn't care less about his motivations. All that mattered was that he was here. He was here to make love to her, and she was going to enjoy every sinfully glorious minute of it.

She only hoped she would be able to maintain her composure through it all, and not push him to explain why he was so against loving her, or feel heartbroken when he left. She had made it her goal to be strong and patient, for she certainly could not force him to love her.

Her husband closed the door behind him and locked it, then sauntered confidently like a lion to the bed. All Sophia's senses prickled with awareness of him as a masterful, sexual being.

"Any luck finding a new maid?" His voice was low. Husky.

"Not yet." She tried to keep her voice from revealing the quickening of her heart as he approached. "But there are two more ladies coming tomorrow."

"Excellent. The housekeeper's been cooperative, then?"

"Yes, very." She had the distinct feeling that James might have spoken to the housekeeper himself, to ensure the hiring went smoothly.

He sat down on the edge of her bed and stroked her forearm with a finger. "How are things otherwise?"

Gooseflesh shimmied up her back. "Fine, though I still have a great deal to learn."

"I don't doubt you'll master it in your own time and in your own way."

"My own way? I don't think your mother would approve of that."

He grinned. "I don't expect you to be my mother. In fact, I'd prefer it if you weren't."

The flirtatious look in his eye fired another hot thrill straight through her.

She scrambled to keep her mind alert to what he was saying, when all she really wanted to do was stare at him in awed silence. "Do you mean I can do things the way I want?"

"Within reason."

"What do you mean by that?"

James raised a leg to rest on the bed. "I've been watching you the past week. I've seen you go riding and visiting tenants. I know about the scullery maid you sent away on holiday."

Sophia felt her cheeks flush.

"I can only guess what kind of opposition you went up against to accomplish that," he added.

"The housekeeper wasn't impressed. Nor was your mother."

He laughed. "I don't imagine she was, but it's good for Mother to have someone stand up to her. You did a brave thing, let her know you're not a jellyfish. If you hadn't, she would have had strings tied to your limbs and joints in no time, and the servants would continue to look to her for direction."

"They still do. They listen to me when I'm alone, but when your mother is in the room, they glance at her for a final nod about whatever request I make."

He touched her cheek. "They're set in their ways, Sophia, and they expect things to be done the way they have always been done. They'll adjust to you eventually, as you will adjust to them."

His fingers were a soft, soothing caress, and Sophia for the first time in weeks felt the comfort of having someone acknowledge what she was going through, and care enough to try and ease her woes. She wanted to preserve this feeling of closeness and understanding.

If only James could come to her like this every night and talk to her, this strange, new existence would be so much easier to bear. She needed this emotional closeness. She needed *him*.

Sophia cupped his hand in hers and kissed it. "Thank you, James. I've been feeling so lost and—"

He stopped her words with a kiss, and Sophia responded instantly, burying her fingers into the hair at his nape. She wasn't sure why he had stopped her—if it was because he wanted to make love to her and couldn't wait, or if he simply did not want to talk anymore about personal matters. She suspected it was a little bit of both, but whatever his reason, she would accept it, because she wanted him now, more than she'd ever wanted him before. She wanted the warmth and the touching, and no amount of pride or rational restraint was powerful enough to make her refuse him.

He withdrew from the kiss and fondled her earlobe between two fingers, sending a rush of titillating shivers down her spine.

"I presume you know why I'm here," he murmured. She nodded.

"And you're willing this evening?"

In some indirect, roundabout way, he was handing the reins to her, letting her be the one to decide what would or would not occur in this bed tonight. Letting her know that he was in this small way, her servant.

"I'm more than willing, James. I've been waiting for you. For days, now."

His eyes became sexual. Predatory. "And what, *exactly,* have you been waiting for? This?" He slowly and tenderly pressed his mouth to hers again, parting her lips with his own and probing inside with his tongue. His fingers played in the wisps of hair around her temple, igniting her senses with tantalizing, tingling desires.

Sophia clutched at his head, deepening the kiss.

"Or this?" He growled out the words as his hand slid down her neck and into the warm confines of her nightgown, stopping to relax upon her breast and massage it gently.

Awakening to a sudden and intense onslaught of

need, Sophia sucked in a breath. She couldn't speak to answer his sexually charged question.

"Or perhaps you've been waiting for what I've been waiting for . . ." He eased her down onto the bed and leaned over her.

"And what was that?" she asked breathlessly, her heart racing, seeming to burn a hole inside her chest.

James smiled wickedly. "Everything. Beginning with this, I believe." He gathered the hem of her nightgown in his huge hand and carefully drew it up, sliding his fingers up the side of her leg as he did so, then he found the damp center between her thighs. "Is this what you've been waiting for, too?"

Completely disabled by his skillful touch, she nodded.

He slid his finger inside her, then slowly . . . teasingly . . . drew it in and out, again and again until she was slick with burning need.

"And what about this—what I'm doing now?" he whispered in her ear. His breath was hot and moist, sending waves of gooseflesh all over her body.

Sophia melted like butter in his hands. She closed her eyes and barely managed to whisper a reply. "Yes, James, that."

She gave in to the overwhelming, erogenous power he had over her—the debilitating pleasure he knew so well how to bestow, the pleasure that was now forcing her senses into a whirlwind of eroticism.

He slid under the covers, tossed his robe to the floor. Sophia's desires screamed inside her head. She wanted him inside her now, quenching her impossible lust.

Dizzy with a need so fierce, it would have knocked her off her feet if she were standing, Sophia tore at her nightdress with frantic fingers and pulled it off over her head. She had no idea where she threw it. The cool air met her bare breasts, and the sensation enflamed her already savage desires. She wiggled down and indulged in the feel of her husband's hot skin as he lowered himself upon her, and the bone-hard feel of his arousal pressing against her pelvis.

"I've missed you, James."

"I've missed you, too," he whispered into her mouth.

She gloried in the atonement, however small it was, then at last parted her legs to receive him. He blinked down at her, rubbed his nose over hers, then—as if he couldn't hold out against the waiting any more than she could—he entered her with a single, violent thrust that took her breath away.

He pushed into her once, as deep as he could, then went still against her womb. "Don't move," he commanded. "I need a moment."

Motionless they lay there in the candlelight, while Sophia thought her heart was booming loud enough for the servants to hear.

"There," he whispered, then smoothly withdrew and slid back in.

An instantaneous orgasmic swell enveloped Sophia as she arched her back and pressed her fingers into her husband's smooth, sweat-drenched back to push him deeper inside. They moved together for an immeasurable length of time, until a sweet ache shot through her in a series of swells, followed by an overpowering tingling. She cried out in a perfect, shuddering release.

James drove into Sophia again and again, reveling in her tight, slick heat as she tightened and pulsed around him. The feel of her fingernails in his back and the sound of her amorous cries brought his own pleasure to the fore. For days and days he had waited for this. Finally, he thrust hard and deep to spill into her and feel at last the trembling, debilitating pleasure of his own release.

He relaxed his weight upon her and waited for his breathing to return to normal, while Sophia lightly stroked his back. Her gentle fingers soothed him. Made him want to hold her closer.

A few minutes later, not wanting to crush her precious, slender body beneath his own, he rolled off her and kissed her cheek.

"Will you stay all night?" she asked, in a quiet, careful voice.

"Yes."

He pulled her close and held her, and again like the first time he'd made love to her on their wedding night, he began to forget who he was. James fell asleep, but it was a restless sleep, full of the usual dark dreams.

Sophia woke in the middle of the night, and James was gone.

Naked, her bare arms chilly on top of the covers, she sat up. The moon in the window cast a light upon the bed, and she leaned over the side to reach for her nightdress, in a heap on the floor. She pulled it on over her head and sat for a moment, thinking.

He had left her again. She should not be disappointed, for even though he had said he would stay, she somehow knew he would leave.

Yet, it seemed that her head could not always control her emotions. She was coming to realize that giving James the space he wanted was impossible. In her family, whenever something was bothering any one of them, they always talked about it and worked it out and everyone felt better afterward. There was never this silence, this ignoring of emotions, pretending everything was fine. She needed to talk openly to James about their relationship. Her own happiness—and her mental equilibrium—depended upon it. She needed to understand why he did not want to love her, and she would not accept that loving one's wife was simply not done.

Sophia climbed out of bed and padded across the cold stone floor for her shawl. Shivering, she struck a match to light her candles, wondering when she would find the time to undertake the installation of hot-water heating. Before the snow came, she hoped, because this coal-in-the-fireplace procedure was just plain primitive.

Carrying her candles out into the silent, dark corridor, Sophia walked to James's room. She knocked lightly, but did not wait for a reply before she pushed the door open. A welcome heat touched her face as she entered.

James sat in front of a roaring fire, staring at the flames, a full glass of brandy in his hand. "I couldn't sleep," was all he said.

A spark snapped loudly in the grate.

"Neither could I." She set down her candles and knelt on her knees in front of him. "I was cold."

"Come here, then." He pulled her onto his lap.

Sophia sat for a moment, enjoying the relaxing feel of his chest rising and falling beneath her, his thumb rubbing her shoulder. She wondered anxiously if she should try to be content with this level of intimacy—which was the best she'd had since they arrived here—rather than push him for more. She decided to keep things light, at least to begin with.

"Is it always this cold in October?"

"No, this is unusual. I won't be surprised if the snow spoils our shooting party."

"Will we still have it?"

"Yes, the guests come for much more than the game."

She could smell the brandy on his breath and had to fight the urge to kiss him, for if she started that, they'd never get to talking. Sitting forward, she turned to face him, and moved a lock of his dark hair away from his forehead.

"Can I say something to you?"

His hesitation revealed an unease. "Of course."

She gently combed her fingers through his hair. "You won't get angry?"

A hesitation again. "That depends on what you say."

She paused, thinking about how she should begin and how she could phrase things to avoid sounding like she was attacking him. She needed to burrow in gently.

"I've been thinking about the things you said to me before you went to London, and the way I reacted, and I wanted to apologize for my behavior—for being so angry."

She took note of his Adam's apple bob as he swallowed, and knew she had knocked him a little off kilter.

"You have nothing to apologize for. All of this must be a difficult adjustment for you."

She gazed at the firelight reflecting in his eyes, and nodded. "I'd be lying if I said it wasn't difficult. But I do want you to know that I'm doing my best, James. I want to be a worthy duchess."

His expression softened, and she knew she had broken through at least one barrier. All the better to reach a deeper one.

He brought her hand to his lips and kissed it. A quivering of warmth moved through her. "You've been more than worthy, Sophia. The tenants adore you."

"But your mother doesn't," she said with a smile, still burrowing. . . .

"Mother is a tough nut to crack. In fact, I'm not even sure if she is a nut. A stone, more like it, but stones do break." He squinted with humor. "If, for instance, they're dropped from a high tower."

Sophia laughed out loud. "Are you saying I should push her out the window?"

"Of course not," he replied, laughing, too. "Though I shouldn't joke about such things. It has happened."

Sophia felt her amusement drain away. "It has? When?"

He shook his head as if to dismiss it. "It was a long time ago."

"Someone was murdered?"

"No, not murdered. The second duchess of Wentworth took her own life. She threw herself out her window."

A cold chill moved through Sophia as she remembered what Florence had told her about James's father drinking himself to death, and his grandfather shooting himself in the head. She couldn't imagine life being so horrific that a person could lose all hope. But as she thought about that portrait of James's ancestor in the hall, Sophia began to feel a deep sympathy for the woman.

"She jumped from *my* window?" she asked as an afterthought, curious about the details.

He grimaced. "I shouldn't have said anything. It was a long time ago. Things were very different then."

How different? she wondered uneasily.

Sophia settled her head on his shoulder again, distracted from all the things she had wanted to say when she'd tiptoed down the hall. The flames in the fireplace leaped and danced as a gust of wind blew down the chimney. James picked up his glass and sipped his brandy.

"Has your mother always been the way she is now?" Sophia asked.

"As long as I can remember."

"That must have been difficult for you, growing up. What was your father like?"

To Sophia's dismay, James gently lifted her off his lap and rose from the chair.

"Worse," he replied.

She felt the coolness of his departure like an icy frost on her skin. He crawled onto the bed and pulled the covers back. His voice was erotically appealing. "Come and lie down with me."

Something he had said to her the night before he left for London repeated in her mind: *You don't know me.*

It was true. She didn't know her husband. She knew nothing.

The desire she usually felt when he looked at her the way he was looking at her now eluded her. It was a need to understand him that was overcoming her.

"Was he cruel to you?" she asked bluntly.

"Who?"

"Your father."

The seductive look in his eye vanished with the sudden realization that she wanted to talk. "Yes, viciously cruel. I'd presumed you would have heard the gossip about him in one of the London drawing rooms, or at least from the Countess of Lansdowne. You were staying with her, after all, and you'd heard just about everything else."

Sophia remembered something Florence had said: "Who knows what secrets live in that vast country castle of his? I would wager quite a few."

Sophia wished she had pressed her for more information about that. "No, I didn't know. Only what you told me that day in the park."

His chest heaved with a sigh. Was it annoyance? Or defeat?

"Well, now you do. Why not come to bed?"

"Was he cruel to your mother, too?"

James let his hand drop onto the covers. "He was cruel to her; she was cruel to him. Everybody was cruel to everybody. But my father's dead now, and I think I've managed to exorcise this house of at least some of its demons."

"What kind of demons?"

"The kind that spoil my sleep. Are you going to keep torturing me like this? The least you could do is lean back while we're talking, so I can't see down your dressing gown."

She realized she was indeed leaning forward. Her gown was unbuttoned at the neck, and James could surely see everything. She pressed her hand to her chest with a sudden sense of modesty. "I'm sorry," she said ridiculously.

He shook his head at her and spoke with a seductive smile. "Don't apologize."

He rose from the bed and approached, then pulled her hand away from the gown so it fell loose around her breasts. He reached a hand inside and touched her.

Sophia gazed up at him standing before her in the

firelight, wearing only his black silk robe, his hands warm as he fondled her nipple. She remembered the man he had been on their honeymoon. That man had not been real. The real James had been wearing a mask and she had been completely unaware of that fact.

Now, at least she knew.

She also knew that the mask was tilting, just a little—for she understood something about his family and the events that had shaped him. Perhaps it was possible that a bond could grow between them, that the man she had fallen in love with did exist somewhere beneath this cool shell of indifference.

"Did he beat you?" she asked, surprising even herself with her persistent interrogation, but she wanted to know as much as possible.

"Yes. He had a temper. He beat my mother and my nurses and governesses, who all took it out on me." James pulled her to her feet, and she wondered how he could speak so casually about all of this.

"What about Lily?" she asked, trying to fight the ache in her heart at the horror of what he was telling her.

"Probably. Though I was gone by that time."

"Gone where?"

"To school. Then abroad in the summers."

She took his face in her hands. "Not all families are like that, James."

"Perhaps not," he said, meeting her gaze. "But for us, it's been a contagious disease that has been passed down for generations, and it needs to be snuffed out."

"Snuffed out?"

"Yes." He took her by the hand, led her to the bed, pulled her nightdress off over her head so she stood naked before him. He took her face into his own hands and leaned down to kiss her lips, whispering at the last moment, "By me."

He did not appear to be emotional about it—he seemed only to be calculating and determined as he spoke those words and eased her down onto the soft coverlets. Sophia wondered fleetingly how he intended to go about such a thing, then gave up her thoughts for a more tangible, pleasurable pursuit. She promised herself she would learn more about it later.

James—having spent a lifetime pushing his emotions away—felt their violent assault like a cannon going off inside his brain. He was embarrassingly distracted while he kissed and fondled his wife, and he had no choice but to acknowledge the reason why.

She had deliberately opened a wound.

He shouldn't have said so much, he thought, feeling the silky warmth of her skin beneath him, smelling the sweet scent of her arousal as he dropped kisses along her flat belly. His beautiful American wife had come here to nudge her way into his life, and he had permitted it. He had answered all her questions, and now he felt exposed.

Strangely, he still felt like he was in heaven when he entered her—despite the trembling, emotional vulnerability that was sliding like a snake around his heart.

He brought her to a climax shortly before he allowed himself to give in to his own, but none of their lovemaking was as simple as he would have liked. Yes, he found pleasure in her body, but at the same time there was an odd urge to leap into a deeper relationship with her—like he used to leap off the stable roof into the haystack below when he was a boy. What a joy it was—to sail through the air and land softly in the dry, crackly hay, even though there was fear, the second before he jumped.

Would I land softly with Sophia? he wondered, as he drew himself out of her with a sigh and rolled onto his back.

James thought of his father. He'd become a monster because he couldn't be with the woman he loved, and because the woman he married was cold, distant, and cruel. Similarly, James's grandfather had lost his head when his wife had run away with her lover. The jealousy had driven him to unthinkable acts of madness, and he'd ordered their deaths. Of course, no one had ever been able to prove that they had been shot by anyone other than highwaymen. There were only whispers. . . .

Sophia was neither cruel nor cold nor distant. Nor had she ever given him any reason to think he could not trust her to be faithful. She seemed to want love. With him. At least, that's what she'd said.

With a happy little moan, Sophia snuggled closer to him, and he held her tightly in his arms and kissed her forehead. He would sleep the rest of the night with her, he decided.

He wondered if his father, in all his obsessiveness, had ever felt a tender yearning like this.

Tender yearning.

James felt a tremor of bewilderment deep inside his chest. *Is this love, or the beginnings of it?* he wondered. For tender was how, in his purely logical mind, he'd always imagined real love would be. For those who were capable of it.

That night, Marion sat at her desk by candlelight, laying an exquisite opal-and-diamond necklace into a box and wrapping the box in tissue paper. She wept quietly, so as not to wake her maid, lamenting the fact that the necklace was a family heirloom, and sending it to Paris was going to break her heart. She would never see the necklace again, but what choice did she have?

If it would keep *him* from coming, it was worth the price of her tears.

Chapter 19

Lily returned to Wentworth Castle the day before the guests were due to arrive for the shooting party. Overjoyed to see her sister-in-law—and thinking ruefully of the things James had told her about their childhood—Sophia ran out to the courtyard to hug Lily and welcome her home.

"I suppose the Earl of Manderlin is coming," Lily said to Sophia, after they hugged and exchanged pleasantries.

"Yes, I invited him."

Lily pulled the hood of her cloak off her head so it draped down her back. "Oh, bother. I guess that's why Mother was so adamant about my returning."

"She's not trying to marry you off to him, is she?"

Sophia remembered the earl's very unromantic proposal back in London. Heavens, the man was at least twice Lily's age. Did no one here believe in love? She supposed with some melancholy that none of them really knew what it was.

"Finally!" Lily said, hooking her arm through Sophia's to walk to the house. "Someone who sees things the way I do! Mother just doesn't understand, nor does James. I'm so glad you're here, Sophia. You won't let them force me, will you?"

"Force you! Good Heavens, Lily, this isn't the Middle Ages."

Lily gave her a doubtful, sidelong glance that sent an uncomfortable shiver up Sophia's spine.

She decided to be more careful with her words from now on. "I'm sure James and your mother have your best interests at heart. They just want you to have a happy life."

"I wish that were so, but I know for a fact that Mother's first priority is to attach me to the highest-ranking eligible peer around, no matter *what* he looks like."

Sophia recalled her own flight from New York to escape the decidedly dull Mr. Peabody, who wouldn't know what a smile was if it bit him on the nose.

"And James . . ." Lily continued, "James won't listen to me about what would make me happy. I can't talk to him. He doesn't want to hear. . . ."

"The Earl of Manderlin doesn't seem like your type," Sophia said.

"My type. Exactly. What a perfectly modern phrase. Is it American? Tell me, what do you think my *type* is?"

Sophia laughed. "Oh, I don't know. You'll have to decide that for yourself. But I suspect you'll know him the very minute you see him. In your eyes, he'll be the most handsome, most fascinating man in the world.

Let's just hope you're lucky enough to fall in love with a man your mother will approve of."

"Like you did," Lily said with a giggle.

Sophia had no reply.

They hurried up the steps together and, after greeting the housekeeper at the door, went straight up to Lily's room. Lily told Sophia about her trip to Exeter and her aunt and some of the trouble Martin had gotten into, then they sat down on the bed together.

Sophia took her sister-in-law's hand. "May I ask you something, Lily?"

"Of course. We're sisters, remember?"

Smiling, Sophia nodded. "A few nights ago, James told me about your family . . . about your father."

Lily pulled her hand away and glared at Sophia. She stood up and went to the window to look out. "What did he say?"

"He told me that your father was . . . not a kind man."

"It's true, but I don't see the point in talking about it."

"Sometimes, talking about things can make you feel better about them."

"How?" she asked harshly, turning to face Sophia.

"Sometimes it helps to know that you're not alone, or that certain things that were difficult are over and done with, and won't happen again."

Lily faced the window. "I can only hope."

Sophia moved to stand beside her. "What did happen? James didn't tell me very much."

Lily answered with a softer tone. "James saw the worst of it. By the time Martin and I came along, Father stayed in London mostly. He had his heir and his spare, so there was no point remaining here when he despised all of us."

"Why would he despise you?"

"I'm not certain. Martin has heard things—gossip mostly. He said James has broken a few jaws over things people have said about Mother, and has had his own jaw broken in return, no doubt." Lily gazed out the window for a moment, her expression melancholy. "He was always getting into fights when he was younger."

"What gossip did Martin hear?" Sophia asked.

Lily hesitated. "Promise you will not repeat this, especially to James. I wouldn't want him to know I spoke of it to you."

Sophia agreed.

"Supposedly, Father loved another woman, but Mother refused to turn a blind eye like most wives do. She wouldn't let him see the woman, and threatened to ruin him if he did."

The cavalier manner in which Lily spoke of her father's adultery lodged uncomfortably in Sophia's heart. At the same time, Sophia was not surprised that Marion was determined to ensure her husband's faithfulness. Not because she loved him—though maybe she did in her own way—but because she likely could not bear to see rules bent or broken.

"How did James see the worst of it?" Sophia asked, her thoughts dashing back to him as they always did. "What happened to him?"

"Everything erupted when he was a baby. James told me that he was a difficult child—that he used to throw temper tantrums and that it didn't help matters, because Father was at his worst then, and the governess was bad, too. She used to lock him in a trunk to punish him, and once when he was nine, she slammed the lid on his hand and broke it. He didn't cry out or anything. He stayed inside for over an hour, waiting. When the break was discovered, it had swollen so badly, the surgeon thought he might have to amputate. Thank goodness he didn't. Father at least fired the governess, but the next one was no better. I don't think anyone knew what to do with James. Martin and I had different governesses, who were quite kind, and we were quieter children, but we did occasionally feel the back of Father's hand."

"Lily, I'm sorry."

"It could have been worse. It was for James, but it's better now." Lily smiled at Sophia. "You're going to be a good mother, aren't you? Tell me you would never let anything like that happen to your children."

The hair stood up on the back of Sophia's neck. "Certainly not. I'd steal them away first."

Lily's brow furrowed, as if she was puzzled by such a thought. "You can't steal the heir to a dukedom. James wouldn't allow it."

The thought of her and James ever being at such odds shook Sophia. For a moment, she felt disconnected from the floor.

Lily began to unbutton her bodice to change for tea. "Is there anyone new coming to the party this year?" she asked, changing the subject.

Sophia sat down on the bed. "Yes. A friend of Lord Manderlin's."

"Lord Manderlin has a friend?"

Sophia struggled to focus on Lily's questions. "Apparently, there is a man from Paris renting a cottage from him. He's quite well-off, the earl said, though he has no title. He's here simply to travel and see England."

Lily sat on the bed beside Sophia. "Really? From Paris? Have you seen him yet? Is he very handsome?"

"I don't know," Sophia replied, trying to forget what they had been talking about earlier. She forced herself to smile. "He could be old or have no teeth, or perhaps he doesn't even speak English. All I know is that he's a bachelor, and his name is Pierre Billaud."

Lily flopped onto her back. "*Pierre* . . . how very French. Oh, how I long to go to Paris. I would do anything to see it. It's such a romantic place, don't you think? Does Mother know he's coming? I can assure you that when she was duchess, Lord Manderlin would never have asked to bring a stranger. People feel more relaxed with you, Sophia. It's quite refreshing."

"Thank you, Lily, and no, your mother doesn't know. She doesn't ask me about things, so I don't feel it's necessary to inform her of all the details. She'll meet Monsieur Billaud when he arrives."

"Monsieur Billaud. I love the way you say it—with such . . . Frenchness."

Sophia laughed again. "I was educated in Paris for three years."

"Oh, Sophia, I envy you. And you truly speak French?"

"*Mais oui,* Lily. And German, too."

"So if he doesn't speak English, you could translate."

"Yes, I could, but I'm sure he will speak wonderful English. Now I've got to go and dress for tea. I'll see you downstairs."

Sophia left her sister-in-law to her daydreams and felt a pang of painful longing for her own childhood dreams, and for the childhood joys James had never known.

* * *

When the guests began to arrive for the annual Wentworth shooting party, Sophia began to feel a renewed sense of purpose. There were people coming to stay, people from all over England, some from as far as Wales, and she was determined to make them all feel at home like never before at Wentworth Castle. It was time for some good old-fashioned American hospitality.

One of the first guests to arrive was Lord Whitby, who stepped out of his coach with an exaggerated, sweeping bow. "Duke! Duchess!"

Sophia waved from the top of the steps.

"You invited Whitby?" James asked dryly.

"Of course."

James nodded, then he stuck out his hand to greet Lord Whitby. "Good of you to come."

Sophia sensed the tension between the two men. She had hoped they would have put aside their differences by now.

"I wouldn't miss it for the world," Whitby said. He turned his attention toward Sophia and kissed her hand. "You look as radiant as ever, madam."

She felt a flash memory of the excitement during the all-too-brief London Season—the parties, the balls, the anticipation, and the glitter. It seemed like a long-ago dream to her now as she stood on these cold, stone steps with her heavy woolen shawl around her. She'd given up carrying her colorful, lacy parasols ages ago. The servants would probably have laughed her off the premises.

"You know you can call me Sophia," she replied, feeling the weight of James's gaze upon her.

She and James escorted Edward into the front hall, where a footman showed him upstairs.

The moment he was out of sight, James spoke softly. "You didn't put him in the Van Dekker Room, did you?"

"Yes, it's where he stayed last year."

"But last year, your rooms were occupied by my mother." There was a hard edge to his voice.

"What are you getting at, James?"

"Nothing." Then he left her alone in the hall and climbed the stairs to his study.

James sat down to a pile of letters on his desk, wanting to get through all of them before dinner. The first one had come from his aunt Caroline in Exeter. He broke the seal and read the long and involved description of what debauchery Martin had been up to, and how she could no longer see fit to have him in her home. Along with the letter was a bill for an enormous debt Martin had incurred at a local tavern, which naturally, she was refusing to pay.

James leaned back in his chair and rubbed his throbbing temples. Martin was on his way home, the note said, which meant James would have to deal with this and exact some kind of discipline.

Bloody hell, Martin.

Another coach pulled up outside, and James glanced out the window. He watched the Weatherbees get out and saw Sophia go to greet them. Thank God, because he didn't think he'd be able to welcome anyone at that minute, when his blood was boiling in his veins.

What did he know about discipline? He certainly wasn't going to beat Martin to a pulp or lock him in a trunk, so where did that leave him? He'd already tried talking to Martin when he was in London, and that had done little good. He'd sent him away to Exeter as punishment for getting suspended, but the lad continued to act irresponsibly, even under the watchful eye of his aunt, who was as stiff and dutiful as her sister—James's own mother.

James laid the letter aside and went through the rest of his correspondence, hoping fresh wisdom would somehow descend upon him before Martin arrived. He was not looking forward to it, for he had distanced himself from his younger brother for most of his life and had no idea what to say to him.

He was almost through all his letters when a knock sounded at his door, and Sophia entered. "May I have a word with you, James?"

"Of course." He gestured for her to sit down. "The guests are settling in?"

"Yes, but I wanted to tell you about the cook. Mr. Becon slipped on a cabbage leaf and bumped his head. I've sent for the doctor, but Mr. Becon said that with all the work to do before this evening, your mother would not approve, but I assured him that *you* would agree with me about his seeing the doctor."

James laced his fingers together. "You were right to call the doctor. Of course, I agree."

Her shoulders rose and fell as if she were relieved, and the fact that he could support her in this way brought him a small measure of gratification, which he greatly needed at the moment.

"Thank you. I'll leave you now." She stood up to go, but stopped. "Is there something wrong, James? You look troubled."

James gazed up at his wife, wondering what he'd

said or done to give himself away. He swiveled in his chair and handed the letter about Martin to Sophia. She read it quickly, then gave it back to him. "What will you do?"

"I'm not sure. I'm at a loss, I'm afraid."

She sat down again. "Is this the first time anything like this has happened?"

"I wish it was. Martin was suspended from Eton twice, and both times, I've sent him to his aunt's, hoping she would have a positive influence on him. Obviously, I was a little too hopeful."

"I see."

James stood and paced the room. "I cannot ask myself what my father would have done, for my father's methods will not do, but nothing I have tried so far has made any difference."

"What have you tried?"

"I've sent him to people and places I felt would help him mature."

"Have you considered keeping him here for a while?"

James stopped pacing. "I don't suppose I'll have much choice. I'm running out of options."

"This might be the best place for him, with a family who loves him."

There was that word again.

"If he is unhappy about something," she continued, "we can find out why, or perhaps we'll discover that he is simply at that age."

"Boys will be boys, you think."

She shrugged. "Perhaps. But if it's something more, having him close to us will help us see what it is."

Sophia rose from her chair. James was amazed to

feel the tension draining out of him where he stood.

She moved toward him and kissed him on the cheek. "I'll see you in the drawing room before dinner."

Then she left him behind to contemplate just how much—if he let himself—he could depend upon his wife.

"Remember," Lily said to Sophia when the dressing bell rang, "that when everyone lines up to go into the dining room, you must take your place near the front. Mother will go with James in front of you."

"I thought I outranked your mother."

"You do, but James is the highest-ranking man, and he is required to be matched with the highest-ranking woman who is not his wife, and that would be Mother."

"There's so much to remember."

"You'll do fine. You will walk with the Marquess of Weldon, and behind you will walk Lady Weldon with the Earl of Manderlin, then I will follow with Lord Whitby. I once had a crush on him, you know."

Sophia stopped midstride between the bed and her desk. "Really? Lord Whitby?"

"Yes," Lily replied with a blushing grin. "He and James have been friends for years. I first saw him in London when I was very young, and I thought he was the most dashing young man I had ever seen. He and James were always off somewhere, causing trouble."

"Trouble?" Sophia asked, thinking of Martin's recent behavior.

"They spent a lot of time in the gambling halls, and Mother was always furious with them. They've matured, though," she said with a smile, "as I have. But oh, there was a time I did fancy myself very much in love with Lord Whitby. Perhaps it was the rebel in him—and the fact that Mother didn't like him."

Sophia watched her sister-in-law rearrange some tiny cat statues around on the mantel, and wondered how Lily was such a romantic when her brother and mother were so drastically the opposite.

Sophia returned to the subject of the formal dinner. "I hope I don't do anything wrong tonight. Thank you for helping me with the seating arrangements."

"You're very welcome. Now I must go and dress. I'll see you in the drawing room."

Sophia summoned Alberta, her new maid, but before Alberta arrived, another coach pulled up in front of the house. Sophia went to the window. Two gentlemen stepped out, so she hurried down to greet them, for she recognized the older man as Lord Manderlin.

She was descending the stairs just as they entered the front hall. "Good evening, Lord Manderlin, and welcome."

"Duchess, it is a pleasure to see you again." He bowed, and it was as if his awkward proposal had never occurred. Lord Manderlin turned to introduce the gentleman behind him. "May I present to you, Pierre Billaud."

Monsieur Billaud moved forward, and Sophia stared unblinking at his handsome face. His eyes were dark, his hair and mustache even darker, and he had the look of a flirt.

He bowed his head and spoke with a thick French accent. "I am honored, Your Grace."

She held out her hand and he kissed it. *"Merci, Mon-*

sieur Billaud. J'espere que votre voyage au Chateau de Wentworth sera très agrèable."

"Why, your French is excellent. I am certain I will enjoy my stay verv much, *merci.* I hope I will not be intruding upon your . . . how do you say? . . . hospitality."

"Don't be silly. The more, the merrier."

"The more the merrier," Pierre repeated. "That must be an American expression. It is charming. *You* are charming, Your Grace."

Sophia noticed Lord Manderlin stiffen at Pierre's candid flattery, but it didn't faze her. She grew up in Wisconsin, where the local blacksmith flirted goodnaturedly with little girls and elderly women more than he flirted with his own wife.

She instructed the footman to show the gentlemen to their rooms, then went quickly to her own room to dress for dinner.

Wearing a dark crimson gown and a parure of matching rubies, Sophia entered the gilded drawing room. All the guests were assembled and conversing with one another; James was at the far end of the room, her mother-in-law was standing by the marble fireplace talking to Lord Manderlin, and Sophia felt a rush of nervousness overcome her.

She reminded herself of something Florence once told her—that American manners amused the Marlborough House Set, so she set out to be amusing.

She moved into the room and greeted Lord Whitby.

"Duchess, you look ravishing this evening." He reached for her gloved hand to place a kiss upon her knuckles.

"Thank you, Edward. I hope you have settled in comfortably."

"I have indeed. And yourself?"

"Me?" she replied with a laugh. "You forget that I live here."

"But you haven't lived here very long. No disappointments, I hope. No bouts of homesickness."

"Of course not," she answered smoothly. "I'm very happy here."

He regarded her quizzically for a moment. "Yes, I'm sure you are. James is a good man, and no doubt he has done everything in his power to ensure your happiness. See to all your needs."

A footman with a tray of champagne passed by, and feeling slightly knocked off-balance, Sophia seized the opportunity to reach for a glass and change the subject. They moved on to safer topics about the weather and the dinner menu.

A few minutes later, Pierre Billaud strolled in and stood in the doorway, assessing the crowd. Realizing he would be acquainted with no one, and happy to have a reason to excuse herself from Lord Whitby, Sophia went to lead Monsieur Billaud in and begin the introductions.

They made their way around the room. They finally reached Marion, who raised her spectacles to garner a better look at the handsome young Frenchman. With one glare at Sophia, she revealed her disapproval that someone new had been invited without her knowledge.

"Marion, may I present to you one of our guests, Pierre Billaud. He is visiting us from Paris."

Marion accidentally dropped her spectacles. Sophia

continued the introduction: "Monsieur Billaud, this is the Dowager Duchess of Wentworth."

Marion was silent, then she grew pale and, without warning, collapsed in a heap of skirts and petticoats at Sophia's feet.

Chapter 20

James tried to bring his mother around by fanning her with a dinner menu, but it was the smelling salts that did it. Three vials appeared instantly under her nose from three nearby ladies.

Sophia knelt on the other side of his mother, and their guests stood over them with concerned expressions, whispering to each other.

"It's the heat," Marion explained as she started awake, her cheeks flushing with mortification. "Tell the footman to put out the fire!"

James raised a finger at a footman. The next instant, the coals were hissing with smoke and steam.

"Are you all right, Mother?" James asked, helping her sit up.

She touched her cheek with a trembling hand. "I think I would like to go to my rooms."

"I'll take her," James said to Sophia, as they helped her to her feet. "You stay and see to the guests."

They moved slowly toward the door, his mother leaning heavily upon him. "I hope you're not ill," he said.

"I'm fine."

As they turned toward the stairs, James glanced back into the drawing room and noticed Sophia speaking with a stranger. "Who is that man? The one with the dark hair and mustache?"

"I don't know," the dowager replied breathlessly. "He's French. Someone your wife invited. Perhaps she met him when she went to Paris for her trousseau."

James glanced back at them again and felt a knot form in his stomach.

His mother continued. "You of all people should know how she always introduces herself, and now she's invited strangers to our house, James. It is time you spoke to her and prevailed upon her that her American ways will not do here. She is a duchess now, and she still goes around doing as she pleases, causing all kinds of problems you could not even begin to guess at. She doesn't understand the significance of her rank or the importance of our traditions. You need to take a firmer hand with her."

"Mother—"

She sighed. "Consider what your father would have done. He would never have permitted the situation to get so out of hand. I cannot imagine what would have occurred if I had taken the liberties Sophia has taken."

James gazed icily at her. "May I remind you that I am not my father, nor do I ever wish to be. And you are no longer mistress of this house. Sophia is mistress now. She is my duchess, and *I* will be the one to decide what courses to take with her."

The dowager hobbled weakly down the hall beside

him. "You have not changed, James. You still do everything you can to hurt me, don't you?"

"Mother," he said, stopping in the corridor, "Sophia has provided us all with a future, and I am not just referring to her father's generous marriage settlement. She has entered into our family with high hopes and a kind heart, and the desire to do the very best she can, and I will no longer allow you to make what is already a difficult transition for her a harder one. Do you understand me?"

His mother glared at him with incredulity, then gathered her skirts and stormed off down the hall. James stood in silence, feeling acutely satisfied that he had spoken so candidly and truthfully to a woman whom he had rarely in his life spoken to at all.

He felt strangely connected to Sophia at that moment, as if they were on the same side together. As if they were a new contingent in this dark, cursed house.

Surprised by his change of heart, James backed up a few steps, then started toward the stairs. As he descended, he found himself staring through the open doors of the drawing room below, searching for Sophia. Wanting to see her face.

He spotted her. Smiling brightly, she was conversing with Whitby, then she turned to speak to the French gentleman.

James could not deny the discomfort he felt at seeing her speak to a man who had sent her three dozen red roses a few short months ago, a man who had been openly pursuing her with the goal of marriage. Then another man whom James himself knew nothing about.

She was glowing with cheerfulness and vitality as she always did when she spoke to people. Just like she had glowed for him when they'd first danced in that London ballroom. It was that very charm that had turned his head and sucked him in.

He reached the bottom step and walked toward the gathering. The image of her with the stranger—from France, of all places—brought a frown to James's face, for he did not like being shut out or kept uninformed of things that pertained to his household or his wife.

Even more than that, he didn't like the sharp, irritating—and irrational—sting of jealousy that was prickling at him now.

Marion passed through her bedchamber door and slammed it behind her. "Eve, I want tea. Go and see to it," she said to her maid.

The woman hurried from the room.

Marion moved quickly to a chair, her hands still trembling from shock. Genevieve had sent Pierre *here*! How could she have done such a horrible, horrible thing after she'd been paid the sum she'd requested, and Marion had assured her there would indeed be more installments. Had Genevieve decided that money would not satisfy her need for vengeance? Would she attempt to take the dukedom as well?

Marion covered her face with her hands and contemplated what to do. Should she tell James?

No, she couldn't possibly. If he knew, he would be furious with her for keeping the truth from him all his life. He might even allow the secret to get out, for he had never been one to care about scandals or what others thought of him.

Knowing how he felt about his ancestors, Marion couldn't even be sure he would defend his peerage. He might simply say good-bye to it and sail off into the sunset with his rich, new American upstart wife.

And leave me to cope with the aftermath.

That night, after all the guests had retired to their rooms, James picked up a candelabra and ventured into the hall. A strange and unfamiliar apprehension curled in his stomach, and though he had spent most of his life keeping emotions at bay, he recognized the cause of it. He was on his way to his wife's bedchamber this evening, not to produce an heir, not even to satisfy his own lustful hunger for her, but to reassure himself that she belonged to him and no other.

He found her door and entered. Sophia was already in bed with the lamps out, and his appearance must have startled her. She sat up and hugged the covers to her chest. "James, what are you doing here?"

"Can't a husband visit his wife when he feels the urge?"

She was quiet a moment. "Of course. Please come in. I . . . I didn't expect to see you tonight."

She didn't expect it, he thought, because this was the first time he had come to her two nights in a row. She had, like him, embraced the idea that their lovemaking was about duty and duty alone.

Good God. A week ago, he had believed that wholeheartedly, or at least he had believed that he was capable of *ensuring* it was based on duty. Now, he wasn't quite so confident in that assumption. Somewhere between saying "I do" and watching Sophia talk to Whitby and that Frenchman tonight, his feelings had begun to change.

He moved fully into the room and set down the candles. "May I join you?"

She seemed almost confused by the request as she turned the covers back for him. James removed his robe and slipped into the cool sheets beside her. "You were an excellent hostess tonight."

"Thanks to Lily. She's been wonderful, James, helping me with the rules of precedence and so much more."

James lay on his side with his cheek resting on his hand, facing Sophia. "I'm glad she's been a friend to you."

"So am I. And she's been confiding in me, James. I feel like we share a bond. I could not have hoped for a finer sister-in-law."

He smoothed a lock of hair away from her face. "I'm glad." *Glad that someone has been kind to you, when I have been absent.*

"Do you know," Sophia said, "that Lily told me she once fancied Lord Whitby?"

James felt his brow furrow. "Whitby? Certainly not."

James had known Whitby forever, and consequently, he had seen the earl at his worst. James was right alongside him for most of it, of course, but still, the memories lingered and it was hard to imagine Whitby being good for any woman, let alone James's younger sister.

"She told me it was a girlish crush," Sophia continued, "and that when the two of you were at school together, she thought his rebellious ways were rather exciting."

"Now *that* doesn't surprise me," James said, amused. "Lily is a romantic, and I am now certain that she has inherited her father's horrifically wild side."

Sophia laughed. "How wild, exactly?"

James shrugged. A month ago, he would have avoided answering such a question. He would never have brought up the subject of his father in the first place, but Sophia already knew a part of what she had married into, and she had not, thank God, fled back to America. "My father married late, well into his thirties, so he had a number of years to adopt a rather scandalous manner of existence."

Curiosity gleamed on Sophia's face, so James continued. "He gambled and drank and frequented the worst establishments imaginable, and when my grandfather couldn't stand to watch him behave in such ways, he sent him abroad to France to live with an old army companion. A man who was no doubt equally as strict as he. My father later returned to England and married my mother, and at least for a little while kept up appearances."

"Lily told me he had a mistress."

"Many, no doubt, but the one he kept the longest was from Paris—a woman he met there."

The candles flickered in the night, and James admired Sophia's creamy complexion as she lowered her gaze to her hands on her lap.

"Speaking of Paris," James said, "who is Pierre Billaud? Is he someone you met while you were there?"

Sophia's gaze shot to his face. "Someone *I* met? Good heavens, no. He is here with Lord Manderlin, who wrote to me a week ago to ask if he could bring a guest. Apparently, Monsieur Billaud is renting a cottage from him, and he's here to travel and see England."

"So you've only just met him?"

"Yes, today. Why? Did you really think he was a friend of mine?"

James realized at that uncomfortable moment how

irrational he had been, jumping to conclusions, giving in to a ridiculous jealousy which had no foundation in reality. Surely his wife must be thinking the same thing. "I didn't know one way or the other."

Sophia reached up to stroke his cheek. "Well, now you do, so you can forget about it and think of something else. Something more immediate, like making love to your devoted wife."

The melody in her voice—it reminded him of their honeymoon, when he had permitted himself simply to adore her, and she had reveled in that adoration.

She had been different since then. So had he. *Everything* had been different.

She inched down and wiggled her bottom while she pulled her nightdress off over her head. All at once, James was gazing down at his wife's full breasts in the candlelight, her nipples already firm and waiting to be touched. She raised her arms and placed them behind her head. He was very thankful that she was indeed *devoted.*

With the thought of making love to her, his mouth lifted in a smile. "You realize I'll be staying tonight."

"Good, because I was going to tie you up if you tried to leave."

He smiled again. The time for talking was over. The need to have her became powerful beyond belief. He could not have fought it if he'd wanted to, for he was overcome by a carnal, ferocious compulsion to possess her. In every imaginable way.

He pulled her into his arms and covered her mouth with his, feeling his blood race through his veins as his tongue mingled with hers. His instantaneous erection pressed against her warm, fleshy thigh, and as he stroked her belly with his hands and teased her nipples with his tongue, he contended with emotions and susceptibilities he would have preferred did not exist—like the desire to make love to Sophia for the sheer purpose of proving that she was his, and that she would remain his forever.

Forever.

It was frightening.

All of it.

Because it was exactly the thing he had been carefully avoiding all his life. Uncontrollable, unmanageable passion.

He rolled on top of Sophia, and felt her arms and legs wrap around him and pull him as close as humanly possible. Then he entered her and felt a monstrous surge of heat and pleasure move through his body, rushing through his soul. He had never in his adult life felt so hellishly, inconceivably vulnerable.

For Sophia, the following few days were the happiest since she and James had arrived at Wentworth Castle. The guests had brought laughter and conversation to the dinner table; for once she was not embarrassed to wear her Worth gowns and her jewels. Above all, James had been remarkably attentive, coming to her room each night and staying until dawn. It was as if his cruel withdrawal was a thing of the past, and he had settled in to the idea of having her in his life, accepting the fact that he was a married man now, and he was willing to open himself up to at least an outward appearance of intimacy.

Even his lovemaking had changed. He smiled and laughed like he had on their honeymoon. He talked to her about Martin and Lily and changes he wanted to make in the running of the estate. She and James amused themselves in bed at night over all the little foibles during the party, how Lady Fenwick had gotten her heel stuck in a crack under the front portico, and how the dowager had tried to pull her free. The two ladies had grunted and groaned, each of them mortified beyond words, then immediately afterward, tried to pretend it didn't happen. James and Sophia laughed so hard over it, he had fallen off the bed.

Of course, James had never told her he loved her, nor had she spoken the words to him since he'd returned from his trip to London, for somehow she sensed that he was not ready for that. But with all the changes in the past few days, she began to feel that there was hope for such sentiments in the future. That alone gave her the strength to push on with a smile.

She wondered if he realized how different he was. If he would ever mention it, or acknowledge it. Perhaps he would one day.

For James, the shooting party was fast becoming the best one on record, for there had been a certain relaxed feel to the celebrations. Thanks to Sophia, there was a conspicuous lack of high-browed, tight-laced expectations—the kind his mother had always so carefully communicated in the past—and James was enjoying himself tremendously.

Like a breeze of fresh air, Sophia, his duchess, had released the tensions of previous years. She'd hired an American accordion player whom she accompanied on the piano while the two of them played lively little ditties in the evenings (his mother had winced at every one of them). Sophia arranged games like Clap In, Clap

Out and Blind Man's Bluff, which—after a few glasses of wine—had everyone laughing uproariously by midnight. He could not remember a time in his life when he had laughed as often and as outrageously as he had this week.

One particular afternoon, he and the other gentlemen were out with the guns, and Whitby moved to stand beside James. James and Whitby had avoided each other for most of the party, speaking casually whenever necessary, both of them recognizing the fact that their friendship had been maimed. The last time any honest words were spoken between them, Whitby had expressed his outrage at James for proposing to Sophia, and James had simply walked away. Afterward, he had put it behind him, as he did with so many other unpleasant things in his life.

Whitby aimed his rifle and pulled the trigger. The shot rang out, and one of the lower birds in the flock fell from the sky.

"Good shot," James said.

"Not as impressive as that last one of yours, but you always did aim high."

James felt his shoulders tense. He reloaded his rifle.

"So how is married life?" Whitby asked. "Everything you thought it would be?"

"Everything and more. Sophia is a fine duchess."

Whitby aimed and fired again. "I never doubted it." He lowered his gun and looked at James. "She's certainly made some drastic changes around here."

James merely nodded.

"I can't imagine your mother is taking it well."

"Mother is taking it in stride." *God, this is awkward.*

"Well, she couldn't argue that Sophia has neglected

any details in planning this shooting event. The sheer volume of food devoured this week has been matchless, James. The shrimp soup was fantastic. Your wife has a talent in that regard, to be sure. She's an excellent hostess."

Whitby reloaded while James waited for the beaters to send out another flock.

"Who is the Frenchman, by the way? He's been here for all the dinners, but never stays for cigars. Is he a friend of Sophia's?"

"No, he's *Manderlin's* guest," James emphasized. "Billaud is renting a cottage from him."

"I see." Another flock flew across the sky. Both James and Whitby aimed and fired. "Kind of a strange fellow," Whitby said. "Doesn't talk much, only to the ladies. Not into shooting, I take it?"

"I presume not, or he'd be here, wouldn't he?"

They were quiet for a few minutes, each concentrating on their shots, then Whitby lowered his gun. "Look, James, we've been friends a long time, and I feel I should apologize for making presumptions about certain things. Everything turned out the way it was meant to, and I would like to forget about it if you're willing."

James gazed down at the brown grass. He had not expected this today. Nor had he let himself admit how wretched he had felt over his estrangement from his oldest friend.

With a deep sigh, James faced Whitby. He held out his hand and they shook on it. "Of course I'm willing. And I'm sorry, too, my friend. I hope you weren't . . . hurt by any of it."

"Hurt? Me? God, no. The Marriage Mart is nothing but a cutthroat competition, especially when heiresses are involved. My pride was a little dented, that's all."

James smiled. "I'm glad to hear it."

Another flock went up, and they both aimed and fired.

As they reloaded, Whitby nudged James. "I haven't given up, you know. There's always next Season. No doubt, another steamshipful of American beauties will be making the crossing as soon as the weather turns."

With a smile, James looked at his friend. "And you'll be there to greet the ship of gold?"

Whitby raised a cunning eyebrow. "Naturally. True love awaits me, just over the blue horizon I believe. Or at least I can always hope."

Two guests arrived late for the final two days of shooting, so Sophia stole a moment to return to her boudoir and consider the new seating arrangement for dinner. She sat down with her leather pad, which had slots cut into it for the insertion of name cards showing who would sit where, but when Sophia came to the new guests, she wasn't absolutely certain where they should be. She suddenly had the worst fear that she would turn the whole table into a fiasco, and some pompous peer would scream bloody murder.

She needed *Debrett's Peerage,* which assigned a number for each peer and his family members. Unfortunately, Marion preferred to keep it in her room, since like everything else, it had belonged to her first.

Sophia left her room and went to the dowager's boudoir. She was about to knock on the door when she heard a gut-wrenching sob. She put her ear close to the door and listened. She heard it again, another sob from inside, and she knew that it was Marion who was crying.

Sophia harked for a moment, thinking she shouldn't intrude, but when she heard another sob, a pang of sympathy for the woman tugged at her belly, even though she hated the fact that she felt it. Sophia couldn't help but knock on the door.

There was a brief silence. "Yes? Who is it?"

Sophia didn't bother to answer, because she knew Marion would only tell her to go away. Instead, she gently pushed open the door and peaked inside. "It's me. Sophia. Are you all right, Marion?"

The dowager dabbed at her eyes and sat upright in her chair. "Of course I am. I did *not* say you could enter."

Sophia stood in the doorway. "I heard you crying. Can I do anything for you?"

"No, all you can do is leave. I want to be alone."

Swallowing over the desire to do the simple thing— to do as she was told and walk out—Sophia instead lingered. Then she remembered why she had come. She stepped more fully into the room. "I came to borrow *Debrett's Peerage* again. I need to change the seating at dinner."

"Why? Is someone leaving?" She sounded overly hopeful. Perhaps she was tired of the noise and wanted her house back.

"No, Lord Witfield arrived this afternoon with his wife."

Marion cleared her throat, taking a moment to collect herself, then she slowly rose from her chair to go and retrieve the book from her desk. She handed it to Sophia, without any of her usual criticisms or carping. Her eyes were red and swollen.

"Marion," Sophia said softly, "please tell me what's wrong. Maybe I can help."

The dowager's lips pursed. "There is nothing wrong. Certainly nothing *you* would understand. So please leave."

Sophia held firm. "I can't. Not knowing that you are suffering."

The dowager seemed to flinch at Sophia's declaration, then turned away and walked to the window. "I don't wish to talk about it."

Why was she so cold to everyone, Sophia wondered, when a little warmth might open up a world of happiness for her? Sophia supposed Marion had never been taught how to convey warmth toward another human being, and had never in her life been on the receiving end of it. She would therefore, not know what she was missing.

Sophia moved closer. "You can trust me, you know. Whatever you tell me won't go beyond these four walls."

"I have nothing to tell."

"Marion, I can see plainly that that's not true."

The dowager remained at the window. "Why must you be so bold, Sophia? It is not becoming of a duchess."

"In my heart, I am your daughter-in-law first and foremost," Sophia said. "I am a duchess second. As your daughter-in-law, I want to help you."

Marion was quiet, then at last she turned. The hard lines of her face were completely contorted; she was on the verge of another sob.

Sophia took an anxious step forward. "What is it, Marion? What could possibly be so bad? Please tell me, and I promise I will keep it between us. It might do you good to let it out."

The unthinkable happened. Marion dropped her face into her hands and wept, as she walked unsteadily into Sophia's arms.

All the world seemed to shift under Sophia's feet as she hugged her mother-in-law, felt the wracking sobs shake her. Sophia rubbed Marion's back and whispered soothing things.

After a moment, Marion calmed and backed away. She kept her eyes downcast, as if she were ashamed of her emotions, and blew her nose into a handkerchief. "I do apologize. I don't know what came over me."

"There's nothing to apologize for, Marion. Something has upset you. What is it?"

Eyes still downcast, she shook her head, refusing to say. Sophia took her hand, led her to the bed, and sat down beside her. "Obviously, there is no one here you can talk to. Please let me be the one. I can help. I know I can."

"How can you possibly help?" she said weakly. "I have kept a secret, and I cannot reveal it. To anyone."

"But you must, for your own peace of mind. You must have *someone* on your side. You must have at least one true friend in your life, someone you feel you can trust, even if all they ever do is provide a sympathetic ear."

Marion again shook her head at Sophia, as if she couldn't believe any of what she was saying.

"Is there no one you trust?"

Marion stood up and walked away again. Sophia supposed it was her habit to walk away, to avoid intimacy—a lifetime habit, hard to break.

Sophia sat on the bed, waiting patiently for Marion's reply. The dowager paced the room for a moment or two, then finally returned to sit on the edge of the bed. "There is something that no one knows, not even James."

Sophia swallowed nervously.

"He is not the true heir to this dukedom."

Chapter 21

Sophia's stomach coiled nauseatingly. She had expected something trivial, like an embarrassing error in protocol during the shooting party, or a minor scandal. Perhaps one of the guests had been carrying on an improper affair with another guest. But this. . . .

"Are you sure?"

"Yes. There is a secret in our past, and I've spent all my life fighting to keep it from the world."

"What is it?"

Marion bowed her head. "It was all because of my husband, Henry. It's *his* fault this has happened. *His* fault we are all in dire straits." She met Sophia's gaze. "I was not his first wife."

Sophia tried to contemplate what this meant. "You mean he had a child from his first marriage?"

"Yes. A son. But he didn't know that when he divorced her. He'd gone to live in France when he was a younger man, and he married Genevieve, a woman no one would have approved of. She was an actress, and she performed in one of those vulgar penny gaffs. Knowing Henry, he probably married her just to spite his own father, for believe me, that man was no saint."

Sophia squeezed Marion's hand and rubbed the back of it.

"Anyway, Henry never told her that he was a duke, nor did he tell anyone from England that he had become a husband. He all but changed his identity and lived another life. He married Genevieve in Paris, where they lived in a horrid place in the worst part of the city, but when he found out he'd inherited his title, he divorced her and returned to London, and married me rather quickly. I don't think Genevieve was sorry to see him go, for she never told him about the son. It was years later that she discovered who he was, but by that time she was running a brothel and he, of course, didn't wish to bring that kind of scandal back home, where his respectable English son was being groomed to inherit. So he began an affair with her. That's where all of our money went, to keep her quiet."

Marion began to weep again. "After Henry died, I didn't hear from her, but she wrote to me not long ago, insisting that I continue to support her financially, or she would reveal her son to the world. And I just received this telegram, asking for more by the end of the week."

"But that's blackmail," Sophia said, taking the telegram from Marion and reading it for herself.

"Call it what you want, but paying her what she asks for is the only way I can keep James from losing everything. Oh, I wish she would just disappear!"

Sophia squeezed Marion's hand again. "Are you sure you shouldn't tell James about this? He might be able to do something. Perhaps there's a way. Maybe their marriage wasn't legal. You say she didn't know Henry was a duke. Did he use a false name? Because that could render the marriage contract void."

"He used his family name. I've seen the marriage certificate. I looked into it years ago. They *were* legally married."

"But why wouldn't she just come and claim her son's birthright? Why insist you pay her? It sounds suspicious to me."

"She's always known the estate was not profitable. She wouldn't want this kind of life in the country. She only wants money or jewels, so she can have the kinds of luxuries she enjoys and continue to operate as a . . . a businesswoman."

Sophia shook her head. "You really should tell James."

"No. I've worked all my life to protect him from this filth, and I will not see him lose what belongs to him. He has a certain sense of justice, and I fear he might . . ." She didn't finish.

"You fear he might give the dukedom to his half brother?"

"He might."

Sophia stood up and began to pace the room. "But it would at least be his choice."

Marion sucked in a breath. "You promised you would keep this between us, Sophia."

Good God, she *had* promised. "Yes, I know, but—"

Marion rose and approached her. "You promised, Sophia. I would never have told you any of this if you hadn't convinced me that I could trust you."

What was she to do? Keep this secret from her husband in order to win the approval of her mother-in-law, who had never been anything but hateful toward her up until now? What if James found out?

But perhaps this was why Marion had been so hateful all her life—because she had no one to confide in, no one to trust. How could anyone be anything but hateful without ever knowing love in her life?

Sophia smoothed her hands over her skirts, not knowing what to do. With pleading, vulnerable eyes, Marion watched her and waited.

Debrett's Peerage sat on the desk. Sophia's duties as hostess were waiting.

She went to Marion and held her hands. "I will keep your secret for now, but I will also try to help somehow." Perhaps, once Sophia proved to Marion that it was better to trust people than to shut them out, Marion might decide to trust James, too. Sophia would work on that . . . getting Marion to tell James. "You were right to have told me."

The rueful desperation in Marion's eyes dimmed slightly. She leaned in to hug Sophia, who tried not to gasp at the surprising, unexpected gesture from this cold, unfeeling woman.

Marion stepped back. "There is one thing more."

One thing more? What else could there possibly be after the last shocking deluge?

"The brother that James doesn't know about . . . His name is Pierre. He's Pierre Billaud."

After tea, the guests took an evening stroll in the gardens, then retired to their chambers to dress for dinner. Sophia was a little late getting back to her rooms, as she had to converse with the cook about the turtle soup and remind him that four of the guests that evening were strongly averse to onions. All this, while her mind was still reeling over what Marion had told her. Pierre Billaud was James's half brother?

She recalled all the times they had conversed over the past few days. He had done nothing to suggest he was visiting with some ulterior motive in mind. He appeared to be what he said he was—a visitor from France, nothing more. He had not even spoken to Marion about his identity. There had been no threats from him, no devious looks. There had only been the telegram from Madame La Roux, demanding another payment.

Why was Pierre here? Simply to put pressure on Marion? Or was he here to look over the estate he hoped to inherit?

Entering her room at last and closing the door behind her, she began to unbutton her bodice. How was she ever going to convince Marion to trust James and tell him about the blackmail?

She was about to summon Alberta to help her get dressed, when a voice caught her off guard and caused her to jump. She whirled around to look at the bed.

"Is there time?" James asked, a wicked grin lifting the corner of his mouth. Shirtless, he was lying on top of the coverlet, looking relaxed, with one long leg crossed over the other. He was still wearing his riding breeches and boots.

Absorbing the meaning of his enticing proposal, Sophia let out a breath and teasingly sauntered away from him to stand in front of the mirror, continuing to unbutton her bodice. "Time for what?" she asked, pretending to sound innocent. Pretending that there was nothing on her mind beyond what was happening in this room at this moment.

With an engaging smile, eyes alert, he swung his legs off the bed and stood. "Time to have dessert *before* we go down to dinner."

She gazed at him in the mirror's reflection while she removed an earring. Sounding completely serious, she said, "I didn't realize you liked raspberry custard so much. I suppose I could have one of the maids bring up a couple of servings."

James's intense gaze became voracious. "Creamy custard in a cup wasn't what I had in mind. I was thinking of quite another flavor." His voice dropped to a husky whisper. "I've been thinking of you all day, Sophia. I was a lousy shot this morning because of it, and that dress you wore at luncheon—"

"The green one . . ."

"Yes, the green one. I wanted to pull you under one of the tables and find out what color stockings you were wearing beneath it."

Sophia faced him as a flash of beautiful, warm light exploded inside her heart. It was the first time since their honeymoon he had admitted that he was the least bit out of control where she was concerned—where anything was concerned—and she felt suddenly buoyant. The worries in her mind began to recede as they were replaced with a fresh, honeyed lust. "I've been wanting you, too."

They were both quiet, staring at one another in the dim evening light that poured in through the lace curtains. James smiled, and Sophia thought of the smooth way he had worked his hands over her the night before, how he had brought her so much pleasure, she had wanted to cry out loud with happiness. She felt a tingling in her nether regions . . . a fierce, womanly need.

He took a single step forward.

"My maid will be here soon," she said.

He paused and considered that, then walked to the door and locked it.

"We'll be late for dinner," she added.

He slowly crossed the room toward her and touched her lips with the tip of his finger. "But we'll work up a superb appetite."

Sophia swallowed over the wildly hot thrill rising up within her.

Scooping her up into his arms, James carried her to the bed. Sophia didn't even try to resist or argue. All she wanted was to feel his damp skin next to hers and look upon his beautiful nakedness in the fading daylight. She sat on the edge of the bed and shamelessly began to unbutton his trousers where his erection was bulging and waiting to be freed. Within seconds, he was out of his boots and the rest of his clothes, and she was gazing up at his magnificent nude physique with longing.

He gently pushed her back onto the bed, and she could never have fathomed the wicked pleasure of feeling a man's naked body upon her own in the full light of day, while she herself was still completely clothed.

Not for long, however. James began to unbutton her bodice, then unhooked her corset in front. Soon he was stroking her breasts, kissing them, tasting them until she became obsessed with blazing desire. The rest of her clothing came off in a hurry, and her body began to throb with a deep, potent, powerful longing.

Within minutes, James was inside her with a swift, satisfying thrust that shook her.

His lips found hers and she drank in the exquisite taste of him, the feel of his tongue sweeping into her mouth. Orgasmic response came quickly, after two or three deep thrusts and withdrawals, and her climax shivered through her. He matched hers with his own, then whispered her name, "Sophia."

She heard affection in his voice, and as her body returned to its normal rhythm, a quivering of guilt found its way into her blissful state of being.

She was keeping something from her husband, something dreadful, when she didn't want to keep anything from him at all. She wanted his complete trust and love, and she wanted to trust and love him openly in return.

But she had promised Marion, and she felt she was close to bridging the gap between them. She couldn't possibly betray her now.

Why had this happened, when she and James were finally moving forward?

Sophia hugged him close. She needed time. Time to comprehend what all this meant, and how she could best serve this family.

In the drawing room where the guests were gathered before dinner, Sophia mingled through the crowd toward Pierre. Marion hadn't known why he was here, for he hadn't revealed himself to her or made any demands, nor had he told anyone that he had any previous connection with this family. Pierre simply attended the luncheons and dinners, made light conversation with the other guests, and took long leisurely walks alone while the men were out with the guns.

"Monsieur Billaud, how are you enjoying England now that you've had a few days to explore it?" she asked when she reached him.

"Very well, Your Grace," he replied in his thick French accent.

He was a handsome man, but there was little resemblance to James.

Except for his dark coloring, which was exactly the same. *But how many men have dark hair?* she wondered. Almost half the population, surely.

Lily approached and gave a dazzling smile. "Monsieur Billaud, you didn't stay for the entertainments last evening. You must stay tonight. Musicians from London arrived this afternoon, and I do believe there will be dancing. Isn't that right, Sophia?"

"Yes, we've opened the smaller ballroom in the east wing."

Pierre raised his eyebrows. "Dancing, you say? Well, I suppose I shall have to attend, with the promise that you will do me the honor, Lady Lily?"

Lily's eyes beamed. "I would be delighted. Will you excuse me?" She turned to go and greet some of the other guests.

Sophia caught a glimpse of Pierre watching Lily walk away.

No, not just watching her. He was devouring her with his eyes.

Sophia felt momentarily sick at the sight of his expression. Did he not realize that Lily was his half sister? Sophia supposed he didn't think anyone else knew.

Then she wondered if he knew it himself. Could that be true? Could his mother have kept the truth from him and sent him here to threaten Marion without knowing that's what he was doing?

Sophia pasted on a smile. "Tell me about your home, Monsieur Billaud? What part of France do you come from?"

For the next few minutes, she asked him other questions about his life, but nothing seemed out of the ordinary. He was a skilled liar, if that in fact was what he was, for he never mentioned a mother who operated a brothel. Nor did he mention a father who abandoned him before he was born. He said his parents were successful merchants.

Some other guests joined them, so Sophia was safe to move on. "If you will excuse me."

Feeling no more confident about what was really going on, she turned away and spotted James just inside the door of the drawing room, staring at her. They met a few minutes later by the fireplace.

He took her gloved hand in his and kissed it. "Madam, your magnificence astounds me."

"And your ... hmmm ... your virility astounds *me,* Your Grace, especially when it shows up on my bed unexpectedly before dinner."

He smiled. "I'll try to give you notice next time."

"No notice necessary. I like surprises. I also like being ... astounded."

His eyes sparkled flirtatiously at her, then they began to circle the perimeter of the room. Sophia purposefully chose the direction opposite to where Pierre was standing.

They mixed and laughed with the guests until the dinner gong rang out, then with a strict adherence to the order of precedence, they all walked into the dining room for dinner.

The next day, James waited in Sophia's bedchamber for her to return after the usual evening stroll with the guests, but even after most of the others had come in, she still did not arrive. When the hour grew too late to fit in any marital "activities" before dressing for dinner, he grew frustrated and went to the window.

There, outside on the lawn, returning from an apparent stroll through the secluded south garden, was his wife and the French fellow. Sophia's arm was looped through his, and she was laughing at something he had said.

James felt an unwelcome pang of jealousy, even as he told himself it was irrational. He trusted his wife, truly he did. He did not for a moment think that she would be encouraging a flirtation with Monsieur Billaud. But still, he did not like to see her walking with another man, holding his arm in the pink twilight, when she must have known her husband would be waiting for her.

He swept the foolish notion aside and pulled on his shirt, deciding it would be best not to be here when she returned. He did not want her to know he had been watching her, nor did he wish to ask prying, accusing questions about where she was and why she had been gone so long. That was something his father would have done, knocking over a dresser concurrently, and James was not his father. He was not overly suspicious, he told himself, nor was he irrational, and any murderous temper he might have inherited from the man, he had crushed long ago when he'd crushed so many other things in his nature.

Then why did he feel the need to avoid seeing Sophia now?

He walked back to his own bedchamber, remembering a day in his childhood, when he had been five or six years old at best, and his mother had found him at the window in tears because some visiting children had gone out to play and had not invited him to join them. His mother had thrown him into the trunk and told him not to cry or his father would hear of it. He supposed that day, he had learned to conceal his feelings.

James pushed his own bedchamber door open, but stopped dead at the sight of a male visitor sitting in front of the fireplace.

"Martin, I didn't expect you until tomorrow." Nor had James had sufficient time to decide how he was going to handle Martin's awkward homecoming.

His younger brother stood quickly. His eyes wavered back and forth between confident rebelliousness and fear. "I'm here today, just as scheduled."

James moved fully into the room and closed the door behind him. Thompson, his valet, was in the dressing room brushing lint off one of James's suit jackets. "Thompson, that will be all for now."

As soon as the man was gone, Martin flopped into a chair and slouched against the back.

James could see that his younger brother's guard was up, even though he was trying to convey a carefree appearance. It reminded James of all the times he had faced his own father in situations like these, grasping for his dignity when he knew it was about to be crushed.

God, he'd never imagined himself on this end of the discussion.

"I suppose you want to exact some form of punishment now," Martin said. "Well, go ahead. I'm waiting."

James crossed the room and stood in front of the window. "I understand you have some debts to pay."

"No more than any other man my age."

He was *barely* a man, James thought, looking down at his lanky young brother, sprawling in the chair.

"What your friends are up to is no concern of mine," James said flatly. "There is responsible behavior, and there is recklessness. I would prefer to see you in the first category."

Martin swiped a hand across the chair arm and got up. "You would like to see me bored to death, here in the country with nothing to do but wander around or go fishing." He turned a cautious, uncertain glance at James—no doubt to test the waters of James's anger—then continued. "If I recall, you were no better at my age, you and Whitby. I know the kinds of trouble you used to get into. I know how often you were suspended from school."

James breathed deeply, searching for calm. "Indeed I was suspended. That, unfortunately, was the least of my punishments."

Martin dropped his gaze to the floor, knowing well enough what James was referring to. "Nevertheless, I am no worse than you," he said. "Yet you look at me like I am a great disappointment, like I should know better, when you didn't know better when you were my age."

James paced the floor. "So what . . . am I supposed to simply let it go by? If we are comparing you to me, I assure you, no one let any of *my* misdemeanors go by."

Martin raked a hand through his hair. "It's bloody dull here, James."

"In what way?"

"There's no one my age."

"Lily is less than two years older than you."

"Lily talks about dresses and fairy tales."

James closed the distance between himself and his brother. "Surely you know there must be consequences for your actions, Martin. You were caught a second time with brandy and a woman in your room at Eton, and your aunt has been completely unable to steer you back on track." James turned away again. "You will have no increases in your allowance for the rest of the year, nor will you be permitted to leave Wentworth until I deem it appropriate."

"You're going to lock me up?"

"Nothing quite so dramatic as that. I will hire a private tutor so you can continue your studies, and when I am convinced you've turned a corner, I'll consider your wishes. Until then, I suggest you take a liking to the country air."

"This is dashed cruel of you, James."

James whirled around to face him. "Cruel of me? Would you prefer I take a stick to you instead? Or hold your hand over a burning candle until you screamed an apology and promised never to do it again?"

Martin's lips fell open with astonished realization. Quietly, he said, "No, James." Then he straightened his shoulders. "May I go now?"

"Yes. You're welcome to join the guests at dinner if you like."

Martin paused at the door. "I'm rather tired after my journey. I'd prefer to have something sent up to my room."

"Fine. The guests will be gone by tomorrow, so I would ask that you plan to join the family tomorrow evening. I'm sure Lily and Sophia will want to see you."

Martin nodded and walked out.

James went to dress for dinner.

Chapter 22

He was still in control of his passions, James assured himself as he watched his wife converse with some of the guests on the other side of the ballroom. Why he was telling himself that now, he had no idea. Perhaps it was because he had been watching her all night long, and couldn't get over how brightly she sparkled as a hostess. She had a way with people—a radiant glow that brought smiles to the faces of everyone in the room.

Everyone except his mother, who was sitting along the far wall with some of the other matrons, fanning herself. Not enjoying herself one bit. But that was nothing new.

He glanced at the door when an impressive young gentleman entered, and with some surprise realized it was Martin. Strange, how a black suit with tails could mature a young man so instantly. Martin stood tall and confident, his white gloved hands at his sides while he surveyed the room.

James went to greet him. "You decided to join us." They began to walk together around the dance floor.

"I couldn't help it. I was trying to fashion a water bomb to explode over Lord Needham's door when he opened it later tonight, but the music and noise was dashedly distracting. I couldn't concentrate."

James halted on the polished wood floor. Martin halted, too, shaking his head cynically. "I'm joking, James. What do you take me for?"

Just then, Sophia approached. Her face illuminated with a smile; she held her gloved hands out to greet her brother-in-law. "Martin! How wonderful to see you! I haven't seen you since the wedding. James told me you'd returned. I'm so glad you've joined us!"

Martin's face lit up at the warm welcome as he leaned forward to kiss Sophia on the cheek. She looped her arm through his and walked beside him.

"How was your journey?" she asked him. "The train trip wasn't too tedious, I hope."

Martin described how tedious it was, in fact, and Sophia agreed with everything he said, nodding and telling her own little stories about similar experiences. Before long, Martin was smiling and laughing, and James wondered how it was possible he could have been so blessed to have found such a wife, who was not only obscenely rich but brilliantly charming as well. A woman who could effect miracles . . . like making his cynical younger brother smile.

They all walked together around the back of the room.

"There are a few single young women here," Sophia

said. "Would you like me to introduce you to any of them?"

"That would be splendid," Martin replied.

They found a group of ladies at the far end of the room. They all smiled at Sophia, unable to take their eyes off her while she made some light pleasantries, and James realized that the whole world seemed to be entranced by his wife.

"Lady Beecham," Sophia said, "may I present my brother-in-law, Lord Martin Langdon? Martin, this is Lady Beecham and her daughter, Lady Emma Crosby."

Martin bowed cordially, then requested the next spot on Lady Emma's card. When the music began, he escorted her onto the floor.

"You are a remarkable woman," James said to Sophia, as they ventured off to steal a few minutes alone together, outside on the balcony.

They found an empty corner near a potted baby elm. It was a warm evening for October, without a hint of a breeze. An autumn fragrance of freshly fallen leaves floated in the air.

"How so?" she replied flirtatiously. "And spare none of the details."

He grinned. "You make people feel appreciated and esteemed, as if you have been waiting all day just to talk to them. Everyone adores you."

Sophia rested her graceful hands on the balustrade and smiled modestly. "Me? An American? Who would ever have thought?"

He covered her hand with his own. "That's sadly true, my darling, but you have won everyone over. You have conquered England."

She laughed. "Oh, James, I never meant to conquer anything, only to find happiness."

"And have you?" He was ardently surprised at his desire to know her answer, for he had never intended to care one way or the other if she was happy. He hadn't wanted to feel *anything* where she was concerned.

Yet, he had found joy with his wife these past few weeks. He would not wish to give it up.

Sophia laid her warm palm on his cheek. "Yes. I have never been happier. I'm pleased that we have been able to find some . . . enjoyment with each other."

Enjoyment. He remembered using that word a month ago—the night before he'd left for London without saying good-bye to Sophia. He had told her there was nothing wrong with enjoying each other, but that he had never intended to love her.

She, in turn, had claimed that she loved him. He had not believed her that night. He had not thought it possible. Love could not be so easy to feel, nor could it advance so quickly. He had been certain she'd married him for his title.

Yet, this rapture he felt now as he gazed into her eyes . . . it had come upon him like a great tidal wave, the force of it compounding with every night spent in her arms and every morning he woke to the glorious warmth of her sweet company beside him.

Was this love?

If it was, when had it begun? The first time he'd seen her in London? Had it been growing and deepening all this time?

He remembered a night not long ago in his bedchamber, when she'd asked him questions about his childhood. He had made love to her afterward and a small door inside him had creaked open. Perhaps that had been the turning point. He had felt an unfamiliar tremor of tenderness that night, and because he had not banished it, it had grown into something more.

"You were very good with Martin, just now." He raised her gloved hand to his lips and kissed it. "Thank you."

"You have nothing to thank me for. I was truly glad to see him. I hope he will know how much we care about him, and that we truly want him to stay."

James felt another tremor deep within himself. "I've never known anyone like you, Sophia. No one has ever been so willing and unafraid to express their affections."

She gazed directly into his eyes. "Perhaps you should try it sometime."

He basked in her warmth and beauty, then leaned down and pressed his lips to hers. It was the only way he could express how he felt at this moment, for he wasn't sure he understood it enough to articulate it.

Later that night, he went to her room. She was sitting by a roaring fire, naked in her chair, waiting for him.

As he approached and she stood up to walk into his open arms, he knew without a shadow of a doubt, that the tidal wave had crashed upon his shore.

This, God help him, was love.

Late the next morning, Sophia looked out her window and saw Pierre Billaud heading toward the gardens with a large group of ladies and a few of the husbands.

If only she had been able to gain some information or a clue about his intentions when she had gone walking with him the day before. He had said nothing the least bit incriminating, which continued to bother Sophia, for what kind of blackmailer had no secret plots? Maybe he was not as dangerous as Marion believed. Or maybe he was more so.

She went out into the hall to deliver instructions to the butler about the guests' departures, but stopped just outside of Pierre's guest chamber door. The silence in the house curled around her. She stared curiously at his door, wishing there was some way she could learn something about him . . . anything. Anything that would help her convince Marion to cease keeping these secrets and go to James with her problem. If they were ever going to grow close as a family, they all needed to open up to each other and trust each other.

But that was Sophia's problem. She wanted to tell James what was going on, but she had promised Marion that she would not, and her shaky relationship with the woman was barely beginning. She could not betray her now, or all hope for a deep, personal alliance would be lost.

She gazed at the doorknob to Pierre's room.

Would there be a clue in there about what he knew or what his intentions were? A diary perhaps?

A diary. That was hoping for too much.

Nevertheless, if she was going to talk Marion into trusting James with the truth, Sophia needed to know what that truth was. She could not continue keeping this nebulous secret from him forever, especially when she was working so hard to bring *him* closer to her heart—to help *him* open up to her and learn how to trust her and love her.

Sophia listened for sounds in the corridor, knowing this was an opportunity that would not come again. Perhaps she could just take a quick peek.

She checked over her shoulder to make sure no one was watching, then quietly pushed open Pierre's door.

The bed was made, the fireplace swept clean. His carpetbag sat open on the floor beneath the window; his razor and brushes were placed neatly upon the dresser.

Sophia tiptoed toward the carpetbag. She picked it up but there was nothing inside. She went to the wardrobe and pulled open the doors. A few expensive suit jackets and shirts were hanging there. With an unpleasant surge of guilt, she stuck her hands into the pockets, looking for God knew what. . . .

All the pockets were empty.

She closed the doors and moved to the dressing table where she found a travel book about London. Her eyes perused the room, but there appeared to be nothing out of the ordinary.

Not wanting to risk being caught, she decided it would be best to leave. She went to the door and opened it a crack to peer out into the hall and make sure no one was walking by. All seemed quiet, so she sneaked out.

She had barely made it halfway down the hall when she heard James's voice. "Darling . . ."

Halting fast, she felt a stinging heat erupt on her cheeks. She forced a smile and turned around.

Her husband was walking toward her. "Do you have a moment?"

Had he seen where she was? she wondered frantically. "Of course."

He caught up with her and kissed her on the cheek. "You're overwhelmed with hostess duties I suppose."

"Overwhelmed, yes. Everyone will be leaving after luncheon, and I'm still scrambling to get the carriages organized at the right times. Some of the guests will be catching the early train, while others are catching the late one . . . it is an organizational nightmare."

"Can I do anything to assist?"

"No, truly, I'm fine."

He glanced back at Pierre's door. "I noticed you coming out of Monsieur Billaud's bedchamber just now. He is finding his visit satisfactory, I hope."

The beating of her heart resonated to a full cacophony. "Yes. I was just checking the ink jars in all the rooms, to make sure they were full."

"And were they?"

Her eyebrows flew up. "Yes."

He gazed at her for a long time. She did her best to smile and appear relaxed, for she did not wish him to know that she was keeping anything from him. That would put them back at square one.

He kissed her on the cheek again. "You're busy. I won't keep you, but I will look forward to a quiet dinner this evening. It will be nice to have the house to ourselves again." Then with an appealing glint in his eye, he turned and walked in the other direction down the hall.

Sophia continued on, immediately worrying over what she had just done. Maybe she should have confided in James. If only she could have had a moment to think about it, instead of staring up at him and being forced to reply to an accusation (and she wasn't even sure if it was an accusation) that she did not wish to acknowledge just yet.

Soon, she promised herself. Soon he would know everything, and with luck, they would all work together to bring an end to this disturbing problem.

* * *

Ten minutes later, James was gazing pensively out his study window. Had Sophia truly been checking ink jars?

What was it that made him suspect otherwise? The color in her cheeks? The tone in her voice?

He sat down in the chair in front of the unlit fireplace, rubbing his chin with his thumb. It didn't matter what it was. He had known there was something wrong, and he was sure he was not being irrational or excessively suspicious. His wife had just lied to him, and he had known.

The fact was, something about Billaud rubbed James the wrong way, ever since the first moment he'd laid eyes on him. He didn't trust the man, and that circumstance had nothing to do with Sophia.

But why was she skulking around in Billaud's room while the man was out walking in the garden? Was there something going on between them?

Bloody hell.

James rose from his chair and returned to the window. He hated that he could even entertain such a thought.

God!

This would *not* be the beginning of a slow descent into hell. . . .

No, no.

No! He would not jump to ridiculous, melodramatic conclusions about something he had no good reason to suspect. Sophia had been nothing but caring and dutiful since the first moment she'd agreed to be his wife, even when she was faced with the cruel, shocking reality of the temperament he had hidden from her. To suspect her of anything surreptitious would be absurd.

James tipped his head back against the window frame. Perhaps he should go to Pierre's room and end this curiosity. He could check the jars for himself.

A moment later, he was letting himself into the blue guest chamber and perusing the room with an alert, searching gaze. He glanced at Pierre's empty carpetbag and looked all around at everything, then at the ink jar. It was empty.

Sophia had said it was full.

He gaze fell to the bed, where a note lay on the pillow with a single red rose upon it. He immediately picked it up. It was written on the ducal stationery.

"My Darling Pierre," the author wrote in an elegant script that looked very much like his wife's. "I enjoyed our walk in the garden together, and only wish we could have stolen a few more moments alone. Please don't leave for London yet. Stay here at the castle a few more days, for I am not yet ready to say good-bye."

James sat down upon the edge of the bed and read the note again. He did not want to believe what he was seeing, nor did he wish to feel the ice-cold chill that was moving slowly and painfully through his veins.

Perhaps Pierre had begun a *tendre* with one of the guests, whose writing bore a resemblance to Sophia's, he thought with a desperate, fleeting hope.

But no, the note was asking Pierre to stay at the castle. Everyone else was leaving.

A servant, perhaps?

Anger, deep and unbidden, began to simmer. This was the ducal stationery. A servant would never use it.

James squeezed his forehead between his thumb and forefinger. This was insane. He would not believe it. He would not.

What, then, would he do?

James did the only thing he could possibly do to prevent himself from losing his mind. He went all over the house, searching for Sophia, and when he found her in the dining room, checking the place settings at the luncheon table, he confronted her.

"May I have a word with you, my dear?"

"Certainly." She kept her eyes upon the settings as she continued to move down the long table.

His shoulders rose and fell with a deep intake of breath. "In my study, if you please."

Chapter 23

Sophia followed James into his private study. He sat down at his huge, mahogany desk and gestured for her to take the seat on the other side.

For a second or two he said nothing while Sophia sat with her back poker-straight, squeezing her hands in her lap and feeling as if she'd just been called into the schoolmaster's office after being caught cheating on an examination. This was strange. Surreal. She did not feel like she was looking at the husband she had come to know in the past week.

Finally, after what seemed like an interminable silence, James reached into his breast pocket and pulled out a letter. He rose from his chair to hand it across the desk to Sophia.

"I wish to know the meaning of this," he said coolly.

Sophia read it. Her blood began to wash noisily from her toes to her head, until her temples were throbbing. "Where did you get this?"

"On Pierre Billaud's pillow."

"When?"

"Just now."

She swallowed nervously. "Why, may I ask, do you expect me to know the meaning of it?"

"It looks like your penmanship, does it not?"

What had a moment ago been anxiousness, exploded into outright fury, but she kept her voice calm. "You think *I* wrote this?"

"You did not?"

"No! I would never write a letter like this to another man!"

He raised an eyebrow. "How can I be sure of that? We have not known each other very long. We still know each other very little, to be honest."

This was too familiar. It was just like that horrid night when James had brutally yanked his heart out of her grasp, before fleeing to London. He had been cold and unfeeling then, just as he was cold and unfeeling now. He had the same look in his eyes—the look that told her he did not care whether she loved or hated him.

"If you do not know me well enough to be certain that I would not write something like this, then I am gravely disappointed." She stood up to leave.

"Stop right there," he said, rising also. "This discussion is not over."

She would have liked to walk out despite his order to stay, but when Sophia heard the dark, commanding tone in his voice, she halted.

After all the progress she and James had made the past few weeks, the fact that she felt afraid at this moment was heartbreaking.

"Sit down," he said.

Sophia returned to her chair. James waited for her to be seated before he sat down as well.

"What were you doing in his room? And don't tell me you were checking the ink jar, because you lied about that and told me it was full when it was not."

"You went in there to check up on me?"

"When we met in the hall, it was clear that you were not completely honest with me. I merely intended to ease my mind. Unfortunately, that was not how it turned out."

Sophia picked up the note and read it again. "I assure you, I did not write this. It wasn't on the pillow when *I* was in the room, or I would have noticed it."

"You have neglected, Sophia, to explain what you were doing in Monsieur Billaud's room in the first place."

Panic descended upon her with frightening speed. What was she to say? She had promised Marion that she could be trusted, and if she told James now, he would go to his mother posthaste in all his fury, and meet her head to head. It could not end that way. Any hopes that the family could be eased into leaning upon each other would be shattered.

Sophia bowed her head. "James, I truly do not know who wrote this letter. It could have been anyone. Yes, the penmanship resembles my own, but it was not done by my hand. I can only ask that you believe me."

"Fine, I believe you. Now you can tell me what you were doing in Pierre's room." His voice was as sharp as steel, and it sent a shiver down Sophia's spine.

Tears pooled in her eyes, not because he was forcing her to say what she did not want to say, but because he

was speaking to her with such coarse, heartless re-
serve. How was it possible a man could bury his feelings so easily? Did he even possess feelings? Perhaps
that was it. He did not even care the least bit for her.
He only enjoyed using her body to find his own shal-
low, short-lived pleasure, and he had spoken the truth
that night, when he'd told her that he never intended
to love her. She should have listened. Oh, how she
wished she had.

Salty tears spilled from her eyes and ran down her
cheeks. She wiped them away, despising herself for this
weakness in front of a man who despised emotion. She
swallowed hard, but could not keep her voice from
shaking when she spoke. "You're right. I lied about the
ink jar."

She felt him stiffen, even though she was staring at
her hands.

Sophia forced herself to continue. "But that's not
the worst of it. There is more. I admit that I am keeping
something from you. Someone has trusted me with a
secret, but I cannot tell you what it is and betray that
trust. I can only promise you that I will endeavor to do
the right thing and find a way to tell you as soon as I
can."

He rose from his chair and walked to the fireplace,
leaning a hand upon the mantel. He kept his back to
her as he spoke. "The person with the secret . . . is this
her letter?"

She shrugged. "I honestly don't know." She couldn't
imagine that it was.

"Frankly, I don't care who wrote it, as long as it
wasn't you."

Sophia tried to breathe evenly, thinking that she

might have found comfort in his words if his voice had not been edged with a razor-sharp warning. He was telling her that she belonged to him and no other. She was his possession, nothing more, and if she was an intelligent woman, she would never test those boundaries.

She remembered the story about the duchess who had thrown herself out her window. That woman had been in mental shackles. Was that what awaited Sophia, if she continued to displease her husband?

"I will not force you," James said, "to betray this person who trusted you with her secret, but I will have you know that if this secret involves you or me or my family in any way, I will act quickly to put out that fire one way or the other, and I will give no heed to whether or not your *friend* feels betrayed. Do you understand?"

Oh yes, she understood. She understood that their glorious, pleasure-filled nights were at an end, and James was not going to forgive her easily when the wicked, scandalous truth awakened like the sleeping dragon that it was.

By four o'clock, all the guests were gone, including Pierre Billaud. The family dined together as usual, with the added company of Martin, who was quiet but not rudely so. In Sophia's opinion, he was not unlike most of the young men she had known when she was that age—cool and reticent, only beginning to learn the charm that would inevitably come as they matured.

James was also quiet, but she could not dismiss his silence to such a simple origin. Yes, he had made eye contact with her since they'd sat down, and he'd made some light conversation about the success of the party, but it was all very aloof and polite. It was as if he were making sure she knew that he was not angry with her, the more relevant point being that he did not care at all.

Nevertheless, Sophia put on a bright smile as she always did and listened to Lily talk about how much she enjoyed the shooting party and especially the games in the evenings. All the while, Sophia was wound up tighter than a tin clock, lamenting over how she had handled everything since Marion had confided in her. She wished she could go back and not have pushed to know what was bothering her mother-in-law, for this knowledge that Sophia now possessed was threatening to ruin her marriage, when it was already so fragile to begin with.

Late that night, Sophia waited in bed for James, hoping he would come, but he chose to stay away. She was not surprised, given the tone and outcome of their conversation that day.

Briefly, she considered going to his room to try to patch things up, but how could she? She couldn't tell James the truth, not yet, so how would she ever fix what was broken?

She would have to talk to Marion first. Sophia turned the key in the lamp and lay in the darkness, finally deciding that first thing in the morning, she would go and see the dowager. Somehow, Sophia would come up with a way to convince Marion to trust her son.

A number of knocks in quick succession startled Sophia awake. Heart pounding, she sat up in bed and clutched the covers to her chest. "Who is it?"

"It's Lily!" the voice on the other side of the door whispered. "May I come in?"

Sophia climbed out of bed and opened the door. "What's wrong? It's the middle of the night."

"I know, but I couldn't sleep, and you're the only person I can talk to."

Sophia invited Lily in, then lit the lamp. "You're not sick, are you?"

"No, no, it's nothing like that." They both climbed onto the bed. "Or perhaps it is something like that. I do not feel myself. Oh, Sophia, thank goodness you're here. I could not possibly trust anyone else with this secret. Promise me you will keep this just between us."

Warning bells began to go off in Sophia's head. She'd already promised to keep one secret, and it had driven a wedge into her marriage. She couldn't make this promise again. . . .

"Lily, maybe I'm not the best person to—"

"You're the only person, Sophia. I can't live with this longing anymore. I feel like I'm going to die from it!"

As she stared in silence at her sister-in-law, a sinking feeling descended upon Sophia. "What do you mean . . . *longing*?"

Lily flopped backward onto the bed. "I'm in love."

"With whom?" Sophia asked, fearing that she already knew the answer.

Lily sat up again. "With whom do you think? Pierre! Couldn't you tell that we were mad for each other?"

The walls seemed to close in around Sophia. If what Marion had told her about Pierre was true, then Pierre was Lily's half brother.

She tried to keep from stammering. "Are you sure? I mean, did he feel the same way? I hardly saw you speak two words to him."

Oh, pray that this is all one of Lily's romantic fantasies!

"He does feel it, Sophia. That's why I am so delirious now that he's gone. How will I ever survive being away from him?"

The letter. It had come from Lily. . . .

"How do you know he's . . . in love with you? Did he say it?"

"He didn't have to say it in words. We communicate with our eyes and our hearts. It's magical, Sophia. I had no idea love could be like this."

Sophia shook her head, still hoping that Lily was imagining any romantic feelings on Pierre's side. "Did anything happen between you?"

"Nothing you need to worry about, though I don't know what would have happened if he hadn't left when he did. We took walks together while the gentlemen were out with the guns, and please don't tell Mother, we sneaked off alone sometimes when we could. Don't worry, he was a complete gentleman, which only makes me love him more!"

Sophia cleared her throat. "Love is a strong word, Lily. Don't be too quick to use it. I know Pierre is a handsome man, but we really know very little about him."

Lily's delicate brow furrowed. "I thought you were more of a romantic, Sophia. I thought you believed in passion."

"I do, but we must be very careful not to let our hearts rule our heads, or sometimes we can get ourselves into trouble. Pierre is a foreigner, and no one here can truly recommend him as a—"

"You're a foreigner, Sophia. I didn't think that would matter to you, of all people."

Sophia waved her hands, trying to backtrack. "That's not what I mean . . . it doesn't matter that he's from another country, it's just that . . . that we don't know anything about him. He could be a criminal for all we know."

"A criminal! He's not a criminal, Sophia! I would know if he was."

"How would you know?"

"Like I said before, we communicate with our hearts. It's like we are connected by some cosmic force."

Oh, good God. "You still haven't told me what happened between you. Did he . . . did he kiss you?" Sophia asked warily.

For a long time Lily gazed off into the distance, then she flopped backward again. "Yes! And it was fabulous!"

Sophia's muscles tightened like vise grips around her bones. "You've kissed him? Lily,"—she tried to speak gently—"that was not wise. You should not have been alone with him."

Lily made a face. "Oh, pooh, Sophia. You were alone with James before he proposed. That night at the political party. I saw you go into the conservatory with him."

Sophia swallowed uncomfortably. "That was different. I'm older than you."

"It's no different. You were an unmarried young woman, and the rules are the same." She waved a hand flippantly through the air. "It doesn't matter anyway. Everyone does it."

"No, they do not! And if they do, they certainly don't speak about it!"

Lily's wide-eyed gaze narrowed. "Sophia, this is not

at all like you. You're usually so open about everything." She sat up, a look of concern clouding her expression. "Is it Pierre? Do you not like him?"

Raking fingers through her hair, Sophia scrambled for a reply. "I don't know enough about him to like or dislike him, and neither do you for that matter."

Lily sat on the bed for a few more minutes, looking morose, as if Sophia had just stuck a pin in her euphoric bubble of delirium.

Well, good, Sophia thought, not allowing herself to feel guilty about it.

"I thought you'd understand," Lily said, sounding altogether brokenhearted.

Sophia sighed. She touched Lily's soft cheek. "I'm sorry, Lily—I do understand how you feel. It's just that . . . I think you need to be cautious before you allow yourself to fall too deeply head over heels in love with a stranger."

"Is it because he has no title?"

"Of course not."

"It will matter to Mother, you know, and to James. They would never allow me to be with him because of it."

Sophia merely nodded. "It's not something that needs to be worked out now. There's plenty of time."

But it *would* be worked out, Sophia thought with grim determination.

"Would you talk to James for me?"

"About what? About Pierre?" *This can't be happening!* "I don't know Lily. . . . I can't answer that now."

Lily gazed at Sophia, a look of intense disappointment coloring her eyes, then she put on a smile and inched off the bed. "I understand. Truly I do. Maybe you can think about it, because I would not want to . . . I would not want to alienate my family. I would need to have at least one person on my side, no matter what."

Shaken and completely distressed by everything Lily had said, Sophia bid her sister-in law good night, giving her a kiss on the cheek before she left the room.

As soon as Sophia saw Lily disappear down the hall, she picked up her lamp and took off in the opposite direction to Marion's bedchamber.

"Marion! Marion!" She rapped hard on the dowager's door. "Open up! It's urgent!"

The door opened at last. Marion stood glaring. "What in God's name is going on?"

"We have to talk. It's about Lily."

The angry lines in Marion's face deepened. "What is it?"

Sophia gathered her robe together at her chest and entered the room. "You have to tell James the truth about Pierre."

"I will *not*," Marion replied haughtily.

"This is serious, Marion. James has to know the truth. Everyone has to know, at least everyone in this family."

Marion's face grew tight with fury. "Why? It's a scandal from years ago! Why taint all of them with it now, and risk losing our proper place in the world?" She slammed her open palm down on the desk beside her. "I should *never* have trusted you! I knew you would not understand what any of this means."

Sophia took a step toward her mother-in-law. "I understand very well what it means, Marion, and you were lucky to have told me, because if you hadn't, you would never know what I am about to tell you now."

Marion struck her with an icy glare.

Sophia would not be warned off. "It's Lily—she's in love with Pierre."

Chapter 24

Marion took a few steps back as if she had been punched. "You're lying."

"Why would I come here in the middle of the night to lie about something like that?"

"It can't be true. He's her . . . her half brother!" Marion covered her mouth with a hand. She looked like she was going to be ill.

"Are you absolutely sure he's your husband's son, Marion? Did Pierre speak to you at all? Did he mention who he was, or allude to the blackmail?"

"No, not once. It was as if he didn't know me at all."

Sophia set down her lamp. "Well, maybe he doesn't know he's a relation. Perhaps Genevieve never told him."

"He must know."

"But why would he kiss Lily if he thought she was his sister?"

"He *kissed* her? Dear Lord." Marion collapsed onto the bed.

Sophia rushed to her side to help her lie back. "Can I get you anything? A drink of water? I could ring for tea."

"No, don't ring for anything. I don't want anyone to see me like this."

Sophia rubbed Marion's forehead.

"He *kissed* her? Are you certain?"

"Lily told me herself. She obviously has no idea what she's doing, and we can only hope that he doesn't either. To think otherwise is purely . . . well . . ."

Marion waved a hand in the air to hush Sophia. "We will be ruined! All of us! What are we going to do?"

"What you should have done years ago. You must tell James. He will be able to handle this."

Marion began to weep. "I can't tell him."

"Why ever not?"

"Because I've kept it from him all this time. He knows nothing about his father's secret marriage, or the fact that he might not even be the rightful duke, and he will despise me for not telling him."

Sophia didn't mention the fact that Marion's relationship with her son wasn't exactly rosy at present. "He will despise you more if you continue to keep it from him when Lily is now in danger. Marion, you *must* tell him. For the sake of your daughter."

Her mother-in-law turned her face toward the darkened window. "There must be another way!"

Sophia gripped Marion's shoulders and forced the woman to meet her gaze. "There isn't, and we don't have time to plot and scheme. There's been enough of that, and look where it has taken you. The situation is out of control now, with Lily involved, and you cannot continue to deal with it alone. You need help. You must trust James. He is the duke, and he is strong. He will know how to take care of this."

"Do you really think so?"

"I know so."

Marion hesitated. She bit her lip. "All right. I'll tell him. For Lily's sake. But I must have you there with me when I do, for I don't know how he will react. It will be a shock, to be sure."

Sophia nodded and helped Marion up off the bed. "I know it's late, but we should go now. James will want to take action first thing in the morning."

A few brief minutes later, they were standing outside James's bedchamber, and for the third time that night, a door was knocked upon in a frantic manner. "James? It's me, Sophia. I'm here with your mother. We must speak with you."

He did not answer immediately, so Sophia knocked again. "James? Please open up."

Still, he did not answer. Sophia turned the latch and opened the door for herself. Carrying the lamp, she walked into the room, but found the bed empty. It had not even been slept in.

It was long past midnight when James and Martin entered the London house. The servants, who had been notified by telegram that the duke and his younger brother were on their way to the city, scurried to see to the luggage and make sure that His Grace and Lord Martin were given a proper welcome.

James gave his overcoat to a footman, and gestured for Martin to follow him to his study. He immediately went to the side table to fill two glasses with brandy.

"You're sharing?" Martin said with some surprise

as he accepted the glass. "What's going on, James? You've invited me to come to London without a moment's notice, nor an explanation as to why we are even here. You barely spoke on the train, and now you want to drink brandy with me? Something is definitely not right. This isn't my last liquid meal before I'm sent to the gallows is it?"

Exhausted, knowing he would not get any sleep if he tried, James managed a smile for his younger brother, and clinked his glass with Martin's. "No gallows for you tonight. Though I will admit to considering such a tactic when I received that last letter from Aunt Caroline."

Martin yielded with a nod and a look in his eye that held a hint of an apology.

"The truth is," James said, "I need you here with me. I need someone I can trust."

"And you thought of *me*?" Martin inclined his head. "I find that difficult to swallow."

James sat down by the roaring fire and crossed one leg over the other. His brother sat down across from him. "I need a family member, Martin. Someone who knows how to tell lies and keep secrets, and I reckon you've mastered the art of both while you were at Eton."

Martin put on an innocent air. "Why in the world would you think that?"

"Because I learned the art well enough myself at your age. Moreover, from what you tell me—and from what I've struggled to forget about *myself* these past few years—we have very similar dispositions."

Martin looked down at the amber liquid as he swirled it around in his glass. His voice was quiet, pensive. "I thought you were ashamed of me, James."

James reached out and touched his brother's arm. It would never have dawned on him to do anything like that before he'd met and married Sophia, and that fact resonated noisily in his mind.

He was not quite sure what to say, then found himself asking, *What would Sophia say at this moment?*

"I was never ashamed, Martin. Frustrated, yes, only because I felt I couldn't reach you, but that was my own fault. I have never tried to be a brother to you. I've always kept my distance, not just from you but from Lily and Mother, and I know now that I must find a way to change that. I must find a way to talk to you, so that when there is something wrong, we will discover what it is and fix it, rather than try to bury it."

"You've changed," Martin said, still looking down at his glass.

James only nodded.

"It's Sophia, isn't it? She's brought something to the house. It's not like it was. I knew it the moment I stepped inside."

God. Hearing those words . . . hearing Martin say it . . . James felt a deep surge of emotion rise up within him. His heart began to ache; he breathed shakily.

But why?

Was it happiness?

Or pain?

He was unaccustomed to any kind of intense onslaught of emotion—emotions that affected him physically. He had no idea what to make of them.

Martin filled the silence with a few softly spoken words. "She's special, James. You chose well."

He nodded again, only because he wasn't sure he

would be able to speak. Here he was, conversing openly with his brother, whom he had never, in all his life, really talked to before. And they were talking about Sophia, who James loved. Loved!

The frightening thing was, she had the power to reduce him to this. To reduce him almost to tears, and he was still pushing her away, like he had always pushed everyone.

He had left again without saying good-bye.

God, he wanted to make it right. If only he knew how.

If only he knew how to let go of the fear of loving her and the fear of being loved in return. Fear of the great beyond.

Martin leaned back in his chair. "You still haven't told me why we're here, James. All I know is that you want me to lie and tell secrets, and that sounds bloody interesting."

James found it in himself to snicker. "Interesting, yes, and I hope that's *all* it will be."

"It's nothing dangerous, is it?"

"I won't know until I find out who the devil Pierre Billaud is, and why he was keeping a letter in his side table drawer—a letter addressed to Genevieve La Roux."

Martin's eyebrows drew together in a frown. "Should that name mean something to me?"

"I doubt it, but it means something to me." James leaned forward and rested his elbows on his knees, rolling the brandy glass back and forth between his palms. "I think it's time, Martin, that you learned something about your late father."

* * *

He had done it again. He had gone off to London without saying good-bye, and this time without telling anyone why he was going. The butler had that morning informed Sophia that His Grace had left shortly after dinner the night before, and had taken Lord Martin along with him, which Sophia found surprising, given James's desire to keep his distance from his siblings.

She also found it disturbing that he had left so quickly, considering her last conversation with him, when he had accused her of writing love letters to Pierre Billaud. As if she would prefer him to her own husband, whom she adored—though she sometimes wished she didn't.

Was that why James had left? she wondered, as she paced her room after breakfast. Because he still did not believe her about the letter? Because he was angry with her for admitting to keeping a secret from him and couldn't bear to be in the same house with her?

She supposed he had good reason to leave. She would be hurt, too, if the tables were turned.

But her husband was not capable of being *hurt,* she realized miserably, stopping in the middle of the carpet when a dull, throbbing ache settled into her heart. He had revealed nothing so sensitive as that in his study the previous day, when he'd handed the letter to her in a calm, detached manner. He had sat on the other side of that big desk like a powerful administrator of a huge business enterprise, conducting the most minor of obligations.

The morning passed slowly. Marion slept, and all Sophia could do was pace in her room, while she tried to decide what to do. She wasn't quite certain how urgent this problem was at the moment. Pierre had left with the other guests, so there was no danger to Lily now, and for all she knew, James might return on the evening train tonight and she could talk to him then.

Heavens, she hoped Marion would still be willing to tell him the truth.

Oh, James, why did you choose yesterday of all days to leave?

Quite unable to stand another minute in her boudoir feeling anxious and powerless, Sophia left to go to the luncheon table. She sat there for quite some time, however, with no one to talk to until finally food arrived.

"Watson," she said to a footman standing against the wall, "where is everyone?"

The man bowed slightly before he spoke. "The dowager requested lunch in her rooms, Your Grace, and Lady Lily . . . she is expected at any moment."

Sophia gazed across the table at Lily's empty plate. "It's not like her to be this late for luncheon. Might she be unwell?"

"I don't know, Your Grace."

Smoothing her napkin out on her lap, Sophia wondered if Lily was napping, catching up on the sleep she'd missed the night before.

Sophia picked up her fork and tried to start her meal.

Her appetite, however, was utterly absent. For some reason, she was worried, and she could not possibly eat without knowing where Lily was and exactly what she was up to.

"I shall go and look in on her," Sophia said with a polite smile, placing her napkin on the table and pushing her chair back. "Just to see if she's all right. It was a busy week you know, Watson, and everyone is quite exhausted."

He held the door open for her as she departed.

Gathering her skirts in her hands, she whisked up the stairs, hoping to find everything as it should be: Lily in her room, merely dawdling. If she was dawdling, it was probably because she was kissing her pillow and calling it Pierre.

Sophia had to admit she would be relieved to find that that was the case. She wanted to believe that most of what Lily had told her last night had been mere fantasy. The alternative was too disturbing to contemplate.

She reached her sister-in-law's door and knocked.

Silence.

She knocked again.

When still no answer came, Sophia entered the room. It was empty. "Lily?"

Sophia glanced around the tidy, cream-colored bedchamber. With everything that had happened with Pierre, Sophia couldn't help but be worried. She walked to Lily's huge, oak wardrobe and opened the doors.

Good Lord. Gowns were missing.

Sophia picked up her skirts and hurried from the room in search of Lily's maid. "Josephine!" she called down the corridor, not really sure where she was running or where she would end up, only that she needed someone to answer her calls. She reached the front staircase.

Mrs. Dalrymple, the housekeeper, appeared in the main hall and stopped at the bottom of the staircase with her hand on the newel post, looking up. "Your Grace? What's the matter?"

"Where's Josephine?" Sophia asked as she flew down the stairs.

"She went to the village this morning."

"Was Lady Lily with her?"

"No, Lady Lily asked to be left alone. She was very tired, Your Grace, and wished not to be disturbed."

All at once contemplating the ramifications of what was happening, Sophia reached the bottom step and labored to calm herself. It wouldn't do to have every servant in the household knowing Sophia's impossible fears—that Lily might have eloped with a complete stranger, who might very well be her own brother.

Please, let me be wrong about this. . . .

Lily would be ruined. Worse than ruined.

Sophia inhaled deeply. "I see. Well, I won't disturb her, then. Perhaps I will go and see what Marion is up to."

She smiled and headed up the stairs again, forcing herself to walk leisurely, not run, but as soon as she was out of sight of the housekeeper, she began to sprint. She reached Marion's door and knocked hard.

Looking wearied, Marion appeared. As soon as she saw the frantic expression on Sophia's face, she stepped back to wave her in. "What is it? What's going on?"

"Do you know where Lily is?"

"No, I've been in my rooms all morning. Did she not come to the luncheon table?"

Sophia put a hand to her forehead. "You'd better sit down, Marion. I'm afraid something terrible might have happened."

The dowager's face went pale.

"There's no time to waste. I will have to be blunt. I just came from Lily's room, and she is gone."

"Gone! What do you mean, gone?"

"Her gowns were missing from her wardrobe, and Mrs. Dalrymple told me that Lily had sent her maid into the village this morning. What if . . . what if she's run off and done something foolish?"

Marion backed into a chair and sat down. "No, she would never do anything like that . . ." Her voice trailed off into nothingness; she stared blankly at the wall.

Touching Marion's shoulder, Sophia knelt. "We have to assume the worst and do what we can to find her." She made a fist and pounded the chair arm. "Oh, where is James! Why did he choose this day of all days to be in London!"

Marion clutched at Sophia's sleeves. "We have to send for him. What about a telegram?"

"Yes, indeed. A telegram. We'll tell him to return home immediately, that it's urgent." Sophia rose to her feet. She crossed to the door, but stopped to look back at her mother-in-law, who was now weeping. "Pray that I am mistaken about this, Marion. Pray that Lily has simply gone off for a long walk somewhere to be alone."

Marion shook her head. "No. I know my daughter. She has the hot Langdon blood. I fear the worst."

Chapter 25

Exhausted and weary from his journey, James stepped out of the crested coach. He ran up the steps of Wentworth Castle, taking two at a time, and entered the hall, handing his overcoat to a footman as he passed. "Where is the duchess? I must see her immediately."

"In the drawing room, Your Grace."

James strode across the hall. The telegram had been disturbingly vague and frantic, and he had entertained some of the most unpleasant thoughts on the train. Was Sophia ill or injured? Perhaps it was his mother . . .

James had left Martin at the house in London, with instructions to carry out the investigation regarding Pierre Billaud. Martin had in his possession a brief list of names of people who knew their father and would have known about Genevieve. James—wanting to know the true connection between Pierre and Genevieve—had laid all his trust in his younger brother. Martin had seemed grateful to have been given a purpose. He had embraced James as he was going out the door.

It was a moment James would not forget. Nor would he waste this opportunity for a new start with his brother.

Heart pounding uncharacteristically fast, James entered the drawing room.

His wife was sitting on the chintz sofa.

It was all like some kind of strange, unsettling dream. She was weeping.

Onto Whitby's shoulder.

James halted. Sophia looked up. Her eyes were red and swollen. "James, you're back!" She got up from the sofa and crossed toward him. "Thank God!"

The fact that Whitby kept his distance on the other side of the room was not lost on James. He gazed down at his wife's stricken face, then over her shoulder at his old friend. "What's going on?"

"You received my telegram?" Sophia asked, but he could barely form an answer, his blood was rushing so tumultuously in his head.

"Yes, it's why I returned." He gazed at Whitby. "Why are *you* here?"

Whitby took an uneasy step forward, as if he didn't know quite how to answer the question.

Sophia reached for James's hand. "He's here because I sent for him. I needed help, and I didn't know when you would arrive. You never replied to the telegram."

"I didn't know you required a reply."

She shook her head as if to dismiss what was a meaningless quarrel, then turned to Whitby. "Would you excuse us, Edward? I must speak with my husband alone. We'll go to the library. Please, have another cup of tea."

Looking ashen, Whitby nodded.

James felt a heaviness descend upon his chest. "What the devil is happening?" he asked Sophia, as soon as they were out in the hall. "You both look like someone has died."

Sophia shook her head and put a finger to her lips to hush him.

They reached the library. She closed the double doors. "I'm so glad you're back, James. Something terrible has happened. You might want to sit down."

"I prefer to stand." He had no patience left. He had just walked in on his wife weeping onto another man's shoulder—a man who had openly admitted to wanting her for himself not long ago. James wanted to know the truth.

"Your message was urgent," he said. "Why?"

How was she to begin? Sophia wondered, gazing with apprehension at her husband's exacting face. She moved slowly to the center of the room.

"There is a great deal I need to tell you, James, and there's no easy way to say it, so I'll just come out with it. Your mother confessed something to me not long ago, something to do with your family. There is a secret you don't know about."

James's gaze darkened, but Sophia would not be daunted.

"It's about your father. This may come as a surprise, but your mother . . . your mother was not his only wife."

James put his hand up to halt Sophia. "Wait just a moment. You sent for me, insisted I return from London immediately, to tell me *this*?"

"Well . . . yes . . . but."

"I've known for years about my father's scandalous first wife, Sophia. What I didn't know was that my mother knew." He shook his head with disbelief. "And she told *you*?"

"Yes."

"How in God's name did you ever get her to admit something like that? To *you*! No, wait, you don't need to tell me. You have a true gift, Sophia. You get under people's skin whether they want you there or not."

She stood motionless, staring at her husband, completely unsure of his meaning. Had she just been insulted or paid a compliment?

"James, it doesn't matter why she told me. The fact is, there have been developments."

"What kind of developments?" He sat down.

She hesitated. "You knew about Genevieve. Did you know about the blackmail?"

Her husband slowly blinked. "Blackmail? I suggest you explain."

Sophia paced across the room, afraid, desperately afraid of what this news, coming from her, was going to do to their marriage. He had known she was keeping something from him, and he had allowed her to keep her secret, but now his sister was possibly in the greatest danger of her life, and Sophia had done nothing to prevent it.

All this after the most glorious week with James, when Sophia had let herself believe that there was actually hope for happiness in her marriage. Hope that her husband would one day grow to love her.

She felt certain that those hopes were about to be ground into a fine, dry dust in the next few seconds.

"Genevieve has been threatening your mother," she

said. "Genevieve claims she has a son who is the true heir to the Wentworth dukedom, and if Marion does not pay her what she asks for, Genevieve will reveal him to the world and take everything away from this family."

Sophia watched James for a long time. He did not move from his position on the sofa. All he did was make a fist in one hand. "*This* is the secret you did not want to tell me?"

"Yes."

"That you believe I have a brother?"

She nodded.

The muscles in his jaw clenched. He stood up and walked to the window. "This was not a game, Sophia. You should never have kept such serious information from me."

Her voice quavered as she tried to explain. "I didn't *want* to keep it from you. I pleaded with your mother to go to you, but she would not."

He turned to face her. "*You* should have come to me! As my wife, you have a duty to me, first and foremost, above all others!"

Sophia jumped at the frightening timbre of her husband's anger. He had never raised his voice to her before, even when he'd thought she was writing love letters to another man.

"I know that now," she said, wringing her hands together in her lap. "Looking back on it, I wish I had. But as you know, my relationship with your mother has not been a congenial one. I've been lonely here, James, far from my own family, and I wanted desperately to feel as if I belonged. I wanted your mother to care for me like I was her own daughter, just as I longed to care for her as a mother. So when I made that promise to her—

to keep her secret no matter what, before I knew what the secret was—I had no idea what I was agreeing to. Afterward, I felt that I was close to fixing the problems that existed between Marion and me, and—"

"It's not your place to fix this family," he said icily. "You are an outsider. You do not understand our history."

Sophia felt the sting of his words like a hot iron burning into her soul. She gritted her teeth together. "Perhaps an outsider was exactly what you all needed."

He did not respond to that. He merely turned and looked out the window again.

Sophia wanted to scream! She rose from her sitting position and strode toward him, pulling him by the arm to face her. "What is the matter with you? Have you no heart? Can you not see that this is as painful for me as it is for you? That I want, more than anything, to be a part of this family, yet I must contend with your cool, steely reticence day after day when all I ever wanted was for you to love me? And now, I feel as if I have spoiled any chance of that ever happening, and put Lily in danger, all because of my deep—and not unreasonable—desire to be accepted!"

His gaze narrowed. "What do you mean, you've put Lily in danger?"

Sophia felt sick. This could not possibly have gone any worse. "Lily is missing."

"Missing!"

"Yes, that was the next thing I was going to tell you. It's why I sent the telegram."

Now, for the first time, his voice shook. "Madam, you will explain the rest of this situation to me."

Sophia nodded. "Lily came to me the other night to tell me that she was in love."

"In love with whom?" he demanded.

"With Pierre Billaud. The man Genevieve claims is her son."

James's eyes blazed with fury. "Good God! She says Billaud is her *son*? And you think Lily has run off with him?"

"It's only a suspicion at the moment, but as I said, she is missing, and some of her gowns are gone."

He raked a hand through his hair and strode toward the door. "Is that why Whitby is here?" he asked while he walked. "Did you tell him all this?"

Sophia followed. "Yes, I was desperate. I needed someone to go to Pierre's cottage and search the village, and I was afraid to trust any of the servants. I knew Whitby has been your friend for many years, and he was the only person I knew to call upon."

Returning to the drawing room, James burst through the doors.

Whitby stood, appearing startled. "You know what's going on?"

"Yes," James replied. As soon as Sophia entered the room, James closed the door behind her and turned to Whitby. "You went searching for Lily?"

"I did, but she was nowhere. Pierre's cottage was empty, and Lord Manderlin had no idea where the man had gone or when he had left. Took off without paying the rent he owed, I might add. Then I searched the village. I was discreet with my questions, I assure you. No one has seen her."

James turned his fierce gaze upon Sophia. "How long has she been gone?"

"Since yesterday morning."

"And no one knows anything? Where's her maid?"

"I was afraid for Lily's reputation, so I've been scrambling to keep everything quiet. I sent her maid home for a holiday. The servants seem to accept things like that coming from me. Other than that, we've been playing a cat-and-mouse game, making them all think that Lily is still here, but I don't know how much longer we can keep up the charade."

He nodded. "You did the right thing. Whitby, I'm going to need your help."

"I am at your disposal, James."

James paced the room, thinking. "Does Mother know?"

"Yes," Sophia replied. "She's been in her room weeping constantly."

"How certain are you that Lily went anywhere with Billaud?"

"Not positively certain, but my instincts tell me that's what has happened. After she came to me the other night. . . ."

"What did she say?"

"She told me how much in love she was, and she asked me to speak to you about it, to convince you to accept Pierre."

"*Accept* him? If everything you've told me is true, he is involved with blackmailing this family, and, worse than that, he might be our half brother!"

"I know that! I tried to caution her!"

"Well, madam, your counsel was ineffective."

Sophia bristled at her husband's accusing tone. The anger and fury that had been snowballing for weeks pounded into her with all the force of an avalanche.

"This is not my fault, James!" she said furiously. "As you said, I am merely an outsider. Your father's scandals and your mother's secrets and this horrendous blackmail—all of it was going on long before I set foot on English soil. None of you would be in this mess if you simply talked to each other!"

The men were silent, then Whitby moved toward the door. "Perhaps I'll leave you two for a moment."

James held up a hand. "No, Whitby, stay."

No one said anything for a long time. It seemed like hours to Sophia, who was breathing fast and hard, trying to control the fear in her heart—fear that she had pushed her husband too far. That he would never be able to forgive her for speaking so frankly at a time like this, even if every word of it was true.

James walked toward her, staring into her eyes. "Perhaps my wife is right," he said slowly.

Sophia gazed at him in disbelief. Had she heard him correctly?

"There have been too many secrets," James continued, "and we are in one bloody horrible mess because of it."

A raw and violent wave of emotion overwhelmed Sophia. James had heard her. He'd listened, and he'd accepted what she'd said.

It was not much, but it was something from her husband—a small offering. Not quite an apology for everything that had gone between them, and nothing close to a declaration of love, but it was something.

He touched Sophia briefly on the shoulder. The small gesture went straight through her and made her heart lurch with painful longing and desire for him as a man. As her husband. How she wanted all this behind them. She wanted Lily returned to them, safe from harm, she wanted Marion to stop crying. She wanted to break through the impossible barrier her husband had forged between them.

James faced Whitby. "We need a plan."

Whitby spread his hands wide. "I'm all for it. Where do we begin?"

Chapter 26

A heavy rain had just begun when James entered his mother's boudoir. Her window was open. Powerful gusts of wind were billowing the white lace curtains into the room. The rain was getting in.

His mother was hunched over in her chair by the unlit fireplace with a blanket wrapped around her legs and a handkerchief to her nose. She still wore her dressing gown and nightcap, and her eyes were puffy and red.

James strode across the room to close the window and shut out the noise of the wind. He turned to look at his mother.

He had never seen her look so distraught and vulnerable before.

Something tugged painfully inside his heart. It was an unfamiliar sensation in reference to his mother, and he marveled at it.

He marveled at everything about himself lately.

After crossing toward her, James knelt on the floor and placed his hand upon hers. It was cold and marked with age spots and blue veins. He stared at it for a few seconds. The look and feel of it surprised him.

Had he never touched her hand before? he wondered warily. He wasn't sure. If he had, he could not remember.

He waited for her to lift her gaze. "I'm home, Mother."

She nodded. "I see that, but you're too late. We are ruined James, and it's all my fault."

"We are not ruined."

"Lily certainly will be. That's if we ever see her again."

"I shall do my best to prevent that from happening. I'm going to find her and bring her back."

"How? How will you ever find her? Whitby went looking already, and he found nothing, not even a clue about where they might have gone."

"That's why I'm here. I need to see the letters from Madame La Roux. All of them."

Her throat bobbed as she swallowed. "Sophia told you?"

"Yes, but I already knew about Father's first marriage, as well as what continued to go on between them while he lived. It was no great surprise to hear of it."

His mother's eyes grew wide with horror and shame. "Did you know she was blackmailing me?"

"That, unfortunately, I did not know about, and I wish you had told me. I would have put an end to it. I would have spared you all these years of anxiety. Why did you not tell me?"

She raised the kerchief to her eyes and dabbed at the corners. Her voice was shaky.

"You were just a child when it began. I knew I could never protect you from *him*, but I could at least protect you from scandal. By the time you were old enough to understand or do anything about it, I was too entrenched. It had become a regular part of my life—to receive the letters and send what she asked for. I didn't want to upset the arrangement. I was afraid of what she would do, and on top of that, I never felt I could confess the truth to you. I feared you would hate me more than you already did. I feared you would be like your father and react with a temper."

James lowered his head to his mother's lap. He felt the unfamiliar sensation of her hand upon his hair—then her fingers shakily, awkwardly combing through it.

How many times, when he was a child, did he wish he could run to her and do just this?

"You never had to fear me, Mother. I would never have hurt you. I made it my purpose in life to control that aspect of my nature."

She continued to sniffle as she stroked his hair. "I was wrong about you, James. I see now, with my own eyes, how deeply Sophia cares for you, and it makes me realize that you could not possibly be *anything* like your father."

James closed his eyes and held them closed for a long, significant moment.

He lifted his head and took her hands in his. He kissed them. "Thank you."

She managed a melancholy smile.

James rose to his feet, touching his mother's cheek as he did so. "The letters now, Mother. I need to see them. For Lily's sake."

She nodded and pointed across the room. "I understand. They are in that box over there, and they are yours to do with what you must."

"I must meet this woman for myself," James said to Whitby and Sophia, later in the drawing room.

"But Madame La Roux is in Paris," Whitby said. "Can you risk the time? What if Lily is with Pierre somewhere nearby?"

Sophia sat forward on the sofa. "Wait—I remember the first time I mentioned Pierre to Lily. She was desperate to see Paris. Perhaps they might have gone there together. They certainly wouldn't stay here. They'd both know we would be looking for them."

"That is precisely what I was thinking," James replied. "From what Mother has told me, she paid nothing to Pierre. She never even spoke to him. She was always instructed to send the funds directly to Genevieve, which leads me to believe that Pierre will wish to return home to reap the rewards of his journey."

"But why take Lily?" Whitby asked, his tone reeking with fury. "You don't suppose he meant to kidnap her for ransom, do you?"

James's shoulders heaved. "It is a possibility. He might have seduced her only to lure her away. But why do that, when the blackmail was working?"

Whitby leaned forward to rest his elbows on his knees and clasp his large hands tightly together. "Maybe he truly did fancy her. But if he is a relation . . . God, if that's the case, James, I would like to wring his sick, French neck."

"There are too many questions," Sophia said, trying to calm everyone down, "and the only people with the answers are Pierre and Genevieve. I think you're right,

James, we should go to Paris and speak to Genevieve in person. If nothing else, we can find out where Pierre lives and search for Lily there."

James held up a hand. "Hold on, I never said you could come. I plan to take Whitby. You should stay here in case Lily returns."

"Your mother will be here," Sophia replied, "and Martin is at the house in London, doing everything he can there. You can't leave me here, James. You need my help."

"No, absolutely not. I can't be sure that—"

Whitby stood up and tried to leave again.

"Sit down, Whitby," James said forcefully. "I need you here to help me plan this. Perhaps, Sophia, you should go and check on Mother."

"I'm not going anywhere! I am a member of this family, James, and Lily has confided in me, and me alone. You need me with you in Paris, if for no other reason than to be there for Lily when you find her. I believe she will need a . . . a feminine shoulder to lean on."

James stared at her for a long, tense moment. "You do seem to have developed an intimate rapport with her, and if things have progressed to a . . . to an *inappropriate* level with Pierre, she might be afraid to see me. She would talk to *you*, though. All right, it's settled."

James and Whitby unfolded a map of Paris and began to make plans, while Sophia sat in silence, listening, working hard to slow her pulse. She had just stood up to her husband a second time, and he had bent to her wishes. Again.

What a tremendous relief that she would be going

with him! Not only to help search for Lily, but to find a way to mend what was broken between them.

She decided she would do her very best to utilize the time alone with him—to reach into his heart again, where she was sure he needed her the most.

The waters were calm across the English Channel, but as Sophia stood alone on the deck of the ship with her gloved hands on the rail, the cold mist biting into her cheeks, she wondered if this was in fact the "calm" before a more serious storm.

Would they find Lily in Paris?

What if they did? What would be done?

She turned to see James approaching, his strides long and slow and relaxed on the damp deck. He looked every inch the aristocrat. An exceptionally handsome man he was. Dressed in an expensive wool greatcoat and elegant hat, he carried himself with a deep, innate confidence, as if he believed without question that he would succeed in this quest to rescue his sister.

His face was clean-shaven; he must have unpacked his razor and used it in the cabin while Sophia was on deck, watching England disappear into the fog.

His piercing, blue-eyed gaze met hers, and he came to a slow stop beside her, then faced the sea. "It's a damp afternoon, Sophia. Would you not prefer to be in the cabin?"

"I wanted to breathe the sea air for a little while," she replied.

He stood beside her, watching a gull soar and swoop down near the gray water.

Sophia sighed heavily.

"You enjoy the sea," he said.

"I do. I like the vast, open space and the salty smell of the water." She leaned out to look over the rail. "Who knows what's down there in those dark depths? Sometimes I wish I could dive in like a mermaid and find out."

For a long time he watched her. "You look at people the same way, Sophia, always wanting to know what's in the depths of their hearts and souls."

His comment caught her off guard. Trying to deny the power of his charismatic presence beside her, and how he affected her just by breathing, she gazed up at his beautiful profile, the fullness of his lips, the strong line of his jaw. She could have stood there and stared at him all day and long into the night. It would have been intoxicating.

"I suppose I do want to know what's in people's hearts," she said. "But only if they want to show me."

He faced her and slowly brought a finger up to stroke her chin. The caress was tender, and her heart ached with yearning. It had been so long since they'd been alone together and physically intimate. How she wished their life was normal at this moment, so she could clear her mind of everything but the feel of his large, strong hands upon her skin.

"I have shown you very little, haven't I?" he said softly.

Sophia's knees went limp from the sweet, smooth sensation of her husband's touch, and the gravity of his words. "And I promised not to ask for more than what you were willing to give," she replied.

He nodded with understanding and faced the sea again. Sophia faced it, too.

"I have reconciled with my mother," James told her. "There were things that needed to be said."

Sophia wondered why he was telling her this, and clung to the hope that he was intentionally trying to reveal something of his own heart to her. "That's wonderful, James."

"We spoke about the woman my father loved—if he indeed ever knew how to love—and Mother told me why, all her life, she had kept the truth from me. She believed she was never strong enough to protect me from my father, but that she had the power to protect me from scandal, and that was her only consolation when she felt weak and ashamed of herself for what she allowed to occur in our home."

Sophia reached for James's hand, raised it to her lips, and kissed it. "She loved you, James. She still loves you."

She released his hand and gazed into his eyes.

"I spoke to Martin, too," he said. "I believe we have found the beginnings of a friendship. He is very much the same as I was when I was his age. He reminded me of that."

"I'm glad you found the opportunity to talk to him."

James shook his head. "It was not opportunity I was lacking, my darling. It was understanding. Empathy. And courage. I had not wanted to hear what I feared might make me angry or feel pain, and because of that, I distanced myself from everyone. You have shown me, by merely talking to me and drawing me out, how to open up to my family, Sophia, and I thank you for that."

A bright, euphoric glow alighted within her.

If there had not been others milling about on the

deck, Sophia would have wrapped her arms around James's neck and thrown herself into his embrace. But there were others, and she was still cautious in regard to her husband, so a warm smile had to suffice.

She was learning the English way. . . .

"That means a great deal to me, James."

"I was hard on you," he continued, "when you told me about Lily, and for that I apologize. You must understand that it was difficult to hear. Difficult to know that I had not taken adequate care of my family."

"It was not your fault. You are here now, doing everything in your power to bring your sister home, and that is all you can do. You are only human, James, and you have suffered a great deal yourself. You told me it was not up to me to fix what was broken in your family. I shall say the same to you, now. You cannot be expected to fix everything either."

He touched her cheek. "You told me at home that you wanted to be accepted by our family, and I came out here today to assure you that you are. We would not wish to lose you, Sophia."

Did he truly think he would?

"I don't wish to lose you, either."

The ship sliced through the calm waters below; a whistle blew from somewhere on deck.

James gazed down at Sophia and spoke in a deep, sultry voice. "Come now, back to the cabin with me. I've been without you for too long, and I am weary. I cannot bear to think about what has become of Lily. I want to feel the warmth of your skin next to mine."

A passionate fluttering arose within her breast. Her husband wanted comfort from her, not love, but she would accept that for now. She would glory in the act of giving him comfort as well as pleasure, for he would surely give her the same.

He held out his hand, she placed hers inside it, and followed him below deck.

Whitby, James, and Sophia registered in a tiny inn on the outskirts of Paris under false names, to hide their purpose in France and prevent anyone from knowing that Lily had likely eloped to Paris with her alleged half brother.

After a quick meal at the inn, they hired a coach to take them to the return address on Madame La Roux's correspondence, and the location James had for years known was her place of business. This was, however, the first time he would pass through its doors.

The coach rattled noisily along the cobblestone streets, down narrow, twisting avenues lined with decrepit old buildings and littered with refuse. James reached for Sophia's hand and held it tightly.

He did not know how he would have gotten through all this without her. No one would have had the slightest idea where Lily had gone; his mother would never have told him the truth about the blackmail. He would have been lost.

More importantly, he would not have found comfort anywhere. With anyone.

That's what Sophia gave him, after all—over and above the pleasure she gave him in bed.

Comfort.

Solace.

Love.

Novel concepts for James, who had never wanted or needed any of those things. Never expected to need them. He had been frozen solid inside, and those things Sophia offered held warmth. He had not wanted warmth to touch his hardened heart. He had wanted to avoid it at all costs. To remain frozen. Untouchable.

He would not wish to go back to that hard shell now, not after experiencing the astonishing joy that came with the knowledge that someone in the world cared for him. Someone was there for him no matter what, and would *always* be there for him.

He had learned a great deal about Sophia these past few weeks, and he had discovered that she possessed integrity, devotion, and compassion. She would walk through fire for those she loved, and thank God in heaven for blessing *him*—for making *him* one of the people in this world whom she loved with that enormous, healing heart of hers.

He gently squeezed her hand.

She gazed into his eyes.

A thousand questions were written on her face. She deserved answers. He owed her those answers. There were so many things he wanted and needed to say to her. So many apologies. And promises, too.

They came to a halt in front of Madame La Roux's brothel. Neither Whitby nor Sophia had voiced a concern that Lily might have been brought here, for it did not need to be said. They all knew it was a disturbing possibility.

James leaned forward to climb out of the coach. Whitby tried to follow, but James held him back. "Stay here with Sophia, if you will. I don't want her left alone anywhere near this place."

Whitby nodded and sat back.

"Good luck, James," Sophia said, just before he closed the carriage door behind him.

He ascended the steps on the outside of the brick building, and was admitted by an Oriental porter. James glanced around at the lavish furnishings in the front hall—a crimson carpet to match the red-and-gold wallpaper, a red velvet settee, a glittering crystal chandelier overhead. To his right, a large portrait of a nude woman lying on a riverbank, her legs spread wide, hung on the wall.

James requested a meeting with Madame La Roux, and was ushered into a back room, where he waited.

A moment later, a brocade curtain on the other side of the room lifted, and a slim, impeccably dressed woman appeared. Her hair was naturally golden and shiny, pulled into an elegant twist on top of her head. She wore no face paint, and her complexion was flawless, her bone structure the envy of any woman past twenty. She was, he had to admit, a striking beauty for her age, and not at all what he had expected.

As soon as her eyes fell upon him, her face paled. She brought a hand up to cover her mouth. "It's you."

James made a slight bow. "Indeed."

Madame La Roux collected herself and fully entered the room. Her voice took on a charming, sultry tone. "I beg your pardon, Your Grace, but I had not expected the resemblance to be quite so . . . startling. You look exactly the way your father looked the first time I met him, over thirty years ago."

"I assure you, the resemblance ends there," he replied.

She forced a polite smile, went to the side table and picked up the decanter. "Would you like a drink?"

"I will decline."

She turned over a glass for herself. "I hope you won't think it rude if I take one myself."

Judging by the way her slender hand was shaking as she poured, he suspected she needed it. "Not at all."

Genevieve took a long sip from her glass, then moved gracefully across the room to the mantelpiece. "What brings you to Paris, Your Grace?"

"I should think you would have been expecting me. Eventually."

She gave him a devious look. "You wanted to meet me?"

He laughed. "I will admit to a certain curiosity about the woman my father married—against the advice of his own father—but that is not why I'm here."

"His father was a bastard, but I'm sure you knew that. He was your grandfather, after all."

Odd, he thought, how a woman such as herself could exude such feminine sophistication while uttering profanities. Quite unexpectedly, he understood why his father—given his wild, defiant nature—would have been attracted to her all those years ago.

"Did you wish to know more about your father's other life?" she asked with a flirtatious, teasing tone. "Did you come looking for a memento of him?"

In actuality, James would have liked to learn about his father from Genevieve, but there were more important issues to consider at the moment.

In any event, it wasn't likely that he could sit here for long and casually sip tea with the woman who was blackmailing his family.

He took a step forward. "I don't have time for games, *madame*. I understand you have been corresponding with my mother, the Dowager Duchess."

Genevieve raised an eyebrow. "Ah, yes, she's the dowager now, isn't she? I heard you took a wife. An

American. She was quite the rage while she was here, James, shopping for her trousseau."

The woman's knowledge of Sophia infuriated him. Her use of his given name only added to the flame.

He took a deep breath into his tightening lungs.

He was through with idle pleasantries.

"I will have you understand, Madame, that there will be no more letters to Wentworth Castle. If you dare to make another request for payment, or try to contact any member of my family ever again, I will return to Paris myself and crush you. Do you take my meaning?"

Her shoulders heaved with a sigh. "What makes you think I have requested any kind of payment? I swear," she said casually, "I have not thought of your family since . . . almost forever."

"Let us dispense with the lies, Genevieve." He strode forward and yanked the opal pendant from her neck. "I recognize this, and I will return it to its proper place in my mother's boudoir."

With a look of shock and horror contorting her face, Genevieve clutched at her throat. "How dare you!"

"How dare *you*, madame. Your secret is out, and there will be no more of it."

He could see her bosom heaving with indignation, a look of defeat finding its way to her huge, green eyes, but James was not finished with her yet. "Now, *madame,* you will tell me where I can find Pierre Billaud."

"I don't know who you're talking about."

"I believe you do."

She called out to someone. "Armande! Come in here!"

A hulking gentleman in a suit came bursting into the room. James reached into his coat and withdrew a pistol. He aimed it at the man's chest. "You will remain outside the door, sir, until I am through with your employer." The man didn't move. James pointed the weapon at Genevieve. "Or I swear I will shoot you both."

After a tense few seconds, Genevieve waved her servant away.

James lowered the pistol to his side, but kept his finger on the trigger. "I need an address."

"Why? He's nothing to you."

"Nothing? The man you claim is your son? The man who is allegedly my half brother and the rightful heir to my title? He means a great deal to me, *madame,* and I will have one of two things. A birth certificate, or his address. Now." He raised the pistol again to point directly at her heart.

Genevieve breathed heavily while she stared at the pistol, considering her options. "I don't have a birth certificate to show you, but that doesn't prove or disprove anything."

James raised the pistol even higher to point at her face.

"All right, all right," she said, holding a hand up. "He lives on rue Cuvier. But good luck finding him. I haven't heard from him since he left Paris. For all I know, he's still in England."

James turned to leave, but Genevieve called after him. "You're wrong about something, you know! The resemblance doesn't end with the way you look. You're *just* like your father, in every way!"

James pushed through the front door and descended the front steps. He did not look back.

* * *

Twenty minutes later, the coach pulled up in front of a shabby, broken-down boardinghouse across the city.

"Good heavens," Sophia said, looking out the window of the coach.

Whitby slid across the seat. "I will not stay in the coach this time, James, not if there's a chance Lily is in that detestable place with that worm. We will both come with you, Sophia and I."

"Yes," James replied. "If she is there, she might require some convincing, before she leaves with us. But may I remind you both, she might fancy herself in love with that worm."

Whitby made a wry face.

They all three of them stepped out of the coach and entered the boardinghouse.

"Madame La Roux said she has not heard from Pierre since he left for England," James said. "I am not hopeful."

The stench of stale urine assaulted their nostrils as they climbed a narrow set of stairs with a wobbly banister and reached room six at the top. A baby was crying in one of the rooms. A cat scurried past their legs.

James knocked forcefully on the door.

The knob turned.

Then—quite to his surprise—James found himself staring into the face of Pierre Billaud.

Chapter 27

This is too easy, James thought. Pierre was either a vapid moron, or he'd wanted to be caught.

Pierre tried to slam the door on him, but James stuck his foot in to block it. "Don't be a fool, Billaud. Where's my sister?"

"James!"

He heard Lily's childlike voice from within, and shoved Pierre out of the way. Sophia and Whitby followed him in. Lily hurled herself into James's arms, and he held her tighter than he'd ever held her before.

She squeezed him and began to cry. "How in the world did you find me?"

"It wasn't difficult, my dear. There was a trail of letters, sent over many years, that led us here."

"Letters? What kind of letters?"

He wiped a tear from her soft, pale cheek. "That, I will explain later."

Pierre seemed to gather his courage at that moment,

and took a step forward. He stopped between Whitby and James, who were both at least six inches taller than he. James had to credit the man.

"What's the meaning of this?" he said. "Lily, this is not what we planned."

James frowned down at Billaud.

"I'm sorry, Pierre," Lily replied, "but this was not what I thought it would be like."

"He didn't kidnap you, Lily?" Whitby asked.

She bowed her head in shame. "No, I came to Paris with him, willingly. He said he wanted to marry me."

"Why didn't he?" James asked, glaring at Pierre for an answer. Pierre was curiously silent.

Sophia reached for Lily's hand. "It's all right, darling. We're here now to take you home. Everything will be fine."

Lily sniffled and wiped her nose.

James turned to Pierre. "Whitby, take Sophia and Lily to the coach. I will be along shortly."

They moved toward the door, Sophia with her arm around Lily to guide her out. Lily stopped however, and returned to speak privately to James. "It's not all his fault," she whispered through her tears. "Please don't hurt him. He did say he wanted to marry me."

James felt a tremor of uneasiness move through him. *Please don't hurt him.* Lily was afraid—afraid of the family legacy.

James glanced at Sophia, who gazed at him uncertainly. His gut twisted into a tight, coarse knot. Was she afraid, too? Afraid he would explode with uncontrollable, raging violence, like his ancestors?

The truth was, he had no idea what he was going to do. All he knew was that he had to deal with this man. It was necessary. He only hoped his sister would understand when she learned the whole story. And that Sophia would stand by his actions, whatever they may be.

"You needn't worry, Lily," he gently assured her, kissing her on the forehead. "I only require an explanation."

She accepted that and started for the door, but paused to kiss Billaud on the cheek. She burst into tears immediately after, and Whitby gathered her up into his arms and carried her down the stairs. Pierre watched them go with a look of hostility in his dark eyes.

James looked at Sophia, who was lingering by the door. "I'll be down in a moment," he said. "Wait in the carriage, if you will."

She hesitated, then turned to leave. James stared after her, knowing this would be a defining moment in their marriage, for he was about to discover for himself what kind of man he was.

He turned to face Pierre. James regarded him through narrowed eyes. The man was his own age, perhaps a year or two older, but he was weak. James wasn't altogether certain what Lily had seen in him. Then he remembered the flirtatious manner Pierre had exhibited during the shooting party—socializing with the ladies, complimenting them endlessly in his thick French accent—and James supposed that Lily, in all her romantic innocence, had been easily charmed.

"You removed my sister from her home, good sir," James said. "You transported her out of England to this hovel, without my permission, nor with the accompaniment of a proper chaperone. I will have clarification from you."

Pierre spoke with a contempt that grated upon James's already frayed nerves. "I fell in love with her, Your Grace."

"Then you should have requested permission to court her properly."

"I beg your pardon, but you wouldn't have given permission, and I didn't want to say good-bye to her."

James had to fight hard against the fury he felt—brought on by an intense need to protect his sister and the unpalatable knowledge that he had failed the first time around. He tried to distract himself from it by seeking to understand more of what had happened and *why* it had happened.

"What is your connection to Madame La Roux?"

He'd found his mark, James noticed. Pierre stiffened. "I don't know what you're talking about."

"I think you do." James stood before Pierre and looked him up and down. He studied the man's eyes, the set of his jaw, the line of his nose. "Do we resemble each other at all?" he asked.

"Not really, Your Grace."

"Some might think we do."

Pierre said nothing.

James tapped a hand on his thigh and wandered around the room. Pierre began to fidget.

"You had this letter in your side table drawer when you were a guest in my home." James pulled the letter addressed to Genevieve from his pocket. "I took the liberty of reading it. You said that your assignment was going well, and that you would be returning to Paris on the seventeenth. You returned earlier. With my sister in tow."

"Like I said, we fell in love."

"Which was not part of the 'assignment.' "

A bead of sweat trickled down Pierre's head as he shook it.

"So why did you leave your assignment unfinished? You found a more profitable bounty?"

Pierre's mouth tightened into a hard line. "Your sister was eager, Wentworth. She practically begged me to bring her here."

"Watch your tongue sir. I will ask you point-blank, are you Madame La Roux's son?"

A sneer colored Pierre's eyes. "I don't know what's going on in your sick family, and to tell you the truth, I don't really care. All I know is that I'm not that whore's son, I've got an entirely different whore for a mother. So if you're worried about Lily and me being related, we're not. What happened between us was—how shall I say it?—decent and natural."

James had to work hard to swallow his blinding fury. "How did you find out about the shooting party at Wentworth Castle? Unless you want to face the full force of my wrath, I suggest you tell me the truth."

Pierre considered it, then sauntered toward the small window that looked out over an alley. "I met Genevieve only a few times, then she came looking for me, to ask me to attend your party. She knew all about it and made the arrangements for me to stay with Lord Manderlin. She paid my expenses and bought me clothes. She instructed me to say nothing about my purpose, and I would receive five hundred English pounds when I returned. As well as a few other 'favors.' "

"But you have not gone to collect your reward."

"We only just arrived in Paris last night. I didn't want to leave Lily alone."

James took a threatening step forward. "Thank you for the facts, sir. I will let myself out."

Foolishly, Pierre grabbed James's coat sleeve as he passed. "Wait. There is still the matter of your sister. What if I intend to fight for her?"

James's eyes burned as he glared down at Pierre's hand on his arm. "Spell it out, Billaud."

Pierre did not let go. "She's got a reputation to think of. If anyone found out where she'd been, she'd be ruined."

James met Pierre's narrow gaze. "First of all, I recommend that you let go of my sleeve. Then, sir, you will tell me exactly what it will cost me to have the pleasure of never seeing your face again."

Pierre's eyes glimmered as he released James's arm. "A duke like you with a rich American wife? Fifty thousand pounds should keep me quiet."

James let out a long sigh. "You, too, Pierre. Have the French nothing better to do than dream up endless plots of blackmail?"

Proudly adjusting his collar, looking as if he'd just bagged a lion, Pierre smiled. "It's better than pushing a potato cart around town, Your Grace."

"Ah. But is it better than this?" James drew his pistol and pointed it at Pierre's head. "I would wager that pushing potatoes would be preferable to being buried with them. Am I clear?"

Pierre raised his hands in mock surrender. "She's *your* sister, Wentworth. Are you sure you want to risk this getting out?"

James pushed the barrel of the pistol against Pierre's clammy forehead. "There will be no risk. Because if you do not agree, you will be dead."

Pierre's hands trembled as he stared at the pistol.

"I will have your word, Billaud, and with it, you will have my promise not to hunt you down and spill your brains all over those dowdy new clothes of yours."

Pierre's Adam's apple bobbed noticeably. "If you hadn't come here, I would have married her, you know."

"With the expectation of an allowance from me, no doubt."

"With or without it."

James flinched, then raised his chin. "Do I have your word, sir?"

After a tense second or two, Pierre judiciously agreed.

A moment later, James walked out of the boarding-house and stepped into the private coach that was waiting on the street. Inside its safe confines, Sophia sat beside Lily, who had recovered from her tears and was now looking nervous and frightened at the prospect of facing James's wrath.

He took a few seconds to roll his neck and relax the muscles in his shoulders, and allow his raging pulse to settle down. His hands were shaking.

But he was in control.

He gazed at Sophia, so beautiful even now in this horrid coach. God, if she only knew what she had done for him. He never would have been able to trust him-self to deal with all of this before Sophia had come into his life. She had given him so much, taught him so much. She was the greatest gift he had ever known.

He felt a blanket of calm slowly descending upon him.

Whitby, Sophia, and Lily all sat in silence, waiting to hear what had occurred.

As soon as the coach was in motion, rumbling down the street and turning a corner, James spoke. "Pierre will keep quiet."

Lily covered her mouth with a hand. "You didn't harm him did you? Because . . . because he wasn't bad to me, James, truly. As I said, I went with him of my own accord. He was always very charming toward me."

James noticed Whitby stiffen with outrage. He was no doubt wondering what James himself was wondering— had Pierre robbed Lily of her virtue?

"I did care for him," she continued. "I just realized, after we left England, that I wasn't quite sure who he was."

James sat forward and squeezed her hand. "You don't need to explain everything to me now, Lily. There will be time for that later. We're just glad to have you back." He raised her tiny hands to his lips and kissed them.

God, it was so hard not to see her as a child.

"You must all think me a fool," Lily said. "Or hate me entirely." She turned her sheepish gaze toward Whitby. "And *you* came."

"Of course I came," Whitby replied gently. "I've known you since you were a wee girl, Lily. You're like a sister to me."

Sophia pulled Lily into her arms and hugged her. "You mustn't worry. You're safe now, and we're going home."

"I give you my word, Lily," James said, "that it will be a different home than it was before. I've not been there for you in the past, and for that, I am deeply sorry."

*   *   *

Not wanting to leave Lily alone, Sophia shared a cabin with her sister-in-law during the overnight crossing, making it necessary for James and Whitby to take separate cabins on the other side of the ship.

Sophia was still unsure about what exactly had happened between Pierre and Lily, and whether or not they had been physically intimate. It was certainly possible—likely even—for Lily had been more than a little besotted with Pierre.

She had not wished to talk about it, however, and Sophia agreed not to push. She would wait until Lily felt ready.

Thankfully, it did not take long to ease Lily into a restful sleep, for she had not slept a full night since she had left her home with the intention of eloping. At long last, Sophia was able to sit down in a chair and consider all that had happened in the past week.

She did not remember a more distressing time in her life. She had kept secrets from her husband and feared he would condemn her if he found out.

She had teetered on a wobbly precipice between winning her mother-in-law's affection or guaranteeing her hatred forever.

Lily had gone missing, and Sophia had blamed herself. They had all exhausted themselves traveling to France, confronting the most despicable people, setting foot in foul, filthy places they would never have set foot in otherwise.

Yet, so many wonderful things had come of it. Sophia had discovered that her mother-in-law did in fact possess a softer side, though it was deeply buried beneath a mountain of fear and guilt. Sophia had even managed to bridge the gap that had existed between them from the beginning. Marion had revealed her regrets to James, and they had reconciled after years of ill will and circumvention.

James and Martin were embarking on a brotherly friendship. James had apologized to Lily for not being there for her, and he had thanked Sophia for her role in all those reconciliations.

He appreciated her. He'd admitted it openly during the last crossing. When they had made love in their cabin afterward, she had known that he still wished to find pleasure in her body and give her pleasure in return.

She should feel satisfied, she told herself, grateful and fortunate at this moment, for she had made a difference in James's life and the lives of all his family members. Against the odds, they had rescued Lily, put an end to a devastating blackmail plot against their family, and were on their way home to begin a brighter future together.

Feeling tired and despondent, Sophia sighed and leaned her head against the chairback.

Something was still missing.

She knew she should feel fulfilled and lighthearted, but she did not, for James didn't truly love her, not the way she loved him. She wasn't even certain he was capable of loving her, after declaring on so many occasions that he was not.

Yet she loved *him*. More than she loved her own life. Why? It made no sense. He had done everything in his power to keep her at a distance.

She supposed it was because she knew that James possessed a myriad of beautiful, hidden depths, just like the ocean itself. Why else would he have retreated so ardently from his family after the ordeal of his childhood?

Clearly, his heart had been shattered by all that he had suffered. All that had crushed the inherently noble expectations he had possessed as a child.

Yes, deep down, he was truly noble, she thought. She had witnessed it these past few days when he had put everything aside—even a lifelong chasm between himself and his mother—to protect his family.

She felt a tremendous throb in her own heart at that moment. An aching need to know her husband as intimately as she knew her own soul. She wanted to be his true mate throughout their lives, and to know what lay beneath his guarded surface. She wanted to grow old with him and see him become the man that he was capable of becoming.

She only wished he would let go of the demons from his past and embrace her like he had embraced the rest of his family.

Sophia, James, and Lily arrived home in a carriage driven by James, describing for everyone their journey to Scotland for a much-needed holiday alone—without maids or valets—after the busy social schedule during the shooting party.

It was "an American thing" Sophia had claimed—to travel spontaneously without servants after a lengthy party. Quite to their surprise, everyone who greeted them on the massive front steps of the castle had accepted that it was true. They all nodded knowingly, saying "Ah," and "Of course, Your Grace."

Sophia had felt a swell of joy and satisfaction when her husband winked at her, pleased with her creative little lie. She smiled lovingly at him, feeling rejuvenated, as if a great many of her American ways were being accepted and appreciated lately.

"We are home, Sophia," he said softly in her ear as they crossed the front hall toward the staircase. "I can't tell you how glad I am to be here, to have you with me, at my side."

His warm breath at her neck gave her gooseflesh; the adulation warmed her heart and soothed her soul.

They climbed the stairs together, and when they reached the top, James kissed her on the cheek. "I am going to take a long bath now, and rest my weary bones," he said. "I will see you at dinner?"

"Of course. A bath sounds splendid, James. I shall enjoy one myself."

Sophia retreated to her own bedchamber, summoning her maid to arrange for the tub to be brought in and filled with water. She would look forward to some time alone, to cleanse herself of all the dirt and grime of the past few days.

Later, as she lay in the tub with her head tipped back upon the bowed rim, a note came sliding under her door. Sophia opened her eyes to the sound of the paper swishing across the floor.

She rose from the tub and stepped out, dripping water everywhere as she bent to pick it up.

My Darling,

When you are finished bathing, please come to me.

James

Sophia stared at her husband's elegant script upon the ducal stationery, then raised it to her lips and kissed it. "I am finished, now, my love," she said aloud, knowing he couldn't hear her, but needing to say it all the same.

She rang for her maid to return and help her dress and pin up her hair. A half hour later, she was at James's door, knocking.

"Who is it?" she heard him call from inside.

"It is I," she replied.

"Come in."

Sophia turned the knob and pushed open the heavy door. A wave of moist heat touched her cheeks as her gaze fell upon her husband, lying in his huge brass tub in front of the fire. His arms were up out of the water, gently resting along the rim, and his black hair was wet and slicked back. His chest was magnificent in the afternoon light beaming in the window—brawny, golden and robust.

Sophia's breath caught in her throat as she stood in the open doorway, staring at her impossibly gorgeous husband, naked before her. A swell of avaricious lust moved through her.

"You sent for me?" was all she could manage to say when her carnal senses were awakening.

His expression was blithe and open. "I did. Come in, if you will, and close the door before some unfortunate soul walks by and gets an eyeful."

Clumsily regaining her composure, Sophia obeyed.

"Lock it as well." A hint of seductive allure softened his voice.

She did.

Standing not far away, she let her eyes luxuriate in the clear view of his enormous arousal under the water, felt the beginnings of a hot, crazed lust, and understood fully the overwhelming force of sexual desire. No wonder it could push people to act without sense or logic, to tumble into mad acts of delirium. It was burning through her brain and knocking away all her emotional doubts and misgivings about her marriage. None of that mattered now, when beneath the layers of her clothes, her body was trembling with a sudden, tempestuous need.

James's head fell back against the edge of the tub, but he kept his gaze on her, watching her with complete mindfulness, allowing her to stare at him as long as she wished.

Taking full advantage of his rare, unguarded offering, she let her gaze travel from his dark, arresting eyes to his smooth, broad shoulders, gleaming with clean droplets of water. His sinewy chest rose and fell with slow control, and she noted that every time she glanced up at his eyes, he was still looking at her—blinking slowly with an invitation that was just over the horizon. Watching her expressions as she quivered and delighted in the perfection of his raw nakedness.

Her love for him at that moment was excruciating. Blinding.

The corner of his mouth curled up in a grin. Sophia trembled as he lifted his hands from the rim of the tub and held them open. "Would you like to come in?"

With a grateful smile and a nod, Sophia unbuttoned her bodice and slowly undressed in silence in front of James while he watched. Heart racing, she laid her clothes out neatly upon his bed, reveling in the sizzling, deliberate anticipation of undressing in front of him, knowing he was enjoying every sweet second of it, too.

Naked at last, she stepped into the tub and slid down to sit between his legs. His erection was firm against the small of her back. She let her head tilt back upon his huge shoulder.

James picked up the washcloth and dipped it in the water, then squeezed it over Sophia's breasts and let the warm drops caress her nipples. The delicate sound and the tickling sensation of the water lapping up against her skin brought an erotic whimper to her lips.

"You are the most beautiful creature I have ever encountered in all of my life," James whispered hotly in her ear.

"I love your seductions," she replied with a teasing smile.

James lay in the tub, quiet and still for a few seconds. "It's not just a seduction, Sophia. Not today."

He kissed the side of her head, and Sophia felt her forehead crinkle with curiosity. "What is it then?"

"It's an apology. And a surrender."

Sophia sat up and turned sideways in the tub to look at his face. She wanted to ask him what he meant, but no words would form in her brain. She was stuck in some kind of questioning stupor.

James stroked her cheek with the backs of his fingers. "I have many regrets, Sophia. I have not been a good husband to you."

"You've been a wonderful husband, James." Of course it wasn't entirely true. There was still so much missing from their marriage, but she felt his need to open up to her, and she would not dream of discouraging him.

"You are very kind and good-hearted to lie like that," he said.

"It's not all a lie," she replied. "I've been treated very well here. You have given me so much."

"But not enough. I've not given you my heart."

Sophia swallowed nervously. "James . . ."

"Please," he said, holding up his hand. "Let me speak the words I should have spoken ages ago."

Heart suddenly pounding in her chest, hopes flooding her senses, Sophia waited patiently for him to continue.

God, she was afraid.

Afraid to hope.

She tried frantically to control it.

"I know that from the beginning, you've wanted more," he said. "At first I tried to tell myself that you only wanted my title, but I always knew there was more to you than that. There were things that you openly revealed to me, while I revealed nothing. I didn't tell you about my family or my fears, because I was ashamed. I didn't tell you the truth about Florence, because I thought it would scare you away. But most of all, I didn't let myself love you, and I am sorry, Sophia. You deserved more, and I failed you. My only excuse is that I did not want to give in to my passions and become like my father. I didn't want to hurt you the way he hurt my mother and me."

Sophia's heart ached painfully with love and compassion for her strong, noble husband. "You will never be like him, James. You have been put to the test in every way, and you have not failed. Think of it. You believed I had written a love letter to another man, yet you never lost control of your temper, when you must have been raging inside. And think about your siblings. You have done everything in your power to protect them from harm, because you care for them, deeply and truly. Your father never cared about you like that. He never tried to mend what was broken between you, nor did he take any responsibility or worry himself over the fact that you were off getting into trouble as a young man. You have worried constantly over your loved ones. Think of what you have done with Martin. You tried everything you could to get him through this difficult time, and you ultimately succeeded. There is hope for him, now."

James rubbed her back. "You always look for the good in people, Sophia."

"I have no trouble finding it in *you*. Still waters run deep, James."

For a long moment he stared into her eyes. "It amazes me that you have never given up on me. That you ever cared for me to begin with, when I was so determined to keep everything superficial."

She touched his face. "I was captivated by you, from the very first moment I saw you walk into that London drawing room in all your elegant grace. You were so handsome, James, so tall and confident and untouchable. I wanted to know who you were. I wanted to know what was beneath that calm surface, and why you seemed so cynical when you looked around yourself at the world and everyone in it. For some reason I sensed that the world would change for you, if only someone would just *talk* to you."

"You wanted to rescue me from my reserved English way?" he said with an amused tone, lifting his eyebrows.

"I suppose I did. But I wanted you to rescue me, too, from the endless boredom of my perfect life in New York. I never had to work for anything, my father always gave it to me, and I was weak. I'm stronger now."

"You were always strong, Sophia."

She smiled. "You also rescued me from the marriages my mother kept trying to arrange for me. I wanted passion, and I saw it in your eyes. I knew you possessed an abundant wealth of it—that it was bottled up inside you, just waiting to be released. I wanted to reach in and find it."

James cupped her cheek in his large hand. "You did, Sophia. You found it. You reached inside, and here I am now, vulnerable in front of you."

He gazed at her for a shuddering instant before devouring her mouth with his own. The kiss was deep and wet and probing, and Sophia knew that the barrier was breaking down.

She gave in to the erotic allure of the open kiss, while her hand at the same time found its way down to his erection. Indulging in the glorious feel of him in her palm, she carefully stroked him under the water until she felt out of control with the searing need to feel him inside her.

Sophia turned in the tub, then sat up on her knees to move a leg across and straddle him. He watched her face the entire time as she took him in her hand again and placed him at her eager opening.

A pounding frenzy of desires cascaded over her as she arched her back to wiggle down around him. Slowly, teasingly, she took him inch by inch into her throbbing insides and let out a delirious little cry at the feel of the hot, wet friction against her sensitive, feminine tissues.

The water sloshed up against the sides of the tub as Sophia rose up, then drove slowly down again, pressing herself hard against his pelvis to enhance her own pleasures. He held her hips, guiding her up and down, thrusting his own hips forward to meet each marvelous, grinding plunge.

The room and the daylight disappeared around

Sophia. She closed her eyes. All that existed was the dizzying sensation of floating in hazy darkness with James, while sheer, extravagant lust besieged her senses.

"Sophia."

She could feel him with her, beside her, hear his soft voice in the passion-filled haze; she could not stop herself from moving in a slow, pulsing rhythm over him, so lost in the pleasure was she.

"Sophia," he said again.

She opened her eyes, looked into his face. He was watching her.

"Yes," she whispered.

He said nothing for a moment while he gazed at her tenderly. Lovingly.

Sadly.

Sophia stopped moving. She squeezed herself around him.

A tear trickled from the outside of his eye, down over his cheekbone.

She stared at that tear with heart-seizing, soul-reaching comprehension.

"I love you," he whispered softly.

Sophia couldn't move. She could only stare at him, blank, astonished, and profoundly shaken. Her mind and body seemed to stop functioning.

"My heart is yours," he said. "I am in your hands."

Through the roaring din of joy washing through her like a waterfall, Sophia somehow found her voice. "I love you, too, James. I will *always* love you, till the day I die, and beyond that."

All at once, her heart swelled irrepressibly with that love. She threw her arms around James's neck and wept as she hugged him.

He held on to her as if he never wanted to let her go—his strong arms wrapping around her back, his face buried in her neck.

"No one has ever touched me like you have," he said. "I never believed it was possible. I am yours, Sophia. For eternity."

Her own tears began to fall, and she sat back to look at his dark, beautiful face. She sobbed and laughed at the same time, and wiped the wetness from her cheeks. "I am so happy."

"I intend to make you happy every day for the rest of my life. You are my one and only love, Sophia. You have saved me."

Sophia couldn't stop crying. "I was so afraid to let myself hope that you would ever love me."

"Before I met you, I never thought I could love anyone. I was wrong, Sophia. I love you, more than life itself."

"James, I never dreamed . . ."

He held her and kissed her and stroked her hair, and for the first time, she felt as if she were truly home. This was where she belonged. In England. With James. Here in his arms. As his wife, his duchess.

He shifted his body minutely beneath her—the smallest trace of a movement—but it was enough to transform their shared tenderness into a burning arousal, in one sweeping, wondrous instant.

James closed his eyes; Sophia grabbed on to the sides of the tub and began to stir herself over him. Fiery eroticism returned with a vengeance. She let her head fall back, then felt James's hot lips suckle her breast and work her expertly with his tongue. Her breaths came in short, quick succession until at last she felt the coming onslaught of orgasm.

But it was different this time. It was more intense, more resonant, for there was love between them now. James had told her he loved her. He loved her! The pleasure was unfathomable.

It descended upon her with all the force of a tidal surge, storming through all her muscles everywhere, tightening, tingling to a potent climax, then finally releasing her. James cried out, thrusting deep inside her and shooting his seed into the very center of her womanhood.

Sophia closed her eyes and rested her forehead on James's shoulder. He had made love to her. Her husband. He loved her. She could barely contain the tremendous euphoria that was flowing through her body and soul.

Feeling elated, basking joyously in the sound of his breathing and the feel of his heart beating against hers, Sophia sighed.

A short time later, they got out of the tub and dried off, then moved to the bed and made love again, tenderly and with great consciousness of each other's needs and desires. James said the magical words again—*I love you, Sophia*—as he gazed into her eyes and held her face in his hands.

Then they helped each other dress, and went down to the drawing room to gather with the family before dinner. Sophia requested that the leaves be taken out of the dining table, so the family could sit nearer to one another, tonight and every night, far into the future. In all her life, Sophia had never felt so happy.

Martin and Lily walked in, and James hugged each of them in turn, then his mother entered the room and he hugged her, too, while she released years' and years' worth of anxieties and wept openly in his arms until her tears became tears of joy.

She moved to Sophia and hugged her, too. "Thank you," she said to her daughter-in-law. "Thank you."

Sometime near dawn the next morning, James pulled Sophia close. "It's a new day," he said, "and the world is already a brighter place. All because of you. How was I ever so lucky, to have found you when you lived your whole life on another continent?"

Sophia smiled up at him. "We were meant to be, James, and nothing was right until I came here."

"Are you glad?" he asked, touching her chin with his finger and lifting her face to look into her eyes. "Even though it was difficult in the beginning?"

"Of course. This is my home now, and I am gloriously happy to be here with you. You're the only man I ever could have loved."

"And I am gloriously happy to have you, my darling. May I show you how much?"

Sophia rolled onto her back and ran her finger up his bare chest. "If it would please you, Your Grace."

"The point, my dear, is to please *you*."

She smiled seductively. "Far be it from me to argue with a duke."

Epilogue

April 15, 1882

Dear Mother,

Greetings from merry old England. I hope this letter finds you all happy and well, and enjoying spring in New York.

James and I are getting anxious, awaiting our little one's arrival. The doctor says the baby will arrive sometime in July, but I think he will come earlier than that, because I am so anxious to meet him. James thinks it will be a girl. I think a boy. Either way, we will both be overjoyed when he arrives. We are overjoyed with everything in our lives these days. God has blessed us with so many wonderful treasures.

How are Clara and Adele? Have you given any more thought to their coming to London for the Season? I would love to introduce them into the very best society, and Lily would be pleased to have the girls at her side, for this will be her second Season, and she is somewhat nervous about the whole affair.

Say hello to Father, and I will await your reply.

Your loving daughter,
Sophia

P.S. May I tempt you with the news that the Prince of Wales informed me personally that he will be "decidedly disappointed" if Clara and Adele do not come?

Your determined daughter,
Sophia

Author's Note

For years I've wanted to write about American heiresses searching for husbands in aristocratic London, ever since I read about Edward VIII abdicating the English throne for the woman he loved—Wallis Simpson, an American divorcee. I was fascinated by the couple's passionate romance, their difficult struggle for acceptance, and, in the end, a king's decision to give everything up for love.

Later, I read *The Buccaneers*, by Edith Wharton, a brilliant novel about four American girls invading English society in the late-Victorian period. Again, I was enchanted. The romantic notion of English lords falling head over heels for American girls because they were beautiful, exciting, and different (and filthy rich) intrigued me, as well as the darker side of history that was more often the case, where young American women gave up their home and country for a life of loneliness abroad, with strangers who never truly accepted them and husbands who had married them only for their money.

In actuality, between the years 1870 and 1914, approximately one hundred American women married British nobles, and of those one hundred, six set their sights high and captured dukes—the exalted cream of the nobility crop. These women were the glamor icons of the late-Victorian period, and not unlike Princess Diana, had to dodge photographers and raving admirers who wanted to glimpse the fairy-tale "dollar princesses." You can read about five of those American heiresses—whose stories are engaging, inspiring, and sometimes tragic—in the book *In a Gilded Cage*, by Marian Fowler.

All the characters in my book are fictional, with the exception of Edward, the Prince of Wales ("Bertie" to his friends and family), who was in fact a key player in the overall acceptance and success of the American heiresses in England. His mother, Queen Victoria, gave him very little to do regarding the affairs of the country, so he had to amuse himself somehow, and being half-German himself, did not possess the usual prejudice toward foreigners. He enjoyed beautiful women and found the American heiresses more than capable of keeping him entertained. They could afford to host frequent, lavish parties when many of the English aristocrats were suffering financially from an agricultural depression and the negative effects of the industrial revolution. (Fast-moving steamships were bringing competition from American beef and grain; consequently, farm prices in England fell. On top of that, the tenant farmers were trading in their pitchforks to work in factories.)

Mrs. Astor was also a real person—the matriarch

of high society in old New York. She eventually had to accept the *nouveaux riches,* because among other things, many of their daughters were wearing English coronets.

I hope you enjoyed reading about Sophia and James, and will look for the sequel about Sophia's sister, Clara. This will be the second book in my series about American heiresses in England.

COMING IN JULY—
SUMMER'S HOTTEST HEROES!

STEALING THE BRIDE by Elizabeth Boyle
An Avon Romantic Treasure

The Marquis of Templeton has faced every sort of danger in his work for the King, but chasing after a wayward spinster who's run off with the wrong man hardly seems worthy of his considerable talents. But the tempestuous Lady Diana Fordham is about to turn Temple's life upside down . . .

WITH HER LAST BREATH by Cait London
An Avon Contemporary Romance

Nick Alessandro didn't think he would ever recover from a shattering tragedy, until he meets Maggie Chantel. But just when they are starting to find love together, someone waiting in the shadows is determined that Maggie love *no one* ever again. Now Nick has to find the killer—before the killer gets to Maggie.

SOARING EAGLE'S EMBRACE by Karen Kay
An Avon Romance

The Blackfeet brave trusts no white man—or woman—but the spirits have spoken, wedding him in a powerful night vision to a golden-red haired enchantress. Kali Wallace is spellbound by the proud warrior but will their fiery love be a dream come true . . . or doomed for heartbreak?

THE PRINCESS AND HER PIRATE
by Lois Greiman
An Avon Romance

Not since his adventurous days on the high seas has Cairn MacTavish, the Pirate Lord, felt the sort of excitement gorgeous hellion Megs inspires. Though she claims not to be the notorious thief, he knows she is hiding something—and each claim of innocence that comes from her lush, inviting lips only inflames his desires.

REL 0603

Avon Romances—
the best in exceptional authors and unforgettable novels!

Discover Contemporary Romances
at Their Sizzling Hot Best
from Avon Books

Avon Romantic Treasures

*Unforgettable, enthralling love stories,
sparkling with passion and adventure
from Romance's bestselling authors*

Have you ever dreamed of writing a romance?

*And have you ever wanted
to get a romance published?*

Perhaps you have always wondered how to
become an Avon romance writer?
We are now seeking the best and brightest undiscovered
voices. We invite you to send us your query letter to
avonromance@harpercollins.com

What do you need to do?

Please send no more than two pages telling us
about your book. We'd like to know its setting—is it
contemporary or historical—and a bit about the hero,
heroine, and what happens to them.

Then, if it is right for Avon we'll ask to see part of the
manuscript. Remember, it's important that you have
material to send, in case we want to see your story quickly.

Of course, there are no guarantees of publication,
but you never know unless you try!

*We know there is new talent just waiting
to be found! Don't hesitate . . . send us
your query letter today.*

The Editors
Avon Romance